SUN DOG MEMORY

SUN DOG MEMORY

Douglas Armstrong

LEXINGTON HOUSE PRESS

For more information about the historical basis of this novel, visit www.douglasdarmstrong.com.

ISBN 979-8-218-18436-0

Cover design by: Patrick Armstrong
Library of Congress Control Number: 2023906298
Printed in the United States of America.
Lexington House Press.
Whitefish Bay, Wisconsin

For Pap

Reckoning

New Orleans – May 1930

The house has a tranquil, dignified air in the dappled light. Velvet drapes are drawn tight across the depravity inside, but this time, Jed Albright is not fooled.

"Out," the Musgrave detective snarls. The eye in the sea of burgundy-stained flesh is like a branding iron. As the detective leans across Jed to open the Chevy Coupe's door, a ripe odor escapes his tweed suit. "Now!"

Jed's wrists are cuffed behind his back and his bladder is threatening to explode. It's difficult to move. The impatient Musgrave shoves him out onto the sidewalk, where Jed lies still a moment, thinking about his deranged brother-in-law, probably inside. The lunatic took a carving knife. And the girl.

The Musgrave removes the Peerless model cuffs now. Jed kneels quickly to re-tie his shoe on the cobbled path and make sure the little two-shot Remington Double Derringer is still concealed in the ankle holster beneath his pants leg. He hopes to hell it won't be necessary.

One

Simmering Kettle

April 1930

The delivery pouch bounded like a jackrabbit across the depot platform at Breckenridge, skidding and tumbling to a stop in a weed patch at the end. Dammit, Jedidiah Albright muttered, and squinted into the slipstream of soot and smoke huffing out of the engine and flying past his cinder guard as he reeled in Breckenridge's outgoing pouch.

Then he rolled the mail car door shut, mopped the damp strands of his hair with a handkerchief, and scanned the tinder of paper, cardboard, and canvas inside the car like a forest ranger. This old crate could go up as fast as a hay barn if a hot cinder nested in it somewhere. And there'd be no place for him to flee if it happened. More than one railway mail clerk had met the Postmaster in the Sky that way. Jed had no interest in feeling the sharp lick of another flame again as long as he lived.

He pulled out his pocket watch. 8:11. Frisco 630, three minutes behind.

Even without a blaze inside, the old car felt like a blast furnace with the door closed. A merciless sun beat down on the roof, and the collar of Jed's starched shirt chafed like sandpaper. The door would have to stay shut, however, until the train turned north out of the headwind pushing locomotive sparks directly down the line of cars behind it.

Jed dumped the Breckenridge outbound pouch onto the sorting table and set to work on a mound of mail to far-flung places, addressed in indecipherable handwriting. He paused briefly at an envelope destined for downtown Kansas City. It made him think of his brother again and the shock he would get tonight when he saw the girl for the first time. At least that's what Jed was expecting.

Despite the heat, Jed craved another jolt of coffee. And he had ample time, twenty-six minutes to the next exchange at the Town of Hunter, even if Junior kept the boiler stoked and the throttle wide open. The pile of bulk items in the corner could just wait. Catalog distributors shouldn't expect first-class handling if they didn't pay full postage.

Jed lowered his drop stool and poured a cup of joe from the vacuum flask in his valise. His regulation .38 rested atop his change of clothes. Such a silly regulation. Why should he have to carry a pistol on a two-bit milk train? He'd never discharged it except for sport out the mail car door to scare ornery red-winged blackbirds off fence posts. No bandit in his right mind would stick up a train that didn't carry government gold. And this definitely didn't. Tucked beneath the pistol was the letter he'd sweated over to the bank.

4/12/30

Mr. J.J. Pierpoint
Citizens State Bank
Rolla, Kansas

Dear Sir,

I apologize for my delayed reply. I did not receive your past due notice until I returned to Enid yesterday. Run outs for the post office keep me away for up to a week at a time. Enclosed is a postal order towards the amount indicated. I hope you will extend me the courtesy of considering it sufficient until the remainder can be remitted at the end of the month. Until then, I remain

Respectfully yours, Jedidiah Albright

Pierpoint's blubbery face would probably pucker at that load of BS. On the other hand, determination to avert foreclosure might impress him. Give him pause. Wouldn't he be better off not putting another mortgage into default? The sheer number of foreclosures was threatening to bring the little bank down. A payment was a payment. Blood from a shriveled turnip. Like all of the other borrowed-to-the-hilt farmers of Kansas, the Albrights were in the crosshairs of freefalling grain prices in the aftermath of the panic and crash on Wall Street. Hundreds of farms were about to fail. Winter wheat was being left to rot in the fields, forty cents a bushel not enough to cover the expense of harvesting it.

Jed ran his thumb absently over the raised imprint on the money order before penning a postscript to the letter. Make sure the old boy's bulbous beezer caught a whiff of what was in the wind. The man had to read the newspapers.

My prospects remain strong, as you know. Your patience will be rewarded.

Jed blew over the wet ink before refolding the letter. He'd show it to Arthur after the business with the girl was done. But the girl first. Definitely. It wasn't easy to catch Arthur flat-footed, and his unguarded reaction to this remarkable creature would be a litmus test of the situation for Jed. Tell him if he'd lost his marbles.

The mail car swayed suddenly at a fork in the rails and hot coffee sloshed out of Jed's cup, stinging his hand and splattering his clean white shirt. Junior was driving the engine like a rodeo cowboy this morning. The coffee cooled to reveal a second wet spot in the crotch of Jed's trousers. *Jesus wept,* the hapless clerk thought. He couldn't go into the depot at Ark City looking like this. His work overalls had more dignity than a spotted suit. *This is what comes of trying to primp*, he thought. *Old fool.*

He'd stood and dropped his suspenders to step out of his spoiled pants just before the hatch to the Railway Express compartment clicked open and Lester Barnhart's scuffed boots appeared in the opening. The rest of Lester squeezed through as Jed stuffed the money order and letter back into the valise and snapped it shut.

"My interrupting sumpin'?" Lester snickered with a bemused

glance at the trousers pooled around Jed's ankles. He resettled the plug of tobacco bulging in his bristly cheek. "Those knobs yer knees, Jed?" he said with a smirk.

The man was trespassing in a postal facility. U.S. Government property. A federal crime. The car was strictly off limits to members of the train crew. Not that it mattered to Lester, who was in constant pursuit of the forbidden. Nothing was safe from his sticky fingers.

"What are you doing in here, Lester?" Jed asked.

"Mind puttin' on yur pants?" Lester chuckled and settled onto Jed's vacated stool. Getting him off it again wouldn't be easy. "Come to tell ya," Lester said, "fellas is plannin' to raise a toast to Ol' Man Volstead tonight. Back room a the pool hall. Thought you might like a invite. What ya say, Jedidiah? Up for a little snort?"

With a watchful eye on his shifty visitor, Jed fastened the buttons on the fresh shirt he'd packed for the next day. "Bathtubs aren't just for brewing gin, Lester," Jed said. "You might fill yours with water sometime and try getting in it."

Lester ignored this. "She-et, Jed. 'T'aint rotgut. This here's gen-u-wine aged Scotch. Billy got holt of it."

Billy. Lester's organ grinder monkey. Fireman on the train. Several scoops short of a full firebox. To hear Billy say where the hooch had come from would be laughable and sad. He never could repeat a story exactly as Lester had given it to him to tell. The bottle had obviously been pilfered from a passenger suitcase resting in the baggage car. And it would go unreported since Scotch was, by definition, contraband under the Volstead Act.

"Could use some air in here," Lester said and got to his feet to open a high window. He had to close it immediately when a spark blew in. He stamped the ember into a splotch with his boot heel to join the others speckling the floor. "So, wha'da ya say there, Jed? Two bits'll get you fixed up nice. Help keep you reg-oo-ler too, old man! Get ya off your stewed prunes." His laugh hissed like a deflating truck tire.

"Time you were on your way, Lester," Jed said. "You knew what my answer would be without even asking." Jed didn't drink or socialize with the men of the train crew. A chance to drink a bottle of stolen whisky with the brakeman was not an incentive to change that policy.

"There's more to life than Victrola records, Jed," Lester jeered, dragging the girl into it now, which was probably what he'd come to do. Throw down the gauntlet. Lock horns with an old man. "You a little long in the tooth for such tender nookie, ain't ya?"

Jed felt his shoulders tense and his knees coil.

"You ain't her pappy, is ya?" Lester taunted when Jed twitched but declined to throw a punch. *Put up your dukes, old man, or swallow your pride.*

Jed snorted instead and made a show of dragging the Town of Hunter delivery sack slowly to the door. Fisticuffs in the mail car? Over a girl? When word of it reached his superiors, he'd get the sack. "Busy tonight," Jed said matter-of-factly. "My brother's coming in."

Rings showed in the armpits of his denim shirt as Lester leaned back and laced his fingers together behind his head. "She-et, bring him along. Interduce him to the boys."

Jed smiled. "Not sure they'd care for that."

"Yeah?" Lester chortled, feigning puzzlement. "He a tea-totaler, too? Bible thumper?"

It was the federal badge in his wallet they wouldn't be happy about, Jed thought. "Hardly your business, is it?" he said. "Now, I've got work to do."

He tightened the drawstring on the Town of Hunter pouch and opened the door. Smoke and the clatter of wheels poured in. Jed waited for a signal stanchion to pass before cranking out the catcher arm. A collision would tear the apparatus off, and the cost of replacing it would come out of Jed's pay. Hunter's station wasn't a stop. Junior slowed to a leisurely pace for the catch and throw. Lester retreated to the hatch as Jed executed it.

"Gotta git," Lester said. "This place ain't safe. If Junior goes and rams sumpin' bigger'n a cow, that kettle a his will cut through here faster'n a knife through hot butter." He spat tobacco juice on the floor for emphasis. "Think again on that drink," he said, and disappeared through the hatch like a worm going to earth.

Jed's lips fluttered in exasperation. How could the girl be

taken in by the little goon's counterfeit parlor manners? His cheap toilet water? The gifts he brought her were stolen! Thank God the girl's *maman* made her give back the stolen cameo brooch Lester had taken on an Enid-to-Denver train. Some hapless porter had gone to jail for it when fingers were pointed. But the girl's face had lit up when she opened the jewelry case, and Lester had shot a lurid wink Jed's way.

The train wheels gave a hollow report drumming across the Salt Fork trestle. Jed dumped the Town of Hunter outbound onto the sorting table, wondering if his determination to protect the girl was actually about his failure to properly protect his sister years before. The girl was a dead ringer for her. Carrie. Their encounter outside the Beaumont station had stunned him. How could his missing sister simply step out of the distant past—not a day older?

There was another explanation, of course. It turned out the girl had a tough little Cajun woman she called Maman. The woman had clearly not given birth to this girl. But this wild theory was a stretch as well. He'd have to see what Arthur thought after he saw them tonight.

Jed sprinkled sawdust on the splatter of Lester's tobacco spit. He swept the gooey clump into a pail. The stain left by the man's words was not so easily removed.

You ain't her pappy, is ya?

* * *

The midday sun was baking the color out of the squat brick buildings at the Arkansas City depot as Jed dragged the bundles of periodicals to the mail car's door. He tossed down three bulging mail sacks to the postal station manager, who loaded everything onto a hand truck. Jed locked the car and then descended the iron ladder.

11:55. Fifteen minutes behind schedule. Junior would try to make up lost time by departing as soon as the locomotive had drunk its fill from the water tank. The spot on Jed's pants had dried. He straightened his vest, tilted his bowler to a slightly jaunty angle, and sauntered inside. At the lunch counter, a square white box tied up in string was waiting for him. He took a stool by the cash register, tucked his legs under the counter, and waited.

Ruby's hair was the color of an old penny and her face a testament to hope in a wearying world. But her customary smile wasn't there today. "Look at you," she said. "Getting married later?"

The levity stung. He'd dressed up specifically for her. See what might come of it, and she'd called him on it. It seemed out of character. "Is something wrong?" he asked.

"Railroad's raising the rent on this place," she said. "Manager has to lay one of us off."

What could he say? He set his empty milk pint on the counter for her to place with the other bottles in a tray below. Their little ritual. "Long as it isn't you," Jed said hopefully.

Her look suggested how foolish this comment was. She sighed and said, "Your lips to old man Franck's ears." Jed could almost picture the awkward goodbye that awaited them, neither sure whether a hug was appropriate.

They gawked at each other for a time, before movement out the depot window drew Jed's attention. Billy the fireman was limping quickly along the platform from the rear of the train toward the engine.

Ruby squinted. "What's he up to?"

Jed had locked the mail car's outer door, but the Railway Express hatch inside remained unsecured. "Gotta run," Jed said, grabbing his box lunch.

He sprinted across the platform, ignoring a handcart piled high with mail pouches. At the caboose down the platform, Roscoe had his timepiece open in his hand and his eyes on Jed as he hurriedly unlocked the mail car door. Junior was leaning out of the engine cab, blasting the whistle, and waving his arm like a cop unsnarling a traffic jam.

Inside, it was clear Jed's valise had been opened. The revolver and letter were gone. "Son of a bitch!" he spat.

Roscoe arrived at the mail car door, tugging at his conductor's cap. "What's the problem here? Get those mail sacks on board, Albright! We got to clear this siding. The next train's coming in."

"Can't leave!" Jed yelped, distraught. "Been a theft."

Roscoe blinked. "From the mail car?" Serious trouble.

Junior came stomping down the platform, his face pink and twisted. "Get those sacks on board, Albright, or I'll do it myself. Never mind your damn rules. We're leavin'!"

Roscoe said, "Hold up there, Junior. We got a problem. You're gonna have to blow off the steam and simmer the kettle."

"Why the hell would I do that?"

"Because Lester stole my revolver," Jed said.

"What in tarnation!" Junior bellowed. He yanked off his denim cap and swept it through the air so hard it spun him completely around. Junior glowered toward the locomotive, where Billy peered around the coal tender from the steps. "Billy!" Junior yelled. Circles of white opened in the eyes of his coal-smudged face. "Where the hell's Lester at?" Junior barked.

Billy hopped down awkwardly and stumbled. Beset since childhood by a badly set bone break in his leg, he began to limp away around the front of the engine.

Four pairs of rails squeezed through the narrow Ark City yard. Billy began to cross them. The last was the through-line of the Atchison, Topeka & Santa Fe, where a freight hauling steel chuffed into view. Billy raced recklessly at it. If he could clear the train before it passed, his pursuers would have to wait out a long string of cars. The ground shuddered under the behemoth 2-8-4 Berkshire class's rumbling weight. Its bell clanged. Its whistle shrieked. And the iron teeth of the cow catcher in front nipped Billy's gimpy leg as he dragged it over the last rail. Then there was only Billy's cap dancing along in the air, fanned by flatcars. Too late came the squeal of brakes and the skid of wheels, no match for Newton's law of inertia.

Shreds of gray-striped denim began to scatter in the cinder-blackened gravel beneath the train, and then Billy's battered boot, chewed and spit out. Jed, Junior, and Roscoe raced past it, jogging alongside the slowing train. Then, what nobody wanted to see, the prone figure of a boy, thrown clear of the tracks, legs and arms at disagreeable angles.

"Stay put, Billy!" Junior ordered idiotically and ducked under a boxcar as it rolled to a stop. Jed was right behind.

"I'll get a doctor," Roscoe called out.

Junior bellowed, "What kind of fool stunt you pullin', Billy?

Mighta got yourself killed." Jed thought, *might have?* One of Billy's legs twitched as Junior snatched a slip of paper out of the boy's hand. "What's this?"

"Money order," Jed suggested. "If it's made out to Citizens State Bank, it's mine." Junior fixed on him a look of infinite fatigue and disgust. Junior's habit was to snarl at everyone first and buy them a whisky later.

Mama, Billy moaned pitifully.

"Wha'd you boys go and do now?" Lester called down from atop a Santa Fe boxcar. "Christ, Billy! You okay?"

"Get your ass down here," Junior ordered.

Lester slid down the boxcar ladder as if it were a firepole. "What the hell, Albright!" he scolded. "Why'd ya run the poor sumbitch into a movin' train?"

"I didn't. This is your fault!"

A chunk of Lester's chaw splattered at Jed's feet. "Bullshit."

"I'm going to need my revolver back now," Jed said.

"Don't know what you're talking about, old fool." To Junior he said, "Albright shoots his pistol out the mail car at jackrabbits. Prob'ly in some crick where he dropped it on accident."

"What about it, Albright?" Junior said, siding with his crewman, it seemed.

"Did I throw my money order out the mail car, too, and Billy run back to get it?"

Junior's head swiveled back in Lester's direction.

Lester laughed raucously. "Old fool thinks he can frame me. 'Fraid I'm gonna steal his boardinghouse girl before he can get to her coonie himself. Dirty old man." Amusement danced in his cocky eyes. *See, old man? You can't touch me.*

The crack of Lester's teeth beneath Jed's fist reverberated long after the impact. Lester staggered backward and over. Jed gripped his stinging knuckles with his other hand, hoping Lester wouldn't get up. But he did. Sunlight glinted on the blade of a knife that snapped open in his hand. "Don't never wanta do that," he growled.

In the blink of an eye, a slash opened in Jed's vest, his white shirt showing through. Jed's belly tingled where the blade narrowly missed his skin. "Jesus!" Jed said in a strangled voice.

Lester's arm lifted and the knife was pointed at Jed's throat now.

Then suddenly, inexplicably, Lester was on his back in the dirt. And Junior waggled a large pipe wrench over him that he'd smuggled into the party to deliver the blow. Lester's eyes rolled back in his head and took a long look at his troubled soul.

"Stupid bastard," Junior said.

Two

The Girl

Beaumont, Kansas

The tangy vinegar and pepper afflicted his tongue like turpentine. Jed mopped his eyes and forehead with his handkerchief and pushed beans, rice, and sausage around aimlessly on his plate once more as the girl watched. It was a rare moment alone with her. She'd generously offered to reheat his supper and serve it to him on the sly at the kitchen table. The other boarders were in the parlor or their rooms. Maman was off on an errand.

"I don't understand," the girl said. "Why would they arrest Mr. Barnhart if Billy took the money order?"

Mister Barnhart—like the brakeman ran the railroad.

"You'd have to ask the police, Miss Robichaux," Jed said. What else could he say? It would sound like sour grapes if he griped about Lester's crimes—the mail car theft, a knife slash in response to a punch. The girl was in the thrall of the boy and her instinct would be to find fault with the messenger. "It's some sort of mixup, I guess," Jed said, and tried to wash away the aftertaste of the greasy sausage with his coffee, which had gone cold.

Madeleine lifted a doubting eyebrow at the *mixup* remark, exactly as Carrie might have done if she'd been there. As if it was 1912, not 1930. Had Carrie made a pact with the devil to escape aging? Was the price of the bargain erasing her memories of the past?

Madeleine picked up the serving bowl and took it to the sink, kerplopping it into the cloudy dishwater with the rest of the dinner crockery. The girl kept a spotless kitchen. Leaded glass cabinet doors sparkled. Imported floor tile shone. Deep grooves in intricate medallions of plaster were free of dust.

"Don't tell Maman that Mr. Barnhart was arrested," the girl begged. "Please? You know she doesn't like him." He agreed, hoping they could get off the topic of Lester and onto her story.

The maman was Jed's unlikely ally now. With a word, he could set the woman's tiny teeth to gnashing, spitting out arcane Cajun curses at Lester. Jed could fix it so the door would be slammed in Lester's face if the sleazy brakeman showed up here again.

Jed tilted an ear toward the parlor, listening for the maman's return. The woman would come after him with a rolling pin if she found him alone with the girl. The indications were that she was not back. If she were, she'd be putting an end to a disagreement in full boil in the parlor between kindly Old Man Tilman and Widow Baker over how to get the nation and the economy back on track. The widow's knitting needles clacked angrily.

"Could I ask," Jed said to Madeleine, "is there a picture of you and your mother when you were little?" The house was void of keepsakes and souvenirs. Nothing sitting out cast the faintest light on the girl's past. "Did you look more like her when you were a baby?" Jed asked, crossing the bounds of tasteful inquiry.

The girl was tall and willowy with emerald green eyes and hair the color of caramel. The maman was small and dark with more than a trace of mustache. When you got right down to it, Jed bore a greater resemblance to the mother than the girl did.

"It's not so good warmed up?" Madeleine said of his dinner, sounding suddenly irritable. She snatched his plate away before he could object and scraped the remains into the compost bucket. Was she going to blame him now for Lester's arrest?

Up at dawn to cook, clean, and mend for the snippy lodgers, the girl had her short-tempered moments. Who wouldn't as captive labor? Abused like Cinderella in the fairy tale.

Jed took another swallow of cold coffee and daubed his lips. "Thank you for saving my dinner," he said. "Now I must get back to the depot for my brother's arrival."

"What? Your brother is coming? We haven't prepared a room, and yours is too tiny!"

Not to mention up two flights of stairs and overrun with arthropods and mice.

"Not necessary," Jed assured her. "He's taking a room at Forstein's. But I'd find it most agreeable if you'd accompany me to meet him." Most agreeable indeed. Jed wanted Arthur's first glimpse of the girl to be out of the maman's steely sight. "What do you say?"

"I'm sorry, Mr. Albright," Madeleine said. "I can't. I have the dinner dishes to do. And I must draw Mrs. Baker's bath. And Mr. Blanton complained to Maman that the hall hasn't been properly swept in a week …"

"All that can wait just a bit, can't it?" Jed nodded encouragement. "You could slip out and return without your maman ever knowing." The answer would have been yes, he suspected, if it had been Lester asking. Jed was long past knowing how to speak to a young woman.

"Oh, she'd find out," the girl said, "and she's already mad at you, you know. She set a place for you at dinner and you didn't come. You'd have done without if it had been up to her."

Yes, he knew. The woman disliked him from the start, even before Jed had haggled with her over paying a full month's room and board up front. In cash. "No exceptions!"

"But I won't be here even half those nights," he'd argued.

"This ain't a hotel!" she snapped.

Had she seen him across the street, lurking like a pervert on the night he'd followed the girl to the boardinghouse from Beaumont Station? The girl had seemingly slipped out of a wrinkle in time clutching a butcher-paper-wrapped bundle to her bosom like a talisman. Jed's knees buckled. This was not some vaguely similar face in a crowd. Not some woman in the distance whose stride resembled Carrie's. No, it was his sister's face, and he'd seen it up close. Unmistakable. He fell in behind her like a common stalker as she walked on. Propriety be damned.

The grand brick and stone house she led him to had a hand-lettered sign in a window advertising *Rooms*. Her family had fallen on hard times. Or was she a boarder? Jed stood across the road wondering what to do next. Acting on impulse seldom ended well for him. He should mind his own business. Move on. But after years of agonized questions about his sister's disappearance, he couldn't just give up. He needed to find out who this girl was.

A short, dark woman answered the bell stinking of cigar smoke. A silver skull amulet hung on a crude length of black string around her neck. "No solicitors!" she snarled and began to shut the door.

Jed stopped it with his hand. "Room?" he inquired, nodding toward the sign.

She scowled as she sized him up. Then she led him up two narrow flights of stairs to a dingy space carved out under attic rafters. Former servants' quarters. Coal stove. Kerosene lamp. Lumpy mattress. The stink of misery past.

The landlady smiled mischievously. No one would take a room like this. She turned to lead him back down, but as she did, the girl he'd followed was coming up the stairs carrying bed linens. A housekeeper's apron was cinched around her waist.. She looked Jed in the eye, and his heart leapt into his throat.

"I'll take it," Jed said, and reached for his wallet. "How much?"

The old woman squinted hard at him and then spoke angrily to the girl in French. The girl responded with troublingly deference. *Yes, Maman. No, Maman. Right away, Maman.*

"Sure you won't come with me?" Jed said, not really surprised by her refusal. "Okay, could I ask another favor?"

The girl continued bustling about in the kitchen as though he hadn't spoken.

"I'll pay you," Jed said. "And I won't tell your maman that I did, either."

He'd torn his vest and shirt on a hook in the mail car, he said. Would she have time to mend them before his departure in the morning? He produced two quarters from a small leather coin purse.

"That's too much," the girl said. But he pressed the coins into her hand.

* * *

Beneath the depot's mossy water tank, a workhorse Hinkley locomotive was taking a breather after the long, slow uphill climb. The ripe smell of depot cattle pens was strong in the muggy, night air. Jed maneuvered around the engine and jerked to a halt at the sight of Lester Barnhart chatting with a freight handler down the tracks. Lester lifted his cap to show the nasty welt on his skull. How could he be out of jail?

Jed reversed course and cut through Beaumont's former red light district and past the boarded-up saloon. A vagrant was asleep in the doorway where hookers had once swarmed as thick as mosquitoes on an August night. At the billiard hall, the hustlers tipped their hats. Jed had taken two dollars from Lester at snooker there months before, answering his challenge, the sap too drunk and cocky to see he was his own worst enemy.

Junior answered the door of his room at Forstein's in his undershorts, a dog-eared pulp mystery in his hand. His hairless legs were ridiculously scrawny under his barrel chest, like a giant toad with a black mustache. Junior's eyebrows pinched together when he saw it was Jed.

"Thought you'd want to know," Jed said, "Lester's out. Over at the depot now showing off the gash where you whacked him."

Junior's expression didn't change, as if waiting for Jed to come to the point.

"Why would the police let him go?" Jed asked. What plausible answer could there be?

Junior cocked his massive head. "Seeing as how they didn't find your gun on him or on the train or anywhere in the yard, his story must have seemed more likely to them than yours."

Did Junior not believe him either? Was he determined not to admit his train crew had a thief who routinely stashed stolen goods under his very nose? Did Junior not care that Jed would be written up for firing potshots out the mail car door (a possible expulsion offense) or for failing to lock the hatch door to the Railway Express compartment (demerits and a fine at a minimum). Junior's loyalty was to his men, not some loner postal clerk.

17

"Come on, Junior," Jed said. "You know Lester has confederates. At least twenty passengers got off that train at Ark City; any one of them could have smuggled my gun away. And you know Billy didn't steal that cheque. Lester gave it to him."

Junior tilted his head back and peered down his nose. "Your word against Lester's, and he says it ain't so. And Billy ain't talkin', course." He'd ceased his moaning and writhing—*Mama!*—before police and a doctor arrived.

Jed sighed.

"Ain't saying you ain't right, Albright, but where's your evidence? Can't expect John Law to lock a man up on account of some other guy's say-so." He shook his head. "Only the big shots who run railroads get to do that."

"What about him slashing me with a knife, Junior? You saw it. You told them."

"After you cold-cocked him," Junior said and rocked on the balls of his feet, a man running out of patience. "Accused him of every crime in the book, too, as I recollect. Man has a right to defend himself. Hell, don't matter. He's out. Nothing more to be said." He started to close the door and paused. "Only I don't want no trouble tomorrow. Got it? Lester's still on the crew, and we all got jobs to do. That's something to be grateful for these days, in case you hadn't noticed." Then the door snicked shut.

The passenger train from Kansas City was parked on the platform siding when Jed emerged from Forstein's. The passengers had disembarked, but Arthur was not among them. The night telegraph operator, feet propped up on a desk, metal key clacking with signals for stations down the line, flagged him over.

"You Albright?" he said.

"Yes."

"This come for you. I was about to find a boy."

Jed opened it. From Arthur. One word. *Delayed.*

* * *

It was not one of Mrs. Robichaux's scratchy Zydeco records playing on the Victrola when Jed returned to the boardinghouse. It was something jazzy and fresh. Melancholy solos on a trumpet, saxophone, and piano. Snappy percussion.

Madeleine was swaying in the center of the room, seemingly lost in the music. Her apron was off and a ribbon was in her hair. "You like it?" she asked Jed.

He did, but there was Lester on the long velour divan, his hand tapping in rhythm on his thigh, smiling smugly. He'd washed his face and combed his hair. Put on a clean shirt. The garish welt left by Junior's wrench was painted iodine purple, like a hairy plum had sprouted there.

"Mr. Barnhart brought it for us!" Madeleine bubbled merrily.

Lester winked at Jed. *See, old man? You're out of your depth.* His knee was practically touching Widow Baker's, who didn't seem to mind one bit.

Madeleine handed Jed the record sleeve. Her emerald eyes sparkled. *Hoagy Carmichael and His Pals.* "Stardust." She went back to swaying dreamily to the music.

Jed's voice was gruff. "What happened to that party you had planned for tonight, Lester? One with the boys?"

Lester's smile drooped. "After a train run over Billy?" There were gasps. Lester scowled. "That slip your mind, Jed? Boy all busted up in a hospital? Half dead."

His tongue was finely honed. like his switchblade. "What say we step outside, Lester? You and me. Have a private chat."

Puffs of pipe smoke rose over the bleak headlines in Mr. Wallace's newspaper.

Lester got to his feet, grabbed Madeleine by the waist, and began to foxtrot her around the rug. He was smooth on his feet, and Madeleine looked positively jubilant.

The needle made a scrape as Jed lifted it off the disc. "Outside, Lester. Now!"

"Mr. Albright!" Madeleine pleaded. "Don't spoil things!"

Mrs. Robichaux hissed something at Madeleine in French from her perch on the parlor's Queen Anne chair. A needle and thread were drawn taut through a garment in her lap. Jed was startled to see it was his vest.

"Now, Lester!" Jed said. "Outside."

Lester smiled indulgently. "Guess you can't blame a guy for wantin' a bit of privacy if he's got things to get off his chest," he advised the boarders. "Ain't every day a man chases some dumb cripple into a moving freight train."

Madeleine's eyes burned into Jed's face.

"You really want to do this here, Lester?" Jed said. "Maybe you should tell everyone first how it started when you stole my service revolver."

Mr. Wallace's newspaper crumpled. Mrs. Robichaux set aside her mending.

"Shoot, Jed. There you go agin. You know you dropped it in some weeds shootin' at a farmer's dog from the train." Lester spoke calmly, as if instructing a child. He turned his head toward Mrs. Robichaux. "Police tole me that."

"No, Lester," Jed said, "they didn't." He lifted Hoagy Carmichael and talented pals off the turntable and thrust it at Madeleine. "Time to give Mr. Barnhart his record back. He's leaving."

"Naw," Lester said, "I ain't. Ain't done dancin' with this fine young lady. And what right you got, orderin' her around for? Ain't like yer her pappy, is ya?" His grin was evil. "Is ya?" He chuckled. "Naw. She's too purdy to be yours."

Jed's cocked fist froze at the sound of the maman ratcheting a shell into the chamber of a shotgun she produced from under her chair.

"*Sortez!*" she shouted, looping the barrel in a lazy circle at Lester's chest. "Out! *Tout de suite!*"

"Toot sweet!" Lester chuckled and smiled in Jed's direction. "Toot sweet!"

He shrugged impishly, a man unjustly accused. At the door in the front hall, he plucked a new straw skimmer off the coat tree (purloined, Jed suspected). Hand on the knob, he said, "Have that word with you now, Albright. Outside."

The evening had turned clammy. Lester stopped in the spill of a streetlight, hands thrust into his pockets. Had the police confiscated his switchblade? "Listen, old man, dangle a bit of cash and things might have a way of turnin' up. Get me?"

"Like my gun, you mean?" Jed asked. "How much money?"

"Five hundred," Lester said.

Ludicrous, Jed thought. A new one was only thirty dollars.

But a troubling feeling passed through him when Lester didn't wait for an answer, turning on his heel and disappearing into the night.

Three

Arthur

Beaumont, Kansas

Arthur arrived just before eight in a late model Buick roadster with government plates. His wingtip oxfords gleamed in the morning sun and the angle of his gray trilby hat brim suggested a man of the world. He looked trim and athletic in a boxy-shouldered, single-breasted suit. He tossed a nonchalant wave to Jed at an attic window and rested his foot on the Buick's running board to say something to the driver. Then he turned up the walk.

Madeleine stopped sweeping the front hall to answer the door before Jed could race down the stairs. But he stopped at the landing in time to see Arthur gallantly lift his hat to the girl. Then, as if he'd been slapped in the chops by a ghost, Arthur's eyes nearly popped out of his head and the placid, unruffled expression on his face turned tight.

"Who the hell was that?" he said, after Madeleine dashed off to the kitchen.

"Landlady's daughter," Jed told him.

Arthur kept his gaze in the direction the girl disappeared. "You might have warned me."

Jed said, "Let's go get my hat and valise. Upstairs. You can say hello to the spiders."

Arthur trooped along in Jed's wake and grabbed his sleeve.

"How old is she, that girl?" he asked.

Jed smiled. His brother's first thoughts mirrored his own. Not crazy then. In addition to the remarkable resemblance, there was an implication suggested by her age. A breathtaking possibility. "Seventeen," he said. "Same age as Carrie when she disappeared."

"What's her name?" Arthur stammered.

"Madeleine Robichaux." Jed spelled it for emphasis. "I can tell you more on the way to the station. I haven't much time. If you want, we can talk about it in the mail car on the ride to Ark City, and you can be on your way from there."

Arthur puffed pensively on a cigarette by the mail car door as Frisco 635 rumbled south and west over the monotonous Kansas countryside. He finished his smoke, grabbed the safety rail, and leaned out into the rushing air like a circus acrobat to flick the butt into the roar of noise, steam, and soot. Hadn't he had his fill of thrill riding when they were boys? Jed had and was happy to have the heavy door shut again and the horrid racket muffled.

It was a lot for Arthur to take in, Jed could tell. "So, she only knows what the maman has told her?"

It was a concise summation of their conundrum.

"What's the mother's story?" Arthur continued.

Jed relayed what he'd learned about the Cajun seamstress who rented out rooms in the big fancy house. It belonged to the town's banker, Calder Maxwell, her brother-in-law, who vanished in the midst of a depositor run on the bank on November 2, 1929. "Pleasant man," Widow Baker told Jed, "and ramrod straight—or so everyone thought." Until a rumor spread that the books had been cooked. A line of depositors wanting their money back formed before the bank opened the next morning, and an hour later, the door to the bank was locked and chained. "No one saw a penny after that." The sheriff put up a hand-lettered sign in the window, "Closed Till Further Notice." A brick sailed through in answer to that. Sheriff's deputies turned out in force then with long rifles to disperse the angry crowd. Arthur said he hadn't heard of it. One bank failure among many. Bank robbery was more his line of work. The apprehension of bandits. Jed wondered why his agency didn't spend more effort on thieves who used pen and ink as weapons.

"Does this Maxwell have family?" Arthur asked.

The way Widow Baker told it, the banker's wife managed to flee before the assembled mob could reach the Maxwell family home. "Left without a word to Babet." Babet Robichaux and her daughter Madeleine had been living with the Maxwells as cook and maid since the Great Gulf Hurricane five years earlier had taken the life of Mr. Robichaux.

"Went down with his fishing boat," Widow Baker said as her knitting needles continued to clack away like a character out of Dickens. "The past is always present," she said, ambiguous fortune cookie axioms another of her trademarks. "If you know where to look," she added. Jed had no idea what she was hinting at.

The widow's husband had been a very successful Beaumont cattle trader in his day. "Before the market crash ruined everything," she griped. She still had a collection of expensive jewelry, which she wore to bed at night like a daffy princess. "Babet smokes cheroots in the cellar," she muttered when Jed asked. She flicked a hand at the combustible materials all around them. "In this world, you must be prepared to escape with what you have on your back." Her phobia had the unintended benefit of protecting her jewels from Lester's prowling kleptomania, of which the widow seemed blissfully unaware.

"Thanks to the Maxwells' looting," she complained, "the town has gone to the dogs. The cattle trade dried up without a bank to finance it. And the shops on Main Street closed when the cattlemen left. And this fine house got carved up like a Christmas goose. Taken over by squatters! Not that I blame Babet. She didn't have much choice. She, too, would be out on the street with no roof over her head if she didn't pay the property taxes." She gritted her dentures in a scornful smile. "Taxes never stop! Good thing Calder Maxwell can't evict us without showing his face somewhere. So I sleep like a baby in his comfortable bed—a small reparation for the thousands he stole secretly mortgaging my home and gambling away the proceeds in the stock market."

A postcard bound for Iowa sat atop the pile of mail on Jed's sorting table. He reread the address, trying to remember whether Keokuk mail was supposed to be routed through St. Joseph in the latest scheme or Topeka. With Arthur fidgeting nearby, it was hard to concentrate. Frisco 635 swayed and clacked. "The girl is not stupid," Jed said. "She knows she's adopted. Her maman even yells *batarde* at her when she's mad. You don't have to know French to understand what that means."

Arthur nodded. "And you wanted me to see this girl so I wouldn't doubt your theory? Was that it? Well, it could just be some weird fluke of nature instead. A doppelganger."

"Yes," Jed said, not in the least persuaded. Seeing Arthur's reaction in the front hall had told Jed all he needed to know about Arthur's true opinion.

"Still, on the longshot chance that she's … well—" Arthur hesitated. "We need to know the truth."

"Yes," Jed said. "We should probably set up a trust in Carrie's name. Put aside a fourth share of the royalties. We could set it up with us and Tim as beneficiaries. Let any royalties accumulate."

It was clear Arthur didn't care for the idea. Less for him. He dragged over a bundle of magazines to sit on. With his snazzy fedora off, his age showed. Thinning hair. Worry wrinkles. A web of blue veins on his nose. Jed might not be fond of what he saw in his own mirror lately, but he wasn't slipping as fast as Arthur. "You said there was something else you wanted to tell me?" Arthur said irritably.

"Yes, the brakeman on this crew stole my service revolver yesterday. Took a swipe at me with a switchblade when I confronted him about it. Then, last night he offered to get it back for five hundred dollars."

"Five hundred?" Arthur repeated, his brow furrowing. He lodged a thumbnail between his front teeth and gazed into the dust motes afloat in the light of the car's high windows. "It's not the player with the worst cards in a poker game who loses his shirt," he said. "It's the player with the second-best hand, the one who bets his last nickel on what he thought was unbeatable."

What did any of that have to do with Lester? Just who was Arthur calling a sucker here? "What's that supposed to mean?"

Arthur shrugged, as if explaining was more trouble than it was worth.

They'd been close once. It had been their younger brother

Timmy who was always the one out, preoccupied with pursuing his junkyard inventions. But Jed and Arthur had been companionable rivals as boys back in West Virginia with their endless rassling matches and footraces. The quarreling began on the long, difficult trek across Kansas in the wake of their parents' deaths. The stakes had shot sky high, their survival on the line homesteading arid government-granted land in western Kansas. In the end, three boys who had shared a bed in West Virginia found they could no longer share a single opinion in western Kansas.

Arthur asked, "Did you hear back from Tim? Did he go for it?"

"Yes, he signed a lease with Cantor, too."

"So this Marxist collective you've cooked up—it's a done deal?"

"The register of deeds is processing it." The unitization agreement guaranteed that revenue from any well on the four adjacent quarter sections would be split equally three ways among the brothers, no matter where oil or gas was discovered. "Musketeers," Jed had quipped to cajole Arthur. "One for all and all for one." But Arthur sneered at this "insidious socialist arrangement." Like this was Russia. "Why shouldn't I be entitled to a larger slice for a well that hits on my quarter? I have a family to support. You two don't." But Jed had outmaneuvered Arthur by enlisting Tim's support. "Tell me, Arthur, would you be satisfied to get a paltry check if the only well to come in was on Tim's land? Keep in mind that Cantor is under the impression that we own Carrie's quarter, too." A fight over dividing royalties risked exposing a secret best kept buried. Don't play with matches if you've papered over impropriety.

Carrie was still missing and presumed dead eighteen years after she'd walked away. Her brothers felt they were entitled to her quarter section. They'd helped her improve it and they'd managed it in her absence. Wouldn't they be its rightful heirs under common-law? Did it really require the government to stamp its approval?

Not long after Carrie's disappearance, Arthur moved on. He'd openly plotted his escape almost from the day they'd arrived, burning the midnight oil on law school correspondence courses. The frontier life, holed up in a dugout, held no appeal for him. So, the day his land was proved up and legally his, he departed for greener pastures with his young bride. Only with the discovery of oil in a nearby county a decade later was his interest in their farms rekindled. But even good fortune could not quell Arthur's bickering.

"It's a swindle," he claimed, looking over the offer for their mineral rights that Jed favored. It paid less cash up front in exchange for a larger royalty percentage over the life on the contract. And with Tim's backing, Jed held a two-to-one majority. Tim cared little about money, his head in the clouds and his hands busy on his endless projects.

"And if we hit nothing but dry holes?" Arthur pointed out. "We'll get next to nothing!"

"True, because it had been just a pipe dream all along."

The train slowed as Jed wound his pocket watch spring and Arthur paced the mail car's narrow aisle. "We'd better hope nobody comes around asking questions about Carrie's land grant," he said. Arthur seemed not to hear him. "Is something troubling you?" Jed asked.

For all his practice, Arthur was not a good liar. "Nope," he said, his nostrils flaring guiltily.

At the shriek of the engine whistle, Jed realized the catcher arm was not in position for a pickup at Latham. He yanked the door open and hastily kicked out the destination pouch. There wasn't time enough to lock down the catcher arm. So he swung it like a baseball bat at the pouch suspended on the frame. A nasty jolt shot up his arms and into his shoulders, the pouch as heavy as a medicine ball, nearly dragging him out the mail car door. A botched pickup like this had yanked an Ohio mail clerk out of his car recently outside Akron, throwing him under the wheels of the train.

Jed had to sit on his drop-down stool until a surge of dizziness passed. "Any of that whisky left?" he asked Arthur. His brother had been taking furtive nips from a flask all morning when he thought Jed wasn't looking.

* * *

Arthur descended the short ladder outside the mail car door at the Ark City depot and went in to see about a train to Kansas City. "I'll wire you later," he called over his shoulder.

Avoiding two thick-shouldered railroad bulls in leather jackets on their way to roust a hobo from a boxcar, Jed nearly collided with a man in a derby hat coming out of the telegraph office. His bushy mustache seemed familiar. "Mr. Wallace?" Jed asked. What would a reclusive boarder from Beaumont be doing here?

"Oh, Albright!" Wallace said, stuffing a handwritten telegraph form into his pocket. "Didn't see you!" He tipped his derby hat. "You'll have to excuse me, but I'm in rather a hurry. So, I bid you good day, sir!" He doffed his hat again, and departed for the front door.

Ruby had Jed's box lunch waiting at the register.

"The devil's half-brother was just here asking about you," she said, glancing nervously around the depot. She'd gotten her hands on a tube of lipstick and gone overboard with the rouge on her plump lips. "But I don't see him now, thank God."

"Was it Clarence Darrow?" Jed suggested.

Ruby giggled. "How can anyone as gloomy as you make me laugh?" She slid the box across the counter with a wink. Copper highlights shone in her hair. "Prosperity might not be around the corner, Jed, but a piece of homemade lemon pie is." She patted the box with a nod.

Lemon pie. A sick feeling rose in him as he tried to summon a smile.

"On the house," Ruby said, misreading his distress. She reached to touch his hand but drew back at the sight of his wedding ring.

"Thank you," he said. "It's very kind." What had he been thinking, leading this kind woman on? Dressing up to impress her, this waitress who slipped drifters baloney sandwiches behind the boss's back. "Seriously, Jed," she called after him. "Be careful."

There was ice water in the cooler tank of the mail car. He filled a paper cup twice trying to subdue the sour ache taking root in his

29

belly. Lemon pie. Was his past determined to punish him for his unfaithful thoughts? The words of the widow returned, as if prophetic. *The past is always present.* It just lurks beneath the surface.

Frisco 635 lurched, the gapped couplers clanged, and the train slowly gathered speed out of the station. Alone amidst piles of sealed personal communications, Jed untied the string around his box lunch and nearly gagged at the sharp, sweet smell of lemons. In the mail car toilet, he lifted the lid of the commode and dropped the wedge of pie down the hole to splatter on the rough cedar ties racing beneath.

Four

Sun Dog

Rolla, Kansas – July 1911

The Leghorn they call The Duchess insists on laying her eggs at the edge of the clearing in a parched, matted clump of buffalo grass. Her unbending routine comes to a dramatic end, however, the morning that the only trace of The Duchess is a ghastly smattering of bloody feathers and bits of broken eggshell where her prodigious yield is usually found.

"Did a hawk get her?" Anna Carrie asks. Her fingers fuss at the gingham skirt she cut and sewed by lantern light in the dugout, using a mail-order pattern. The black mourning dress has been retired, lifting everyone's spirits. But Carrie's chin trembles now and tears seem close as she considers The Duchess's violent end. She tugs tight the apron in which she's cradled all of the other eggs. She didn't need this reminder of the fragility of life. Of the suddenness and finality of death. None of them did. Not after Ma passed three months back, days after the mine explosion that took Pa.

Jed fans his face with his broad-brimmed hat, trying not to let his veneer of optimism slip. It's hard not to think of this as a bad omen. Bad things happen in threes. He watches a killdeer circle lazily in the empty sky. Whatever attacked The Duchess has long since departed to enjoy its feast. And not close by, from the looks of it, not with the gelding out on the hobble, tranquilly grazing on bluestem. A coyote did this, Jed suspects. More than one has announced itself in the night with its yipping serenade and mournful howls. He keeps this conjecture to himself. There's no point in riling Carrie up more. Coyotes scare her half to death. "Look for a red tail with a big grin," Jed says. "That'll be the one."

"Don't josh," Carrie scolds. "She was our best layer."

"So, I trust you'll hatch us a new champ," Jed says. Carrie has a keen eye and a sixth sense for candling eggs. Trouble is, The Duchess was a freak of nature and the end of her line. "We must build us a coop, and soon, before whatever did this comes back for another meal," Jed says. "It's that or share our beds with the chickens," he adds ruefully.

A pile of stray fender pieces remains from the rickety secondhand buckboard they'd bought in Kansas City. They'd used it to haul their teetering mound of possessions across Kansas on the Santa Fe Trail. Decrepit furniture, winter clothes, chamber pots, and keepsakes—all of it sent to the trailhead from Thurmond, West Virginia, by rail freight. At no small expense. It wouldn't have been possible without the wad of greenbacks Tim discovered in a powdered milk tin in the lean-to kitchen back home. Ma's secret cookie jar for a rainy day. The smithy who sold them the buckboard after a lot of dickering agreed to buy their father's spare mining kit so the "youngsters" would have a bit of bankroll left for food and other supplies.

Picking through the lumber in the salvage pile near the dugout entrance, Jed finds enough to fashion a slatted roof and a chicken wire doorframe, if he's careful. It will have to be tiny, sided with hay bales until the rock-hard ground softens under a passing storm and they can cut additional sod bricks. They'd used what few they'd been able to make before the long dry spell for the dugout's face and roof. Planks from the buckboard bed had been cannibalized to hold up the roof. Lumber is a luxury in these parts. There are no trees. The landscape is largely featureless here, as flat as a griddle cake, as if some evil force passed through and scraped away everything except scraggly underbrush. Jed misses the sounds of West Virginia songbirds and the rattling aspen leaves in the breeze and wonders if this place will ever truly feel like home.

The sweat collecting under his muslin shirt is trickling down his back, reminding him there's no time for daydreaming. By midday, the blistering sun will be unbearable and force them to take cover in "the hideout," as Tim calls it. He alone likes the novelty of living beneath the earth.

"Reckon we shouldn't have sold Pa's spare mining helmet and lamp," Carrie has joked more than once when a clump of loose soil dribbled out of their ceiling. An above-ground soddy and tin roof will have to wait. It's all they can do now to keep up with what they've planted and put away stores to last the coming winter. Next spring, they can think about building something else, this time on Arthur's quarter section.

One day they'll all live in a large white frame house at the intersection of their four quarters, Jed believes, nestled amidst orchards of fruit trees and bountiful gardens and pens for livestock, surrounded on all sides by row upon row of profitable sorghum, as far as the eye can see. Arthur will be mayor of Rolla. Carrie will have a dress shop. And Timmy? He'll help Jed work the farm. The endless sea of prairie grass will be gone by then, plowed into oblivion for cash crops. But right now, this year, all that the Albrights can manage is a patch of broomcorn on Tim's quarter and Carrie's beleaguered vegetable garden close by. The rest is raw determination and a hole in the ground where they can lay their heads at night.

Arthur appears on the footpath calling out his return from town, a book from the Rolla library tucked under one arm and a sack of cornmeal slung over his shoulder. He has bartered yesterday's eggs and one barren chicken at Burlingame's for the meal. On other occasions, he's traded for beans, sugar, pork, seeds, and tools. Hearing Arthur's call, Tim materializes.

"What are you doin', Jed?" Arthur asks and drops the meal sack to the ground. "What's happened here?" The shoulder of his shirt has a golden smudge where the gunny had rested. Jed leads him to The Duchess's plundered nest, and Arthur explodes. "If we lose our best layers, we don't eat!" Like Jed is to blame. Or too stupid to realize. An insult either way.

Jed feels something akin to a toothache coming on. The close quarters and long days have whittled down his patience.

Everything and everyone they'd ever known who might provide help or comfort is a half continent away. Arthur has their father's flinty eyes—minus the coal dust that blackened the rims. A lecture from Arthur is something Jed is not prepared to suffer.

"I thought I'd cut up what's left of the fenders to build a coop," Jed says.

"What about the privy?" Carrie objects. "You said that's what it was for."

It's true. He'd promised—foolishly. Now he has to go back on it. It's hardly a real choice, though, a young lady's modesty or food on the table for them all. "I'm sorry," he says. "The privy will have to wait. Circumstances have taken an unexpected turn." His words sound ridiculously pompous, even to him.

"Right," Arthur interjects, and begins bossing everyone around. "Timmy can build the coop. Carrie should finish her chores. You and I, Jed, we have to get after the bull thistle and bitterweed in the broomcorn." They could ill afford to have anything competing with their cash crop for nutrients and the depleted moisture in the soil. They'd already had to replant the field after a terrible, gritty wind uprooted the seedlings. There hadn't been enough grain left to refill every furrow they'd so laboriously plowed. The field had shrunk. Turning a profit was going to be a serious challenge. Arthur says, "Best we get going, Jed. It's gonna be a scorcher."

They stomp past wilted prickly pear and drooping spikes of yucca on the way to the cornfield, carrying their mattocks like rifles. The buffalo grass underfoot has been baked to a sickly, wilted brown from a month of dry heat. Aridity has also unmoored a Russian thistle from its roots, and it is bounding overland in the breeze, scattering seeds as it rolls. Tumbleweed.

"This is all cockamamie, you know," Arthur says, straightening up between the rows he's working. He stretches this way and that, trying to work a kink out of his back. His weed bucket is half full.

"What is?"

"This." He gestures with contempt at the vast landscape, and then singles out the stubby corn emerging from the rock-hard soil under their boots. "This farm. The corn, which should be twice as tall as this by now." Dust has collected in the shallow cleft of his chin.

The sun feels like a weight on Jed's shoulders. He and Arthur are drenched in sweat.

"Not now, Arthur. Not today." Jed feels too close to capitulation, as if Arthur's doubts might eat him up and finish the job. (What has he gotten them into?) Between the heat and exasperation with the bull thistle, he's tempted to throw down his hoe and walk away. He wishes Arthur would at least give it a rest, but he is unrelenting.

"Come on, Jedidiah, look around you. This isn't fit land to farm. It'll be nothing short of a miracle if this damn broomcorn makes it."

Prophetic words, as things turn out.

"Rain follows the plow," Jed says meekly, but he can't look his brother in the eye.

"Bah!" Arthur mocks. His eyes narrow to slits. "That's claptrap, and you know it. Cornball superstition. Rainfall here is just fifteen inches a year. Back home it's almost fifty."

Unwilling to concede the point, Jed says, "Just last year the Johnsons grew fat, juicy watermelons. Yonder, not three miles from where we're standing."

"Last year was wet, as it happened. This year it will be dry, if only to prove this climate is fickle. It's the law of averages, brother. The map we had at school labeled this the Great American Desert."

Jed remembers it clearly. The pale blotch conjured up images of sand and scorpions and steer skulls bleached white by the sun. But it isn't like that at all. The soil here is rich and thick with vegetation. Not sand. "Dry farming works, Arthur. And this is the right crop. Give it time. I wager rain will be here by the end of next week. We just have to put our backs into this, keep tilling, and hope for the best." When Arthur continues to grumble, Jed leans on his hoe's hilt and says, "I seem to recall it was Ma's dying wish that we stick together. Watch out for each other—especially Carrie and Tim. And we agreed, this was the way."

Arthur shakes his head. "You can be stubborn as a mule, you know?"

Stubbornness is not a bad thing. His stubbornness kept them out of the mine after Pa made them quit school to work as breaker boys for the mining company, one step short of going down in the shaft with him. Jed's refusal to mine coal led to whippings and to both boys being forced instead to pluck slate out of the coal ore ten hours a day, six days a week, fingers bloodied by the sharp, jagged rock riding past on the conveyor with the coal. Jed still has nightmares about Billy Edmond falling into the apparatus and being crushed in its gears. If Jed hadn't been obstinate, they'd be buried right now with Pa under thousands of tons of rock, just a slender vein of calcium compressed between the seams of heavy bituminous coal. "Determination," Jed says. "Not the same thing as stubbornness."

"Yeah, in your case, it is. You've even got a mule's pointed ears."

A taunt meant to provoke him. But Arthur knows Jed won't throw a punch, even if he's itching to. He can't afford to start something that would risk retaliation or hard feelings. Their survival depends on peace and cooperation. Jed can't manage things out here without him.

"Met a fella in town," Arthur says, as if he has something up his sleeve. "Neighbor of ours. Scruggs. Elmore Scruggs. Cattle rancher. Says animal grazing is the only thing this land is good for, why the buffalo could thrive here for eons before a bunch of mad Yankees slaughtered them for sport and left the corpses to rot where they fell. Grazing, he says, is the only use of this Godforsaken prairie that isn't doomed to failure and misery. And I believe him."

"Okay, but how are we supposed to get into the cattle business? It takes a lot of capital. And we literally don't have chicken feed—for our own chickens." It's true.

"We invest our broomcorn profits once the harvest is in."

"That money is as good as spent three times over already—*if* it materializes."

"Yes, I figured you'd say that. Turns out there's another way."
"Yes?"

"Scruggs offered me one of his calves. No charge."
"And why would he do that?"

"He asked if his cattle could graze on some of our land. We have more than a hundred idle acres, and his is already overworked by the beeves he's got. And he's looking to expand. He knows we're a couple years away from cultivating out to the edge. He'll throw in some cash if we go along. You know we could use the money, Jed. Get that store-bought window for the dugout wall before winter. Pay down a bit on the cookstove at Burlingame's. Buy the tools we'll need for digging the well."

"How would we keep his steers out of our broomcorn?"

"Scruggs says he'll fence it off for us."

Arthur has an answer for everything. Jed's not surprised. He says, "There's a big difference between leasing some grazing rights and jumping into ranching ourselves. We don't know the first thing about the cattle business, Arthur. You ever neutered an animal that big?"

"We'd learn. Start out with the one calf, and watch how Scruggs does it. You know it makes sense, Jed. What have we got to lose?"

If Jed says no, there is nothing to stop Arthur from splitting off his own quarter section and going it alone. And if he puts barbed wire around his place to pen in a herd, the barrier could lead to more division. Arthur has him over a barrel. "All right, Arthur. You've obviously been thinking on this for a spell. I need a day or two to ponder it myself, all right?"

In the heat of this discussion, Carrie has sidled up the path unnoticed. Behind her in Jed's line of sight is the dugout's stovepipe, jutting out of the earth like a metal tree stump. For fuel, they burn dried buffalo dung in the stove. The stuff is plentiful for now. Heifer City coal, the locals call it. It should be stockpiled, too, before the snow flies or they won't have heat this winter. "Ponder what?" Carrie asks. "What are you two jabberin' about?"

"Farming," Jed says evasively, not inviting her to widen this into a family debate. Carrie might well align herself with Arthur, if he dangles promises of lace curtains and china-laden sideboards from the fat profits that he believes ranching might bring.

A tiny pinch of doubt creases Carrie's beautiful brow, acknowledging that this is a dubious response at best, a cucumber to steep in the brine of her skepticism to make a pickle for Jed later. "Here's something else to ponder," she says. "Vermin are nibbling on everything in the garden. And it's looking mighty parched, too."

"Okay," Jed says. "We'll barter for more water. Two buckets at a time from Burlingame's. If the garden doesn't produce, we'll never make it through the winter." Right now, the root cellar they dug is just another hole in the ground.

* * *

The rooster crows in the dead of night, wrenching Jed from a troubled dream. His eyes sting and refuse to open. The chickens are making a ruckus, squawking and flapping their clipped wings hard. Sitting up on his straw tick, he awakens to a molten orange light on the western horizon, as if the sun is coming back up right where it went down a few hours before. A whiff of smoke hitchhikes in on the breeze, and Jed's heart thuds as he steps out into the starless night. He's struck dumb by the sight of dancing flames and massive showers of sparks in the distance. It's breathtaking. The words he needs to alert the others refuse to form on his lips. This can't be happening. The blaze seems as wide as Kansas itself, as if the entire state has caught fire.

The scrape of a boot behind him and an abrasive voice in the darkness addressing him break the spell. "Albright? That you, Albright?" A man-sized bug has invaded their yard with a limp black flag hoisted. Something straight out of a child's nightmare. It has a splotchy dark shell that tapers at the neck and a monstrous leathery skull with seams for ears. Its eyes are flat circles in which the jagged lines of fire dance.

"What the hell?" Jed stammers.

"It's Scruggs," says the bug out of a corner of its mouth. And then Jed can tell it's the neighbor in a motorcyclist's helmet and goggles. The shell is a blood-stained leather apron. "What are you waitin' fer, fire to run up your pant leg?" Scruggs looks around. "Where's your well at?"

Jed says *don't have one,* loud enough to be heard over the ruckus of chickens.

"Don't have one?" Scruggs bellows back. "Don't have no plow! Don't have no well! How long you 'spect to survive out here?"

Again Jed can't find words. *Hell,* he mutters to himself. Is it a badge of shame that they borrowed Redmond's heavy breaking plow and oxen to turn their soil? And had to trade away eight good laying chickens and the promise of a quarter of the crop for the privilege? Jed's head clears away the nighttime cobwebs. "Not everybody is blessed with an artesian spring on their land, Scruggs. We got the river yonder." The Cimarron. And drinking water from Burlingame's.

Scruggs snorts. "That crick? Case you hadn't heard, that little dab of nothin' dries up in July and freezes over in December— if'n the Lord sees fit to send us a single drop of rain after May 1. Hell, none of that is gonna matter a hoot in an hour if that there fire keeps acomin'." He nods in that direction. "I'd get moving, I was you."

"Won't the break at the section road stop it?"

"Feel that breeze, Albright? Fire's suckin' in the oxygen it needs, creatin' its own wind, like a cyclone. When it gets to that spit of dirt you're talking about, it'll leap it quicker'n a grasshopper."

Scruggs has an empty gunny sack in his hand and a wet towel tied to the hoe over his shoulder. A filthy red bandanna hangs limp around his neck. Why has he come this way, moving toward the fire rather than away? Shouldn't he be rounding up his herd? Moving them to safety? Jed, tongue-tied, doesn't ask.

Scruggs looks toward the dugout entrance and says, "Best be getting the others up quick. Not a minute to spare. You're four, right?" The teeth in his suddenly leering mouth are as dull as stones. "Countin' the young lady?" He squints behind the goggles. He's taken the measure of everything apparently. "Seen her over to Burlingame's. She your wife?"

Jed's disgust with Elmore Scruggs grows. "Sister," he says with a mind-your-own-business tone.

Scruggs pays no attention. "Anybody spoke yet for her hand?"

Jed stares in disbelief. "Thought you said there wasn't a minute to spare."

"That's right," Scruggs says, as if he has his answer. "So quit your lollygaggin'."

                                  * * *

Mice scamper past underfoot, a hundred feet from the flames. Snakes, too, are slithering to safety. The sparks float like lightning bugs in the night. But when they land on exposed skin, they sting like hornets. Jed stamps his boots on any that he sees settle around him in dry buffalo grass. The smoke and heat become unbearable as the Albright boys reach the fire line behind Scruggs. They quell the flames in one spot, only to be outflanked in another. Staying below the thicker smoke is only marginally better, Jed discovers. Every breath rakes like sandpaper down his throat. Fits of coughing interrupt him as he lashes at the flames with a charred gunny sack. Scruggs has his bandanna pulled up over his nose and mouth now like a bandit. His goggles keep the ash and smoke out of his eyes. He's done this before. It's a puzzle where all these other stern, determined souls have come from in the middle of the night, these sweaty strangers with blankets, shovels, and stray tools better suited to other tasks. They scoop pails of dirt on the advancing flames until wind gusts fan the flames to a whooshing roar and drive them all back. They dodge fiery tumbleweeds that roll out of the line of flames like Roman candles. "Watch out!" a man on horseback calls before he gallops by dragging the split carcass of a cow through the flames. He circles back and makes another pass before dashing off to rescue a group of women and children encircled by flames and shouting their voices hoarse for help.

"Fire behind you!" a girl shrieks at Jed. He flees as if he's been shot out of a cannon with Arthur and Tim. They run through an opening in the flames, but Jed collides with an old man in a nightshirt and tumbles into prickly pear that snags his dungarees. Flames lick at his back. He cries out in shock as much as pain. And suddenly Arthur is there slapping at him with his blackened cornmeal gunny and yanking him out of the thorns. Scruggs appears. "This way," he orders. "Fire's shifting!" His tangled, dirty hair hangs out the back of his leather helmet.

The flames are headed for the Albrights' broomcorn despite the brothers' efforts to blunt its relentless advance. Soon, their precious field is breached. But with only stunted stalks and no dry grass to burn in the tilled space, the fire weakens between the meandering rows. It dies out entirely at another capricious shift in the wind. Some of the crop, such as it is, has been saved. The ragtag fire brigade moves on to other outbreaks.

At dawn, the brothers collapse at the door to their dugout. The blackened fields continue to smolder. Their faces and hands are dark with soot. "We look like we've been down in the mine," Arthur says and laughs. His eyes are bloodshot and maniacal in his miserable face. He removes Jed's singed shirt and applies petrolatum ointment to the burn blisters on his back, where the scars from Pa's strap are still visible. "Scruggs is going to be up against it now," Arthur says. "Not much chow left for his beeves to munch on." Scattered patches of grass remain, untouched islands in the charred landscape where the fickle fire has jumped or split.

A drizzle starts up, seemingly out of thin air. Smoke and mirrors. But real moisture. The soot on their faces streaks as it drips. The ash is bitter on their lips and tongues. Rain. Now. Sure.

"Look at that!" Tim shouts and points at the eastern sky. "Did you ever see the like?" There appear to be two suns in the sky. The larger of the two is a faint silver orb poking weakly through the veil of cloud and smoke. The smaller one is surrounded by glowing rings that flicker. "Sun dog!" Tim exclaims. "A sign from God! Ma saw one as a girl."

Jed is all but certain it's an atmospheric deception. But after the night they've just been through, the effect is so unsettling, so unexpectedly bizarre, it swamps him with bewilderment. He feels dislocated from reality. He literally can't believe his eyes. Another sign, perhaps, he thinks, unable to turn away. All is not well with the world. Is it ending?

"It's a mirage," Arthur scoffs, not one easily bamboozled. "Like those vanishing lakes we saw all along on the trail coming here from St. Louis. Light bent, as if through a prism."

"No!" Tim shouts. "It's a sign from God, Arthur! Ma told me all about it. Ain't got nothin' to do with pretend lakes. That's God's halo up there. He's blessing us."

"Jesus Christ," Arthur blasphemes. And laughs ruefully.

"Arthur," Jed says. "Please. Not everything is literal or scientific. Mystery and magic are two of the great joys of life." Not that he agrees with Tim. This is not a blessing. If it is God, it's the wrathful one of the Old Testament, smirking. The one who's just seen fit to burn their farm.

Carrie leads the gelding safely back from town. Its tawny hooves have boots of gray ash. Jed tries to intercept his sister before she can see the devastation of the burnt-out yard. Only a charred pyre remains of their horse cart with its axle and sagging springs. The chicken coop is nothing but embers and ash. When Carrie notices it, she breaks into a run.

"Nothing to be done, Carrie," he says, catching her in his arms. "They're gone."

Carrie cries out and wriggles free from his grip to pound his chest with her fists. Her eyes are full of tears and accusations. *You! This is your fault.*

He can see the others feel the same. Someone is always to blame when things go wrong.

Without a word, Jed gathers up the gelding's reins, mounts, and rides off.

He might well have stopped long enough to wash his face, he sees in the glass of the front door on his way in.

A ferocious bronze eagle above the teller cage bares its talons at Jed as he sits before the banker's desk and carefully explains the situation to the fastidious J.J. Pierpoint. Pierpoint's skin is as polished as a pearl. Not part of last night's volunteer fire brigade, then.

"We can't lend you money against land you don't own," Pierpoint says with a trace of amusement. His chair squeaks as it rocks. He taps a ledger open on his desk and nods unhelpfully. A reasonable man. The brass pendulum of his office clock leisurely ticks along.

"It would only be till October when our broomcorn comes in," Jed says humbly. Not begging. Conscious of his youth and his West Virginia accent. "How's a man supposed to improve his land if he can't borrow a little money to do it?"

A portrait of Pierpoint's grandfather in full Union regalia hangs on the office wall behind him. The ancestor's dark beard puts Jed in mind of Ulysses S. Grant. He can't recall which side of the war Kansas fought on, just that there was some kind of local massacre over the issue.

"Until you've worked your claim for two years and proven it up at the land office, received your patent," he explains patiently, "you lose that land if a disaster like a wildfire drives you off. And should this crop of yours fail, how would you pay us back? The bank would be left holding an empty bag."

The door to a vault full of greenbacks, silver, and gold stands open behind the teller cage grid. Jed glances that way as he stands. The seat of Jed's dungarees sticks to the chair as he rises. "Thank you for your time," he says in a rather sarcastic way.

He rides the gelding slowly past Burlingame's, the hotel and livery barn, the drugstore and the smithy's shop, and out onto the open plain. He promises himself he'll return someday and shoot Mr. J.J. Pierpoint between the eyes, even if hanging is the price.

Five

Vinegar Pie

Enid, Oklahoma – May 1930

Jed was not pleased to discover it was Arthur knocking on his apartment door uninvited at suppertime that night in Enid. Not after the sullen silence he'd put Jed through that morning in the mailcar. "Suddenly find yourself in the mood to talk?" Jed asked.

"Get your hat," Arthur said with halitosis that could wilt flowers. "We've got a train to catch." He took a puff off his cigarette.

"We do?" Jed replied. First he'd heard of it. But Arthur was in the habit of springing plans on people. One of his tricks for controlling outcomes. Agent training at Quantico had refined and enhanced this natural gift for bullying. Born for bureau work, Jed thought. He informed his brother of a niggling little hitch. "I have potato soup going on the stove."

"Ah." Arthur sniffed the air and nodded. "I thought you might be ironing. It smells like laundry starch." He had an impish grin. "Not interested in a wild-goose chase then?"

"And where would this wild-goose chase take us?" Jed asked, playing along. "Louisiana?"

"No flies on you," Arthur said. He tossed his trilby hat up with a flick of the wrist and caught it as neatly as a carnival juggler. "Forget the soup. I'll buy you a steak on the train. Let's go." When

Jed didn't budge, Arthur said, "So, you'd rather I just went by myself?" If the carrot didn't work, reach for the stick.

Cut Jed out. Do something that suited Arthur's purposes only. No, Jed had to go, to see for himself if Carrie was truly alive. Put an end to the torture. Hear the exact words that came out of her mouth about what had happened. Arthur wasn't one to take fliers. There had to be something solid here or he wouldn't be going. "Don't be in such a toot," Jed said. "Give me a second."

Arthur cast a fretful glance down the hall as if their train was idling there and about to depart down one of the stairwells.

"Come in, dammit," Jed said. "Just for two minutes. I have to call my supervisor. I'm scheduled to work the Enid-to-Beaumont run tomorrow, and he'll need to find a sub."

There was a time in his childhood when Jed had relished the "missions" Arthur cooked up, walking out of town on the Chesapeake & Ohio tracks that ran through the very heart of Thurmond. The front steps of the hotel, shops, and the church led down to the railroad tracks, since there was no Main Street. In fact, no road went in or out the coal company town of Thurmond except for those rails. You could follow one of the footpaths that clambered overland through the hills. But otherwise, the railroad was the town's connection to the outside world. From the Albrights' front porch, Jed and Arthur had watched the enormous chains of coal cars rumble by and tried to guess their destinations or where the empties were returning from. The boys became experts at walking atop the narrow steel rails—another source of competition. The first one to step off onto a cross tie lost. Thinking themselves indestructible in the armor of adolescent hormones, they'd ventured once, and only once, across a 200-foot trestle high over New River, where one false step off a rail would be a loss to end all losses. Done on a dare. *Bet you can't do it! What's a matter? Scared?* Jed had never forgotten Arthur's arms windmilling in panic ten feet from the trestle's end on the far side of the river, fighting for balance after the train whistle blasted out of the tunnel just beyond the bridge. No time to go back. Jumping into the river far below might have sent them to their deaths. "Forward," Jed yelled. The rocky outcropping at the mouth of the shaft had just enough ledge for them to cling to. They pressed their faces to the rock as the freight locomotive barreled past. If they'd been in the tunnel, they'd have been trapped with nowhere to run. The indelible incident was never mentioned again.

"That line is busy," a Central operator reported. Jed slipped the receiver back onto the hook and made space for the pot of soup in the icebox. He rounded up his valise and hat. "I'll have the manager at the station pass the word," he said.

They raced on foot to the depot, Arthur wheezing and huffing. The flask made an appearance on the platform and Arthur lit a cigarette that somehow helped him catch his breath.

"What's our destination in Louisiana?" Jed asked. "And why all the cloak-and-dagger rush?"

"Listen," Arthur said, and took another swig of his spirits as their train came into view. "I just realized, I didn't pack. You know, I should go home. And you should, too. Have your soup. Forget the girl. Get on with your life."

"Too late," Jed said. This clumsy attempt to pull the plug only made Jed more determined. "We're going. This was your idea."

Arthur's jaw was tight as he stared at the oncoming train. Out of the blue, he asked, "Did you tell Amanda about the girl?"

Amanda. It was the second time that day Jed was forced to think about her. Confront his regrets. She had arrived in his life as a silhouette in the doorway of the dugout, a girl lifting the canvas flap the morning after the fire. A wicker basket is on her arm. Drizzle is falling outside. Her musical *yoo-hoo* for attention halts a heated argument between Jed and Arthur about selling the surviving broomcorn to Scruggs for forage. Arthur claims it's worth more as fodder for steers than bristles for brooms. Jed calls that bullroarer. The girl's melodic voice instantly cools the hot tempers.

"I'm sorry, am I intruding?" the young lady asks in a cheerful tone.

The hem of her calico dress has dragged through wet wildfire ash and is streaked with it. But Jed's eye is drawn to the way it gathers at her narrow waist, accentuating her bust. Her face disappears beneath the brim of her rain hat as she glances down the slippery slope into the dugout. Wisps of fine auburn hair are loose on her slender neck. When she lifts her face, Jed is taken by her beauty. A vision has arrived bearing gifts! How like cornered rats they must seem to her in their dingy hovel. Jed recedes deeper into the shadows, wishing he'd washed his face.

Carrie puts down a pot to catch water dripping from a spot in the ceiling.

"Please," she says to their visitor, "come in. How do you do? I'm Carrie. Anna Carrie Albright. And these are my brothers, Timothy, Arthur, and that's Jedidiah back there in the shadows being shy. Here, let me take that."

Before she can, Tim wrestles the basket from the visitor's grip and pulls back the cloth covering its contents. A peculiar, insistent odor—something a bit off—invades the dugout to mingle with the robust smell of damp soil. A pie and two Mason jars of cool sweet tea are visible. "Ooh," Carrie trills, "refreshments!"

"It's a vinegar pie," says the visitor. "It's, uh, what you might call a local specialty. From Mrs. Trutcher's prize recipe. I hope you all like it. Our apple barrel went bad, unfortunately, and fruit is in short supply just now."

"*Vinegar* pie?" Tim wrinkles his nose and backs away.

Jed's thoughts go down a rabbit hole in search of a compliment. Whoever heard of vinegar pie?

"It looks wonderful," Carrie says, coming to the rescue. "Thank you. And, please, set a spell?" She gestures to a trunk covered with one of their mother's chenille-bordered tablecloths. "Maybe have a glass of the sweet tea you've brought?"

"Oh, no, that's all for you." Her manners are prim. The girl has been brought up properly. "Because of your heroics last night, those of us closer to town were spared the lick of the flames. Thank you!" She looks around. "I almost didn't find your place, though. If your brother hadn't ridden this way on horseback, I might still be wandering around. My stars, your dugout is all but invisible, the way it's tucked into this little rise! And so cozy inside! You have lovely things. And what do we have here?"

Gently, she picks up a newborn chick that has pecked its way out of its shell on the incubator table. Its damp, matted feathers haven't had time to fluff out. Its scrawny chest heaves with effort. "Why it's so tiny and adorable."

"And it'll grow into a fine, plump chicken in a few months," Jed says. "Why don't you take it with you, Miss uh …?"

"Oh, my! Where are my manners? I've neglected to introduce myself! I'm Amanda Elizabeth Vanderhorn. My people call me Mandy." Jed has heard of the Vanderhorns. They are working claims on a section northeast of the Albrights. "This chick is so darling. Are you sure you want to part with it?"

"Yes, it's yours," Jed tells her. "Take it as a token of our gratitude for the refreshments, Miss Vanderhorn."

He walks her back out. The prairie fire has scorched a belligerent mark on the canvas flap over the door, the material just tough enough to deny the flames entry.

"Hard to believe right now, Mr. Albright," Amanda Vanderhorn says, "but everything that burned will come back extraordinarily lush and beautiful before you know it. It's just nature's way." The chick peeps softly in the basket. Amanda Vanderhorn smiles sweetly. "Your family was very brave."

Jed feels the flattery turn his soot-smudged face into a source of pride, proof of his courage and fortitude in the face of last night's blaze. He is worthy of her admiration! His mind thrashes about for a way to detain her. "We are much obliged for the pie and tea, Miss Vanderhorn," he says again, wishing she would stay.

She giggles. "Miss Vanderhorn is my aunt," she says. "Please call me Mandy." With that, she sets off for home with a crisp goodbye. Amanda Elizabeth Vanderhorn has a jaunty, quick step, and her arm swings in an arc that suggests she is grasping the empty air in front of her and using it to pull herself along faster.

"Is that Cupid's arrow I see sticking out of your back?" Arthur asks, materializing at Jed's elbow. "What the hell are you doing giving away one of our last clutch!"

Of course Arthur would find a way to spoil things. "One less mouth to feed," Jed says and smiles, thinking his joke suits the occasion perfectly. Arthur doesn't find it funny. His eyes are burning a hole in Amanda Vanderhorn's lovely back. Jed says, "Don't worry, Arthur, one of these days we'll stew a rooster or two for Sunday dinner. In the meantime, we need all the friends we can get."

* * *

"Well?" Arthur yelled over the screeching brakes of the

southbound train as it pulled to a stop at Enid station. "What's the answer? Did you tell Amanda about the girl or not?"

"What? No." They hadn't spoken. Not in ages. Arthur knew that. And why should it matter? Jed retaliated for Arthur's offense by asking an equally idiotic, offensive question. "Does your mother-in-law still make her legendary vinegar pie?" Arthur and his mother-in-law don't get along either.

"Jesus! Is that a joke?"

Famished, the Albrights had each tried a piece of the pie that day. Arthur had gagged and run from the dugout to spit his out. But Tim, who thought it tasted like lemon custard, volunteered to finish it all.

Their train, bound for New Orleans, was twelve cars long. It had crossed Minnesota, Iowa, Missouri, and Kansas before arriving in Oklahoma. "Tell me, Arthur, what makes you think this wild-goose chase will turn up our sister?"

"Coincidence," he replied.

"Yes?" Jed said, waiting for the rest. The porter lowered the bottom step. "That's it?" Jed said as Arthur mounted the steps without another word. Jed had a queasy sensation as he followed him up. Were they about to open a can of worms? Poke at the proverbial sleeping pooch? Choose a cautionary cliché. If Carrie was still alive (which Jed was finding hard to fathom), why had she never contacted them? Since she hadn't, there must be reasons.

Arthur showed his federal badge to a gravelly voiced conductor and arranged for their deadhead rides. The old trainman had a glint in this eye as he ushered them to a pair of comfortable armchairs in a smoking car decked out like a gentlemen's club. Curtains at the windows. Ashtrays on stands between the plush seats. The conductor nodded toward a deeply tanned man at the end of the car and whispered, "That fella there's a professional golfer. Don't like autograph hounds. So, you two mind your own business." It wasn't Bobby Jones. Jed knew that much. He'd seen Jones's picture in the papers many times.

Arthur nipped again at his flask as Jed stared at the full moon out the window. It was racing along like a sidecar attached to the Pullman with invisible wires.

"Your pal Lester Barnhart was nowhere to be found this morning when we stopped at Arkansas City," Arthur said, without preamble. "So I didn't get a chance to question him. And there was nothing on him in the files back at the field office. He doesn't have a record."

"Only because he's slippery as hell," Jed said. "But I need to get that gun back."

"Give me a day or two," Arthur said. "I'll track it down."

The train had gathered speed in the countryside before the conductor came through calling out, "This is the Southern Swift, bound for New Orleans Loose-e-ana. Next stop Little Rock, Arkansas." Jed closed his eyes and pictured Carrie as he'd last seen her in the dim light of the dugout, the family Bible open on her lap, a fingertip lightly tracing the scratchy column of faded ink inside the front cover, the family registry of births, weddings, and deaths. Next to one, she had penned a note, closed the book, and locked it back in the trunk.

It was days later in the desperate aftermath of their sister's disappearance that Jed unlocked the trunk to see what she'd written in the Good Book. The fresh ink from her pen practically popped off the page. A date of death next to her name. The very day she'd disappeared.

Six

Harvest Dance

Rolla, Kansas – October 1911

The fat potbelly stove is wilting some of the early wallflowers in the one-room schoolhouse. The mayor is throwing open windows, trying to entice in a breath of night air. Jed and his family say hello and hang up their coats on the low hooks meant for schoolchildren's wraps.

Orange paper lanterns are strung like fanciful pumpkins across the ceiling beams, courtesy of the Morton County chapter of the Woman's Christian Temperance Union. Peals of excited chatter erupt around the room at each new guest's arrival. Joy and electricity are in the air. The harvest is in, the root cellars are stocked, and all but the last of the nettlesome flies have died off.

"It's time to let down your hair and kick up your heels," their neighbor Walter Redmond says in greeting. "Now, go out there and make some dust!" He points to the empty hard-packed dirt floor, cleared of desks. The agile fingers of the town dentist, Walter Stedman, ripple across the keys of a Hammond piano carted over for the occasion from the Trutchers' parlor. But the Albrights join the others hovering by wooden folding chairs along the wall.

Jed tries his best to smile. His old Sunday school shoes are relics that pinch his feet, and he's embarrassed to be seen in Pa's dated five-button suit. Butterflies take flight in his stomach every time the schoolhouse door opens. Is it her? Does he look the fool? Is she even coming?

"You plan on asking the girl to dance?" Arthur asks. Since Arthur is not one for small talk, Jed assumes he is considering dancing himself.

"Don't know," Jed says. "Maybe." And then, "No!" He laughs at himself. He's completely at sixes and sevens. "And you? Are you going to show us how it's done?"

Hans Knoop, a big Volga German with dark baggy eyes, steps onto the platform where the teacher's desk usually sits and begins belting out a polka on his squeezebox melodeon, stomping his foot in time to the song. The half Cherokee John Blackthorne in an embroidered, pearl-button shirt joins in, valiantly trying to keep up on his fiddle. Dr. Stedman improvises rhythmic accompaniment on the piano. Rounding out the ensemble is Blackthorne's teenage son Little Sparrow, who thumps on a ceremonial drum to the tap of Knoop's boot.

The empty earthen floor yawns wider as townsfolk edge farther back toward the open windows. No one wants to be first to choose a partner and dance. Not with everyone watching. Knoop's wife, Frieda, mutters something in German and goes into the crowd to drag her red-faced son away from his friends. She wrestles him like a rodeo steer out onto the dirt floor and everyone laughs, begins to relent, and joins in as she circles her boy around.

The Albrights look on, Tim clapping joyfully to the rhythm of the music. He gives a friend standing near him a punch on the arm and then doubles over as the other fakes a punch to his gut. The two of them wander off, chuckling over the Knoop boy's woes.

Arthur says, "I'm going for some air." By which he means going for a smoke (his new vice). He'll visit with the men gathered by the horses outside. They'll discuss wheat futures, the Almanac forecast, and such away from the raucous music. Walter Redmond ambles over as Arthur departs. Redmond is the only truly bowlegged man Jed has ever met. He appears surprisingly at ease in a boxy gray worsted suit jacket, his large, rough hands clasped behind his back like an ice skater. His generosity has touched the Albright family in many ways. Above all, he has made Jed feel unashamed about being young and inexperienced.

"I'd like y'all to come try a piece of my wife's spice cake," Redmond says.

"Certainly," Jed replies. "Much obliged."

"Oh, look!" Carrie exclaims. "It's Amanda Vanderhorn! Please excuse me. I must go say hello."

Everything becomes a blur to Jed except the young woman removing her bonnet by the door. Her soft auburn hair spills free and Jed's knees go weak when a smile lights up her face at Carrie's approach. Her splendid blue dress is a ball gown next to Carrie's handmade calico smock. The two young women have become fast friends.

"Coming?" Redmond asks, pulling at Jed's elbow.

Jed has to tear his eyes away. *What?* Redmond pulls him beyond the punch bowl and desserts laid out on the crocheted table runner covering the teacher's desk. "Isn't your wife's cake there with the others?" Jed asks as they go by.

"Yes, but the cake offer was for your sister's ears," Redmond says with a wink. "What I had in mind for us was a little something to cut the dust." Redmond turns his back on the room beneath the bemused lithographic portrait of Thomas Jefferson and produces a dark green bottle from an inside pocket. He extends it toward Jed. "Mash from apples."

Jed accepts it only reluctantly. And only at Redmond's insistence does he tip the bottle to his lips. The tiniest taste sets fire to his tongue. He gulps in reflex, which propels more of the blazing liquid down his gullet. A choking, fumy cough spews from his lungs, and he's still gasping when Redmond says, "Feels dang good goin' down, don't it?"

Like boiling water! Jed thinks.

Redmond hoists the bottle in salute. "A toast to the late Carry Nation, scourge of Kansas." He glugs down a monstrous swallow, smacks his lips, and says, "I hope to hell God's a drinker and He acquaints the good lady with His love of spirits." He eyes Jed closely. "Lookin' a little less peak-id now, Albright." He nods to himself. His face is a roadmap of smile lines. "Tell me how you're fixed, my friend, you don't mind my asking."

"Very well, thanks to you," Jed says. Redmond recruited a half dozen neighbors and friends to help break sod on twenty acres of Albright land to ready it for winter wheat recently, using Redmond's oxen team. In the aftermath of the fire, neighbors had shared food and clothing with his family as well, enough to keep them together, body and spirit, until Jed and Arthur could hire out as hands in the area and establish some additional store credit at Burlingame's. Jed tells Redmond, "We even have a bit of money put by after paying off the well diggers. Tim's got a small but steady income with the smithy. Carrie takes in mending. And she's a coal miner like her daddy—only it's coal of the Heifer City variety."

Redmond laughs and thrusts the applejack at Jed. "Here. Go on, drink to prosperity!"

Jed feels a pleasant, fortifying tingle spread through his belly as he takes another measured swig of Redmond's homemade brandy. He can taste a sweetness concealed beneath the alcohol's sharp teeth this time. The butterflies in his stomach begin to quiet. He decides perhaps another bigger swallow might finish them off entirely and give him the nerve to speak to Amanda Vanderhorn. He's been crazy, torn between anticipation and dread, up to now.

"What do you think you're doing?" a voice behind Jed demands. "Put that away. No alcohol here!"

Mortified, Jed hands the bottle back to Redmond, who is also bathed in the mayor's glare.

"There goes one hen-pecked man," Redmond confides after the mayor retreats. "Wife runs the WCTU, you know."

Jed glances toward the women, worried Amanda may have seen the mayor scolding him and wonder about the cause. What he sees concerns him more, however. She and Carrie have drawn the attention of a pack of prowling farmhands, roustabouts, and flirting cowboys.

"Looks like your sister is in contention for belle of the ball," Redmond observes.

"What? Yes." A raw-boned ranch hand with an embroidered cowboy shirt and a belt buckle the size of Texas has captured Amanda's attention with some amusing banter. Her delighted smile is unbearable. Jed is beside himself with jealousy. The apple mash has left his throat dry and his hands clammy. He balls them into fists and shoves them into the linty pockets of his hand-me-down suit.

Carrie shoos the young studs away after a time. They roll their shoulders and grudgingly disperse. Amanda giggles behind her gloved fingers. Such fun she's having! How cowardly Jed feels, standing across the room like a scarecrow in a baggy suit, wishing he had a clever tongue. How is he to compete for her favors, dressed like a coal miner for church? Carrie whispers in Amanda's ear, and Jed's heart leaps as Amanda steals a glimpse his way and smiles sweetly. A flicker of hope lights a fire in him.

He is not without prospects, as Carrie has enumerated recently. He has an education, she said (sixth grade), a quarter section of Kansas land (slightly arid), and good teeth (as if he was to be graded as a horse). She'd smiled. "You will make something of your life and the land," she'd predicted in all seriousness. The words inspire him now and he stands a little straighter.

"So what do you think, Albright?" Redmond is saying.

"Sorry?"

"About Rolla for county seat? Election's in three weeks."

Jed feels heat rise in his face. He hasn't heard a word Redmond is saying. "Yes, sir. I'd certainly have to agree with you on that." He hopes his exuberant agreement will paper over the snub. His eyes stay riveted to Amanda Vanderhorn, however, engaged now in conversation with a handsome man of apparent means. And he's writing his name on her dance card!

"Excuse me," Jed says abruptly.

Redmond smiles indulgently. "Behave yourself," he chuckles.

Jed has to stop himself from making a beeline for the ladies. It wouldn't do to look overeager. He sidles their direction instead, greeting acquaintances as he goes. His progress is satisfactory until he is stopped in his tracks by Marietta Trutcher, a voluminous and imposing widow with four grown daughters yet to find husbands. A nod and perfunctory *hello* to her are judged to be insufficient.

"One moment, if you please, young Mr. Albright," Mrs. Trutcher says in a tone like cold syrup on day-old flapjacks. "Indulge an old woman a word or two."

Jed's shoes seem to pinch tighter as he stops. To cross her

might have consequences. The cheerful orange glow of the pumpkin lamps darkens in the lenses of her wire spectacles. Her hand has been overly generous with her face powder, he sees. The widow's morose plumed hat and sober black dress are like a steamship's anchor dragging through the sea of buoyancy and merriment in the room. Happiness goes to die in the craters of her eyes. Jed struggles for something passable to say. "How are you enjoying the dance, Mrs. Trutcher?" he asks.

She seems not in the least inclined to reply to that. She transfers a cough drop from one side of her mouth to the other with her tongue and fixes a hawklike gaze on him. She smells like camphor and a dusty attic. He's a rabbit with nowhere to run, and she's the author of the vinegar pie recipe sizing him up for a stew.

"Tell me," Mrs. Trutcher says, archly, "each of you Albrights is homesteading a separate quarter, am I right?" As though she was the county assessor.

"Yes, ma'am." The apple mash has left him feeling a bit sassy. He must be careful.

Fortune has dealt the Trutchers several parcels of land in the path of the railroad that is to be built through town soon, and the widow's sudden unexpected wealth has elevated her family's social status. But it hasn't dampened the snickering gossip about her hornet's nest household. She is under pressure to marry off four homely, spoiled daughters who have piggy snouts, horsy teeth, and dimples in their elbows rather than in their cheeks. Jed suspects she's about to inform him that a full section is too much for his family to manage alone, that the brothers should find themselves wives. She lifts her chin. "I am quite aware of your recent trying circumstances, young Mr. Albright. You have an enormous burden of responsibility resting on your shoulders. How old are you, young man?"

"Twenty-one next month," Jed says.

"Well, there you are," she says as if she has proved something. "You must admit ..." But she doesn't finish her thought. She has noticed a couple on the dance floor and is following along with hooded eyes. Jed is horrified to see it's Arthur, waltzing with one of the Trutcher girls! Emily, if he's not mistaken, the youngest and arguably the least unattractive. It is rumored that Emily has the smallest dowry of the sisters, although that would change if she were to jump the line and produce the first heir. The dowries of the older daughters who are at peril of becoming old maids have been sweetened with extra property to make the young ladies attached to them less unpalatable. Jed spies them across the room in a cluster, watching Emily with narrowed eyes. What in hell is Arthur thinking?

"One hears talk that the track being laid between Dodge and Elkhart will reach Rolla next month," Mrs. Trutcher says, baiting the familiar hook on a prime night for matchmaking. She keeps a Sphynx-like watch over Emily and Arthur. "Won't that be quite a development for our little town?"

"Yes ma'am," Jed says. His eyes sear into Arthur's back.

"Indeed," Mrs. Trutcher continues, veritably trilling the word to stop Jed from edging away, "it would be quite good news indeed for me and my girls, you understand." Belaboring the point. The Trutchers own some adjacent land, too, with untapped commercial potential. Jed would be wise to consider dancing with one of her other daughters before they are spoken for. Jed wonders if Mr. Trutcher went to an early grave merely to escape this woman. "But enough about that. You must tell me about your family, Mr. Albright. One is curious about your youngest brother—Tim, correct? Rather an odd sort. Does he favor the other side of the family?"

Jed grunts. He does not appreciate snide remarks about Tim, especially if they suggest he's not quite right in the head. Tim is eccentric, but brilliant—something of a mechanical genius. Zoltan the smithy has seen it, taken him off shoeing horses, and sent him home with an expensive load of lumber and two heavy, sealed crates stamped Pittsburgh, PA., for a special project. Tim built a shed with the wood to keep out prying eyes and stabled the Albrights' skittish gelding inside to act as an ersatz watchdog. The clang and scrape of tools on metal, accompanied by Tim's annoyingly tuneless whistling, continue well into the evenings behind the closed door. Jed tells the Trutcher woman none of this. He returns the old lady's stare.

Mrs. Trutcher's mouth puckers in disappointment. She tips her head back as if to examine how small Jed might appear down the gunsight of her nose. She says, "One hears rumors of a strange contraption. What is one to believe?"

She already has the answer, of course. When she isn't busy talking someone's ear off, she has hers firmly planted to the ground. The secret is out. "Tim is assembling the component parts of an internal combustion engine, ma'am, modifying it so it can propel a bicycle. Right now, he's tinkering with the design, like an inventor."

She laughs heartily. "Such piffle! As if a bicycle were not ridiculous enough! Motorize one! Pish-posh! Inventor, you say! Please. Everything the least bit useful in this world has already been invented. Your brother, I regret to inform you, Mr. Albright, is not Thomas Edison."

"Perhaps not, Mrs. Trutcher," Jed says evenly. Never mind that an "auto-bike" is already available in the Sears, Roebuck catalog or that Tim and Zoltan happen to think they can improve upon it. "May I get you a glass of punch?" Jed asks, seeking permission to flee.

"No, thank you. One can never be certain what's in it. You go on. You have better things to do than pretend to be attentive to an old lady. And I must speak with Mr. Pierpoint."

The banker has appeared in the doorway in a sporting jacket and jodhpurs, as if he's stepped out of a high street shop window. He adjusts a silly blue silk kerchief on his skinny neck.

The music grinds to a stop so Knoop's son can knock down the dust on the dirt floor with a watering can. The break in the music permits stalled conversations to resume and Jed time to buttonhole Arthur near the punch bowl to implore him not to dance with Emily Trutcher again.

"Honestly, do you have the sense God gave a gnat?" Jed hisses.

Arthur huffs, "No harm in dancing with a girl." He'd spent a long time at the mirror that afternoon fussing with his new mustache. And sculpting his hair so it would drape a certain dashing way over his forehead. It's plastered now to the sweat on his brow.

Jed says, "There is with that one. And you know it."

"Listen, why don't you mind your own business? I know what

I'm doing."

"The mother is a spider and you are a helpless fly."

"So, which is it, Jed: Am I a gnat or a fly?" Arthur grins. "You let me manage the old cow. And *you* go ask that Vanderhorn girl to dance. Get it over with. Stop walking around with a stick up your arse. What are you waiting for?"

Arthur wouldn't understand. It wasn't as simple as all that. If Emily Trutcher had declined his offer to dance, Arthur would have simply moved on, asked someone else, and not felt crushed. For Jed, it's a different story.

With a stomp of Knoop's boot, the little band strikes up again. Jed's heart races. He wonders what suitable phrase he might use when approaching Amanda for a dance. Should he comment favorably on her appearance? Or would that be inappropriately forward?

The new song is in ragtime, and the grinding syncopation coming out of the ragtag ensemble is likely not what the composer had in mind. Nonetheless, couples flock to the floor, including Amanda and Carrie with male partners. Jed's heart sinks. Amanda is in the arms of a handsome townie, a man of means, it appears, and a confident dancer, light on his feet, twirling Amanda between quick steps. She looks pleased and comfortable with him, as if they have more than a passing acquaintance. Could it be a fiancé? The brandy is rebelling in Jed's stomach. The jaunty music rakes across his heart.

Redmond appears. "Thought you could use another little nip," he says, and sways slightly. "A touch of Dutch courage." The bottle of applejack is blue this time and nearly empty. How many did he bring? He edges closer, detached amusement in his glazed eyes. In an awkward boozy whisper he says, "A birdie tells me there's a sweet little thing out there hoofin' just now who'd like you to ask her to dance." He throws Jed an elbow. "You waiting for? Christmas?"

Jed can't look Redmond in the eye. He folds his arms across his chest and tucks his hands into his armpits, watching forlornly as Amanda enjoys the dance.

The ragtime song eventually stumbles to a conclusion with an extraneous note or two thrown in. Amanda's and Carrie's dance partners bow to them and clap for the band. The ladies return to the sidelines, and Redmond gives Jed a little shove in their direction.

"Why, here's Jed now," Carrie says, brimming over with enthusiasm. "Jed, you remember Amanda Vanderhorn?" So, she is keeping his infatuation a secret. Bless her.

"Miss Vanderhorn," Jed says with a chivalrous nod. One whiff of the peach and vanilla fragrance of her perfume brings back the memory of it lifting his spirits in the devastation the morning after the fire. Circumstances in life can pivot on a single breath, he thinks.

"And this is Amanda's brother, Byron," Carrie says as her dance partner arrives with glasses of fruit punch. The tall, handsome Byron Vanderhorn stiffens and glowers at Jed, declining to offer his hand to shake. Amanda introduces her partner as Henry, who is bringing punch as well. He is her cousin, she says. Not a fiancé then! Jed can scarcely conceal his relief.

"Jed is the one who gave me my adorable little chick," Amanda announces. "Only 'she' is now a rather ill-tempered rooster." Carrie laughs, but the men merely smile politely. "Isn't it odd how such a cuddly little ball of fluff can transform itself into something so ornery?"

Jed has to tear his eyes away from Amanda's rouged lips. His heart is throbbing in plain sight on his sleeve. His hope that something clever about chickens would spring to his own lips comes to naught. A barnyard term for roosters has lodged itself in his brain instead. *Cocks!*

"Jed, why don't you ask Amanda to dance?" Carrie suggests, and nods Amanda's direction for approval. Byron clears his throat meaningfully but turns away at a dark look from his sister. "What do you say, Jed?" Carrie asks. "Amanda and I don't want to stand here all night waving off uncouth field hands. And we can't expect the Vanderhorns to keep coming to our rescue!" Her smile at Byron seems rather trusting and flirtatious, Jed thinks. She apparently cannot see that this man thinks they are hicks.

Amanda's patient smile dims only slightly as Jed collywobbles. He's danced just once before, when his mother showed him the waltz steps on their porch in Thurmond and drilled him on them. "Would you care to dance?" Jed asks, thinking Amanda might save them both the embarrassment of dealing with his two left feet by saying she'd rather sit this one out.

"I'd be delighted, Mr. Albright," she replies.

Dizziness unrelated to the apple mash spins the room as she takes Jed's arm to be led out onto the freshly dampened floor. So much static jams his thoughts that he doesn't understand what Knoop is shouting. The band is taking a short break because a string on Blackthorne's fiddle has ruptured. The big German steps off the platform to wolf down some cake and wash it down with glasses of punch. He stifles a series of belches as Jed stands there like a scarecrow, wondering what he's supposed to be doing.

"It's wonderful to see you again," Amanda says into his silence.

Words to pass the time, perhaps, but the hope they deliver to Jed's heart buoys it immensely. Did she mean it? "The pleasure is mine," he replies, safely tucking the tender truth of his feelings under the cover of proper etiquette.

Knoop confers with his wife, Frieda, as Blackthorne tunes up his restrung fiddle. "Not exactly 'Alexander's Ragtime Band,' is it?" Amanda comments with a chuckle. Knoop concludes his marital powwow with a nod and announces in a booming voice that "the wife, she says it's time to play something slow. So we do."

Amanda smooths her gloves and smiles with anticipation. Knoop stomps out a one-two-three beat for the other musicians to follow. A waltz, Jed thinks. Buckaroo Strauss. He takes Amanda's right hand in his left, as he'd been instructed by his mother, and timidly, cautiously places his free hand at Amanda's waist. He doesn't recall feeling corset bones through his ma's dress, however, or a tingling sensation shooting up his arm from his fingertips.

"Pay no attention to my brother," Amanda Vanderhorn tells Jed covertly.

He thinks nothing of this. But in due time he will discover that this advice is impossible to follow. He remains blissfully unaware of that fact at this incredible moment he hadn't believed could happen. He is the luckiest man on earth. Master of his situation.

He says, "I should warn you, Miss Vanderhorn, that I'm not much for dancing."

"That's all right, Mr. Albright," she replies cheerfully. "There's a lot more to life than dancing. The contents of a man's character, for example."

The words are like a blessing and swallow him whole, allowing his feet to unconsciously execute the one-two-three of the waltz with precision. They circle the floor with the other twirling couples like music box figurines. But the gyration of Amanda's hips beneath her satin dress arouses him distressingly. His amorous feelings are out of control. He wishes he could lean in and peck her sweetly on the cheek.

So enthralled is he that he fails to see the white face of the banker's tawny palomino poke through a nearby window to sniff a plate of cookies on the refreshment table. Or see it scoop one off with its tongue. He notices only when Pierpoint goes racing over just before his pony nudges a plate of cookies off the desk, sending them skittering into the dust to be crushed under the feet of the waltzers circling the schoolroom.

Amanda's ringing laughter is infectious, and Jed is quickly caught up in it, losing the flow of the steps. He has to stop when the pompous banker practically falls through the open window struggling to reach his horse's loose reins. Even once Pierpoint has a grip, the magnificent palomino seems determined to back away, dragging the banker with him.

Pierpoint's wayward horse is not the only thing Jed hasn't seen. Suddenly he is face to face with Elmore Scruggs, who has stepped into their path. Scruggs hasn't bothered with party clothes. He's dressed for chores in soiled dungarees and a denim jacket. There is animal hair on his sleeves, manure splattered on his boots, and the smell of estrus fluid and bull semen on his filthy hands.

"Like a word with ya, Albright," he says. His eyes appear misted by liquor and he is tilting his head Carrie's way. "I'm fixin' to ask your sister for a dance."

Not going to happen, Jed thinks. Carrie has already complained about fending off unsuitable partners. "Why you telling me?" Jed asks, not wanting trouble. "I'm not giving you permission.”

“Thought you might say that,” Scruggs says and smiles. “Reason bein’, if she says no, I reckon on heading to the land office in the morning and filing a rival claim for her land.”

Again the sour mash plays up in Jed’s gut, and his head swims. “What the hell are you talking about, Scruggs? That isn’t the way it works.” *Or is it?*

“It ain’t? Between you and me and the gatepost, son, she ain’t made no improvements to that claim, and I have.”

Jed frowned. “You mean that damn fence we let you put up to pen up your cattle?”

“Cost me two hundred dollars, Albright. Fence posts don’t grow on trees.” The stupidity of this remark seems to stun even Scruggs. He staggers back a step and then nearly pushes headlong into Jed as he fights to right himself.

“That wasn’t our deal, Scruggs, and you know it,” Jed says. “Your cattle have been grazing on our land all summer. Their skat is everywhere to prove it. And you haven’t settled up with us for it yet.”

“Cause you ain’t paid me for the fence. And the grass my cows et didn’t cost you a plug nickel. Listen here. You just better hope she says yes.”

With that, Scruggs begins shoving his way through the crowd toward Carrie and elbows Byron Vanderhorn out of the way when he arrives. He seizes Carrie’s wrist and says something that drains the color from her face. Her eyes cut toward Jed. They seem to ask, *why are you just standing there?* Scruggs yanks on her arm and half drags her out onto the hard pack.

Jed watches in horror as another sprightly polka begins. Scruggs can’t take Carrie’s land for the cost of some damned fence posts and barbed wire, can he? Where is Arthur? Jed frantically scans the packed little schoolroom. Arthur has to straighten this out! Right now!

The cattleman’s burly arm is wrapped tight around Carrie’s simple calico dress as he drags her around the floor with ponderous and awkward dance steps, like a drunken stevedore wrestling a barrel. Carrie looks pleadingly at Jed as they go by. She tries to push herself out of Scruggs’s grasp. But he yanks her closer, lifting her off the floor like a misbehaving child, and there are gasps now around the room.

Jed hurtles himself at Scruggs, his fists flying. His knuckles bounce off a jaw as hard as granite and covered in sandpaper. He ducks a swooping, roundhouse left Scruggs throws in retaliation at his ear, but he never sees the uppercut right that follows it until he is flat on his back, staring at pumpkins that seem to float amidst stars, a taste like pennies fouling his mouth.

Later, he would hear the legend of Tim's unhinged fury, riding the cattleman like a bronco, one arm hooked around his neck, squeezing his windpipe until he collapsed. Pain sloshes mercilessly around in Jed's skull, and Amanda's fingers are bloody after she caresses his cheek. Tim yells like a banshee when it takes four men to pull him off the unconscious Scruggs.

Seven

Relativity

Aboard the Southern Swift – May 1930

The remains of Arthur's T-bone were congealing on his plate. He tapped his cigarette over the charred pink flesh, sprinkling a bit of the ash on the fried potatoes and green beans for good measure. His arm was slung over the back of his chair. Cruel amusement danced in his eyes.

"You let that scoundrel Scruggs BS you—so what? How were you to know he didn't have a legal claim? Blame it on whatever you like."

Jed thought Redmond's high-octane mash was to blame for his gullibility that night, as much as anything. He hadn't handled his liquor well at all. Recalling the vile mash now agitated his already queasy stomach. The ripe smell of manure-laden fields out the windows had not aided in his dinner digestion.

"Bottom line," Arthur said, "you put a higher value on our land than on our sister's virtue. And I'd say. in light of recent revelations, that was probably not a bad call."

Letting himself off the hook, as usual. Jed said, "As I recall, Arthur, you made yourself scarce when matters came to a head that night. And it was you who invited Scruggs's damn steers onto our property in the first place. I tried to tell you the man was unscrupulous."

Arthur scoffed. "The deal with Scruggs was on the level, and we benefited. But yes, I did step out for a smoke before that dance. So what? Get your head out of the past. It's over and done with." He seemed a tad more sober and cranky after eating. His breath had improved, but his mouth was still foul. When Jed suggested Arthur's memory was faulty, he countered, "I wouldn't point fingers. Whose memory was not so clear about what happened to his service revolver? I read the police report in Ark City, Jed. It says your gun was lost target shooting out the mail car. I don't remember hearing about that. It also says you chased a crewman in front of a moving freight locomotive, resulting in life-threatening injuries. That true?"

"Don't believe everything you read," Jed said. "And stop glossing over Scruggs." Under the cover of laughter of strangers at another table, Jed leaned forward and said in a lowered voice, "He may well have *raped* our sister."

"Even though an investigation at the time turned up nothing incriminating against him."

Why did conversations with Arthur always feel like wrestling matches? Jed asked, "How about we agree on the fact that that night was the first time we both danced with the women who'd become our wives?" Arthur lifted a butt cheek off his seat to reply with an expulsion of gas, then lit a cigarette. "How long have you known about this girl?" Moving on.

"Couple weeks. It was my third trip to Beaumont. I noticed her carrying a package away from the depot. That would have been the fifteenth or thereabouts."

Arthur nodded and went back to some master puzzle he seemed to be unraveling in his head, fitting in this new piece. For a second or two, the moon ducked behind a cloud and the farm fields out the window went black. It was Arthur and Jed now in the glass, looking like a couple of middle-aged mugs on their way to a convention.

"Say this girl *is* Carrie's daughter," Jed postulated into Arthur's silence. "Who would the father be, if not Scruggs?" Scruggs had come to mind immediately on the day Jed had met Madeleine and his imagination went berserk. "The trail to town went right past Scruggs's place. Out in the middle of nowhere. He could have waylaid her any time she went past."

"We'd have known," Arthur said.

"Not if she was too ashamed to talk about it. Maybe he threatened her."

Arthur rearranged the silverware on his plate with a clank. "No," he said. "She would have howled bloody murder if Scruggs had laid a finger on her. You saw how she reacted when he tried to dance the hoochie-coochie with her instead of the waltz. She wasn't one to take it lying down, if you'll pardon the expression."

"Clearly she wasn't telling us everything that was going on," Jed said.

"*If* this girl Madeleine really is her kid—and that's a very big if—I'd venture that our sister probably had a voluntary liaison or two, not a molestation. And Scruggs wasn't part of it. His mail-order bride had arrived by then." Arthur took a puff on his cigarette. "Look, I say it's not her kid." Arthur was in the habit of nodding when he agreed with himself. "Carrie bolted for greener reasons. She was never going to stay around long, any more than you or I were. She needed a role on a bigger stage. She needed to be the center of a lot of attention. So she snuck off and started a new life."

Or recklessly died trying, Jed thought. Something about Arthur's yapping sounded less like speculation and more like a story he was choosing not to share.

"Who knows, we might get a chance to ask her about it tomorrow," Arthur said.

"Why are you playing this game, Arthur? What is it you're not telling me? Have you seen Carrie?"

Arthur made a sour, hurt face and shook his head. He hadn't. But something was troubling him. Jed could tell.

At the snap of Arthur's fingers, a dining car waiter swooped in to clear the table with white-glove efficiency. Coffee was ordered. Across the aisle, several tables down, the golfer was having dinner with an attractive young woman.

Jed said, "If Carrie was assaulted, I hope it's not too late to set things right."

"Set things right?"

"Punish her attacker. Get her some justice."

"Justice?" Arthur's laugh was scornful. "There's no such thing—not in this life."

Jed folded his arms over his chest and smiled. "And yet you work for the Justice Department."

Arthur smirked. "Correct. So therefore you have it straight from the horse's mouth. There's no such thing." He pulled out his flask, unscrewed the cap, and tilted it over his coffee. A drip, maybe two, trickled out. He gave the flask a little shake, muttered an oath, and put it away. Settled for a cigarette. "I'm only too happy to cash my employer's paychecks in this miserable world if all they ask in return is that I play along with their little charade."

Jed had a feeling that Arthur meant it. Did he not have a single idealistic bone in his body? "I know you have this image of yourself to uphold, Arthur," Jed said, "but that's too cynical even for you. Tell me, could you honestly rest and do nothing if you found out Carrie had been taken against her will?"

Arthur leaned forward and lowered his voice. "What do you want from me, Jed? I'm going against regulations here already. Against my own better judgment. Don't try to sign me up for some vigilante justice scheme. If Carrie got herself in a family way and gave the little bastard up, that's her business."

Such a disgusting, heartless thing to say. *Little bastard.* But they were just words, Jed reminded himself. From a disagreeable man mired in his own troubles. Children like Madeleine were abused because men like Arthur were indifferent to their situations. Jed wound the spring on his pocket watch purposefully and asked, "What time do you have?"

Arthur checked his wristwatch. "8:05." He blew a smoke ring over Jed's head as an irritating joke.

Jed could see it faintly hovering like a halo in his reflection in the window glass. The moon was keeping its furious pace with the train across Arkansas, an illusion of perspective. "I saw somewhere that Einstein got the idea for his famous theory of relativity watching people walking in the aisles of moving trains," Jed said. "If I were to go forward right now toward the front of the train, I would be moving through space faster than the train is, and what I saw out the window would be different from what other passengers saw.”

“Oh, yeah?” Arthur said, as if nothing could be more obvious or banal.

“According to his theories, time and space are actually a loop. The past, present, and future all coexist in the same moment on a continuum. So, it’s a scientific fact that this train is, at present, taking us to our past by propelling us to our future. So it’s unclear whether we are going backward in time or forward.”

“Too clever by half, you are,” Arthur said. “I need a drink. Let’s go.” He stood.

As he slipped his watch back into his vest pocket, Jed said, “You’ll recall, Arthur, that before railroads pushed through the Calder Act in ’18, every local town, hamlet, and crossroads was setting its clock by the sun at high noon—and this patchwork of local times made it impossible for the railroads to write understandable timetables and schedules.” He smiled. “Until 1918, time literally crawled across our vast land from east to west.”

“Thank you, professor. Will there be a quiz on all this?” He snorted and walked away.

“What’s the plan for tomorrow?” Jed asked, following along.

“I have an address. We check it out. We go from there.”

“Are you sure we’re doing the right thing here?” Jed said. “She might have been hiding out all these years because she doesn’t want to see us.”

“Maybe she hasn’t been hiding,” Arthur said, stubbing out his cigarette in one of the standing ashtrays as they reached first class. “Maybe she’s been waiting for us to come and find her. Now, if you’ll excuse me, I’m going to sniff out some hooch.”

Jed tilted his hat forward over his face and closed his eyes in the comfortable smoking car chair. If he’d stayed home, he’d be enjoying a good soak with Epsom salts for his bunioned feet now.

He thought about Carrie’s trousseau trunk, which he’d been lugging from one residence to the next for years. It was filled with eyelet embroidery, bed linen, quilts, corset covers, the family’s christening gown, their mother’s childhood doll. Jed moved it the first time because he thought Carrie might one day return and want it. As it gathered dust in his cellar storage, it had become a burden of the heart, the last remaining piece of his sister. A coffin of memories he couldn't bear to look at. Like the old family Bible with the death date Carrie had written down for herself. Was there a reference in it to some New Orleans cousins that had gone unnoticed?

Around eleven o'clock, the gravelly voiced conductor came through the smoking lounge and took pity on Jed. Arthur had not returned. Jed was led to an unoccupied lower berth in a second-class sleeping car, where he could lie down, maybe catch a little sleep for a few hours. Jed slipped a porter a quarter to bring him an extra blanket and fresh pillow. Then he quickly stripped to his shorts and undershirt in the drafty aisle. He tugged the heavy privacy curtain shut, lay back, and stared at the underside of the upper bunk.

"You know what Dad would have done, don't you?" Arthur had said at dinner. "Beaten her within an inch of her life and thrown her into the street."

A smoker somewhere nearby coughed. The car buffeted to the billowing gust of a train racing in the opposite direction on the adjacent track. In the shapeless moments before awakening, Jed heard a woman giggling in the corridor. Through a crack in the curtain, he saw a flapper dolled up with a dime-store tiara in her hair, sloppy drunk, climbing into a berth across the aisle followed by a gentleman friend. Arthur.

Jed lay back and tried to lose the sounds of the grunting shenanigans by focusing on the sleeping car's clicking wheels. There seemed to be an abundance of available young ladies on this train. Jed was okay sleeping alone.

Each time a passenger went by in the aisle to the toilet, the berth curtain twitched. But then a corner of it was lifted by a meaty hand. "Wrong berth!" Jed barked. Then he wondered if it might have been the rightful occupant. He opened the curtain and stuck his head out to say something, but the corridor was empty.

Eight

The Reverend

and Rose

New Orleans, Louisiana – May 1930

"That's it," Arthur told the cabdriver, like a man well-acquainted with the house.

Good God, Jed thought, catching his first glimpse of it through a wrought iron gate in a brick fence. It was a magnificent two-story French colonial adorned with deep green hurricane shutters at its French windows. A covered balcony ran the length of the facade, buttressed by Greek pillars with plantation-style grandeur. The place stood proud on a boulevard of stately homes. If it was Carrie's, life had turned out well for her. Had she married a captain of industry?

Arthur paid the driver and stepped out into the dappled light beneath a live oak. The air was heavy. Overnight, they'd left behind the tentative buds of Enid's spring for a fully leafed tropical summer, an entire month ripped from the calendar while they slept. Jed felt as off-kilter as the tilted sidewalk slabs beneath his feet, pitched up by tree roots the size of marine ropes. Arthur uncapped his flask and tipped it to his lips. Hair of the dog. Earlier, he'd washed down a handful of aspirins with black coffee as their train weaved through the vast New Orleans rail yard. His

73

scrambled eggs went untouched, and his table napkin was employed only to dab the spot on his chin where he'd nicked himself shaving with Jed's borrowed razor.

Jed waved off his brother's offer of a swig from the flask as the cab drove away. "I try not to drink before lunch."

"You might want to make an exception today," Arthur said. He unlatched the gate and let them into the yard.

"Arthur," Jed called, trooping along behind up the walk, "are you going to explain now?"

Insects buzzed in the azaleas, honeysuckle, and wisteria surrounding the porch, as if tiny critters could play paper-and-comb harmonicas. A drifting petal from the fading magnolia in the yard attached itself to Arthur's jacket as he walked. "You'll find out soon enough," he said, putting to work a brass knocker on the massive front door.

There was a wait. Jed straightened his bowtie and Arthur fidgeted, the kinetic tension in him too great to bear, apparently. He gave the knocker a second hard sequence of clacks.

After a moment, the door bolt shot and a massive man with ink black skin and a preposterous pink silk smoking jacket filled the doorway. His startling hair was as brightly blond as Jean Harlow's, and it stood straight up like the flame of a match.

"Gentlemens," he said in a firm voice. "It's a mite early." When Jed fumbled for his pocket watch, the man said, "Just gone half eleven, suh," sparing him the effort.

He was too tall and wide for Jed to peer past. The wallpapered confines of the foyer ended at a closed frosted glass door beyond. "I'm sorry, does Carrie Albright live here?" Jed asked. He should have left matters to Arthur.

"No one here by that name," the man said, and started to close the door.

Arthur stuck his foot out and blocked it. "Hold on, Tom," he said.

The doorman looked at Arthur's foot as if a serpent had slithered onto the porch. Then he raised his eyes calmly to Arthur's face. "Name ain't Tom," he said quietly. He had the fluid, confident movements of a panther. Was Arthur somehow failing to notice? Was he fooled by the pink jacket and haystack of hair?

"We're here to see Rose Starr," Arthur said, reaching for a cigarette. He lit it in an assertive, tough-guy fashion, eyes locked on the man in the doorway. In the magnolia behind them, a mockingbird trilled a showy serenade that echoed down the street.

"Madam don't receive visitors before six," came the reply.

A bright, young voice rang out from somewhere inside. "If it's that no-good Douglas Fairbanks Jr., make him go away!" The initial peals of female laughter bloomed into a howling chorus. The big man stood like a boulder in the cascading stream of merriment. With a slight scowl, he started to push the door closed again. And again Arthur used his shoe as a doorstop.

"She'll make an exception in our case," Arthur said.

A weary smile came to the black man's lips. "No, suh, she won't." This riposte was punctuated by a brutal stomp on Arthur's foot, sending him yelping and limping around the porch. The front door clicked shut.

"Shit!" Arthur shouted. "Rat fuck!" Gathering himself after a bout of ragged breaths, he reached into his coat and produced a revolver. With his fingers over the trigger guard, he hammered the butt of it on the door and shouted, "Open up, you son of a bitch!"

Jed edged backward until he nearly toppled off the porch. Hadn't Arthur said that Justice Department agents were not permitted to carry guns?

The door reopened with a suddenness that implied serious threats. The man in preposterous pink leaned out the door. Arthur cocked his revolver, tucking it close to his side, out of range of the big man's hands. "Now," Arthur said, voice seething, "you're going to invite us in and you're going to go tell *Rose Starr* she's got visitors, aren't you?"

The doorman's nonchalant expression tightened a fraction, as if settling on a course of reprisal just before Jed reached over and pushed the nose of the revolver down. In a pleading voice Jed said, "Put it away, Arthur. We don't need it." To the bouncer at the door he said, "We're her family. Originally from West Virginia. Maybe you could just tell her?"

The man's dark eyes blinked and he lifted his chin. "Fambly," he said, his voice solemn.

"That's right."

He took a measure of their faces. After a lengthy, discerning assessment, he opened the door wider. "I see that piece again," he told Arthur, "it's the last thing that hand a yours will ever hold. Got it? ... Follow me."

He led them across a black-and-white tiled front hall, between red satin walls and finely tooled French provincial chairs, toward a sweeping marble staircase and a door to the right that opened onto a dim, stale-smelling room stuffed with gilded mirrors, Tiffany lamps, and plush furniture. A kind of horror took root in Jed's heart as he surveyed his surroundings. The room smelled like a gymnasium tucked into a saloon and dusted with a powder puff. This was an establishment, not a home. And it was not one he'd feel comfortable having his sister occupy. Calling herself Rose Starr. "You knew about this?" Jed asked Arthur.

Arthur stopped limping on his tenderized foot and plopped into a tufted red chair. He pushed aside an overflowing ashtray and set his hat on the table.

Carrie's man drew back a drape at one of the windows, drenching the room in brutal sunlight and revealing a large oil painting over the mantel. It depicted a fleshy, reclining nude, which, on closer inspection, shockingly proved to be Carrie, her unmistakably wholesome face at the center of the luridly rendered debauchery, as if the flower of her innocence was available to any man for despoiling. Jed felt his face flush deeply, but was unable to prevent his eyes from seeking out the burgundy nipples afloat on his sister's round, sturdy breasts or the dark smudge between her thighs. She was stunningly alluring. He turned away, closed his eyes, and cupped his lowered head in his hand.

This was the woman he'd saved a musty christening dress for? The chipped-face china doll? The woman who'd inscribed her own death in the crumbling family Bible? She'd given herself to the devil rather than ending it all? The Albright ancestors recorded on the Bible's flyleaf could be forgiven if they'd all turned face down in their graves in horror, Jed thought.

Turning his hat in his hands, Jed said, "Let's go. Coming here was a dreadful mistake." They'd lifted the lid on Pandora's Box.

"Never been in a whorehouse before, Jed?" Arthur asked

disdainfully. This man of the world. (This unfaithful husband!) Arthur removed his shoe and began gently massaging the top of his foot through his sock. "We still haven't seen this Rose Starr," he said. "We don't know for sure it's her."

He'd apparently been too absorbed in his pain to notice the obscene portrait. Jed nodded toward it and watched Arthur's Adam's apple bob deeply.

Carrie's manservant returned. "One of y'all Jedidiah?"

"I am." He got to his feet.

"Miss Starr say to tell you she be down shortly. You gentlemens is to make youselves comfortable."

"Comfortable?" Arthur snapped. "After you smashed my damn foot?" His nemesis chuckled and disappeared into the hall. As soon as he was gone, Arthur hobbled around the room with his shoe off, opening and pawing through end-table drawers and digging deep into the crevasses between couch cushions, like a man on a treasure hunt. He pocketed a cigarette lighter and a small brass figurine in the folds of a handkerchief.

Jed wanted to question him about it, but there were more urgent matters at hand. "How did you know about this, Arthur?" Jed asked.

"Anything I told you would compromise agency confidentiality." The flask made another appearance. "Don't ask questions."

Don't ask questions. What an ass. "Listen, I think we should leave."

"No. I didn't come all this way for nothing."

"I don't think she's coming down."

"Ah, but I am," came a female voice, gravelly and hoarse, a voice being broken in for the day. Her clicking footfalls rolled across the hall. The woman knew how to make an entrance, hips twitching above spiked heels as she strutted into the room. A diamond kneelet sparkled on one leg. Everything else was crimson—shoes, thigh-length dressing gown, cheek and lip rouge—except for her nails, which were lacquered a ripe plum purple. Almost like bruises.

It was startling to see what had become of the vivacious girl in the painting. The ravages of time had gone about their dreadful business, and could be seen beneath a heavy application of makeup. When Carrie's eyes met Jed's, he caught a glimpse of the girl he'd known. The benign expression in them seemed to suggest that her outfit, the gaudy blond hairpiece, and the broomlike eyelashes might all be an elaborate prank. A spoof. Jed's eye lingered, and Rose Starr tugged her gown tighter around her thick body. The room went silent as the dark man in pink slipped in and hovered by the door. Where had eighteen years gone? What was one supposed to say? Long time no see?

"Anybody besides me need a drink?" Rose Starr asked in that husky voice. "A drink wouldn't kill you, Jed, you know." Whorehouse hospitality. Her smile lifted the corners of her mouth and failed to reach her eyes. The reflex smile of a hostess. Hollow. "Reverend, a bloody for the Princess," she said when there were no takers. "But before that"—she squinted and held up her hand with splayed fingers in the direction of the brilliant window—"do something about that. This isn't a theater for surgery."

With a flick of his wrists, the man she called Reverend plunged the room back into semidarkness. Wall sconces were lit, and Rose Starr's appearance softened markedly in the dim gaslight. She was in her element now. She reclined on a tufted chaise longue and again adjusted her peignoir to accommodate her hefty bosom.

Arthur made a little steeple of his fingers. "Well, well," he said, peering over them. "You certainly let yourself go to hell, didn't you?" He could always be counted on to make a bad situation worse.

Knowing Arthur found nothing more insulting than to be compared to their pa, Carrie said, "This from a man with his father's receding hairline and droopy ears. What's new in the world of government file cabinets, brother?"

"Wouldn't you like to know," Arthur taunted. But it came out sounding defensive.

Jed wondered, was he the only one in the room suffering a broken heart? Finding his long-lost sister had done nothing to erase his sense of loss. One bitter outcome had just been replaced by another.

Carrie accepted a tumbler of tomato juice and vodka delivered by The Reverend. She tasted it and set it aside. "Is that Brooks Brothers suit you're wearing a gift from your mother-in-law, Arthur?" she asked. "Seems a little rich for a man on a government salary."

"Keep it up, Rosie," Arthur countered. "See where it gets you."

Jed cringed. The bickering was not making a distressing reunion any easier. "Please," he said, "couldn't you both just be civil for a moment? There's a lot to discuss here." The naked portrait of Carrie seemed to loom over her shoulder.

"We can't turn back the clock, Jed," Carrie said. "A lot of water has gone over the dam."

Arthur bristled. "Water over the dam. Jesus."

She turned a glowering eye his way. "Why did you bring Jed here? Was it to try to shame me? Intimidate me with disrespect? That's below the belt, and you know it." She turned to Jed. "Arthur is having me investigated. He's hoping to put me in jail."

"You could cooperate instead," Arthur said.

Her laugh was the first genuine thing Jed had heard come out of her.

Impatient, Jed asked, "Is this really where you live, Carrie? Is this what you've become?"

"Would you rather have me still collecting buffalo dung on the prairie, another leather-faced old hag in a frilly bonnet with a brute for a husband? Well, this is who I am instead. By my choice. I chose independence, nice things, and a comfortable life. *Freedom.* Independence is the hardest thing for a woman to possess in this world."

"You're a disgrace," Arthur scoffed. "You'd have been better off following through on the promise you made in the family Bible to exit this life."

"Spare me your self-righteous indignation, Arthur," Carrie said, running a finger around the rim of her drink. "Do you have no idea how cruel you are? Or how hypocritical? You think I don't know you came here secretly hoping to collect a bribe? Offer to try to cut me some slack in exchange for getting laid by one of my girls. Tell me you didn't have that in mind."

A girl snickered in the hallway and Jed caught a flash of a scantily clad Kewpie with a chopped-off flapper haircut pulling back from the edge of the door to the hall.

"Back upstairs, Ginger, and the rest of you girls, too," Carrie said sharply. There were groans and exaggerated sounds of stomping feet and giggles in the hall.

Jed said, "If you could just tell me what happened. Back in Rolla, I mean. Maybe it would help me understand."

One shoulder rose in a partial shrug. "What's to tell? I met somebody. I ran off. It was a mistake. And here we are. Let that be an end to it."

Met someone? Jed whispered *who?* and held his breath.

Carrie smiled wearily. "Are you sure The Reverend can't get you a drink, Jed?"

"That's it?" Arthur interjected. "That's how you're going to play it? Stonewalling to the end?"

"If this is your method of conducting investigations, Arthur, it's little wonder you're stuck in Kansas City."

How did she know about that? Jed wondered. Or about government files?

Arthur was seething now. He got to his feet, limped toward Carrie, and stooped to yell in her face. "We may not get to the bottom of what Jed is asking, Carrie," he hissed, "but I assure you, I will get what I need. And then you'll pay. Big." When The Reverend began to advance on him, Arthur jammed on his fedora and limped out of the room in retreat.

Carrie called after him, "Mixing personal matters with business is dangerous, Arthur!"

"You should know," he shouted back from the front hall. "It's your modus operandi."

"Guilt by association!" Carrie retorted before the front door closed with a bang.

Was it Rose Starr's or Carrie Albright's shoulders that sagged at the sound? Jed wondered. She drifted off into her own thoughts a moment and then said, "It was cruel of Arthur to bring you here, Jed. This must have come as a terrible shock. I'm sorry."

"Yes," Jed said, "but I knew I was taking a chance, and there was something I wanted to tell you. And it may come as a shock as well."

"Oh?" She raised her chin.

"Yes," Jed said and plucked a speck of lint off the crown of his hat. "Quite by chance, I came across a girl in a small town I visit who reminded me very much of you at her age."

"Is that right?"

"Yes. The resemblance is so strong, in fact, I thought at first I might be hallucinating."

She said nothing now, holding him in a level gaze.

"The girl is almost eighteen years old. About the age you were when you ran away. Did you run away because you were, well, with child?"

Carrie's face was a mask now. She glanced down and picked up her drink.

"That girl represents a coincidence that can't easily be explained away," Jed said.

When she looked his way again, Carrie spoke with resolve. "I'm sorry to cut our visit short, Jed, but Arthur has put me at sixes and sevens, and I must make some calls as a result." She tugged down her dressing gown, put on her hostess smile, and stood. "Thank you for coming all this way. It was good to see you again. Now, The Reverend will show you out."

"Wait!" Jed said, and lowered his voice. "Did they tell you that it was a girl?"

Rose Starr's hostess smile faded into seriousness. "Listen to me, Jed. I want you to remember a saying we had on the prairie. *Take extra care in deep grass.* You're headed toward deep grass."

The Reverend had Jed by the arm. "I can find my way," Jed said and meant it. He knew where he was going. There was a sweet-natured girl in Beaumont who needed rescuing.

Nine

Torch

New Orleans, Louisiana – May 1930

Arthur was hunting for a taxi on Magazine Street when Jed caught up with him. With no cabs in sight, they moved on, Arthur hobbling and muttering to himself all the way to St. Charles Avenue, where they boarded the first streetcar that rumbled by.

"Someone has to tell Tim," Jed said as they settled onto a seat together.

"That would be you," Arthur replied and unscrewed the cap to his flask. "If word of this fiasco gets back to the bureau, there'll be hell to pay."

Jed snatched the pocket-sized canteen out of his hand and held it out the streetcar window, as if he was set to dispense its contents onto the street.

"Jesus!" Arthur spat. "Don't be an idiot! Give me that!"

"No, it's time you laid off." The drinking was fouling his judgment. "Why would you pick a fight with our sister like that after we'd spent years trying to find her?"

"Mind your own business. And as far as I'm concerned, that woman is no longer our sister. She's Rose Starr, not Carrie Albright. She'll tell you so herself. And when push comes to shove, it's going to be her skin or mine. You don't have a say in it. So, give me that back."

Jed stretched his arm farther out the window. "Not until you tell me what's going on."

"No."

Jed gave his wrist a twist and splattered some of Arthur's gin onto the passing pavement.

"Damn you, Jed!" Arthur shouted. "Cut that out! Hand it back."

"Just as soon as you tell me how you found Carrie, and what that spat was about."

Arthur huffed. Then he sighed. "The woman doesn't pay income taxes, okay?"

"You're a revenuer now?" Jed said. "A lot of people don't pay their taxes."

"Thanks, I'll be sure to pass your comments along to my boss."

"Enough of your wisecracks, Arthur. Why are you going after our sister?"

"Don't ask." He set his jaw. "I told you already, it's confidential, part of a larger case the bureau is working on. A police file that mentioned her landed on my desk. She has a record that reads like an encyclopedia of morals charges. That plump rump of hers gets around. Believe me, you don't want to hear the particulars. One arrest report I saw had her mugshot in it. The name was different but I thought the lady looked familiar."

"So you knew all along she was a … a woman of ill repute. And you didn't tell me?"

"You were obviously in no mood to hear it," Arthur said. "Even now, you can't say the word *whore*." He adopted a superior look, apparently because he could utter the word. "Also, in my defense, I didn't believe it really was our baby sister. You saw how much she'd changed."

"I don't get it," Jed said. "If she's constantly being arrested, how does she stay in business?"

"Palms are greased, of course. Don't be so naïve. New Orleans is a nest of corruption. And that woman Rose Starr is *exceedingly* well connected. Like Huey Long–connected."

"She's friends with the governor of Louisiana?" *The man they say could reverse the course of the Mississippi River if he wished to?* That threw matters into a whole different light. Jed took a swig of some of Arthur's precious gin before handing it back. It all began to make sense. The house. The investigation. The secrecy. Little wonder Arthur was frantic.

The depot clock's hands seemed stuck on the Roman numeral II as the brothers killed time waiting for their train. Arthur snored, sitting upright on the hard bench, his hat down over his eyes. Outside the glassed-in arch of the lobby doors, a hat was lifted to expose a shock of blond hair. The massive black man beneath the hair doing the doffing lowered his sunglasses and tapped a hushing finger to his lips as he shook his head in Arthur's direction. Then he shot a thumb over his shoulder at a curbside newsstand. The set of his jaw said it was more of a summons than an invitation. Jed rather reluctantly eased off the bench and went out.

Carrie's bruiser of a doorman had changed out of his ridiculous pink smoking jacket into a dark conservative suit with a pink carnation in the lapel. Jed wondered if he was, in fact, a man of the cloth. But in a whorehouse? Might be best to let the man do all the talking.

"Y'all fixin' to boogie?" The Reverend asked in a languid Loozianna drawl.

Uncertain exactly what was meant by the question, Jed studied his diminutive reflection in the man's sunglasses and shrugged. "Is there something you want?"

"Yeah," said The Reverend. "Ten o'clock. Carriage house out back a Rose's place. Be there." His stern eyes peered over his sunglasses. "Do *not* bring the cracker."

He pivoted then, crossed Canal Street through traffic, and ducked into an alley before Jed could object.

Arthur pushed his hat off his eyes at Jed's return. "That who I think it was?"

"Listen, Arthur," Jed said, "I've changed my mind. I'm going to stay another night." He saw no point in subterfuge. "Carrie still owes me an explanation. And I intend to collect."

"Fool's errand, brother," Arthur said. "Her lips are the only thing that's still tight on that woman."

                              * * *

A stand of pines screened a dozen luxury cars parked behind
Carrie's bordello, fenders gleaming in the orange light of the
rising moon. Jed stepped through them to a long canopy stretching
from Carrie's back door to the lot. Beyond the fancy cars was a
dark and silent coach house, its ground level doors closed and
padlocked. Jed paused to listen to the friendly buzz of
conversation, music, and clinking glassware spilling out of
Carrie's parlor and felt like slinking off into the night. What had
he been thinking, coming here?

"This way," called a voice out of the dark. On the far side of
the garage, a lamp switched on at the top of an exterior staircase.
The big man was in a tuxedo now, standing in the spill of light at
the top of the stairs by a screen door. Too late to turn back, Jed
thought. He'd crossed the Rubicon.

Inside, The Reverend snapped on a light, revealing a snug
room stuffed with worn furniture that appeared to be castoffs from
the main house. A veritable antique shop. A skunky scent hung in
the air, the kind Jed had smelled drifting out of jazz joints and
roadhouses on the outskirts of some cities. At the screened
window, he looked down on the cars arrayed below.

"Is that an actual Duesenberg out there?" Jed asked, for
something to say.

The Reverend had perched a fez over his blond hair and
wedged his powerful physique into a midnight blue tuxedo with a
gold sash. He might have been an African ambassador going to a
diplomatic reception. His ebony skin was lustrous in the
lamplight. The hint of menace in the blunt contours of his nose
and jaw kept Jed on his guard. A woman's shrill, squealing laugh
from Carrie's parlor cut through the night.

"Johns at this joint shit gold doubloons," The Reverend said,
a comment that took Jed a moment to connect back to his question
about the rare car. "Spot of refreshment?" The Reverend asked.
His New Orleans drawl disappeared and a vaudevillian
impersonation of a Connecticut Yankee took its place. He seemed
to have an aptitude for voices. There was something theatrical as
well about the manner in which he produced a bottle and two
stemmed glasses. The wine he poured was deep red. "Best in the

house," he said, handing a glass to Jed.

The bottle glugged to a halt, however, as he poured himself a glass. He set the empty aside and took one of its drip-streaked, re-corked companions from a shelf of them lined up like wounded soldiers on parade. Unfinished booze from the house. "Shame to waste it."

The Reverend swirled his glass and sniffed at his drink before tasting. "Yup," he said with a satisfied smack of his lips. "Sit." He patted a space on the divan next to him as Jed eyed a chair across the room. "Only got us a couple minutes."

The divan's cushions were cupped and hard. "Miz Rose give us to believe she was orphaned. Said her family died in a fire in Kansas City." He ran his tongue along the groove inside his lower lip and sharpened his eye on Jed. "Yet here you be."

Jed sipped a little wine to be polite, and was surprised to find the taste agreeable. "We did get caught in a nasty wildfire once," he said, "but that was in Rolla, Kansas, and we all survived."

The Reverend thumped a lampshade next to him where a moth was fluttering about the electric bulb. "Heard Miz Rose say this mornin' she run off with somebody. First I heard of it. That true?"

"No idea," Jed said. "Nobody else in town was gone after she left." Running away with someone else was a lie as far as Jed was concerned. He covered over the rim of his glass as The Reverend went to top it up.

"Don't seem like Miz Rose, not lettin' her people know if she was alive or dead," The Reverend said gravely. His brow pinched and he took a gulp of the rescued wine, no longer bothering to swirl and sniff it. *Huh,* he grunted, and Jed wondered if he thought he was being lied to. "Steamy night," the man said and shrugged his tuxedo jacket off his thick shoulders. His stiff shirtfront bowed like a ship's sail.

Jed asked, "She's never spoken about an old flame?"

"Old flame, she-et,*"* The Reverend chuckled, as if he found that hilarious. "Don't have the faintest idea where Rolla's at, let alone who come sniffin' around her hoo-hah back then."

Jed squirmed at the coarse reference to his sister's most intimate privates (and attention they might have attracted). He took another sip of his wine, and again enjoyed the mellow taste.

"Has she ever mentioned a man taking advantage of her?"

The Reverend's pearly smile indulged this turn of phrase. *"Take advantage?* Woman built a fortune lettin' men *take advantage."* He gestured grandly toward the house beyond the cars. "Woman's a natural. Got here with one shoe to her name. Can't close her closet door on 'em all now. Woman a player, son. A titan." His smile went all the way back to his molars.

"What about a baby. She ever mention having a baby?"

The Reverend's brow furrowed. "You talkin' 'bout this acquaintance of yours? This girl?" He snorted dismissively. "Shit happens in this racket," he said. "'Bortions. Clap. Teeth knocked when some fool get rough. Jes' the way it is. But no baby. I'd a known."

"Long before this," Jed said. "Back in Rolla."

"Told ya, don't know nothin' 'bout Rolla. And what's some child to do with you?" he asked sharply. "Don't be comin' 'round upsettin' her, muckin' in stuff ain't your bidness."

Jed set the glass of wine aside. He'd wandered into the tall grass despite Carrie's warning. Her man was fiercely loyal. "But there was something you wanted to tell me?" Jed said timidly. "What was it?"

"Never said that." The Reverend's eyes narrowed a fraction, as if in warning that words could be spoken that could cross a line. He was a powder keg with a short fuse. He refilled his glass. Across the way, the brothel party roared on in the night. The big man's gaze softened with another gulp of the wine, and he stood to cross the room, where he produced a dogeared photo in a cardboard frame after rummaging around in a cabinet. It was a family studio portrait of six dark-skinned figures—prosperous, impeccably dressed, radiating pride and determination. Northerners, Jed thought.

"Fambly," The Reverend said quietly. Mother, father, two sisters, and a brother, artfully arranged by the photographer, the girls in matching white frocks, the boys in dressy tweed knickers and matching jackets. The Reverend as a boy stood out with his short-cropped blond hair, as white in the picture as an old man's. He was skinny and rawboned with a slightly troubled look, as if he feared the camera could peer into his soul. He stood stiffly behind his seated father, an educated man of refinement, from the look of him, but a hard disciplinarian.

Jed held the photograph respectfully. It appeared The Reverend, too, had drifted a long way from home.

"Told Miz Rose they were dead," The Reverend said. "Not true."

He held Jed's eye in a long, piercing gaze. *This is how it goes when a family rejects one of its own,* Jed understood from the look. The moral of the story, as Tim might say. "So, they don't …" He stopped, thinking better of asking. "Sorry, Reverend. I don't know your name."

Carrie's man took the photo out of Jed's hands and put it back in the cabinet. Confession hour was over.

"Name's Jerome," he said after a time. "Don't like luggin' around that ball and chain, though." His chuckle was mirthless. "Folks here call me Reverend."

"But you're not a preacher—are you?"

"No. Got the name quoting scripture when I cast out devils. *At his wrath, the earth shall tremble.* Jeremiah 10:10." He chortled at his own theatrical fierceness. His tongue ran another lap around his lower gum. "Words like that popped outta my mouth first time some white boy at school called me Torch. Said I better hide if the Klan come 'round 'cause they might use me to light their crosses." He tossed down the last of his wine with one big gulp. "Boy thought it was pretty funny 'til I showed him the error of his ways. He found out right quick what a freak of nature could do. *For I am tormented in the flame.* Gonna speak that truth to your brother if he comes back. Tell the man, he's gonna suffer some serious torment."

It was a threat Jed had no intention of passing along. Arthur could find out for himself.

The Reverend said, "Can't let nothin' happen to Miz Rose. Place'd be gone in a minute, if something did. She alone knows the right levers to pull on the machine. Can't have no government bullshit closing her down."

"I expect she knows how to deal with Arthur," Jed said.

"Lady can handle herself, all right," he said. "But somethin' else is preyin' on her mind just now. And hard." He walked a tight circle and returned to face Jed. "But you tell your brother, *anguish shall come upon him and—*"

"Reverend!" Carrie's voice called from the darkness below. "Who you preachin' to up there at this hour?" Her heels began clicking up the outside steps with a rustle of silk stockings and petticoats.

"Talkin' to myself!" the big man hollered. He stuffed a cork in the bottle and stashed it under the divan. Then he gathered up his coat and hurried to the door, where he snapped off the interior lights and went out onto the landing.

Jed listened in the dark.

"You got company? I could smell that grass from my back door. Hope there's some left for later. Time you got moving. The judge is waiting for you to pass judgment and administer some inappropriate justice."

Torch eased his massive torso into the tuxedo jacket under the porch light and pulled the door closed. "Good," he said. "Let him wait. Ponder. Anticipation is the best part."

Jed could see the top of Carrie's head and bare shoulders below when he stood at the screens in the dark. Her voice sounded close as she and Torch made their way across the parking apron, their arms linked. "Would you mind giving Mr. McNally a nudge toward the door before attending to the judge? He's more tipsy than usual tonight."

"He'll be gone in a blink," he said. "Just hopin' His Honor took a bath this week."

Carrie giggled.

"Any of the shrimp left?" The Reverend asked.

"Yes. Saved you some."

They disappeared under the red canopy, headed back into the den of iniquity. He could have been mistaken, but Jed thought his sister sounded content.

He felt a pang of jealousy realizing that Torch had replaced them as her family. Jed sat back down on the divan and let his thoughts drift. He knew what he had to do. There were fences to mend in Joplin, Missouri. Time the waiting ended.

Ten

The Wallow

Rolla, Kansas – May 1912

Jed takes Amanda's hand and leads her a hundred yards off a well-trodden path over small undulations dotted with sagebrush, yucca, and wild rye. He hands her back the picnic basket and asks her to keep watch on the horizon while he spreads his horse blanket over a carpet of prairie clover and goosefoot in a shallow indentation in the soil. The treeless prairie offers little in the way of seclusion, but this old buffalo wallow is deep enough to conceal them if they stay low. Once the blanket is down, Jed reclines on his elbows, the relentless wind barely a whisper above his head. He peers deep into the vast blue heavens and thanks his lucky stars this is happening.

"Pinch me," he says with a smile.

The hem of Amanda's dress rises several inches above her shoe tops, revealing a glimpse of shapely ankles and a hint of calf as she rises onto her knees and peers over the rim of the wallow. "Just checking for snakes in the grass."

"Anyone in particular?"

"Be nice," Amanda says in mock reproof. "He only wants what's best for me."

Byron. "What makes you think I was referring to him?"

They share a nervous laugh at the improbable success of this daring rendezvous—secretly arranged through notes passed at church. Byron cannot abide the idea of his sister taking a West Virginia hillbilly as a suitor. But Jed's ardor is so strong, it sets the Vanderhorns' dogs to barking their heads off as he passes within a half mile of their family farm on his evening walks. On more than one occasion, the brothers have come out in the twilight to investigate, Byron leading the charge. Jed has had to scurry along.

Seeing Amanda at church had been Arthur's idea. "Just go where her family goes." Jed discovered they attended Baptist services in a little sod outbuilding on a neighbor's land. A rough wooden cross had been erected on the roof. The plan was pure genius in its simplicity. "They can't very well beat you up in God's house," Arthur said.

From Amanda's hamper comes a picnic bounty—fried chicken, potato salad, biscuits, a jar of pickles, and a pie. Jed is relieved to see that there are blueberries poking through slits in the pie crust—tinned fruit from Burlingame's—not something concocted out of vinegar. "Wonderful!" he says, savoring a bite off a drumstick. The warm spring sun provides rare, unalloyed contentment. It's a dazzlingly beautiful day, the kind it's hard to even imagine in the depths of a dark, bitter Kansas winter. But Jed isn't one to trust good fortune. Surely, this whole fantastic dream could come to an end at any second, he thinks. Deep down he feels he does not deserve such a day or this beautiful woman.

"Would you like to try some of my uncle's molasses on your biscuit?" Amanda asks.

From the bottom of the hamper comes a dark brown jar of thick homemade goo, which she spreads for him. Jed hates molasses. He tries his best to make appreciative noises, but she sees through the charade. "Nothing is too special for a man who takes his girl to a buffalo wallow," she teases with a wink.

This lighthearted needling reassures him, a token of affection (what he desperately craves) and an acknowledgment of complicity in this deception. But it's true. He's taken her to a wallow. "Really, Amanda, what are we to do?"

"My brothers will change their tune when they see the same man that I do," she says.

That's never going to happen, he thinks. And how long will Amanda be willing to sneak around? His desire to be with her has become an obsession, and the proximity of her flesh in this stolen moment is unexpected torture—within reach, but forbidden fruit. Restraint is mandatory. Precious reputations at stake. But, oh, the temptations of the flesh are strong.

Arthur had it right. "Blue balls, eh?" he said, clucking a sympathetic tongue. Honorable intentions—Jed wants to pledge his life to this woman—don't make his balls any less blue.

"You'll want to hear this," Amanda is saying as Jed emerges from the swamp of his smutty thoughts. "Byron hired on as a surveyor's assistant for the railroad. He'll be around enough to prove up his land, but he'll be away for weeks at a stretch." She hides a sheepish grin behind a chicken wing she's nibbling on. "Byron is a true believer in railroads. He says they are the lifeblood of this country and more important than the government."

Jed feels a fresh wave of exhilaration at this news. He could just kiss her! But he resists, fearful even a friendly peck could break the magical spell they've happened into. "You're very pretty, you know," he says, testing his footing on the tender ground of seduction.

The brim of her straw sunbonnet dips, concealing her face. Jed's eyes take advantage of the opportunity and roam greedily over every alluring contour beneath the purple calico dress, from the rising slope of her bust to her astonishingly narrow waist and jutting hips.

"Thank you," Amanda says, beaming at the compliment. Her lashes flutter and her lips purse. And she abruptly changes the subject. "Is Arthur planning to pop the question to Emily Trutcher? It's the talk of the town, you know—how often he calls on her. She could be a very wealthy woman someday."

Jed has no wish to contribute to the gossip his brother seems to delight in abetting, carrying on the way he has despite accusations of fortune hunting, recklessly poking at the Trutchers' wasp's nest. Instead, Jed surprises Amanda by proposing that they dance.

"Here?" she says and blinks, as if he's just being silly.

"Now?"

Jed is burning with a desire to feel his body pressed against hers. Satisfy some small iota of his terrible hunger. "We'll pretend Knoop's little ragtime band never stopped playing. Or would you prefer to wait 'til next fall's harvest dance?"

Jed offers her his callused hand to help her up. She takes it doubtfully. He begins humming the waltz tune they danced to at the schoolhouse and he can tell it charms her.

He dances her around the blanket's edge and up the gentle slope into taller grass, where her skirt snags on thistle. When she stops to disengage it, Jed impulsively pulls her closer, thinking he can wait no longer. Passion is burning him up inside. A kiss, now! Her eyes dip slowly toward his advancing mouth and her lips part in apparent surrender. But Jed releases the grip he has on her waist. Absurdly, her willingness to allow this puts him off. Is that the sort of girl she is? He stares at his boot tops in confusion. And what kind of thought is that? Amanda gives him a perfunctory peck on the cheek that makes him blush. She says, "We should finish our lunch."

Jed is mortified. "Yes," he agrees, and returns to the blanket feeling like a coward and a fool. He's broken the spell. He furiously shoos away flies that have congregated to sample the potato salad.

The first note she'd passed him at the door of the makeshift church was tucked into the palm of her glove as she shook his hand. It was so unexpected, he nearly dropped it. *Please consider attending regularly*, it said. Passed in such clandestine fashion, it seemed to say that far more than the parishioner engagement was afoot. Jed slaved hours over a reply, but he could not match the note's innocent subtlety. He showed a draft to Arthur. *It is my fervent wish to be a part of this wonderful congregation.* "Don't scare the girl off," Arthur chuckled. Jed hastily crossed out *fervent* and *wonderful*, changed *part* to *member*, and wrote it out again. And then again to smooth out his penmanship. The following Sunday, he left it in the pages of a hymnal under his chair when he was certain she was watching.

A weevil scuttles across a corner of the picnic horse blanket. Jed watches it vanish back into the grass and wonders if his courtship of Amanda Vanderhorn is doomed. Such a fool!

"Funny how similar our families are," she says.

Similar? Other than her high spirits being a match for Carrie's, the families couldn't be more different, Jed thinks. There's no similarity in their circumstances. The Vanderhorns are established and settled in a fine sod house; the Albrights are scraping by in a dugout.

"I mean in the order of siblings," she explains. "Boy, boy, girl, boy. Which I mention because I think you should consider how you and your brothers might resist exercising your protective impulses when the time comes that Carrie has a suitor. Or do you believe someone else would appreciate being hassled by his sweetheart's brothers more than you?"

"Well …"

Amanda lies back with a dreamy look at the vast blue sky, from which seems to tumble a meteorite of a question. "Jed, do you think you'll want children someday?"

He is absolutely unprepared to answer that question, having just been focused on the risk of accidentally producing one.

"Of course," he stammers. The matrimonial implications of the question are clear. Is she really saying she wants to have children by him? "Yes, I'd like children very much."

She continues staring silently into the sky, as if he hasn't spoken or she doesn't entirely believe his reply—he can't tell. She says, "I'd like to be a teacher, I think. Then if I don't have children of my own, I can still—"

Jed holds up a silencing hand. The unmistakable warbling voice of Old Lady Trutcher is ringing out on the open plain. "Young ladies do not strike up conversations with gentlemen who are not of their acquaintance on the street, girl! It's totally improper! And propriety must dictate your every action! Do you understand?"

Amanda does a mocking impression of Mrs. Trutcher's scowl and waggle of the head, silently mouthing the words "propriety must dictate your actions." Then she giggles, leans in, and whispers in Jed's ear, "Is there propriety to be found in a buffalo wallow, sir?"

The intimacy of her moist, warm breath in his ear lifts tiny hairs on the back of Jed's neck, and the electricity rapidly shoots south to his loins. But an encounter with the Trutchers out here would be a disaster, irreparably harming Amanda's reputation. Jed cautiously raises his head and peers over the wallow's rim. Mrs. Trutcher is wedged into the seat of a horse-drawn sulky beside her eldest daughter, Gertrude, a lace-trimmed parasol hoisted above their heads. The family's donkey clops and bobs along stoically behind, tied to the axle. The cart path is a hundred yards away and the Trutchers obviously believe they have the prairie to themselves.

"Really! How many times must one be told? Appearances are everything!"

Amanda cuddles in close as Jed scoots back down into their concealment.

"Everything?" Amanda says softly and giggles again. "Appearances? What about that thing you seemed very interested in doing before? Isn't that something?"

Jed guffaws before he can stop himself, and Amanda clamps a cautionary hand over his mouth. He smells peach and vanilla perfume on her wrist. Her eyes fill with merriment. The danger excites her. For a time, the only sound is the clip-clop of the Trutchers' horse and donkey carried along on the breeze. The wind direction prevents sounds from the wallow from reaching the Trutchers, Jed realizes. It relaxes him, and he realizes he has run out of will to resist this rollicking woman. He removes Amanda's hand, closes his eyes, and presses his lips to hers, feeling a thrill so long denied. Her lips taste like molasses, but they are soft and slick and mingle so wonderfully with his that the kiss feels like a force unto itself. A third party.

Mrs. Trutcher's voice rings out again.

"Does one want to be known as the sort who can be led astray? Stars and garters, girl!"

Jed reluctantly pulls away and lifts his head toward the old woman's scolding. He and Amanda are being very improper, if not immoral, that is certain. He can practically feel the old lady's bespectacled eyes on him. If Amanda's brothers should get wind of this, he's a dead man. With a determined look, Amanda takes

Jed's hand and deliberately guides it over her breast. Presses it there. The world of the Trutchers is instantly dispatched. His hand cannot believe its good fortune, and it celebrates on its own by squeezing the object of its desire. But he cannot fully sense the shape of things squished flat beneath the corset. Instead, her panting guides his movements until her sudden gasp of pleasure takes him by surprise. Lust surges. He is about to vault the gates of propriety into the wallow of wicked abandonment. His hands feel drawn to roam lower. How far will she allow him to venture? Can he stop? He must! He cannot in good conscience take advantage of her. He lifts his head for a sobering glimpse of Old Lady Trutcher's fat carcass rocking along in the sulky to slow himself down.

"Jed, stop fretting," Amanda says quietly, lifting her arms and pulling him back to her with a reassuring smile. "Just hold me, please."

But a thick, hot erection threatens to pop the buttons on his fly and perhaps (in an ultimate humiliation) explode in throbbing jubilation into his drawers. He holds his hips discreetly away, and does not look at her face. She is too beautiful and his nethers are too close to the crest of release. The dam might burst. Nature his enemy.

But then, suddenly, his friend. With a boisterous flapping noise, a covey of sandpipers flushes from cover nearby, a flock of them taking wing overhead. Then the shadow of something far more imposing falls across the blanket.

"My God!" Jed mutters. "It's the Trutchers' donkey!" It towers over them like a colossal, shaggy hound cornering its prey. A tuft of its unruly mane stands up between its two long ears. The dumb thing stands there, stock still, staring at them, the rope that had tethered it to the sulky dangling from its neck.

Amanda jokes, "Who does he think he is, Pierpoint's palomino?"

"Oh, no!" Jed says. "We can't have that animal here. They'll come looking for it." He stands and waves his hat. "Shoo! Yee-hah! Go on! Beat it!"

The donkey plants its hooves and squints its coal black eyes at Jed. It brays defiantly. *Haw-hee-haw.* "Mrs. Trutcher has sent a chaperone!" Amanda howls in a way Jed has never heard her laugh before. As if she might wet herself.

Jed swipes at the dangling rope around the donkey's neck and misses as it trots down the incline and kicks over the picnic basket. It plucks a carrot from the spoils. Amanda laughs harder while it loudly crunches the carrot to a pulp.

"What are we going to do?" Jed says. The donkey bares its yellow teeth in an evil grin. Amanda squeals another wild laugh and points at the donkey's belly, where the long pink extension of its glistening business is sliding into view. It's immense! Jed is horrified.

"The beast has no sense of propriety!" Amanda screams, convulsing with laughter. "Propriety must dictate your actions!"

Jed's face turns pink. His distress might be visible for miles on the flat prairie, standing there with an ornery animal capping off its antics passing gas with a loud, fluting fart.

"Oh, no!" Amanda shrieks on the verge of hysteria. Her eyes are wet with tears, and she's clutching her sides. "It's going to do a plop! Please, make it stop! Make it stop!" She scoots out of the line of fire as the donkey's tail lifts and fresh offense comes pouring out. Amanda squeals, and convulses in hysteria. She has to fight to catch her breath.

Jed delivers a stinging slap to the donkey's rump, hoping that will set it in motion, but he receives a hearty kick to his shin instead. The animal cannot be troubled to move even when Jed scatters the remaining carrots into the grass around them. The donkey turns its attention to a jar of pickles instead and pries one out with its muscular tongue.

They cannot depart without the horse blanket. It could betray their assignation later. And it can't be pulled free with the donkey standing on it. Jed throws his shoulder hard into the animal's ribs and drives his legs forward until the donkey topples over. It scrambles up angry. Jed had no idea donkeys could move so fast. Only by zigzagging and running pell-mell is he able to dodge the animal's snapping teeth at his posterior.

Amanda gathers up the picnic as Jed runs circuits around the wallow, feinting like a bull fighter this way and that. When Amanda has gathered the blanket under one arm and is holding the blueberry pie aloft, Jed takes it from her and offers it to the donkey as a peace offering. Turns out, the donkey loves blueberry pie, enough to allow them an escape.

Eleven

The Musgrave
Detective

Aboard the Ozark Flyer – May 1930

Twenty minutes out of Fort Smith, Arkansas, the Flyer plunged into the deep woods of the Ozark Mountains and began a long, serpentine climb toward the pass for Fayetteville. The steep, rugged terrain out the train's windows reminded Jed of the hills of West Virginia, and he wondered why they had ever left them for the flapjack flatness of Kansas and a misguided dream of a better life.

From Fayetteville, it was another two hours to Joplin and a surprise visit to Amanda. He hoped by the time he arrived he'd have decided how to break the news about Carrie. About a girl in Beaumont, too, who was her spitting image. Would she take it as hard as he had?

Lost in his solitary ruminations, he failed to notice the man who arrived in the aisle until his booming voice rose over the steady clatter of train wheels. "Him!" he said. A second jolt was coming as Jed lifted his head to see a face marred by a grotesque burgundy birthmark.

"Do your duty," he told the train conductor at his side. He was a big fellow in a brash tweed suit. His eye looked deranged, bobbing in its marbled sea of discolored flesh. Where had Jed seen that face before?

"I.D.," the conductor demanded, sticking an open palm under Jed's nose. Four chubby fingers wiggled. "Credentials, mister!" The passenger in the seat next to Jed leaned away.

Jed produced his Post Office I.D. and his deadhead pass, and watched in dismay as they disappeared into a pocket of the tweed suit. "Just a minute!" Jed protested. "What do you think you're doing?" Something about the smug look in the man's eye abruptly connected him to the twitch of a curtain and an interrupted dream on the overnight train to New Orleans. *Good God!* The peeping Tom!

The lapel of the man's tweed jacket peeled back to reveal a badge and a holstered pistol. "Musgrave Detective Agency," he said. "Stand up. Fetch your things. You're getting off."

"In the middle of nowhere?" Jed shot a pleading glance at the conductor.

"Up!" the conductor said.

When Jed didn't move fast enough, the detective lifted him by his suit collar and stuck the barrel of his gun in Jed's ribs. There were gasps from occupants of the surrounding seats.

"You're in violation of 18 U.S. Code 1028," the detective said. "Theft of services in interstate commerce. The United States Post Office did not authorize this trip."

Again, Jed appealed to the conductor. Unofficial trips on deadhead passes were a common courtesy between consenting railroad men when seats were available. But the detective had Jed by the arm, escorting him past rows of murmuring passengers. There were groans when the train began to slow and shudder to a stop in a deep cut through the sandstone hill.

Jed's palms scraped across gravel as he tumbled onto the roadbed from a shove in the back. His valise went one direction and his hat in another.

The detective hitched up his pants and shot his tweed cuffs self-importantly. "Have a nice walk!" he called, tipping his bowler hat with a laugh as the train lurched forward. "You can inquire about the return of your credentials at your supervisor's office, if you ever feel like showing your face there again."

Two hundred tons of brute locomotive strength hauled at the chain of Pullmans. And when it was gone, a deep stillness fell over the cut, punctuated by Jed's curses of futility. What had Ruby said about a detective at the Arkansas City depot? *Satan's half-brother?* Was a Musgrave detective investigating him? Trailing him? Harassing him? Why? What had he done?

There was no way to see any distance in either direction on the curved rail bed, and the steep wooded terrain bordering the tracks didn't beckon. Jed had little choice but to set off the direction the train had gone. Telegraph wire strung beside the roadbed suggested a Western Union office awaited down the line. Before Fayetteville, with luck.

A freshening breeze rattled the leaves on the hillside and seemed like the calling card of an approaching storm. Jed picked up the pace as lightning crinkled and thumped shortly after in the deep distance. Thunderclouds began to show themselves above the treetops. At the crest of the grade, Jed came to a small clearing where trains could stop on a siding after grinding up the hill and refill a locomotive's depleted water tank from a railroad reservoir.

"Aftynoon!" came a call from the shadows beneath the stubby water tower. An old geezer had his back reclined against the wall of an attached tool shed. Jed tightened his grip on his valise and picked up his pace, his eyes cast down at the splintering ties as if they required his full attention.

"I said *aftynoon*," the hobo persisted.

One glance was enough to take in the long stringy hair, tattered clothes, and soiled bedroll. "Afternoon," Jed allowed, still hoping a clumsy encounter could be avoided. Jed's feet were blistered and sore. He was miles from his destination. And a storm was coming. He didn't need to have his ears worn to a nub by some toothless coot and a tale of woe.

"In the first place," the vagrant said, "it's a hump to Fayetteville." There were strains of backwoods Carolina and Kentucky in his accent.

Jed continued to put one hurting foot in front of the other. "Right, thanks," he said with polite dismissiveness. Twenty-five more paces and he would be out of sight.

"Wicked long trestle ahead," the man said ominously. "Got a

blind tunnel jist after, this side a Winslow. Don't want to git caught on the tracks when somethen's comen through. Safer walken t'other way. But Fort Smith is a hump and a half."

"Right," Jed agreed, slowing now, revisited by the childhood terror of a locomotive bearing down on him in the tunnel near Thurmond. Once in a lifetime was enough.

"'Sides that, a train'll be stopping here within the hour. Big ol' freight. Northbound. Git you where you goen lots quicker."

Jed paused to examine the darkening sky as he switched the valise from one raw, burning hand to the other. The tramp had the watery eyes of a drinker, and they had fixed on Jed's bag.

"Just a change of clothes and shaving kit," Jed said, setting it down. "That's it."

"Warn't asken, mister. Don't matter, likely."

"Yeah? What's that supposed to mean?"

"Jist you got a bulls-eye on your back hoofen along out here in those duds. Like you might be a railroad dick. Or maybe some slick jist robbed a bank. Lugging loot around in a fancy bag. Figgerin' on stashin' it in a cave in these parts. What do I know? Don't matter."

Jed unsnapped the case. "Have a look for yourself."

"No need to git all huffy." The vagrant chuckled. "Figured you for a feller might appreciate the straight skinny. But suit yourself. I ain't the only old fossil left for slag rolling through this busted gold mine of a country. So's you know, I hear tell some of these fellers is dishonest. I hear some'll kill ya for your socks." His rotting gap-toothed smile made Jed wince.

A locomotive whistle, faint and distant, echoed from deep in the hills, repeating three times, as was the practice at crossings. So, there was a road nearby, Jed thought. How far from here? The bum's watery eyes scrutinized him.

"You could set a spell whilst you make up your mind. Weather a-comen. Jist no two ways about it. Funny thing. Old tank might be full a water, but she's good for keepin' a feller dry too." He cackled, a man enamored with the sound of his own voice and savoring the opportunity to let some city slick know what was what out in the real world.

A sudden wind gust nearly took Jed's hat off. Large drops of rain began pelting down. Cautiously, Jed meandered under the tank. Up close, the old geezer looked frail. His bristly whiskers were shot with white. The bags under his eyes were like bruises. His knuckles were covered in fresh scabs. Flecks of dried blood dotted his faded woolen shirt. Twenty years before in Rolla, Jed had owned a shirt much like it. The bum smelled as foul as a skunk. Jed kept his distance.

"How'd you end up out here in the middle of nowhere, old-timer?" Jed asked.

The bum cleared his throat. "Jist so happen, my previous ride ended here. They all stop somewheres, right? Don't matter." He coughed. "Got any smokes?"

"No. Sorry."

"No 'shine neither, I s'pose."

"What?"

"Barn brew's okay. Don't matter. Ain't finicky. Beggars and choosers, you know."

A thunderclap shook the support timbers of the tank at the instant a brilliant flash of lightning froze every shadow on the hillside the way a snapshot would. Rain poured down in sheets, forming an opaque curtain where it shed off the sides of the tank. The siding, barely ten feet away, vanished. "Got us a gully washer," the tramp hollered.

Jed thought about pushing him out into it, see if a shower could cut the terrible smell.

So loud was the racket of the downpour, a train might go by without being heard, Jed thought. Then the rain stopped as abruptly as it had begun. The empty siding reappeared. "She's a-comin'," the bum said, cocking his ear to the south. "Got to move."

The old coot snatched up his bedroll and a gunnysack of possessions, trotted across the rails, and jogged up the line, Jed at his heels. The old guy squatted behind a boulder a hundred yards past the spot where the siding rejoined the main line. "Don't let 'em see ya," the hobo said as Jed stood a few feet away trying to decide what to do. "After she stops, stay down 'til she's rollin' again good. Sonsabitches bust your head, they catch you in a car."

With few alternatives, Jed knelt next to his disgusting new traveling companion.

The freight was perhaps fifty or a hundred cars long. Jed stopped counting after two dozen. The engine rolled to a stop under the tank's spout to take on water. The crew jumped off to seek relief in the release of theirs. Jed tucked in closer to the boulder. The old coot grabbed his sleeve and shook his head when Jed tried to peek out.

Cowering like a criminal behind a rock seemed to turn the world on its head in Jed's view. The empty track to the north looked desolate, unpromising. Had his future taken a bad turn?

"Board!" the engineer called to his crew. The whistle shrieked, and the men scrambled back to their places. The engine began to muscle its way forward back onto the mainline. Soon, boxcars were rattling past. Jed popped up to watch for the first one with an open door. "Safer further back," the tramp advised.

He gave no warning, however, before he took off loping toward a string of empties rolling past. Jed sprinted after him, feeling an adrenaline surge unlike any he'd experienced since he and Arthur were boys racing after coal trains and grabbing onto ladders to boost themselves aboard. Just for the forbidden thrill of it. The fun came to a bitter end when they returned home one day caked in coal dust and their father was waiting with the strap. "Think it's a game, do ya?" he screamed, laying the leather on mercilessly.

Jed reached an open boxcar and hoisted himself aboard, and only then realized how far behind the bum had fallen, gasping, the sole of one shoe flapping, a silly gap-toothed grin on his face. Then he stumbled and fell, and he stayed down as cars rolled relentlessly past. Free of him now, Jed thought. He watched the bum lift his head, the smile gone, eyes as glassy as marbles. It hurt just to see it.

"Whatcha doin'?" the old coot wheezed when he was pulled to his feet. His cheek and chin were scratched and bloodied. "Caboose is a-comin'. Don't let 'em catch ya."

"Won't," Jed said. "Let's go." He half carried the man over to the track and jogged back down the line of cars to pull himself into one. Kneeling in the doorway, he reached out to grab the bum's overall strap as he went by. The clasp dug deep into Jed's palm, and he yelped in pain as he rocked back and dragged the feathery bag of brittle bones up and in. The bum felt as light as a bird carcass landing on his chest. And the smell was as putrid as a dead bird, too. With a wave of revulsion, Jed pushed him off.

The bum began coughing as he crawled away across the floor. The spasm dragged on, it digging deeper and deeper into the birdcage chest to expose a pair of withered lungs and a heart with paper-thin walls. The last cough ended in a long, terrifying hiss. The old man's eyes closed. "Tomorrow's another day," he gasped.

Jed thought the bum could use a drink from his thermos. He looked around for it and only then realized he'd left his valise in the first car he'd boarded. Frustration and anger were like stones sinking in his gut. Missing as well were the bum's bedroll and gunny, back where he'd fallen. The poor man had only the clothes on his back now and barely the strength to take his next shallow breath.

"Where you from, old-timer?" Jed asked, thinking someone might have to be notified. "Where's home?"

He seemed in no hurry to answer, and when he did, the response was empty. "Here and there." He cleared his throat. "Don't matter."

"But you have family …"

The bum lifted his chin and turned his head away. "Time ya minded your own bizniss," he said, and folded in on himself in sullen silence.

"Just tell me your name, old-timer," Jed asked to no avail.

The hillside out the boxcar door abruptly angled downward and Jed felt a roller coaster sensation of being launched into space. He made a grab for the boxcar wall to steady himself. Trestle timbers drummed loudly beneath the wheels. The river was visible for a moment, and then darkness swallowed them up and the deafening roar of empty freight cars reverberating in the long tube of rock was the only sound. Just as the bum had described it. First the trestle, then the tunnel.

It was a blackened hellhole choked with coal smoke that seemed to stretch on forever. Blinding daylight finally greeted them on the other side, and Jed gasped for air. Fayetteville was still ninety minutes away, but the train had begun to brake.

"Why are we stopping?" he asked the bum. In the distance, there was only a railroad storage shed and a short siding.

"Tole ya. Winslow."

A freight of this length had no business stopping in a yard this tiny. Unless there was a problem.

"Best you git clear a the door," the bum wheezed.

There were six or seven of them, guns at their belts, billies and bats in their hands. A man with a long rifle stood near the shed, watching the train as it slowed. The brakes hissed when their work was done, and the hired thugs fanned out to begin searching the cars. *Damn bulls*, the old man muttered. The hollow where the train had been stopped was secluded and remote—an ideal spot for an ambush.

"Look-a-here, Vern," one bull yelled. "Filthy thieving tramps is carrying briefcases now! Ha!" He cut short his laugh. "Hey, got ourselves a runner!"

Rapid footfalls crunched past in the gravel. It was a tall, thin man in a sweat-stained fedora sprinting away from a squat bull, whose pistol was drawn. "You there!" the bull called. "Stop!" The crack of a gunshot shattered the air.

Jed scooted deeper into the shadows. He could hear his traveling companion struggling to suppress a cough, and a bull down the line was scraping a billy club along the side of a boxcar. He heard, too, the thump of a stowaway jumping down into gravel and to thrash into the nearby woods. Branches snapped. Twigs crunched. Shouts of *halt* again were ignored and a gun fired.

Jed's heart pounded hard. They were sitting ducks. A shout came from near the shack. "Search every damn car. Bring me the owner of that case." The words lifted the hair on the back of Jed's neck. It was the voice of the man in the tweed suit. The devil's half-brother. Had the train been stopped to look for him specifically? If so, Jed's troubles ran deeper than he'd suspected.

"We've got to make a run for it, old-timer," Jed said quietly, "before it's too late. It's not far to those trees and into the woods beyond."

"Just what them bastards want you to do," the hobo wheezed.

"First ones out always git it worse. Let 'em wear theyselves out conken somebody else's noggin." His long-suppressed cough erupted loudly then, betraying their location.

A flashlight beam snapped on and scoured the car's dim interior. "Come outta there!" a brusque voice demanded as the beam landed on the old coot. "Don't make it worse for yourself."

The bum was in no hurry to scoot across to the door on his scrawny behind, uttering as he went an insulting string of curses about the bull's intelligence and his mother's personal hygiene.

"Shut your trap you old goat or I'll plug you right there!" As if that would be worse.

In the darkness, the old man had managed to slip off one of his disintegrating shoes, and he slapped that leather now across the bull's shocked face. The railroad thug staggered back from the blow and pulled his revolver. He pointed it at the old man's head and stepped forward, as if for the kill. Jed leaped out of the shadows and kicked the gun away. But his feet slipped out from under him as he did, and he tumbled out the door onto the gunman, knocking them both down.

The ricochet zing of a rifle bullet sprayed gravel near them. Jed tried to scramble under the boxcar for cover, but the bull grabbed his ankle and pulled him back.

"That one there," the Musgrave man hollered. "He's the one. Don't let him get away."

The old coot was squatting in the boxcar door, his pant leg peeled back to expose an empty knife sheath at his shin. He jumped onto the bull's back and planted the blade in his ribs all the way to the hilt. The bull's howl filled the hollow with his horror.

A long rifle sounded again, and the side of the old geezer's neck exploded. Blood and bone splattered on the boxcar's wheels and undercarriage.

He collapsed into the dirt, a gaping hole in his neck, beyond saving this time. But Jed might still save himself. He sprinted toward the trees, but a bull with a bat cut him off. From behind, a second bull landed a club to the back of Jed's knees, taking them out from under him. The man in front landed a blow on Jed's head.

Hot cinders seemed to dance in the air above as five men

closed in. The thugs took turns landing blows with crowbars and chains as Jed tried to crawl away. Blow after blow rained down. In the end, they pulled him to his feet and pinned his hands behind. The Musgrave detective was in his face now, joy in the sullen eye in the wine stain. "You're a slow learner," he said. Jed's mouth was too dry to spit in the offending eye.

With a sneer, the Musgrave raised his rifle butt and drove it into Jed's face. Once more, a sound like the thunder of boxcars filled his ears as he hurtled down another dark tunnel at Winslow.

Twelve

Sidetrack

Fayetteville, Arkansas – May 1930

A pitiless thumb pried open his chubby eyelid and stabbed a hot poker of light deep into the darkness. The hands restraining him tightened their grips as he tried to squirm away.

"Pupil's reactive. Mister? Mister! Take it easy! Hold his arms!"

The brilliant light was excruciating. His head was about to explode.

"Looks to be subdural hematoma," said the man with the Yankee accent, letting the lid plop shut. "Prep him for trephine. It's possible we might save this one."

A pincushion full of needles stood in the place where a row of teeth had once been. He could not stop his tongue from exploring it or sampling the disagreeable coppery taste of blood nearby. Had he been in another train wreck? He remembered some terrible racket, but the mail car had not flipped onto its side or rolled like a barrel, had it? There'd been no twisting of steel or splintering wood, things inside flinging from wall to wall like BBs in a toy rattle. No. Only thick, black smoke and a moment of terror before something lowered the boom.

"You checked his pockets?" the Yankee doctor asked. "No I.D. on this one either? Mister! Mister, stay with us!" His merciless hands explored places that roared with complaint at every touch. "Fracture here," he said. "Have the left femur X-rayed. And cauterize the wound to his temporalis. Then suture it."

Jed's legs and arms went rigid at the touch of a sizzling branding iron to his temple. *Did that smell actually come from himself?* Stomach bile regurgitated into his throat. He gasped at the acidity and it clogged his windpipe.

"He's aspirating!" a woman yawped.

"Turn him!" the doctor ordered.

Fighting for a breath, Jed saw Amanda's face, tears streaming down her cheeks. The goblins were on the loose. At the precipice of eternity, his life shrunk down to a few random snippets of the past. Regrets. Failures. Matters left unattended. No time for joy.

A chair scraped and a shoe squeaked on the waxed floor. Why wasn't someone doing something? Then came a blow to his back. And another. He coughed up bile like vomit.

He woke to metal instruments clattering in a pan and a razor scraping away hair on the crown of his head.

"Mister?" It was the woman again, her voice soothing now. Reassuring. "We're going to put you under. Just for a bit."

No! Someone needed to tell him where he was first, mark his departure point from life.

"It's going to be fine," the woman said. "Try to relax."

A skunky rubber mask clamped down on his nose and mouth. He gasped at the sudden assault of noxious fumes. But dismay softened into submission as he drifted away on a cloud of new tires and hospital disinfectant.

He was upright in a wheelchair when he woke, a fresh soap scent coming from flabby arms and a white nurse's uniform holding back her matronly breasts. *Nora* was stitched above one pocket. She wound gauze round and round his scalp, snug as a new fedora, confining a renegade railroad spike caroming inside his head. The world was dark and silent beyond the circle of light of the exam lamp.

"Water," Jed rasped.

She reluctantly consented to "only a sip." The puddle of water in a paper cup was brackish and went down his throat like a wad of sandpaper and turned to lead in his queasy stomach. All hope of refreshment vanished. Repeated swallows were required to keep the tiny sip down. The nurse lowered her hospital mask to reveal that beneath her spectacles was a trustworthy face to go with her sweet, gentle eyes.

When Jed asked what had happened, it felt like the effort dislocated his jaw.

"Skull fracture. Two broken ribs. Several teeth missing. Collarbone broken. You have multiple contusions and abrasions. There's a possible fracture of your left femur. X-rays aren't back yet."

"But how? I don't remember."

Her tongue clucked sympathetically. "Probably for the best. Deputy says it was a car smashup. To which I said, 'Sure, and the Louisville Slugger Company makes cars now?'"

It made no sense. Who would come after him with a baseball bat?

The nurse secured the end of the bandage and stood back to examine her work. "The important thing is you're still with us." A cloud came over her face. "Unlike the other poor fella."

What other fella? She shuttled him down the corridor in the wheelchair to a room with a body under a blood-stained sheet. She helped him to his feet and gripped him around the waist when his legs wobbled. The repulsive whiskery face beneath the sheet belonged to an old-timer who'd been struck down mid-scream, it appeared. His mouth was frozen open. And a chunk of his neck was missing, as if chewed off by a predator. Jed pointed. "Gunshot," the nurse said.

"Who is he?" Jed asked. Why had he feared it would be Arthur under there?

"The doctor hoped you'd know. He wasn't carrying an I.D."

When Jed shook his head, he saw a uniformed deputy behind them in the doorway listening to every word. The nurse pulled the sheet back over the body.

"A detective wants to talk to you," the nurse said in a tone that seemed to counsel caution. "But that's going to be pretty pointless, given the state of your memory." Her words were unnecessarily elevated, as if spoken for the benefit of the eavesdropping deputy as much as Jed. "Don't worry. Confusion and blackouts are natural," she went on. "It's the brain's defense against trauma. It's usually just temporary. But it could just as easily go on for days." Her unstated suggestion seemed readily transparent. *You'd best keep your mouth shut, even if your memory suddenly returns.* Danger lurked.

The deputy walked away then. Jed watched him depart. "Is this Joplin?" he asked, absently rotating the gold band on his finger. Maybe he could summon Amanda to his rescue.

"Joplin? No," she said. "This is Fayetteville."

Fayetteville! What the hell was he doing in Fayetteville? Hadn't he just been fixing potato soup in Enid? Before Arthur turned up, suddenly, unexpectedly. Or had he dreamed that? And had he remembered to turn off the burner under the soup? He raised his eyes to the nurse. "Nora, right?—I'm sorry, I don't know your last name."

"It's Baker. Nora Baker."

He beckoned her closer. "Is there a way I could get out of here, Miz Baker?"

"You can't even walk," she whispered next to his ear. "But I'm sure the doctor would approve of getting you a little fresh air." The corridor was empty, and Nora Baker veered off in a new direction out the door, wheeling him swiftly along the corridor to a loading dock at the rear of the hospital. She disappeared for a time before returning with his clothes. She helped him into them as a car pulled up. "This is my husband, Bill," she said and placed a bottle of aspirin tablets in Jed's hand. "For later," she said.

Two blocks from the hospital, he passed out.

* * *

He clung to a light pole in the night, flotsam at a highway's edge. Passing cars gave him a wide berth, moving across the pavement to the opposite edge when his hitchhiker thumb went up. Hours seemed to pass before a truck pulled over and Jed dueled with sharp pain to climb in.

"Hope you gave as good as you got," the driver said. He accelerated back onto the highway and shifted steadily up the long sequence of gears, a cold cigar stump clamped in his back molars. The numbing fog of the surgical anesthetic was wearing off, and places the doctor had touched reasserted their complaints with vigor. Jed put a cautious hand to his face and groaned when he discovered his nose no longer ran straight up and down.

"You doin' alright there, buddy?"

"Only hurts when I laugh," Jed said, and was surprised to find the cliched joke lifted his spirits. He closed one eye to keep the road from splitting in two out the windshield and listened as the driver ran his mouth harder than his rig. Rants of every stripe.

"Hey! You listenin'? Hey! Buddy! Don't go dying in my cab! You hear me?" Jed's head had lolled to one side to rest against the passenger window, seduced to sleep by the low lullaby of fourteen truck tires humming on concrete. A sign for US 71 shot past in the headlights.

"Woozy," Jed said. "Mind if I open the window?" He thought he might be sick. He brushed at something tickling his neck and was surprised to see blood on his hand. He wiped it discreetly on the leg of his pants. "Just get me to Joplin."

"So you said already. Sure you got the gumption?"

Jed's hat tightened like a vice when the truck jolted over a railroad crossing.

"Damn dinosaur bones!" the trucker grunted. "Time to rip 'em all out and turn 'em into scrap. Save a few at some museum with the other fossils! Give our grandkids a laugh. You're riding in the transportation of the future right here, buddy. The Mack Truck. Rolling everywhere across Uncle Sam's highways tonight. And every night. Getting the merchandise direct to the doorstep … ask me, we got us a New York money panic is all. Jews sittin' on their fortunes, pinchin' every last nickel. I hear bugs crawl out of J.P. Morgan's butt. Honest to God. Anyway, let 'em keep their greenbacks. They ain't gonna be worth the paper they're printed on. Oil is the real currency. Liquid money. Always flowin', you see. Black gold. Means Dallas is the actual financial capital of this country. Mark my words … I hear The Crash made Hoover rich … I tole you, sip it … Is that blood? Okay, time for you to get out. This is as far as I go. Joplin? Down that road a piece. Watch your step gettin' out."

Jed staggered to a chain-link fence topped by barbed wire. He sat beside it and rested his back against the mesh. The fence surrounded a massive lumberyard that seemed to stretch on forever. He closed his eyes for barely an instant and the truck was gone. He blinked again and the horizon had turned rosy pink. A kind of paralysis set in, and his will to move weakened. A car rolled through the intersection where the trucker had let him off and Jed realized he couldn't remember which road the man had said was the way to Joplin. He closed his eyes and sank deeper into despair.

* * *

The chain-link fence was gone and a fluffy feather pillow was behind his back when he awoke again. Someone had tucked him up in sheets that smelled as fresh as April sunshine. A taste of heaven. But it wasn't. The mortal coil remained, unfortunately, and the bugger was stiff and achy from head to toe. He was Rip Van Winkle, adrift in time and place. And hell was one tiny twitch away, he quickly discovered. A slight move of his legs produced agony.

The dim light of the shuttered room was enough to reveal just how badly battered and bruised he was. One arm was taped to his chest, and it was trussed up like a mummy. Slowly, carefully, he lifted the sheet to peek at his throbbing legs, and there he discovered more welts, abrasions, and plumes of sickly purplish yellow. Someone had worked him over good. But where had the gray silk drawers that he had on come from?

He tried to call out, but his parched throat could do little more than squeak. He saw an empty water glass and straw on a table next to the bed and cursed under his breath.

Jaw clenching at each painful scoot, he wormed himself slowly to the edge of the bed. The floor appeared to be a long way down. He looked for courage at a mirror over the dresser, and glimpsed the freak show abomination he'd become instead. Raccoon eyes. Flattened nose. A line of dark stitches across his forehead like a third eyebrow. Stitches were visible on the side of his head, too, where a patch of scalp had been shaved clean and sterilized with something brown. Sewn up like a Raggedy Andy doll. "It's a wonder stuffing doesn't spill out," he told the mirror.

Did he have a cardboard heart now, too?

The oak floor under the rag rug creaked as he guided his foot onto it. He put a hand against the wall to steady himself and set off on a torturous hobble in a direction he thought would take him to the kitchen.

Halfway down a short hall, he stopped to catch his breath next to a framed picture of Amanda Vanderhorn's family, taken in 1911 by an itinerant photographer named Thompson. The family was formally arranged in their Sunday finest at the front door of their crude sod house, arms dangling awkwardly at their sides. Amanda's parents, Agnes and Nathan, were seated in high-back dining room chairs, their children in a row behind them. In the bright sun, their eyes were dark, spooky pits. The soddy behind them was smaller than Jed remembered. He'd forgotten, too, that rocks had to be stacked on the tin roof to keep it from blowing away in the Kansas wind. He felt himself glaring at Byron's cocky expression. It stirred up the same disgust and hostility it always had.

Why had Amanda believed Byron's ridiculous claim that Jed had been unfaithful to her during the time she'd gone home to recover her health? Cheated on her with that bucktoothed Gertrude Trutcher! Outrageous! And the sting of it had never entirely gone away, staying in the nest of troubles that had stolen their happiness.

Thompson had shot a picture of the Albright family that same summer. It made Jed cringe to see it on the hallway wall. In a flash of powder, the camera had frozen for all eternity the ridiculous peevish frowns on his and Arthur's faces. They were annoyed at being called away from their work in the field by Carrie, who insisted they all sit for the camera. She alone was free of dust in a new mail-order dress. Her shoulders back. Her chin up. A chicken dashed through the yard when the shutter was open, blurring Jed's boots. Tim hadn't bothered to remove his hat. His face was a blank gray oval except where the tip of his nose poked out into daylight. How young they'd all been. Like children. Ancient children.

A note was propped up on the kitchen table written in legible teacher hand. Instructions for a pupil. "Home at four. Do not leave. You are in no condition to travel. —Amanda."

A quart bottle of milk in the icebox felt like a fifty-pound dumbbell. It almost slipped from Jed's grasp when the cold liquid hit the exposed nerve of a splintered tooth.

* * *

He'd fallen asleep on the parlor couch and had to be roused at four by gentle nudges. "Mrs. Vanderhorn?" Jed said, caught up in the wool connecting slumber to wakefulness. *Wasn't she dead?* A slightly aggrieved smile from her said she was Amanda, not her mother. Jed muttered embarrassed apologies. "New spectacles?" he asked, hoping for an excuse, for forgiveness, stunned by how much heavier Amanda had become and how gray her hair was now. Her youth, which had seemed timeless, had departed.

"Yes," she said, not fooled. "The spectacles are new since you saw me last." She removed them, but that only made her eyes look more tired and old.

"I'm sorry," Jed repeated, his voice still thick with sleep. Or was it emotion? He cleared his throat and struggled to sit up. "Personally, I feel like Frankenstein's grandfather."

"All right, all right, old man," she said, helping him. "As I recall, you weren't exactly Rudolph Valentino the day we met the morning after the prairie fire."

Jed smiled, forgetting about his teeth. He quickly closed his lips when Amanda winced. "That's good," he said, when she had him upright. "I'm sorry to be an imposition like this. I really have no idea what I'm doing here. Or even how I got here."

"That's one mystery I can clear up," she said. "A former student of mine is a security guard at a lumberyard across town. He found you on his rounds, incoherent and babbling my name. That was three days ago. You don't remember that?"

"No," Jed said and sifted through a jumble of disjointed images and sounds. He recalled the smell of wood and the feel of cold, damp soil, now that she mentioned it. But he thought he'd been lost in a forest. "Wait," he said, "three days?"

"You were out cold for forty hours straight," Amanda said. "The doctor says you've had a serious concussion, and you wouldn't be alive today if a surgeon hadn't drilled a hole in the side of your head to relieve the pressure. Do you remember being

118

in a hospital?"

For some reason, Fayetteville popped into his head. That was ridiculous. Was he losing his mind?

Amanda's lips formed a straight line. "Listen to me, Jed, you should be in a hospital right now. But you wouldn't agree to it the day we found you. You moaned pitifully when the doctor said he was going to admit you. Honestly, Jed, what on earth is going on?"

He wished he knew. He'd been beaten nearly to death and there was no assurance whoever did it wouldn't be coming back to finish the job. He pushed the scratchy afghan off his lap and legs to move away, and there was that mysterious pair of underwear.

"Whose boxer shorts are these?" he asked, slipping a thumb into the waistband.

Amanda's smile was bemused. "Those are yours, Jedidiah."

"These are *not* mine," he countered. He hadn't considered that Amanda might have been with another man. But apparently he'd been an ostrich with his head in the sand. "These are somebody else's drawers," Jed said, "not mine!"

"No, they're *yours*," she shot back. "And I suggest you are in no position to question me on the matter."

She sounded defensive to Jed, as if she had something to hide. "Amanda, a man knows his own damn drawers, and these are *not* mine. These are silk, in case you hadn't noticed."

"I noticed."

"Then you know they're not mine, because I have never, ever owned a pair of silk undershorts in my entire life!"

"I gave those to you as a gift on our last Christmas together, Jed. You never wore them. They've been in a box in my closet ever since."

His face flushed hot. He gritted his teeth to still his runaway tongue, and the jagged remnants in his gums delivered a shot of pain, which he probably had coming.

"So, you thought—" Amanda said before a delighted laugh bubbled out of her.

"No!" Jed said. "I didn't mean," he began again. And stopped. He did mean. "Come on, Amanda. A beautiful woman … alone a long time …"

Her amusement was plain. "Enough," she said. "I happen to know I'm about as appealing as Old Lady Trutcher's donkey. So, you be quiet. And don't change the subject. We need to figure out what's happened and how to get you well."

She waited for him to say something, but he was wallowing in a good sulk now. How many times over the years had they gotten off on the wrong foot when they got together? There seemed to be no way to break the cycle.

"Tell you what," Amanda said. "I'm going to draw you a hot bath, help you out of those bandages, and let you have a good soak. You'll feel better. And your thoughts will have a chance to catch up a little. And I can get dinner started in the meantime. You're probably famished." She paused to assess his reaction, and found it wanting. "The only way things will get better, Jed, is if you go easy on yourself. So, no more talk until dinner."

Jed didn't like being treated as an invalid, even if he was one. He wished he could vanish when he saw the pity on Amanda's face as she removed the bandages.

His cuts stung as they submerged in the hot water before it became a balm for his troubled body. He lay back and closed his eyes, unprepared for a nightmare that arrived out of nowhere. Guns being fired. Billy clubs raining down on his head, back, and legs. A whiskery old face howling in pain as his neck exploded. Jed lurched up trying to flee, and sent a wave of water sloshing over the tub's edge.

The bathroom door opened and Amanda poked her head in. "Is everything all right?"

"Naked as a jaybird here," Jed said, and drew up his knees to scoot lower under the soapy film of the water's surface. His body was a source of shame.

"Okay, Mr. Modesty." She smiled. "Who do you think got you into those silk boxers?"

Once again, Jed's face flushed. "Don't need a nursemaid!" he said indignantly.

"How about a cook, Mr. Sourpuss? Or do you plan on making your own dinner?"

Thirteen

In Sickness

and in Health

Aboard the Kansas City Clipper – May 1930

For some reason, the appearance of a train conductor in the aisle made Jed anxious. Even before he discovered his deadhead rail pass was not in his new wallet. And not in his suit coat either. However, there was a train ticket folded into a note from Amanda.

Jed —

You've had another of your blackouts or you would not be reading this. We discussed this ticket prior to your boarding. The Dr. says these episodes might go on for some time. You are on your way to see your brother in Kansas City. He is expecting you. I told him Dr. Rosenberg thinks nerves bring on these episodes, and he should avoid disagreeable conversations until you are better. I hope you can find it in your heart to forgive me. (And Carrie, too, for that matter.) Or have you mercifully forgotten that already as well?

Love, A

Forgive her? Jed wadded up the note, dropped it to the floor, and kicked it under the seat, sighing so deeply it felt as though another rib had cracked.

Small breaths, he told himself, and closed his eyes. He leaned back, waiting for his fury and frustration to subside. He pictured Dr. Rosenberg puffing on his pipe. "You feel diminished when you forget. Mental turbulence deepens your anxiety and your anger, which brings on your headaches and completes the vicious cycle, you see? Breathe in, breathe out." *The pressure from cranial bleeding damages the brain in ways we don't yet understand.* Hardly the sort of inspirational news you could hang your hat on. The stitches still oozed. Were his brains leaking out?

He'd tucked a list of reminders into his new wallet for moments like this, a master cheat sheet he'd written out of names, dates, things to be done, unresolved questions. A life boat for the choppy seas of an unreliable memory. He retrieved it now to see what *forgive me* might mean. The context was missing.

The first line on the list delivered a jolt. *Tell Tim about Rose Starr.*

Rose Starr. Good God! He'd just managed to put her out of his head. The reclining nude. The fuzzy pumps and pink peignoir. Jed closed his eyes. *Breathe in, breathe out.* "The important thing is to let Tim know there's good news—she's alive," Amanda had said. "That's all. Forget the rest." Maybe Arthur would know how to soft pedal it. He was a master of obfuscation.

Down his list, Jed found a line that said, *How much did Amanda already know?*

But that just presented another puzzle, really. He could remember Amanda being coy after the trip to New Orleans had emerged from the fog of his memory. The memory of the trip brought him to tears. "Perhaps you forgot about it because it upsets you," Amanda said for comfort, but she hadn't sounded in the least shocked or scandalized herself by the news.

Arthur had told her everything when she called him long-distance after Jed arrived half dead in Joplin, she explained. Something about it made Jed wonder how much she'd known before the call. He had chosen not to make an issue of it and risk offending the woman who was nursing him through his night terrors and pain. Bathing him. Feeding him. Shaving him. He could scarcely butter his own toast with his arm in a sling.

"Tickets!" the conductor barked upon arriving at Jed's row.

As the passengers around him handed them over, Jed fumbled futilely through his pockets for his. Where had it gone? Had he wadded it up with Amanda's note? In a moment of frenzy, he thought he saw a man in a tweed suit standing next to the conductor, a man with a nasty birthmark, a badge, and a pistol. He flinched at the imagined pain of gravel scraping across his palms.

"Sir! Ticket." With his head tilted back, the conductor's eyes were the same size as the large lenses of his spectacles.

"Sorry," Jed said. Reaching under his seat for the wadded note, he blanched as the conductor thrust a hand into his sling, rummaged around, and extracted the missing ticket.

He punched the little pasteboard coupon and handed it back to Jed with an icy look.

Musgrave? Jed wrote on the line next to *Arthur/investigation* after the conductor departed. Then he refolded the cheat sheet and put it away. Another headache was coming on. He needed aspirin from the valise under the seat. The leather case had been a parting gift from Amanda, packed with clean and mended clothes. Touched by this kindness, he'd mustered a peck on the cheek for her at the station, and was surprised to receive one in return. He acknowledged her goodbye wave with a nod as the porter helped him up the railcar steps. It had been a difficult visit.

"Still wearing your wedding ring?" she'd asked that first night as he rose from the tub.

"Well, we're still married, you know," he'd replied, sounding rather more gruff than intended.

"In sickness and in health," she quipped, as if he was fussy and citing the fine print. "We're not exactly what I'd call man and wife," she said.

'Til death us do part, Jed thought reflexively. Did she want a divorce after all this time? "Perhaps we should talk," he said.

"No." She wouldn't look him in the eye. "Talking won't change anything."

There was always a chance it might, he thought, but he let it go, too much pride to argue.

"I can't go back to that dugout," she'd said that day years ago when Jed came to fetch her from the Vanderhorns' soddy. She was back on her feet, and Jed threw his arms around her, joyfully ending months of separation. "Did you hear me, Jed?" she said, pushing him away. "I can't do it. Not now, not ever."

The words stung. "What do you mean?" he'd said. "You can't mean it." Her eyes replied with a look of resolve. "Amanda, please. What am I to do? You know I have to stay put or I lose my claim." And there was no way he was moving in with the Vanderhorns.

"You tell that woman of yours to get her butt home," Arthur said. "It's her duty to honor and obey you as your wife."

Jed had other ideas, and set out to build a proper house for her on his land. But before he could finish it, Amanda announced she was moving to Joplin, Missouri, to live with a maiden aunt. A teaching job was open at a school there.

"No!" Jed said. "Please! This will be done soon." They were standing in the shell of the house on the windswept plain, Jed showing her their future. "We can work things out. You can't just leave."

"I'm sorry, Jed," she said. "I need to get out of this Godforsaken wilderness."

When he got past his bitterness at being abandoned and his land was proved up months later, Jed packed some things, put Tim in charge of the farm, and followed his wife to Joplin in the hope of salvaging their marriage. He rented a nice apartment and found work at the post office. And, in time, Amanda agreed to move in with him. But she was changed. Cool. Remote. The magic between them was lost. Taking a chance on love had become a terrible risk.

When an opportunity came to transfer to the Enid post office and a coveted position of railway clerk, Jed accepted. But Amanda would not leave. Joplin was home now. "You don't think a change of scenery might do us good?" Jed asked. Get away from her meddling aunt.

Amanda said something spiteful in reply. And then, "Forgive me. That was cruel." She placed her hand over his. "I'm sorry. It's just that I like it here. My job. My school. The children." She loved them as if they were her own, Jed thought. He'd been treated to endless adoring stories about them almost every night at dinner.

Now, all these years later, Jed felt Amanda's soft, warm body cuddle against his in the guest bed of the Joplin house, waking him. He tried to move away, lost in the delirium of night terrors. "Lie still," she whispered, nuzzling his ear to coo gentle reassurance until his terrifying dreams had passed. "You were moaning again," she said.

The nightmares continued the next night, and Amanda fetched a bottle of sipping whisky from a kitchen cabinet, boldly marked "for medicinal purposes" and obtained with a doctor's prescription. It was Byron's, she explained. He kept it here for infrequent visits. Jed pushed the glass aside on the night table untouched.

"Is this the bed Byron sleeps in when he visits?" he asked.

"Of course," she said. "What did you think?"

He couldn't lie there another second. He pushed her hand away as he stumbled from the bed and swerved along a path to the couch in the parlor, capping off his tantrum with the announcement that he would depart in the morning. Then he sulked in the dark until dawn.

The cheat sheet was back in Jed's hand as The Kansas City Clipper rolled through Fort Scott. Time to get on with things, he thought. The world was literally passing him by. He couldn't just wait around to "feel better."

Carrie's trousseau was on his reminder list. It was time for that damn trunk to go. He'd ship it Railway Express to New Orleans the first chance he got. Let Carrie deal with it.

He began fidgeting absently with his wedding ring, an annoying habit. He stopped and stared at it. It refused to budge over his knuckle when he tried to tug it off. He'd have to try again later with soap and water. And if that didn't work, he'd have it cut off.

Fourteen

'Til Death Us Do Part

Rolla, Kansas – September 1913

The moaning and shrieking inside the dugout stops. Alarmed, Jed puts his ear to the rough-hewn door. Silence. Worse than the screaming. What's happened? The latch lifts and the midwife practically bowls him over.

"She's asking for her mother," she says, wiping her hands on a battered old towel. The woman is rangy and energetic, her iron gray hair pulled into a bun on the back of her head. Not a woman to trifle with. She blocks Jed's view of the bed. "Best be getting after her straightaway. And fetch the doctor while you're about it."

Doctor? Every muscle and tendon in him is stretched taut from listening helplessly for hours to anguished howls. *Fetch the doctor?* The man is a drunk! "I need to see her," Jed pleads. He is quivering to the depths of his guts.

"Well, you cain't! Now git! What are you waitin' fer?"

Reassurance. Someone to tell him everything is going to be okay. He's desperate. The baby hasn't turned over in the womb and isn't due for seven more weeks. *Fetch the doctor?* Turns out some cramps and a few drops of blood were very bad omens.

The midwife puts a hand on Jed's chest and propels him backward. "Git goin'!"

By the time Jed returns from town with Dr. Atkinson, the Vanderhorns' fancy black cabriolet is out front. Byron holds the bridle of a panting horse. He's dressed like Pierpoint and growing a ridiculous mustache. Alerted by the buckboard's rattling approach, Mrs. Vanderhorn emerges from the dugout. Jed wonders if she's cut her hand on something, then recoils with understanding. She motions for the doctor to hurry, and freezes Byron with her bloody palm.

Her hushed conversation with the doctor cannot be overheard with the gelding nickering in his ear as Jed hitches it to the fencepost. Jed tries to follow the doctor into the dugout, but Mrs. Vanderhorn steps into his path. "No," she says. "You stay out here." There is terrible distress in her eyes. She is shaken. "Just wait," she pleads.

But he brushes past her through the door and into the stifling confines. At the incubator table, the midwife is wiping blood and slimy fluids from a scrawny, squirming newborn, smaller than Carrie's childhood doll, kicking his tiny legs and waving his rigid arms, as if he's drowning. His cries are weak and bitter. No one told Jed the baby had arrived. There's been a miracle after all! And he—Jedidiah Albright—is a father! He turns to share his joy with Amanda, but her eyes are closed and her lips are sealed in a shocking shade of gray. The doctor is bent over her, coat off, shirt sleeves rolled up, one hand thrust deep between her bare legs. She arches her back and shrieks a primal howl that threatens to bring the earth down around them. Jed's knees go weak. The ordeal is not over. The crisis is not past.

"You! Out!" the midwife shouts. Her apron has the pitiless stains of a hog butcher's. She sets the infant down on a folded blanket, kicks aside a wad of badly soiled bedding at her feet. She rushes at Jed as he kneels at Amanda's side to pluck a pillow feather from her damp brow. He caresses her cheek just before the midwife seizes his arm in a vice grip and pulls him out the dugout door.

"Let the doctor tend to the poor girl," she says. "Go water them dang horses. Git!"

Jed staggers across the yard, as if a knife has been thrust between his ribs. It's a disaster in there. The daylight is a blinding offense. The legs of his dungarees whisk aimlessly through the bluestem. He sees his own footprints and realizes he's walking in circles. Sweet Jesus. What if she dies? Or the baby? Is he fated to spend his life out here alone?

A bonnet adorned with pink silk roses bounces across the turf like a tumbleweed in the distance. Jed can tell by its direction it has blown off the bench Tim built from glacial field rocks on the rise. Amanda's mother is sitting on it bareheaded, her hair in disarray. She seems not to care that her bonnet has departed or that Jed has arrived.

Her high-button shoes are spattered with blood. There's a smear of it on her shirtwaist, too.

"She's decided to name the boy Nathan, after her father," Mrs. Vanderhorn announces in a dull voice without taking her eyes off the railroad's giant grain elevator in the distant haze.

Misery knows no bounds today. Amanda has given him a son. Then as much as stolen him away the same day. Named him for the man who declared Jed unworthy of his daughter's hand in marriage. It feels like a betrayal, his son forever tied to a man he hates! Did it mean nothing to her, pledging her troth to him at the altar? *To honor and obey?*

Tears stream down Mrs. Vanderhorn's cheeks. "So young," she murmurs. "So foolish."

Out of despair rises anger. The nerve! The Vanderhorns renounced her when she chose to elope and marry Jed. Barred her when she most needed their support. Who is *so foolish?*

"This can't go on," Mrs. Vanderhorn says, as if Jed and Amanda were somehow to blame.

Amanda had predicted that a grandchild would be a peacemaker, a baby in common for everyone to love. "Patch everything up," she'd said. "You'll see." He wonders, was it her plan all along to name the child *Nathan* if it was a boy? Would it have been Minerva for her mother, if it had been a girl? It was her mother she asked for, not him, when her situation looked bleak. Suddenly, he feels hemmed in by Vanderhorns. Squeezed out. Is he married to a complete stranger?

Byron struts up with his mother's bonnet. He's chased it down. The silk roses are bedraggled, but he hands it to her as if he was a conquering hero, this dutiful son.

"Let's you and me take a walk, Albright," he says with one hand resting on his mother's shoulder. The hand seems to say, *Leave this to me, Mother. I'll take care of it.* His cold blue eyes are as hard as marbles.

It occurs to Jed that Byron is the newborn's uncle and may have the mistaken idea he now has some say in Albright family affairs. Does the baby make him a prisoner of his sworn enemies?

Byron strides off with the gait of a man who expects to be followed—this puffed-up, two-bit railroad clerk. Lord knows what financial shenanigans he will cook up next for the benefit of his family. The railroad is awash in cash, and some of it has built the Vanderhorns a large house in town and paid him enough to hire a young immigrant to cook and dust for them. It's rumored that the company also paid a sizable stipend to lease the Vanderhorns' land. The farm remains in the family's name, but the crops belong to the railroad subsidiary that planted them. Rain came this year, and profits will be bountiful. Guaranteed financial rewards for the Vanderhorns will continue without all the backbreaking work of farming. Byron is a rising man about town, and his long-standing contempt for the Albrights of West Virginia is well known.

He stops beside the settling pile of spoil from the dugout.

"This is what comes of your backward, ignorant ways, Albright!" he sneers. "That's my sister in there, in that cold, filthy hole you call home, her life hanging by a thread! Do you actually care so little for anybody but yourself? Wasn't driving your own sister away enough?"

Jed has his arms folded across his chest, riding out this upbraiding, letting the fool run his mouth. But he puts his hand up at the mention of Carrie. "You leave my sister out of this!" he says. "And it wasn't so long ago, Vanderhorn, that your family— Amanda included—had a sod house for a home. Or did you think everyone had forgotten? And don't try to tell me a breech birth can't happen anyplace." Jed digs his heel into the hard turf and spins back toward the dugout.

"Only there's a helpless baby to consider now," Byron calls after him, "a tiny, weak infant. *Your son.* How do you propose to take care of him and your land and my sister out here by yourself?"

Another winter like 1911 could take them all, Jed knows. Only a miracle had saved Tim and Arthur that year from the terrible grip of the fever. Three souls were lost to it in Rolla. Six in Elkhart. Jed says, "This from a man who stands by while his father banishes his sister. You think people will forget that, too? How little *you* cared about her then?"

Byron's nostrils flare. "The people who count in this town will say that it's Jedidiah Albright alone who is putting his family in peril. They are all perfectly aware you stole her from us without my father's consent. So, maybe it's time you thought about giving her back."

Maybe it's time somebody threw a punch at that silly mustache, Jed thinks. He despises Byron all the more for the truth in what he says. He will be blamed. And he doesn't know the first thing about caring for a wife ripped apart by childbirth or how to care for a premature baby. How can he in good conscience take chances with their lives? Pride is harder to swallow than Redmond's brandy. "Not sayin' I'll do it," Jed says, "but what is it you're proposing?"

* * *

The doctor ushers Jed back out only a moment after he steps into the dugout. "We don't know why babies come early, Albright," he says. "But when they do, they often don't make it through the first few weeks. Some survive, it's true." There's gravity in the shake of his head. "But it's not always for the best. This baby's lungs are not well developed. He's struggling. I've done all I can. The rest, I'm afraid, is in God's hands. I'm sorry." The doctor can detect Jed's dissatisfaction with this surrender. "The child won't suffer much, Albright," the doctor consoles. "And your wife still has a good chance of pulling through. She might even be able to have another baby one day. Too early to say. But she's going to need time to recuperate. Understand? Stay off her." Jed understands. "I'll arrange for a wet nurse. Just in case."

Byron drives the doctor and midwife away in the cabriolet after Mrs. Vanderhorn offers to stay behind. She prepares a nursing bottle of watered goat's milk and plays the nipple over the infant's disinterested lips. One puffy eye opens a tiny slit, and the child's brow pinches into a fierce scowl. It's an expression Jed associates with Byron, something else he'd never considered. Will all of his children look like little Vanderhorns?

Amanda's mother hands Jed the softly wheezing bundle that is more blanket than baby. The puny boy no longer wriggles or cries. His breathing is shallow. "It's not a fair world, kid," Jed whispers. "Someone always ends up with the short end of the stick."

Mrs. Vanderhorn closes her eyes in the rocking chair and pretends not to hear this.

Jed passes the long hours of the night with his son in his arms and a kerosene lamp glowing dimly beside them. Life leaks slowly out of the child as Jed holds him close, his heart overflowing with affection and pity. He runs a finger tenderly across the infant's soft cheeks and cupid mouth, and one eye pops open again, inquiring this time rather than scolding. Jed beams him a smile of encouragement. *You can do it.* The infant retains a quiet dignity in the throes of a terrible fate. This little stranger. This tiny blameless boy.

Despite Jed's anxious, vigorous rubbing, the baby's skin goes blue. Two rasping breaths and a shiver signal the end. A terrible hush falls over the room. It seems almost immoral to breathe now that the child doesn't. Without waking Amanda, Jed steals away into silver moonlight with the little bundle in his arms to show the child's unseeing eyes the farm that would have been his one day, had things gone differently. To the east of the dugout, forty acres of bristly broomcorn stand tall in their victory over the stingy soil.

How many times has he anticipated this moment and never seen this coming?

***

Winter's first breaths arrive out of the north on the raw September wind. Back in West Virginia, the leaves will be changing color and beginning to fall. Here, on the treeless prairie, the ground plants are going gray like old men and withering. They will stand like sentinels in snow when it comes and topple in the spring on their way to becoming coal in a few million years.

Jed and Tim walk up the small rise together, shovels in hand.

Jed thinks of the two infants their parents buried back home. Somehow their folks managed to carry on. He and his brother would not be standing here otherwise. On the roulette wheel of life, the mine waited until Jed, Arthur, Carrie, and Tim had been born before exploding. It could have occurred on any of a thousand prior shifts the old man worked. Was there meaning in that?

"I'm sure that baby didn't mean to put Amanda in a bad way, Jed," Tim says. He has ridden the motorbike out from town, where he has a room above the smithy's workshop. "You should forgive him," he says. "I'm sure that little boy's going straight to heaven if you do."

Lost in his own grief—did the baby see his face at the end?— Jed lays down his shovel, sits on the hard, thick turf, and weeps.

Tim's face knots up in confusion. His curly black hair juts out under his leather helmet. He looks slightly wild. He asks, "You going to wait for Arthur to get here from Lawrence?"

"No."

Tim goes to work with the shovel. His brute strength makes short work of it. He says, "That cradle I made for the baby is in the shed. I was thinkin', what if I made a lid for it? We could use it for a coffin." And so they do.

***

Through the drafty door comes the sound of the Vanderhorns' impatient horse pawing the dirt.

"Guess it's time," Jed says. Amanda closes her eyes and seals her lips. She's been refusing to speak or look his way. He cannot divine what's in her head. A chasm is opening between them that runs deep.

Her mother has packed a bag with a few of her things and taken it out to the cabriolet, giving them a moment alone. Jed says, "It's for the best, Amanda. The doctor can look in on you every day in town." He holds her hand tenderly and lowers his forehead to it when his words go unanswered.

He lifts her off the bed and carries her out. Her mother tucks a blanket snugly around her on the rear leather seat. Jed gives her a chaste kiss on the cheek and steps away before he can change

133

his mind.

The carriage takes an eternity to disappear on the flat horizon. Jed stands watching it as long as possible, postponing the moment he will be utterly alone on this forsaken prairie.

Inside, he lays out the baby's handmade clothes on the bed. Nathan. A name like poison.

A rare September rain begins to fall, fat drops thumping the ground. Mud begins to drip from the leaky roof above him, something folks around here call "the black rain."

Fifteen

A Drawer

in the Bureau

Kansas City, Missouri – May 1930

Arthur was bent over paperwork in a back corner of the room. Between him and the front counter where Jed was waiting were rows of desks with candlestick telephones standing sentry on green blotters. This elite corps of federal agents, pledged to stamp out organized crime, performed their labors in white shirtsleeves. Arthur's head rose. Seeing Jed, he zigzagged between the desks to come forward.

"Holy crap, look at you," he said with a grin. He wore a gaudy maroon polka-dot tie that practically yodeled in a room of stifling conformity. "You okay?"

"For a punching bag," Jed said, and straightened his hat on his taped-up skull. The receptionist giggled.

Arthur smiled. "You never were much to look at," he said good-naturedly.

"And you were never Miss Congeniality," Jed replied.

Jed signed the clipboard sheet on the counter next to a brass sign that read, "United States Justice Department—Bureau of Investigation—Kansas City Field Office—Wait Here." Arthur unlatched a gate at the end of the counter and pointed the way to

135

his desk.

Files and notebooks were out on the agents' desks as they strolled past, and Jed saw typewritten words but could not make out what they said. He wondered if any contained mentions of Scarface Capone. Or the notorious Barker Gang. Perhaps they had names of secret informants or addresses of hideouts under surveillance. The Bureau of Investigation was an ideal fit for Arthur's secretive, paranoid, self-righteous nature.

Arthur's desktop was empty. He'd shoved something into a drawer before he came to the counter. Had Carrie's "sheet" been among the papers?

"So," Arthur said and gestured at Jed with his chin, "thought you knew better than to hitch trains." He smiled wickedly. "Did Dad's ghost pay you a visit?"

"Got any aspirin?" Jed asked.

Arthur produced a cloudy, half-filled bottle from a desk drawer, rattled it once, and set it in front of Jed. He leaned forward. "Tell me, was it a run-in with some railroad bulls? Or did that spook from New Orleans work you over?" A vengeful look came to Arthur's eye.

Jed gripped the aspirin bottle between his knees to work the top one-handed. He dumped three tablets onto Arthur's desk, and choked them down. "Forget that guy. Find my gun instead."

Arthur took his time lighting a cigarette and bared his teeth in a pleasurable grimace. A phone rang on a nearby desk. "What say I show you around?"

He led Jed past the windowed office of the special agent in charge to a back corridor. A bulletin board there was plastered with wanted posters for gangsters and bank robbers. In their mugshots, they looked like dullards with droopy eyelids and contemptuous jaws. Hooligans, their mother had called them when she saw posters in the Thurmond Post Office. Jed paused to read one for Lester M. Gillis, AKA George Nelson. AKA *Baby Face*. Was Baby Face a second cousin of Scarface? he wondered.

Down the hall, the door was open to a room full of gray cabinets. A young clerk pulled a file for an agent waiting at the counter. Every item had to be signed out individually and returned by the end of the day, according to Arthur. A tight ship.

Fingerprint Division was lettered in black on the frosted glass of a closed door across the hall. Jed pointed. "Your old office?"

Arthur nodded. "Let me show you an interrogation room," he said, making it sound less like an offer than a command.

Stiff chairs and a battered table were the only furnishings in the claustrophobic space. A smell like gym socks clung to the soundproof panels on the walls. Arthur adopted an expression that suggested the pleasurable portion of the tour had come to an end. "What the hell were you thinking, hopping a freight?" he asked.

"Long story," Jed said. Of which he currently possessed only bits and pieces.

"And you went directly to Amanda's from New Orleans? Don't tell me it was to try to patch things up. No, you went to blab about finding Carrie, didn't you? After I told you it had to be kept confidential—just between us! Damn it, Jed. You really screwed the pooch this time. And I'm the one who'll have to pay."

"I'm sorry," Jed said. "What's the big deal? It's just Amanda. I thought she deserved to know. They were close." And as it turned out, Amanda already knew, which Jed realized after his memory unlocked the riddle of the line on the cheat sheet. Amanda had admitted it. Was Arthur aware the women had remained in touch?

Arthur made a show of his exasperation. "You saw that file room? An entire cabinet is devoted to this case, one drawer to our sister, and it's only the tip of the iceberg." He went to a mirror that ran the length of one wall and cupped a hand next to his eyes at the glass, as if trying to peer through. He sighed, and turned back. "Amanda called me the day you turned up. Frantic. Demanded to know what was going on. What was I supposed to tell her? What *is* going on, Jed?"

The very question Jed had been hoping Arthur might answer. "I honestly don't know."

Arthur came back and sat in the chair across the table. "Well, I know this much. I know you went back to Carrie's that night against my advice. Don't deny it. You were seen. And the next thing I hear, you turn up at your estranged wife's looking like a worn-out pinata. Why shouldn't I suspect it was that coon who roughed you up?"

Jed's head had begun to pound. "Listen, Arthur, that train ride wore me out," he said. Hadn't Amanda asked Arthur to avoid this? "I think I'll go check in at the house."

Arthur ignored this and tossed a photo from his shirt pocket onto the table. "Recognize him?"

It was a morgue photo. Lester Barnhart. Eyes closed. Face a lifeless gray. On a slab.

"Dead?" Jed said, stunned with disbelief and, surprisingly, a trace of remorse.

"Accident, they say. In Enid. Same night we left there for New Orleans."

"Accident? What kind of accident?"

"Fell under the wheels of a train." Arthur made it sound suspicious.

"Lester? No. He was an acrobat around trains."

"Drunk, I'm told." Arthur was watching him closely. "And trapeze artists can fall. Especially if they're pushed."

"Pushed," Jed said. "You don't think …"

"If you want my help, you need to tell me everything," Arthur said.

"Okay," Jed said. He tried to pry something loose from the cobwebs. "I do remember one odd thing. For no real reason, I was thrown off the Ozark Flyer in the middle of nowhere by a man who I believe was also on our train to New Orleans." The memory was as faint as chalk on a hastily erased blackboard.

Arthur leaned forward. "Can you describe him?"

"Your height. Stocky build. Gruff manner. Oh, and one thing stood out. He had a burgundy-colored birthmark around his eye like the map of Cypress."

Arthur's brow pinched. "You're sure?"

Jed nodded. "Yes." More was coming back to him. "He said he worked for the Musgrave Detective Agency. Carried a badge and a big revolver."

"Shit," Arthur muttered and took a long, thoughtful drag on his cigarette. He returned to the long mirror and cupped his hand to the glass again. His flask came out, and he tipped it up for a big gulp. "I should never have taken you to New Orleans," he said.

"So, you know who it is?"

Arthur did not say. He came back to the table and stubbed out his cigarette in an overflowing ashtray. "Railroad dicks are investigating Lester's death. Maybe that's all it is. But the local cops have their noses stuck in there, too. And the union. And the ICC. It's a regular law enforcement convention, everybody tripping over everybody else's feet. Two guys on the same train crew get run over a day apart? Hell, whose case is it?"

"And my gun?" Jed asked. "Is anybody looking for that?"

Arthur shrugged.

"I need it back!"

"If it turns up, it will probably be impounded as evidence," Arthur said. "Look, I'm sorry. I pulled some strings and got nowhere. That little punk Lester was a slippery one. I did what I could."

An apology from Arthur was as rare as a hen's tooth, something to be relished. But it was no substitute for what Jed needed. "I need that gun back," Jed said. "Immediately!"

***

Jed stopped across the street from Arthur and Emily's Craftsman bungalow in Brookside Park, checked the time on his watch, and strolled on, hoping he hadn't been seen. At a drugstore around the corner, he bought aspirin and ordered a cup of coffee at the soda counter. The coffee was surprisingly bracing, and he did not refuse a refill. If he lingered long enough, he thought, the children would be home from school when he arrived.

Caffeine jitters undermined the plan, however, and Jed sought out refuge in a movie theater up the block playing a new Mary Astor feature. The poster out front said *The Steel Highway* was a "railroad romance picture." Jed had no idea what that meant, but he liked Mary Astor. A matinee ticket was two bits and a bottle of soda pop a nickel, and he settled into a seat in the dark as the screen flickered to life. He could tell from the opening scenes that *Steel Highway* was a B-movie melodrama. One railroad engineer was sneaking around with another one's wife. Jed inadvertently dozed off and was startled awake by the blast of a locomotive whistle. Boxcars were rumbling by on the screen and there was a nasty crick in his neck. Dream and reality seemed hopelessly twisted in his head when he thought he saw Lester Barnhart riding atop one of the cars on the screen, rugged, athletic, and larger than life. Back from the dead. It drove Jed to the lights of the lobby to clear his head. A box of Sno Caps at the refreshment stand seemed to be in order. One melted in his mouth as he read *The Steel Highway* poster in a lobby case. Mary Astor and Grant Withers dominated the image, but among the other characters in the background was a brash and cocky young actor named James Cagney. Another Lester.

Jed went back into the theater, but the newsreel was up on the screen now.

* * *

Emily Trutcher Albright was watching for him on the Craftsman's porch, arms crossed, disapproval inscribed on her haughty face. She'd been born with the Trutcher family curse of a stick up her ass.

"Dozed off at the picture show," Jed offered by way of an apology.

"For heaven's sake, Jedidiah, we thought you'd had one of your spells!" she said.

"Kids home?" Jed asked hopefully, and heard them thunder down the stairs inside at the sound of his voice. He knelt to gather them in with his good arm and did his best to laugh off the pain when they crashed into his sore ribs.

"Children!" Emily shrieked as Jed tumbled over.

"You don't look so bad!" Alan exclaimed, helping him up. "Oops! Not supposed to say that."

"That's okay," Jed said. "Suits me fine." The boy didn't take after his father. In fact, all of Arthur and Emily's kids were remarkably free-spirited, sweet, and full of fun. What were the odds?

Nancy picked up Jed's valise and impishly handed it to him with expectant eyes.

"How would you like to undo the clasp for me, young lady?" Jed asked. Quick as a flash, she had it open and Jed was handing out the small gifts he'd brought before Emily could object. There

140

was a dime-store barrette for Nancy and a first-day-of-issue Charleston commemorative stamp for each boy in a protective glassine envelope.

"Swell!" Thomas blurted and dashed up the stairs to mount the new stamp in his album.

A one-dollar Zeppelin for that boy this Christmas, Jed thought with a smile.

"Nancy," Emily said, "this would be a good time to take Uncle Jed up to your room to unpack." He was taking the girl's room? If he'd known, Jed thought, he would have gotten her something nicer than a barrette. The girl cheerfully hauled Jed's valise up the stairs. He stayed behind for a moment to speak to her mother at the parlor entrance.

"Where will she sleep?" he asked quietly.

"We'll make up a pallet for her on the floor in the hall."

"I hate to put her out," Jed said. "I didn't mean to be an imposition."

"Don't concern yourself. She'll be fine."

Supper was served promptly at six. "Children!" Emily said sharply. "Put down those forks! We say grace before we eat in this family." Nancy started to talk back, but Emily cut her off, pointing to her eye. "*Seen*," she said, "not heard." *Propriety*, Jed thought, and suppressed a smile.

"Thomas," Emily said, "this is your night."

No free passes. Thomas cast a nervous glance around the table, bowed his head, and began. "Dear Luh-luh-lord," he said, powering through his affliction. "We th—th—thank you f—for this—uh this—uh—this food before us and f—f—for all the blessings we receive. God bless Grandma Trutcher—"

"—and Uncle Jed," Alan put in, swinging his legs back and forth under his seat.

Nancy said, "—and Lord? Forgive all the folks who sponge off the government."

In the short interval of silence that followed, Jed wondered if she had said this with a straight face. Then the children burst out laughing. Alan shot a nervous glance at his mother, and the rebellious merriment stopped on a dime when she cleared her throat threateningly. Jed thought he heard Arthur emit a muffled chuckle.

"We ask this in the name of our Savior," Emily concluded icily. "Amen."

"Amen," they all agreed, and attacked their dinners.

"How is your mother, Emily?" Jed asked.

Arthur jumped in to intercede. "I'll tell you how she's doing. Her tenants are quickly falling behind on their rent, is how she's doing." Which probably meant the same was true of the tenants in the properties settled on Emily when she married. Arthur got up and refilled his lowball glass from a decanter on the sideboard. "We'll have to institute a few economies around here if it keeps on."

It didn't appear that they were exactly teetering on the brink. Roast beef for dinner. A house stuffed with pretentious furnishings and children dressed to the nines. But Arthur, like so many others, had suffered brutal margin calls on the "blue chip" stocks bought at a time when it was thought they were going nowhere but up. That nest egg depleted, his government salary could probably not keep pace with his wife's spending. He liked to believe he wore the pants in the family, but in a serious pinch, Emily's real estate would probably give her the upper hand.

Jed offered to put the boys to bed after dinner, a ritual he enjoyed. Alan and Thomas were like sons he'd been denied in his own life.

"Uh—uh—Uncle Jed. T-tell us about living in a cave with our d-dad." Jed smiled at Thomas and found himself imagining who his boy Nathan might have become, had he lived.

"The dugout, you mean," Jed said.

"Mama says you and Dad lived in a cuh—cuh—cave in Kansas."

Don't forget Carrie and Tim, Jed wanted to say. But didn't. It wasn't his place to tell it. How easily and quietly a branch could drop off a family tree, he thought. "I guess you might call it a cave," Jed agreed. "Did your dad tell you we hatched chicks in it? Whew, what a stink!" The boys laughed and Jed explained about candling and incubating without mentioning it was their long-lost Aunt Carrie who had been in charge of it all. How could he say a word about her without there being endless questions he couldn't answer. They'd never heard of her. And might never now.

"Tell us about the night the wolves attacked," Alan said. He'd inherited his father's appetite for sensation and danger. What had Arthur told him?

Jed shifted uneasily on the bed. "It would only give you nightmares," Jed said gently. "Did your dad tell you our first winter there, we had to use gunny sacks for overshoes and hang them on the stove every night to dry?"

"No, tell us about the wo—wo—wolf!" Thomas begged.

"Let's save that one for another time," Jed said gently, knowing he'd never speak of it. *A secret is not a secret unless it is taken to the grave.*

"That's enough, boys," Emily shouted up the stairs. "Time to turn off the light and let Uncle Jed get some rest, too. He's had a long day."

Their mother's tone silenced them but did not put a stop to their furtive, pleading expressions or address the disappointment in their eyes.

"Another time," Jed repeated quietly.

"P-p-promise?" Thomas whispered urgently.

"We'll see," Jed whispered back. He put a silencing finger to his lips as he gave them each a nickel, kissed their foreheads, and turned out the light.

The radio in the living room was tuned to *The Amos 'n Andy Show*, the speaker crackling with studio audience laughter at the antics of two Chicago ghetto dwellers. "I think I'll leave for Rolla in the morning," Jed said, stepping into the room.

Arthur set aside the newspaper, turned the radio down, and pocketed his reading glasses. A drink was on the table beside his chair. "Tell me something," he said. "You don't want your gun back because you're hoping to plug Elmore Scruggs with it, do you?"

"No," Jed said. But the idea had crossed his mind.

"We don't know that he's the father. Or even that she's the mother."

"That's true."

"Well, if you're dead set on going," Arthur said, "check to be sure Tim harvested my wheat instead of trying to perfect salted-in-the-shell hard-boiled eggs."

Jed said, "If he told you it was done, it's done."

"And you're sure he's on board with the leasing mineral rights?" Arthur asked.

"It's all signed, Arthur," Jed said. "What did you tell the boys about the wolf?"

"Just what a hero you were."

Arthur obviously still hadn't heard the real story.

Sixteen

Wolf at the Door

Rolla, Kansas – November 1911

One appears at dusk, skulking past the perimeter of the yard. Silent. Sniffing greedily at the air. Snout up. Ribs standing out beneath the gray and brown fur. Starving. Desperate.

"What the hell," Arthur mutters, peering through a crack in the heavy canvas curtain covering the dugout window. "It's not leaving!" he complains, just before another appears.

"Jesus, there's two?" Jed says over his shoulder, shocked that the crafty predators would come right out in the open this way. Bold as hell. Were the wolves stalking them? "Do you suppose it's the smell?" Jed ventures.

Tim's foul breath and vile sweat are choking the cramped dugout with a stench strong enough to penetrate gaps in the sod wall like a distress signal. A meal in the making for wolves. Tim lies helpless in the grip of a ferocious fever, and the whole family is now in danger.

"I could go out and bang on a pot," Carrie volunteers. "It might scare them off."

A third marauder appears, larger and thicker through the body than the first two. An adult male. "No," Jed tells Carrie. "Stay put." A growling, snarling confrontation breaks out between the latecomer and the two smaller juveniles to establish order among thieves. After a brief standoff, the juveniles back away and howl in the distance, awaiting leftovers.

The human captives jump at the unexpected sound of the dangerous beast rearing up against their door and scratching at the wood with its claws. The rickety latch holds, but its rattle is ominous. The siege has begun.

"My God!" Carrie shrieks. "Are we safe?"

"Arthur," Jed shouts, summoning help with the washstand as he drags it, wobbling and shuddering, to block the leather-hinged door. The determined pushing and scratching continues.

"Make it stop!" Carrie shouts. "It's frightening Tim." And he's not alone.

Jed pokes the barrel of the Winchester out the canvas window and fires a foot above the wolf's head, not wanting a bloody carcass at the door that would attract every scavenging animal, insect, and bird in Western Kansas. The wolves all scatter into the deep grass at the rifle's pop.

"They're gone," Jed announces. But he wonders for how long.

At nightfall, the young wolves' high-pitched yipping seems to move steadily closer, and the clawing starts up again. Tim, struggling with delirium, moans pitifully.

Arthur says, "I'm going out." He picks up the rifle. "Put an end to this. Kill 'em all. But we'll have to get the big one away from the door first."

Jed helps him wriggle the washstand back, and he bangs the head of an ax against the door like a drum, startling everything outside into silence before Arthur pokes the rifle out and fires. The wolves scatter again. The muzzle flash throws a faint light into the darkness and reveals the last one disappearing into the grass. Arthur takes a step toward it and fires twice.

"I think I wounded it," he says. But he sounds more hopeful than certain, and he does not venture out to verify a hit. It's dark, and at least two wolves remain. They will hunt as a team, one circling to rip out a chunk of leg from behind as Arthur goes for the one in front of him.

When the brothers turn back, Carrie is standing in the doorway, iron skillet in hand.

Arthur collapses onto his horsehair pallet inside next to the wall complaining of a terrible headache. Jed and Carrie exchange a glance. Tim's fever began this way. Arthur barely raises his head again after that. "I'm burning up," he mutters an hour later.

Carrie makes up a cool compress for his forehead. Her face is lined with worry. Her thoughts have gone to a dark place. "What do we do if Tim dies?" she asks. "How do we get him out with wolves lying in wait?"

The ground is too frozen to dig graves, too, Jed thinks. He wonders, did they escape with their lives from a prairie fire only to become a feast for wolves? He watches Carrie pace to the sound of restless activity in the yard. He knows wolves are strong, smart, and agile. They scale ranchers' fences and leap onto moving cattle wagons. Only canvas covers the window! Belatedly, he and Carrie inch the chiffonier across the room and position it over the opening in the sod wall. Jed slides down to rest his back against it, sweating profusely when it's done. What was it Scruggs said? They had no business out here on their own. Is this how it will end?

Jed says, "I'm going to Redmonds for help." He will have to shoot his way out, and Carrie will be left alone with sick, helpless brothers and no weapon. Jed can expect, too, that he will be dogged in the dark by the swift, powerful hunters. But what choice does he have?

"No," Carrie says. She brushes away strands of hair that have drooped into her eyes. She's wearing the same blue muslin dress for a third day, and exhaustion shows in her face. "At least wait for first light," she says. "Maybe they'll leave then. I'll make us some tea."

Before it's ready, fatigue overtakes Jed, and he slips into a feverish, disjointed dream that ends in a gasp when Carrie rouses him, holding a cup of sassafras tea. She looks relieved that he's not in the grip of fever, too. "Arthur just called me Ma," she says. "He's delirious."

Jed sips the hot tea as Carrie returns to the stove. A welcome stillness has come to the yard. Maybe the wolves have given up and moved on. But it's too soon to let down their guard. The stealthy hunters might just be hunkered down out of sight.

"I heated up last night's soup with a few stores from the cellar," Carrie says. Sliced potatoes and carrots stretch the stock. "I hope that's all right." She brings bowls to the table. And there are griddle cakes on a plate. "Thanksgiving is tomorrow. Our first in Kansas. Not much to celebrate with, I'm afraid." She surveys the table wearily.

"I'll bag us a rabbit for stewing in the morning," Jed says optimistically. Carrie takes Jed's hand in hers and squeezes it. She is counting on him, it seems to say. He squeezes hers back, confirming a commitment to courage. They will stand together against the unthinkable. Hope should always die last, their mother used to say.

Carrie tries to spoon a few drops of the tea into Tim. He sputters and coughs and turns away. His breathing is labored, ragged. Carrie kneels next to him and lays her cheek against his chest. Tears well in her eyes. "His heartbeat is very weak," she sobs.

"He's too ornery to die," Jed says, hoping jocularity will scatter his worries. He's distracted by black specks sprinkling into his soup like pepper from above and by strange muffled sounds in the dugout roof. A chunk of the sod tears loose and tumbles onto the table. A dirty animal paw thrusts through the hole that has opened into the night sky. Carrie squeals.

The Winchester is not in its usual spot. Jed's eyes dart around the room and see only the ax in the corner where the rifle should be. One of the makeshift roof supports groans and crackles. The ceiling sags and more soil rains down. Jed manages to jump out of the way just before the wolf tumbles through the hole it's made and crashes onto its side on the table. Its passing claws scrape Jed's forearm, and a sharp, feral scent assaults his nostrils. The wolf's awkward landing has knocked the wind out of it. Jed tries to back away, but his legs get tangled in his toppled chair.

Dust clouds the dugout air now. Carrie edges out of sight behind her dressing screen. The animal rises to its feet on the table with its ears pinned back and a wild look in its glassy eyes. It snarls, baring its array of lethal teeth. There is nowhere to flee. The door and window are blocked. Jed picks up his fallen chair and jabs it at the bristling beast. The wolf's jaws snap at the legs, recalling for Jed the vicious dogfight he and Arthur witnessed as boys through knotholes of a barn outside Thurmond. The gore of the barbaric ring, surrounded by shouting men cheering on dogs in a struggle to the death, reawakens the primitive horror he felt that day. The hair on the back of his neck stands up.

The wolf's sudden lunge nearly knocks the chair from Jed's hand. His cheeks are aflame in the cold night air spilling through the opening in the roof. One of the juveniles is peering through the hole, undecided on its next move. The instant Jed glances its way, the big wolf below springs and knocks him onto Carrie's cot with its teeth clamped around his wrist. Its snout is slick with snot against Jed's palm as he futilely tries to push it off. The teeth have sunk in deep, and he is in agony, pinned under the animal's surprising weight, his wrist crushed in its powerful jaws. The beast snorts its savage breath into his face.

A glint of steel flicks into view in the lamplight, and the wolf abruptly releases Jed's wrist. Carrie's hand rises with her sewing scissors to deliver a second blow to the wolf's back. But the wolf pivots and snaps its bloody teeth on the sleeve of Carrie's dress before she can. A powerful twist of its torso takes Carrie down with a shriek. The animal jerks its head side to side, ripping away fabric before jumping astride her, preparing to sink its teeth into her neck. It hesitates, however, at the sight of the scissors she brandishes.

With a swift, sure hand, Carrie drives the point of the scissors into the wolf's eye. It howls and thrashes its legs scrambling to get away, shredding the front of her dress.

The ax in his hands now, Jed brings the blade down on the animal's neck as if he were splitting kindling. A spasm of shock ripples through the tan and black fur and urine streams onto Carrie's dress as the predator's legs go limp. Carrie stares in horror as the wolf's severed head rolls to one side, oozing blood, and she quickly squirms out from under its spastic surrender to death. *Did that really happen,* her expression appears to ask.

Jed has located the Winchester beneath the legs of the chiffonier. He points it at the opening in the roof, but the juvenile is gone, its appetite seemingly quelled. With Jed's legs no longer willing to bear the weight of his shock, he slides his back down the chiffonier. He tries to stop the blood from pulsing out his wrist with his other hand.

Without stepping behind her dressing screen, Carrie tugs her tattered, urine-soaked dress over her head, immodestly exposing her legs and her skirted corset cover. She doesn't look Jed in the face as she removes her frilly muslin chemise and uses it as a tourniquet for his wrist. The chemise, too, stinks of urine. Carrie's breasts bulge out the top of her armor-like corset.

Jed has not seen so much of his sister's unclothed body since they were little children on bath night, and her body is radically changed, of course. The limits to his knowledge of the adult female form are what he's seen on illicit French postcards of lingerie-clad loose women handed around among men. Carrie possesses the same tantalizing flesh, but her purity and innocence of spirit make hers far more alluring.

She catches the look in Jed's eye, and seems to understand his bashful curiosity about her flesh. She studies him as she unlaces her corset without a word. Jed knows he should turn away and thinks that she must know she should stop. But she doesn't. And his wish to examine her breasts in their fullness is obliged by Carrie, who allows them to swing ripe and free with the corset unfastened.

The sounds of his unconscious brothers' rasping breathing fills Jed with guilt. This is their sister! He turns away then, wondering if a brush with death has cost him all notion of decency.

* * *

At the rooster's crow, Jed drags the bloody carcass of the wolf out of the dugout on a rug. He takes the Winchester with him, in case the juveniles return. Flies gather from out of nowhere in the carcass's gaping wounds as he drags it along.

He summons the strength at the privy to heave the wolf's body down the readymade hole in the ground. He sprinkles lye over it and removes the privy's plank door to vent the fumes. He will lay the detached door over the hole in the roof to temporarily seal the opening.

The sun rises over Kansas for the hundred-millionth time. Clouds scud along in the sky, casting shadows that move across the prairie as if they might be ghosts of buffalo herds that once roamed here.

Jed cradles the Winchester in his arms, observing the natural order to the world and wondering how he will live with the memory of last night, tormented now by what has been revealed of his true nature. Maybe Amanda's brothers are right. Maybe he doesn't deserve Amanda, a man who would gape at his own sister that way. Maybe the Albrights are disgusting, backward hillbillies.

When smoke begins to pour out of the sod from the dugout's black chimney, Jed sets off for town to get help, hoping just this once he doesn't cross paths with Amanda Vanderhorn.

Seventeen

Buried Treasure

Rolla, Kansas – May 1930

Tim's porch was beginning to sag under the weight of parlor furniture dragged out of the house on a hot night long past. Without realizing it, Jed took a step back.

In the yard was a massive broomcorn baler, its spokes threaded with unruly stalks of bluestem and muhly that had grown up around it. An assortment of rusted engine parts, wagon axles, tractor tires, and gear boxes lay scattered in the weeds nearby. Tim's motorbike from 1911, missing its rear wheel, lay on its side like a horse that had been put down. Yesterday's obsession, today's scrap.

Jed unearthed two aspirins from a lint-lined pocket. The journey from town had sapped him, body and spirit. The familiar old footpath was gone, obliterated along with the prairie grasses it once cut through. Everything, absolutely everything it seemed, had been plowed up, right to the edges of town, and planted with needless rows of winter wheat. The vast, wild prairie had been tamed, put to order by the modern mechanized plow. But it was too much. Some fields had already been abandoned, left to bake hard in the sun and wind.

Seen out the window of the train from K.C., the enormity of this "agricultural revolution" was overwhelming, hypnotic. Jed had nearly ridden past his stop. The old depot had appeared suddenly, unexpectedly. A shock. A familiar, unchanged thing in this transformed place!

He'd had to take section roads to get to Tim's, hiking from one unmarked intersection to the next, counting off the squares in his head—two east, one south, and two east again. The spinning copper blades of Tim's eccentric homemade windmill was just a speck on the horizon at first, and it vanished for a time as Jed passed the tall broomcorn in a field west of Scruggs's ranch. The old Victorian still sat squarely on its foundation, white gable ends scraping against the blue sky. Seeing it again unleashed waves of hostility in Jed. He wondered if Arthur was right. Would he have gone to Scruggs's door and put a hole in him if he'd had his revolver?

Jed's gut was sour now from the aspirin. A glass of water would be most welcome, he thought. He looked back at the *No Trespassing* sign posted on Tim's new barbed wire fence and guessed the barricade was there to keep Scruggs's steers out of what might have been the only pristine prairie in Kansas. It teemed with insects and birds like a nature preserve.

Nothing moved in the house when Jed knocked on the door. Nothing was visible in the splotchy windows, either. He strolled to one side of the house, calling out Tim's name. The smell of dog shit was strong in the yard. Privy flies buzzed in the stillness.

A large mongrel dog suddenly bounded around the corner, teeth bared and back legs coiling to leap. A gasp jolted Jed's sore ribs. A whistle cut through the silence then, freezing the mutt in its tracks. Its ears twitched to the sound of Tim's voice calling it off. The dog whined in frustration and glinted at Jed. "You just wait," it seemed to say.

"Jedidiah? That you?" Tim had a vintage six-shooter holstered on his belt and a crowbar dangling from his hand. His eyes were slits from squinting into the scorching Kansas sun for two decades, but his smile remained almost childlike in its sweet sincerity. "Jedidiah! My God if it ain't!"

He dropped the crowbar and charged forward, wiping his hands on his overalls to embrace Jed as he might a posthole digger and bounce him up and down. The valise slipped from Jed's grasp. How had three brothers shared a bed all those years and turned out so different?

"Don't this beat all!" Tim exclaimed. His tight curly black hair was tucked under a denim mechanic's cap. The kinkiness of it had been a source of fistfights back in Thurmond when their mother's marital fidelity was called into question.

Jed kept a wary eye on the dog and said, "I take it I surprised you."

"Well, no shit. A course you did. No matter. C'mon in. Get a load off. Looks like you been tangling with bears."

Beadboard walls, scratched and battered, lined the empty parlor. Tim stomped the dust off his boots, went to the kitchen, and brought back a jar of home brew. "This'll clear your sinuses," he said. They took it out onto the porch and sat on the weathered sofa. The cushions wheezed an aroma of cat piss when Jed sat on it. A sip from the jar misted his eyes over, and the concoction sloshed like gasoline onto the smoldering aspirin in his stomach. Jed coughed. The dog tensed, a growl at the ready in its throat.

"What's his name?" Jed asked.

"Arfur."

It was Jed who barked, trying to choke back a laugh. *Arfur.* Like a comic strip animal. It was exactly the way Tim mispronounced Arthur's name as a toddler. *Arfur.* Tim smiled mischievously.

He grabbed the jar from Jed with a chuckle. "Been aging this batch since '28," he said in mock boast. "Savin' it for a special occasion." He took off his denim cap and tipped the jar up to his lips for a hearty swig. "Guess you're the occasion." He wiped his forehead and blinked at Jed. "What are ya doing here, Jedidiah?"

Not one to beat around the bush, Tim.

"Just thought it was time I paid a visit," Jed evaded. He'd need some time to navigate to the point. Set the stage first. This news wasn't going to be pleasant.

He saw a critter dart for cover out on the prairie, and his distracted thoughts were pulled back to the short detour he took off the road on the long walk from town, crunching into corn stubble to the last vestiges of the old dugout. He got his bearings at the crumbling wellhead. Following a line toward Scruggs's

Victorian roof took him to an egg-shaped stone with a small cross chiseled in it. Jed knelt to clear away some sagebrush. Here was the darkest place in the universe. The scrub-covered landscape began to spin then and suddenly he was facefirst in the dirt, ears ringing.

Tim handed him the moonshine jar again with a worried look. "You okay?" A spring groaned as Jed tried to reposition his backside away from it. He took another swallow from the jar. "Perfected those salted-in-the-shell hard-boiled eggs yet?" he asked his brother.

"Nah. Not enough hours in the day. Got repairs to get out the door. Dipshit suitcase farmers keep showing up who don't know an oilcan from a corncob. Come out here with their heads up their butts hoping to hit it big on a harvest. Strike it rich. So I been busy."

"Your customers don't mind the barbed wire and … ?" He nodded toward the mutt. And there was that threatening Old West six-shooter.

"Had to put the wire up to keep out the railroad," Tim said, sounding angry.

"The railroad?" Jed said. "Why? Railroad's been around a long time."

"Well now they got these fancy pants geologists nosing around places they don't belong." He propped up his boots on the porch railing and scooted down a notch in the chair. The center of one boot sole glinted where a hole had been patched with tin. He scoffed, "But they're learnin'."

North of Tim's land was a section that had been granted to the railroad by government charter. Jed had noticed it was under cultivation, probably by sharecroppers. "You sure these fellas weren't on their own land?" he asked.

"Sure, I'm sure. You think I don't know where the line's at? They were trespassing, plain and simple. Caught 'em red-handed. More than once, too. But I didn't give 'em too much crap 'til they got close."

"Close?"

"To the oil, Jedidiah. To the oil!"

"What oil? They found oil? On your land?" Productive wells in Oklahoma and Texas were operating just a hop, skip, and a jump across the border. Still, when an oil company rep offered Jed a fat check to lease the mineral rights to the family's four section quarters, he almost couldn't believe it. "Here?" Jed had said.

"The future of your land, Mr. Albright, is below the surface, not above," the sales rep said.

"The railroad?" Tim snorted. "No, them shysters can't find shit. I found the oil."

"You found it? How?"

"Come on, I'll show ya." He put his cap on and trotted toward the barn. "Come on! You want to see or don't ya?" There was a red *No Trespassing* sign on the padlocked barn, too.

"Keep a guard horse in here?" Jed teased.

"Very funny," Tim replied and rolled the massive door back on its squeaky track. Inside, under a tarp, was a Rube Goldberg contraption with an old church bell fastened to the underside of a donkey cart. The cart was refitted with bicycle tires. Resting in its bed was a handmade gizmo with pipes and switches and gauges. A crate of dynamite lay in the dirt by one tire. "Grab a couple of sticks, and bring 'em along," Tim said.

He hefted the cart's pulling bar and wheeled his invention forward, calling back from the door, "Well, come on, Jed. Do you want to see or don't you?"

A trail of grooves worn in the soil to the southeast led them into a field pitted with craters. Jed was so distracted by the destruction that he turned his ankle stepping into a divot he hadn't seen. Was this where Arthur's seed money had gone? When Jed had checked his field on the walk to Tim's, he'd seen that it hadn't even been planted.

They limped to a halt in a spot where the grass was heavily trampled. Ten yards beyond was more of the wire fence and the railroad's cultivated field. Tim used a lever on the side of the cart to lower the bell to the ground, exposing wires that ran from it to the black box with the dials. "Give me one of those sticks," he told Jed.

Jed held the dynamite sticks up and out of reach, as if he was dealing with a child. "No," he said. "First, you have to tell me what's been going on out here." The ground around them was like the no-man's-land between the Allies' and Central Powers' armies in the Great War.

Tim shrugged piteously. "Okay," he said, "you know how a coffee cup makes different sounds when you stir it, depending on how much coffee is in it?"

"Yes?"

"Well, that's the idea. Hang on, I'll show ya." He grabbed a stick of dynamite out of Jed's hand, walked between craters for about thirty paces, used a knife to cut a hole in the grass, and lowered the dynamite into the hole. "Come put a match to this when I holler," he said. "I got to turn the machine on, and I didn't think to have you bring the long fuses."

"No," Jed said again. The sound of dynamite going off would travel for miles on the wind. "Tell me how stirring your coffee tells you there's oil here." In their homesteading days, Tim had used a divining rod cut from a willow tree on the Cimarron River to predict where water might be found for a well on their land. He'd walked the property for a week letting his stick decide before the professionals arrived and chose the exact same spot.

"Blind luck," Arthur scoffed. "I could have pointed at random and done the same thing." Arthur. Always the diplomat.

Tim trotted back between the craters. "Okay, see these dials?" he asked, pointing to the black box. "They measure echo time between peak sound waves. Got 'em from a catalog sells to radio stations." He opened a notebook from his back pocket filled with calculations and hand-drawn diagrams labeled with numbers and letters. "First it registers the blast signal," he said, pointing at one figure, "then the echo. The gap between 'em is the key. Lets you see what's down there." He pointed at his diagram. "Like an X-ray. You know what that is, right?"

Jed surveyed the craters around them. "Looks like you've been at this awhile."

"Triangulation," Tim said. "Got to surround your target."

Their mother liked to boast that Tim could tie his shoelaces at two. And that he'd made the heirloom clock on their mantel chime for the first time in a generation at age six when he snuck off with it and took it apart to tinker with the balance wheel.

The kids back in Thurmond bullied him for being "different." But Tim had refused to raise his fists against them. So his brothers had to take matters into their own hands. But when the bullies discovered that *the oddball kid* could unlock doors with a hairpin, they adopted him as a mascot for mischief and hijinks. Keeping Tim out of trouble became the new priority.

"Let's go back to the house," Jed said. "I think I've seen enough."

"You never was any fun," Tim said irritably. He began wheeling his gadget home. "And your hair's fallin' out, you know."

They ate a simple supper on the porch since Tim didn't like being cooped up in his house. "Always hated that dugout," he said. "Reminded me of the mine that took Pa."

"You do know we don't have to find oil ourselves, right?" Jed said. Tim was staring into a plume of gnats swarming in a shaft of sunlight. "It's the oil company's job," he added. Tim had turned silent. Jed said, "I'm happy to hear the repair business is going strong." He wondered if Tim would come clean. Jed had borrowed heavily at the bank to get him started with the proper tools and equipment, and he got monthly operating statements. Deposits had dried up. Checks bounced. If farmers were going broke out here, who was going to pay someone to fix a tractor?

"Arthur sent you out here to check up on me, didn't he?" Tim blurted after a time. Arfur growled at Jed. Tim reached down to pick him up.

"No, he didn't send me," Jed replied. "Why would you think that?"

"'Cause I never did plant that wheat last fall. And he prob'ly heard."

"So why didn't you?"

"Had a fella. Said he'd do it. Took off on me. All for the best, turns out. Wheat's gone bust, you know. Ain't worth a plug nickel. Costs more to get it out of the field than it's worth at the depot. That fella takin' off saved Arthur a lot."

"But you still have the seed?"

"Yeah. And I'm gonna have to throw it in the ground soon.

Dust comes off that land something awful when the wind kicks up. Can't hardly see the barn from here when it blows. But listen, I got an idea, Jedidiah. Why don't we fix up our own drilling rig? Try our hand at wildcatting? Cut out the greedy oilmen."

The odds of Tim finding oil on their land were hopelessly long. And everything in the ground was already pledged to the exploration company that had leased it. The Albrights would get their cut. "Drilling is expensive, Tim," Jed said. "Where would we get that kind of money?" He was done borrowing.

"Just need a drill bit and some pipe," Tim argued. "I can make the rest myself."

He envisioned Tim out here sinking endless dry holes on a relentless, expensive treasure hunt. And if he did happen to strike oil and they could renegotiate the lease, who would they sell it to if not an oil company? Jed admonished, "I'm already your partner in a repair business, don't forget. We need to keep that going."

"Don't be sore, Jedidiah," Tim grumbled. "Never going to make a real living doing that."

"I'm not sore," Jed said. Did he look cross? "Listen, tomorrow I think I'll go into town and buy a few groceries and other supplies." The cupboard seemed a little bare.

"Miss Martha brings groceries on Thursdays."

"Miss Martha? Who's that?"

Tim ignored the question. "You haven't said yet whether you're goin' in with me."

"Going in?"

"On wildcattin'!"

Jed stared some more at the prairie. "You asked before what I was doing here," he said slowly. "I came to tell you something, and there's no easy way to say it. So here it is: Carrie is alive. I've seen her."

Eighteen

Low Ball

Rolla, Kansas – May 1930

Jed counted the words a second time before handing the form through the window to Clarence Ott, whose bald, misshapen head had always put Jed in mind of a difficult birth. Ott was inclined to overcharge you, if you didn't keep an eye on him.

    ARTHUR ALBRIGHT 5631 GRAND AVE KC MO
    ARRIVED SAFE STOP NO WHEAT PLANTED
    STOP WILL EXPLAIN STOP STAYING ON HERE
    STOP JED

"That it?" Ott asked, perhaps disappointed the message wasn't longer and more detailed. Anything Ott sent down the wire had a chance of making the rounds in town, too—if it was juicy enough. In Rolla, the grapevine and the telegraph line were entangled. Jed had tried to cloak his worries with words that were short on specifics. But there might be enough there to set tongues wagging. The Albrights had finally shown up to deal with their crazy brother.

"Yup," Jed replied, letting Ott know he was onto him. He didn't want Arthur hearing the news in Kansas City before the telegram actually arrived (Arthur's rich, busybody mother-in-law lived here, after all, and she could always pick up her telephone and call him).

"Sixty-five cents," Ott said.

"Wait, I don't see a Teletype machine," Jed said.

"You want Teletype, you have to go to Dodge City. Railroad ain't gonna spend a nickel putting a Teletype in here."

Which meant the grapevine had an edge in getting the news to Arthur first. A telegraph key—all those dots and dashes—required the message to pass through multiple human hands, transmitting and receiving. It was inherently slower than words typed at one end that arrived at their destination ready to deliver. Annoyed, Jed said, "Railroad can't be bothered to stop and pick up the wheat either, looks like."

"It ain't that," Ott scoffed, pretending he didn't recognize sarcasm when he heard it.

"Yeah," Jed agreed. "It isn't." Mounds of grain sat here on the platform next to the new cement silos as a result of the market's collapse. Money was gone, squandered on a horrid war. People in Europe were starving in its aftermath, while American bounty piled up like snowdrifts in towns like Rolla. And the lost prairie, plowed under to feed the world, was a collateral casualty.

Jed couldn't shake a streak of sarcasm. "So, is that President Hoover's railcar parked out there? Come out to tell farmers their bumper crop will be needed as soon as this little panic is over?" The dark tinted windows of the green luxury Pullman on the siding revealed nothing.

Ott's lopsided grin was surprising. He wasn't usually one for jokes. "Nah," he said brightly. "That there's your brother-in-law's coach."

He was serious, Jed realized. What? Since when was Byron chairman of the railroad?

Ott seemed to delight in Jed's vexation. The feud between the two men was legendary around here. The telegraph key began to chatter and, reluctantly, Ott turned his attention to it like an obedient lover to a jealous mistress. "Gotta take this," he said, and began jotting down letters and numbers from the stream of syncopated clicks the instrument was making on his desk. His lips moved as he wrote. And his pencil point snapped under pressure.

He tossed it aside and grabbed another from a jar on his desk without missing a beat.

Jed leaned against the Dutch door watching. Across the platform, the luxury green Pullman glinted in the sun. Car 2633. Byron Vanderhorn's? Really? Like a bad penny.

"Another cockamamie telegram for your buddy out there," Ott grumbled when the wire fell silent again. "Third one this morning."

Ott's specialty, setting rumors in motion.

"They're all gibberish, too," he said. "First there's a property description—this one NWQS31T33. That's the northwest quarter of section 31 of township 33. Railroad land. Just east up the line. It's all mumbo-jumbo after that. More of an anagram, than a telegram. Tough on an operator to get it right when the words ain't real."

He held the message up briefly for Jed to see. Something in code, apparently. Ott typed it out on his clattering Remington, inserted the typed version in a yellow Western Union envelope, and shoved his handwritten notes in a file drawer.

"Like to find out what Mr. Big Shot's doing here?" Ott asked, and lifted an eyebrow. "'Cause I got no idea." He cocked one beady eye. "You might ask if you took this out to him." He held out the sealed telegram. "I could get your message out straight away if you do."

After a moment's hesitation, Jed took the envelope. "Word of warning, Albright?" Ott called after him. "I think he's got a bone to pick with your brother."

So, that was the setup, Ott acting as Byron's lackey. "Yeah?" Jed said. "What about?"

"He's been takin' potshots at railroad surveyors, what I hear. Lobbing Army surplus grenades, too. Folks sayin'."

"What are folks saying about railroad men trespassing on his land?" Jed asked.

Ott shrugged as if he wouldn't know about that.

Neither, really, did Jed. Tim had cut short discussion of overzealous geologists after Jed mentioned Carrie.

"She ain't dead?" he'd said, his face tied in an anxious knot.

"No," Jed replied. "She's very much alive."

Tim fidgeted.

"What's wrong? I thought you'd be happy we finally found her."

"Why'd she never come home?"

That was the question, all right. The one Jed wasn't yet prepared to answer.

"She run off with some fella, didn't she?" Tim said.

Jed shrugged and Arfur growled. The dog was a slave to his master's mercurial moods. Two seconds later, Tim bounded off the porch and stalked away, the dog trotting by his side.

Turned out, Arthur was right that telling Tim would be a mistake. But the mistake had nothing to do with Arthur's worry—that his mother-in-law would have to live down the shame of the Albrights' dirty secret spreading over the back fences of her hometown. The worry should have been breaking Tim's heart.

Jed ambled down the platform and across the rails with the telegram, the dutiful messenger boy. But only because he had a message of his own to deliver.

***

Byron's desk was an immense walnut affair situated in front of a pastel mural painted on a partition wall depicting a sleek, new diesel engine and three mythic figures—a farmer, a factory worker, and a train engineer—like partners in a new tomorrow. Heroic. Determined.

Railroad propaganda, Jed thought derisively. He didn't bother removing his hat or waiting for an invitation to sit in the visitor chair. "Hate to interrupt," he said when Byron, in turn, didn't bother to lift his head from over a pile of paperwork.

"What is it you want, Albright?" he snapped, as if he didn't know. As if sixteen years hadn't passed since they last spoke, Byron Vanderhorn still waiting to dance on Jedidiah Albright's grave.

"I came to apologize for drinking up your whisky at Amanda's," Jed said.

"Right," Byron scoffed, and crossed out a line on a memo in

164

front of him. "You didn't come all this way for that," he said in a tone both disinterested and dismissive.

"No," Jed said, "you're right. I thought since you were parked out this way, I'd stop by and tell you to keep your men off my brother's land."

Byron finally looked up. He'd grown a beard that didn't fully conceal the droop of his jowls or the spiderweb of veins on his cheeks. But his blue eyes were as cold and hard as ever, and his expression was serious as he leaned back and said, "My men survey only railroad land, Albright, unless we have an invitation from the property owner."

Once they'd bullied the owner into a corner first, Jed thought. "Is that right?"

"Yes, that's right," Byron said. The thick windows of the plush car muffled the sound of a freight train passing on the main track. "It's good you dropped by, though," Byron said. He plucked a document bound in blue paper from a stack on his desk. Legal documents of some sort. "This is for you. I suggest you consider it carefully before responding." It glided across the desk with a little flick of his finger.

"It's an offer to buy your land," he said when Jed made no move to pick it up.

"The railroad is willing to purchase all four quarters."

So, their land must be sitting on oil, Jed thought. Otherwise, why would the railroad want it? As farmland, it wasn't even worth the taxes owed on it.

"What's the offer?" Jed asked. A price might say something about the value of the mineral deposits beneath. And it felt like the sky was the limit.

"A dollar an acre."

Jed sputtered. "Cut it out, Vanderhorn." It was the price they'd paid the government for the land two decades before. Before they'd invested years of their sweat and torment. Before they'd paid for improvements with borrowed money. "What's your game, Byron?" Jed said.

Byron shook his head. He didn't have to answer questions from riffraff. "I advise you to sign the paperwork before you get out of that chair, because you're definitely not going to like what I tell you next if you get up."

"Are you threatening me?" Jed said.

Byron shrugged. "Just giving you some sound advice, Albright. Because I assure you it's within the power of the railroad to take possession of all of section 39 with or without your agreement, and with or without your family ever seeing a nickel."

If it was so damn easy, Jed thought, why pressure him for a signature, other than to give the theft an appearance of legitimacy? There must be some known flaw in the plan that the contract was intended to patch over. So, Jed would refuse to sign just to discover what the loophole was and exploit it. "Not one damn dime for all that land?" Jed said. "Seems like a reach, even for an organization as underhanded as yours."

A different document came sliding across the desk. The man had a certain style.

"What's this one?" Jed asked.

"A copy of a letter your bank will send you, foreclosing on your property, if you don't sign. The bank will auction off your land, and we will be the only bidder."

Byron had predicted years ago that railroads would run the country. Now they did. They owned the most lucrative means of transportation and essential pieces of adjacent real estate. They controlled legislators, judges, and sheriffs. They owned majority stakes in little banks like Citizens State, too. It was a machine kept well oiled by the vast shipping revenue that poured in. The railroad and the bank would happily carve up the spoils of the Albright land just as it had finally become worth something.

Byron said, "I have contracts here for your brothers and your sister." He patted a pile of papers. "Of course, Carrie won't actually be able to sign hers, will she?" He pulled it from the stack and sent it flopping into a wastebasket.

Jed felt an ache in the pit of his stomach.

"Because it's not as if your sister's signature would match the one on file at the land office, would it? Everyone knows she disappeared long before that paper was signed. And your brother might want to consider the risk to his position in an agency of the United States Justice Department if his role as an accessory to fraud came to light."

The signature on the page that proved up Carrie's land had been forged by Byron's own sister, Amanda. Did he not know that? Jed wondered. Or was he prepared to sacrifice her reputation for the railroad's gain? Byron Vanderhorn rocked in his chair, giving no indication, a steeple erected with his fingers, satisfaction written on his sneaky lips. If he got his way, Tim would lose his home, Arthur his job, and Jed his pride.

A spiky lizard, frozen in a prehistoric stare and camouflaged in a miniature desert in a glass terrarium next to Byron's desk, turned its head almost imperceptibly and stuck out its spiked tongue at Byron.

"I'd humbly suggest, Byron, that you take a second look at Carrie's signature on that land office form before you make a big stink about it," Jed said. "You might just recognize the handwriting."

Byron stared. "A dollar an acre. Not a nickel more."

"Mistake, Vanderhorn," Jed said and rose to his feet. "No deal."

"Don't make me throw your brother in jail, Albright."

There was Byron's ace in the hole. And it stung. Tim would lose his mind in confinement. One last straw. Jed picked up a pearl-handled letter opener off Byron's desk. "That is not going to happen, Byron," he said, and pointed the tip of it at Byron's neck. "Is that clear?"

A third voice joined the conversation from a corner of the room. "Put it down, cowboy." The man with the birthmark emerged from the passageway connecting Byron's office with the rest of the car. The Musgrave detective had his gun pointed at Jed's chest. "Looks like I'm going to have to throw you off another train."

Nineteen

The Lesser of Evils

Rolla, Kansas – May 1930

Tim cranked the Farmall to life and Jed stepped onto its back ledge. Away they chugged, the tractor rolling overland north and east toward Hugoton, away from the partially plowed field on Arthur's land where the Farmall had been abandoned the previous fall. It would take some time for the sheriff's posse to discover their tracks.

Tim wanted to stay and fight. Ambush Byron's men. Set up a crossfire between the barn and the shed. Booby-trap the house with a Kaiser landmine he kept squirreled away in his shop. (*Where had he gotten that?* Jed wondered.) When Tim handed him the old Winchester, Jed said, "I'm not shooting any townsfolk, unless we come under fire." (Not even Scruggs, if he showed up.) They'd be outlaws for life.

Out on the flat, open prairie on a clear day like this, a man standing upright was visible a mile or more. There was a chance they'd be seen. But the tractor seemed their only option. Houdini himself could not have spirited Tim onto a train and out of town with the depot so closely watched. "Byron got in touch with the sheriff first thing this morning," Ott had told Jed. "Planning to have your brother arrested if he doesn't get his way on some deal."

"So, how'd you beat 'em out here?" Tim asked when Jed relayed the story.

"I told Ott you were at Scruggs's ranch helping him brand cattle. I didn't tell him it was two years ago." It was a bit of disinformation Jed figured Ott would blab to Byron, and it might just send his posse off on a wild goose chase.

Tim steered the Farmall toward a gate in the fence, but he began to veer off as they got close. "We got to go back," he said, turning. "I can't just leave Arfur that way."

"There isn't time, Tim!" Jed said. The mutt was tethered to the back of the house, where Tim's new friend Miss Martha would find him. "You'll end up in Leavenworth if they catch you."

"I didn't do nothing!" Tim yelled. "Those galoots were trespassing!"

"Just to provoke you. To draw your fire. It was a setup."

"Bastards," Tim cursed.

"Ott says the railroad is in hock worse than the farmers. They can't pay their bondholders when the boxcars run empty like this. They need cash. Trainloads of it. The company is on the verge of default. They'll stop at nothing to get their hands on all the oil and gas between here and Abilene."

The tractor ground along across the edge of Scruggs's land and onto Jed's. He'd hoped the old dugout could provide a hiding place until dark. But the structure was worse than Jed had noticed earlier. It had almost completely collapsed, and a scent of coyote urine wafted through the front door's tilting planks, which stuck out of the soil like a weathered grave marker. Jed cocked the Winchester and pointed it at the door.

"I'm not going in there," Tim said. "I can't catch a breath just thinkin' about it."

"We have to hide you someplace," Jed said. "Not a lot of choices out here."

"Miss Martha's house has a big old garage out back."

Jed lowered the rifle. "How far is that?"

"Couple miles, maybe." He pointed toward town. "That way."

"Can't go that way," Jed said. "You'd land right in their net."

"What about over by the Cimarron? There's cover there. You could take a little target practice with the Colt. Get the feel of it." It was holstered in Tim's belt. "Plug some jackrabbits. I saw bobcat tracks there last winter. Went right along the riverbed in the snow over to Point of Rocks and vanished. Probably has a den. You kill that, and Scruggs'll give you a reward."

Jed had stopped paying attention, his eye on dust thrown up by a lone vehicle in the distance, motoring hard in their direction on the section road. Was it the sheriff? Jed wondered. He put his finger on the Winchester's trigger and held his breath. The last thing he wanted to do was shoot someone.

"That looks like Miss Martha's Lizzie," Tim said. "I believe it is."

The Model-T bucked like a stallion coming up the short rise, a young woman at the wheel, holding down her Deauville bonnet. The car sputtered to a stop with a series of knocks.

Her hair was bobbed. She had a tight Cupid's bow for a mouth and a snub nose. From the neck up, Tim's Miss Martha could pass for a faux flapper. But when she stepped out onto the running board, it was obvious from the shape of her bold floral print dress she had not forsaken traditional undergarments. And her shoes were old-lady sensible, too. Still, she was not the homely spinster Jed was expecting. She shot him a haughty look. Jed could see how Tim might be smitten by her precisely painted eyebrows and lips, reminiscent of the faces of frilly corset-cover models in old Sears catalogs. He'd inadvertently barged in on Tim kneeling over a torn-out page of the catalog years ago with lowered suspenders and unbuttoned britches, yanking hard on himself in a shed, an intrusion that had embarrassed them both. Drawings of girls in catalogs made no demands. Girls in real life were different.

"Timothy, what are you doing here?" Miss Martha demanded. "That infernal dog is howling its head off back at your house. Did you drive a tractor here? Why, for heaven's sake? Don't lie to me. I've spoken to the sheriff. He came to the parish house looking for you. There's been more foolishness with the railroad, hasn't there?" Her eyes narrowed. "I thought so. Let's go. I'll drive you."

Jed said, "Pardon me, miss. I'm Tim's brother Jed. And he's staying here with me."

The tilt of her head seemed to object to this challenge. Then she thrust out a confident, gloved hand, as if she were a candidate for office. "How do you do? I'm Martha Wanamaker." She gave

Jed's seized fingers a single swift pump, as if working a lever on an etiquette vending machine. "He's told me about you, Mr. Albright. You surprise me. I would not have taken you for Tim's brother in a million years." Her voice had a distinctly waspish quality. "To what does he owe the honor of your visit?"

Her veiled sarcasm caught Jed off guard. His answer was curt. "Family matter."

"Family," she repeated with a belittling chuckle. "I see. Yes, of course. Family matters should always take precedence." She made a mocking face. "However, I've made a solemn promise to bring him to the sheriff. And I believe the law in this case stands preeminent." She lifted a summoning hand toward Tim and turned back toward the Ford.

Tim looked to Jed, who shook his head.

Jed said, "Miss Wanamaker, I don't believe you grasp the true consequences of your actions. The sheriff has no interest in the law here. What matters to him is what he's been ordered to do by some powerful men. And that means locking Tim up and throwing away the key so the railroad can confiscate his land—and mine—just as sure as you're standing on it."

A surprising and undignified cackle erupted from her. "What cock-a-doodle! The world sounds like such a *devious* place the way you talk."

"Well, it is."

Her eyes became daggers. "And I say it's not!" Rather willfully, Jed thought. "Let's go, Timothy. Everything will be straightened out in a jiffy."

"No, ma'am," Jed said, stepping in. How long had this been going on, he wondered. Martha Wanamaker, either knowingly or unwittingly, had been performing surveillance on Tim for the local establishment by helping him with his domestic chores. And today they'd turned her into a stooge. "Miss Wanamaker, Tim won't get a fair shake if he's caught. The sheriff is just a hired gun for the railroad."

"I beg your pardon!" she squealed indignantly. "Take that baseless accusation back right this minute! The sheriff is no such thing! He is a friend of my family, a man of great personal integrity, and a deacon in my father's church."

"And none of that is going to change how this turns out if you betray Tim," Jed said. "I assure you, someone will be collecting thirty pieces of silver."

"How dare you!" She was in a lather. "You are speaking to the daughter of a man of the cloth, sir, and that is unspeakably offensive!"

Tim stepped forward. "Jedidiah didn't mean any harm, Miss Martha." He shot a scowl Jed's way. "He don't know what a good person you are, that you are my friend and someone he can trust."

A small look of triumph came into Martha Wanamaker's eyes.

Jed said, "Miss Wanamaker may be your friend, Tim, but she apparently has no idea who she's dealing with."

"Timothy," Martha Wanamaker said without taking her eyes off Jed, "the clutch in the car has been slipping again. Do you think you could have a look?"

Tim seemed grateful for the chance to disappear beneath the Ford.

Martha spoke softly now. "He's very fond of you for some reason. Don't ask me why, deserting him out here as you did. You can't just turn up out of the blue now and convert him to the ways of the devil, Mr. Albright. Not so long as I'm around." She lifted her chin. "Tim has nothing to fear here if he's done nothing wrong."

The righteous always seem so naive, Jed thought. How could she believe that any man could not be bent by rationalization or graft under the right circumstances?

A locomotive whistled in the distance and the cooling Ford made ticking noises. Jed looked from one to the other. They could skirt the posse to the south beyond the county line in a motor car. Go west sixteen miles to Elkhart and catch an express train to Topeka that would roar past Rolla at 60 miles an hour. The sheriff would be hard-pressed to stop it, even if he'd figured out the Albrights were on it.

"My family did *not* abandon him out here," Jed said. "It was Tim's choice to stay. And we thought he might thrive on his own, without us constantly looking over his shoulder."

She smirked at this. "Really! It must have come as such a

surprise all the trouble he's gotten himself into, then. Admit it, you were counting on strangers to take over the responsibility of watching out for him. The same way he expects me now to take care of his dog!"

"I apologize, Miss Wanamaker, if my family in some way imposed on your better nature. But you can be off the hook by doing us one final favor. Drop us off in Elkhart, and you can say goodbye to both of us for good."

"Bosh!" she sneered. "Not on your life! I'm not going to be party to some flimflam you're planning! I gave my word that I would bring Tim to the sheriff, and I shall!"

Jed seized her wrist as she turned away.

The shock in her eyes turned to bright, angry tears when he squeezed harder. She shouted, "Let go of me! This instant!"

"If you truly care about Tim," Jed said, "you'll forget you ever saw him today!" He released her wrist and practically threw it back in her face.

"Stop it, Jedidiah," Tim said, scooting out from beneath the car. "That's enough. Leave Miss Martha be now."

"Last chance, Timothy," Martha Wanamaker said. "Consider carefully. I'm leaving."

"You're a very nice lady, Miss Martha," he stammered, "but, well, I think Jed's right."

The Lizzy sputtered to life as Tim turned the crank, and loose dirt squirted from beneath the tires when Martha Wanamaker goosed the accelerator and popped the clutch, as if she would have run Tim over had he been standing in the way.

"Well, there goes that," Tim said as she drove off. He shifted back and forth on his feet.

"There goes what?"

"Any chance to marry her," Tim said.

Jed was struck dumb for a moment. Then he asked, "How much gas is in the tractor?"

Almost none, as it turned out. They'd gone perhaps two hundred yards when it conked out. They dismounted and set off on foot through the field stubble. When the Model T's klaxon horn sounded somewhere behind them, Jed said, "Ignore her. We need to keep moving." But they could hear the whine of the Ford's low gear closing in behind them and then a startling backfire from its tailpipe so close it could be felt.

"Get in," Martha Wanamaker said, drawing alongside. "I'll take you to Elkhart."

Twenty

Banishment

Elkhart, Kansas – May 1930

Martha Wanamaker's Model T hit every pothole on the section road going south. The pounding Jed's body took continued to reverberate in him long after the jostling ride smoothed out on the hard-packed gravel of State Line Highway.

"Pride is a sin, too," Martha Wanamaker had muttered to herself when they got into her car. And to her passengers, she'd said, "I'm dropping you at the station. Then I wash my hands of this whole affair."

Pontius Pilate's weaselly words struck Jed as ambiguous at best. Was a Judas moment waiting in the wings? Would she race back to Rolla and expose their escape plan to the sheriff? On the chance she might, they'd have to keep her with them until they were safely aboard the train.

Martha Wanamaker drove with one hand on the wheel and the other clapped over her flapper hat, racing along the border with Oklahoma on a backdoor route to Elkhart that skirted well south of Rolla.

Seated beside his lady friend up front, Tim nibbled on his oil-stained fingernails and whistled a tuneless ditty to himself, an unconscious habit he'd formed as a boy to mask fear in anxious moments. Jed rode with the rifle across his lap in back. He wondered, was Tim really smitten with this prissy, pious woman?

Was he working up the nerve to propose to her? Try as he might, Jed couldn't picture Tim taking a knee. But who knew? Martha Wanamaker had been right about one thing. Jed had abandoned his brother, leaving it to the kindness of others to watch after him. And he had no idea what was going on.

They roared west, Oklahoma on the left, Kansas on the right, an invisible line down the center of the road separating two states. Here and there patches of prairie flowers clung to the sides of the drainage ditches, the last vestiges of what had been stripped away in dreams of greenbacks sprouting from the soil.

They overtook a rusted pickup piled high with furniture, kitchen pots, and suitcases, two children in overalls riding atop the pile lashed down with clothesline. The Lizzie showered it all in dust as it rattled past, Martha doing more veering than steering at the wheel. They crossed a patch of road that undulated like a washboard, and the car's stiff springs shook Jed's innards like a dust mop.

"Were you just going to run off and leave that infernal dog?" Martha shouted over the racket of squeaking springs and the flapping canvas of the top.

"I was hopin' you'd keep an eye on him," Tim shouted back. "He really likes you."

You didn't need a high school diploma to see that the feeling wasn't mutual. Or that Miss Martha was apt to release the mutt onto the plain, where it would menace ranchers and farmers until it came to a violent end. "You were just going to disappear without a word?" Martha hollered. "Without saying goodbye? What am I supposed to do with the ring you gave me?"

Ring? Jed's ears perked up. He already had one difficult sister-in-law.

Martha Wanamaker pulled on a gold chain that dipped beneath the collar of her dress. A jeweled gold band on a necklace popped out. She waved it angrily at Tim.

"Can't get hitched if I'm in prison!" he shot back.

Jed scooted forward, hoping to catch every word over the highway racket. Why put the ring on a chain and not on her finger? Was it to hold Tim within reach while keeping him safely at arm's length? What were the rules of engagement here?

At the fourth section road, Martha Wanamaker skidded the Tin Lizzie around the corner and sped north. Elkhart was visible in the distance. A passenger train was pulling out of the station, heading west, streams of white locomotive steam and black coal ash billowing past the town's towering grain elevators. Martha yelled, "Looks like you missed it."

"There'll be another," Jed answered, secretly pleased she assumed they were going west into Colorado when Jed planned to head east across Kansas all the way to Missouri. "We'll just have to wait," he said. A Topeka-bound train would be along shortly, and, with luck, they'd catch a connection in the capital city and be out of Kansas by nightfall.

Martha Wanamaker thought to hit the brakes for the railroad crossing only *after* they had all been jolted off their seats. She skidded to a stop, throwing them all toward the windscreen. "Cheese and crackers," she muttered, jerking the car backward in reverse. She'd rolled past the intersection where they needed to turn.

"Pull over," Jed said a block from the depot. "Tim, scoot down."

An unmarked black Studebaker sedan of the type favored by police departments was parked in front of the main door under the watch of six old codgers tilted back on the spindle chairs, smoking and shooting the breeze. They paused their jawing and touched their hat brims as a uniformed Morton County deputy emerged.

Jed cocked the Winchester as a way of warning Martha Wanamaker not to shout for help. The deputy stopped outside the door and took his time scanning the street before getting into the Studebaker and driving off. Jed wondered if he'd be back in time to watch who boarded the next train, too.

Before Jed could speak to stop him, Tim jumped out and trotted across the street to take a closer look at a motorcycle parked at the drugstore. He had to touch it all—engine, seat, gauges, muffler, drive chain.

"What will you do now, when we're out of your hair?" Jed asked Martha Wanamaker.

"I don't know. You've put me in a terrible position. I've gone back on my word."

"You've done the right thing," Jed said. "You've saved an innocent man from being wrongly locked up. Your *fiancé!*"

"*Ha!*" she said. "You think you're so smart!" Her eyes grew bright again with indignation. "How could you possibly believe I'd marry a man they call 'The Lug Nut' in Rolla?" Her voice cracked. "Honestly!" she shrieked. "The man is not my *fiancé.*"

Such a horrid, self-righteous woman. "What are you doing with his ring then?"

"It's complicated," she said, as if Jed could not possibly understand.

"Tell me."

"He said he wanted me to take it as an emblem of his dedication to my father's church and his faith in Almighty God. And for me to wear it. Nothing more."

Poor Tim, Jed thought. His affections were being toyed with by this cruel woman. She'd caged him as you might a wild rabbit in hopes of taming it. *She was going to marry me,* Tim had said. Someone had to have planted that idea in his head.

"Where are your people from, Miss Wanamaker?" Jed asked. "I don't recall your family name from my time here." The story went that Martha Wanamaker had turned up at Tim's shop one bitter January morning after the Tin Lizzie broke down going past his farm. According to Tim, the distributor cap had improbably come loose. It took him all of fifteen seconds to find and fix the problem. He refused to take any money for it. So she'd insisted on cooking him dinner. "Just about the best dang meal ever cooked," he recalled.

High over Elkhart, the midday sun continued its slow journey west. Tim was dawdling at the motorcycle. Martha Wanamaker said, "My father and I are most recently from Mississippi. Daddy founded a church in Biloxi, his fourth in the south. Rolla is the fifth. I was born in Pennsylvania many congregations ago."

A regular Johnny Bibleseed, Jed thought, and perhaps a theological con man one step ahead of the law himself.

"So you will be moving on again one day," Jed observed neutrally. Tim's ring would likely disappear with her, and Tim's soul and heart would be left to fend for themselves. Talk about abandonment. "What did you mean when you said you'd wash your hands of the whole thing after you dropped us here?"

"Just what I said. I'm going to have nothing more to do with this." She chose this moment to jump out, slam the car door, and stomp into an alley toward the track side of the depot. Jed tucked the Winchester down between the seats and followed.

Martha Wanamaker stopped to pivot on a step to the platform. "Let's hear about your family now, Mr. Albright," she said in a tone that told him she was playing to bystanders nearby. "Don't think for a minute that I don't know why you all turned your back on him out here," she said, loud enough for everyone to hear. "It was banishment."

"Banishment?" Jed scoffed.

"Banishment!" she insisted.

"I have no idea what you are talking about!"

"Oh, but you do, Mr. Albright. You see, I know your family's dirty little secret. You only thought you could sweep it under the rug."

"Sweep what under the rug, Miss Wanamaker?" The woman was exasperating!

He could see she was relishing this moment. She'd have her sweet revenge for not getting her way. But knowing what she was up to did nothing to prepare him for the words that spun like a tornado from her lips next. "Your brother had carnal knowledge of your sister!" she spat.

Stunned by her outrageous claim, Jed took a staggering step back, and long-forgotten memories began flying from hiding places in his mind like startled sparrows out of a dense hedgerow. There was the inexplicable ferocity of Tim's fists astride Scruggs at the harvest dance. There was the sorrowful, lingering caress Carrie delivered to Timmy's cheek as he writhed, delirious, the winter of the fever.

"No," Jed stammered. "It's not true! Not a word of it!"

"Tim told me," Martha Wanamaker said.

When the memory flooded back of Carrie unlacing her corset and her breasts swaying free for Jed to ogle, his legs collapsed beneath him, and the planks of the platform, piping hot from the afternoon sun, rose up to smack his stunned face.

It seemed only an instant later Tim was bending over him, his face puckered with worry. "You okay, Jed?" from out of nowhere.

Idiot! Fool!

Twenty-One

Unspeakable

Elkhart, Kansas – May 1930

The brutal slap sent Tim reeling backward. Jed's palm burned from the sting of it as he rolled onto his back in a state of high agitation and stared blankly at indifferent clouds adrift in an azure sky. Damn Carrie to hell and back! As if her whoring wasn't shameful enough! She'd included her family in her wanton carnal appetites, too? Right under Jed's nose! He lifted his head long enough to see Tim hovering, his blinking eyes brimming with confusion, shame, and contrition, before slinking away like a beaten dog.

Jed lay back down on the grimy, overheated pine. He was spent, his world shaken to its very foundation. The sting to his hand lingered, even as his fury waned, a rebuke, it seemed, for the haste in which he'd lashed out at Tim, giving him no chance to speak, no room to answer the horrid accusation. He'd decided his brother's guilt for himself, based on the flimsy say-so of a flibbertigibbet he'd just met! A woman whose judgment he didn't really trust. A woman with a grudge. Would she hand Tim over to the sheriff now if he didn't stop her?

Jed sat up. A man on the platform in a western shirt tried coming to his aid, but Jed waved away the proffered hand and struggled to his feet using the wall of the depot building as a brace.

Then he set off in pursuit, passing unsteadily through a circle of murmuring onlookers into the waiting room and out the depot's front entrance. The Model T was no longer on the street. The men in the tipped-back chairs swiveled their heads his way. "Some fella just drove off with a fusspot lady," one of them said with a chuckle.

Jed stared helplessly down the vacated street. Martha Wanamaker had seized the upper hand. West of town, beyond the depot at his back, the whistle of a train bound for Dodge City could be heard, its arrival imminent.

* * *

A stone tablet seemed to occupy the seat next to him on the train to Topeka. *Thou shalt not uncover the nakedness of thy sister.* Was it a line he'd also crossed, an Old Testament taboo, just gaping at Carrie after she'd slain the wolf? So tightly had he locked away that moment in a vault of his denied feelings, he couldn't truly remember how it had been. But doubt taunted him every stop along the slow, tedious ride on the local train back to Enid.

The next morning, he nearly fell out of the mail car door at Salt Fork, sleepwalking through the exchange, reaching out with his bare hand for the outbound pouch when the mechanical catcher arm whiffed by it. Only the Archangel Gabriel, patron saint of postmen, had saved him.

He poured himself a cup of coffee with a trembling hand once the door had been secured again. He blew vigorously over the cup's edge and took his cautious sips. What would Tim have said if he'd been given a chance to explain? So insistently did the question prey upon him that another urgent matter nearly slipped Jed's mind. When it suddenly resurfaced, he drew out a sheet of fresh stationery from his valise and penned a hasty letter.

Arthur - Byron Vanderhorn intends to force us to sell our land to the railroad for $1/acre. If we refuse, he's threatening to accuse us of defrauding the land office. Also, he's arranged to have Tim locked up for shooting at RR men who trespassed on his property. And there's

He deliberately omitted any mention of Martha Wanamaker's accusation. There was no telling what Arthur might do when he got wind of it. He was already fed up with Tim and at war with Carrie. Jed sealed the letter in a two-cent prepaid postage envelope and sighed as he added it to a pile of accumulated work on the sorting table.

At the Lamont station, Junior slowed the train to a virtual halt for the mail exchange. Jed knew he was being mocked for botching the Salt Fork pickup. He could almost hear Junior say to his fireman that the doctor who drilled a hole in Albright's skull obviously forgot to put the plug back in.

* * *

The odor of frying beef patties and onions in the depot greeted him on the platform at Ark City. He could hear the familiar whir of the kitchen exhaust fan. But it surprised him to get the fisheye from Ruby at the counter when he stepped inside.

"Something wrong?" Jed asked as she rang up his lunch in a gruff manner.

"You tell me," she replied sharply. Freckles had exploded across her nose and cheeks during his absence. He'd never seen her without makeup, he realized. Unadorned, her lips were thin and pale and her green eyes faintly withered.

"Tell you what?" Jed said, on his back foot now.

"Is it true you have an illegitimate daughter in Beaumont?" She made it sound more like an accusation than a question.

"Where did you get a crazy idea like that?" How twisted matters could become when your back was turned, Jed thought.

"From the sub on your route." Ruby squinted at him. "He seemed to think there was something to it."

"Well, there's not," Jed snapped. The only child he'd ever

185

fathered was buried out on the Kansas plain. God rest his soul. "And I can't believe you fell for a lie like that. Taking the word of a total stranger." He winced a bit at his own rhetoric.

Ruby wasn't finished. "He also said Lester's death wasn't an accident."

"That might be true," Jed conceded, and wondered what exactly was being implied.

The service bell rang hard. The short-order cook hollered, "Ruby!"

"Ruby, wait!" Jed said, grabbing her arm. "Do you have brothers?"

"One. Why?"

"Did he ever try to pull anything, you know …"

Her expression turned stony. "What's wrong with you? Asking me something like that! Are you sick? You look like hell, incidentally. Get some sleep."

Junior blasted the engine's whistle. Frisco 630 was preparing to depart.

* * *

Jed booked a room at Forstein's with the train crew (opting for fresh sheets once a week for a quarter more) rather than face Madeleine at the Beaumont boardinghouse. He didn't want to answer any questions about his unexplained absence.

He'd stretched out on his lumpy bed for the evening and was reading a sensational murder story in *The Wichita Beacon* when there was a knock on his door.

"There's a girl in the lobby asking for you, Albright," the night clerk said with a leering squint. "She ain't permitted upstairs, you know." He nodded to himself. "House rules."

Madeleine Robichaux was pacing the lobby in a work apron. A smudge of coal soot streaked one cheek and there were rose-shaded patches of perspiration collecting in the armpits of her pink dress.

"We need to talk!" she blurted.

The night clerk cocked an ear.

"Not here," Jed said.

186

He led the girl out the back alley door, through a passage to the next street over, and from there to the coaling trestle at the edge of the scummy Frisco Pond. A grove of trees just beyond offered seclusion. But Madeleine yanked her arm free and refused to go a step farther. "I have to get back!"

"Okay then," Jed said. "What is it you want?"

She stroked nervously at her throat as she lifted her gaze to his face. "I need to know, Mr. Albright—are you my father?"

Startled by the unexpected question and touched by the plaintive, vulnerable look that came over her as she awaited his answer, Jed needed a breath. She'd clearly been wounded by all the whispering about her identity and legitimacy. The poor girl had no idea who her father was.

Jed shook his head. No, he was not her father. It was entirely possible he was her uncle. *Possibly her uncle twice over.* But that was mere conjecture, and he wasn't about to go into it. "I'm sorry, Miss Robichaux," he said. "This is something you should ask your mother."

"I did, and she slapped my face."

The wicked woman. "I'm sorry." What more could he say? He shrugged.

"There's something else," she said. "A letter from a law firm in New Orleans. It made Maman very angry." The girl's expression implied Jed already knew something about it.

"What does it say?" Jed asked, perplexed by the tangle of her assumption and his own suspicion.

"I don't know," Madeleine said. "Maman hid the letter away and she refuses to speak to me about it. She likes her secrets. Just like you." Her eyebrow arched. "You really don't know what it's about?"

Troubled by his hunches, Jed gave her his best poker face. "No," he said, "I don't. Wasn't New Orleans where you were born?"

The girl turned her attention to ducks paddling toward them on the pond, looking for handouts. Someone had been feeding them.

"Yes," she said, and flung a rock in their direction. With

quacks of protest, the ducks ran across the surface of the water, raucously flapping their wings before settling back onto the water a hundred feet away.

"I have to go, Mr. Albright," Madeleine said, and tossed one last pebble into the pond. "Can't you tell me what's going on?"

"Find the letter," Jed said. "See what it says. Talk to me after that."

Madeleine threw her arms around him, squeezed him hard, and took off on a run, back the way they'd come. Her feet splayed as she ran. With trepidation, Jed watched her until she disappeared around the far side of the pond.

Twenty-Two

Stowaway

Beaumont, Kansas – May 1930

The guy ran like a girl. He reminded Jed of that blowhard from the boardinghouse, Cabot, in a peacock pinstripe suit and bowler hat. But smaller. He darted out from the side of the depot, head down, just as Frisco 635 pulled out at 8:32 a.m. His spit-shined brogues clomped across the platform in a rush, coming straight for the mail car. Cabot had barely spoken two words to Jed when they lived under the same roof. Why would he be waving at Jed as if they were old pals? Was he trying to skip town without paying his bills?

"Mr. Albright! Mr. Albright!" he called, his voice all wrong, too. High pitched. Slightly hysterical. He sounded more like a girl, too.

"No one is allowed in the mail car!" Jed hollered as the fool ran alongside the open door with his arms raised up in a plea to be lifted in. His hands and wrists were small and delicate. Everything about him seemed counterfeit. Then the wash of air from the train blew off his bowler hat and a passel of long caramel-colored hair spilled out. Madeleine Robichaux's hair. "Help me," she gasped. "Please!"

Jed's collarbone felt as if it had split open again when he grabbed the girl's hand and hoisted her aboard. The girl yelped, too, when her knee banged the door ledge going by. It was a clumsy maneuver, but it succeeded, and Jed hastily slid the door shut.

"What is it you think you're doing, Madeleine?" he shouted, clutching his wrist to his chest to quell the fiery ache in his collarbone. "Do you have any idea how many federal regulations we've just broken?" With witnesses galore.

"I'm leaving!" she bellowed in return, rocking on the floor, rubbing her knee. A replica of Cabot's mustache was crudely sketched in charcoal along her upper lip. She worked her jaw holding back tears.

"Where did you get the clothes?" Jed asked.

"They belong to Mr. Cabot. I stole them, if you want to know the truth. But that deadbeat owes Maman two months' back rent."

Jed groaned. Two wrongs didn't make a right, he thought, and said, "You can't just run away, Madeleine! Certainly not with me. Not this way. You've put me in a serious pickle here!"

She glared at him defiantly. Then she clawed an envelope out of a pocket of the suit with an air of saucy triumph. Three names— Hannan, Ehrke & Baxter, attorneys at law—were listed in the return address. Mrs. Robichaux's name and address had been neatly typed. A stately Von Steuben commemorative, canceled in New Orleans, had been used for the stamp.

"You found it," Jed said. The heavy stock and embossed printing of the envelope seemed to carry a momentous feel of untold riches or impending calamity.

"Maman will steal my life away from me if she isn't stopped!" There was bitter determination in the set of Madeleine's jaw. "But not this time. Right, Mr. Albright?"

He had no idea what that meant. "Let me see that," he said, taking the envelope. Madeleine busied herself adjusting the padding inside Cabot's suit as he read.

May 12, 1930

Dear Mrs. Robichaux,
We are pleased to inform you that your daughter has
been offered a full scholarship to Tulane University
beginning next term. A benefactor who wishes to

remain anonymous asked our office to coordinate arrangements. Under the terms of the gift, your daughter's books, tuition, and room and board are to be provided at no cost to her and without contingency or obligation, now or in the future. However, Madeleine would be required to relocate to New Orleans, Louisiana, beginning in August.

The benefactor is of the opinion that a higher education is in the girl's best interests and will assure her of an independent and rewarding future. We trust you will agree and accept this offer, made in good faith, and that you will release your daughter into our care and supervision. This condition is not negotiable.

Should you fail to act in Madeleine's best interest, our office is prepared to ask the child welfare board in and of the Parish of Jefferson, Louisiana, where her adoption was authorized, to conduct a thorough investigation of her circumstances. The probable outcome of such an inquiry would be that she would be made a ward of the court. A demonstrable pattern of abuse over many years nullifies your adoption rights, and under such a finding, custody would be transferred to a court-appointed guardian ad litem. The child welfare clause of the adoption papers you signed on October 10, 1912, stipulates that the child may not be required to perform manual labor prior to her age of majority or the completion of her formal education without the consent of the agency.

We strongly suggest that you write to us indicating acceptance of the terms of this scholarship without delay. If we have not heard from you prior to June 1, a complaint will be filed with the child welfare board on Madeleine's behalf.

In the meantime, preparations for Madeleine's fall matriculation will commence.

Yours sincerely,

Thaddeus Baxter, Esq.

It was obvious why Mrs. Robichaux had been infuriated by the letter. It was a mail-order kidnapping. And Madeleine's maman clearly wasn't giving up without a fight.

Jed put the letter back in the envelope under the girl's watchful gaze. "You're this anonymous benefactor, aren't you?" she said excitedly.

He scoffed, "Why would you think a mail clerk had this kind of money?" It was hard to take seriously a baggy man's suit with her face painted up in a ludicrous disguise. "I had nothing to do with this." It was Carrie, most likely, trying to make amends for abandoning the girl as a newborn eighteen years before. But what if she was hoping to groom her as a successor? "You have to go back," Jed said.

The excitement and hope disappeared from Madeleine's eyes. Her lip quivered. "You said, 'find the letter, and we'd talk about it.' Now you're saying you won't?"

"You can't do this, Madeleine. You have no idea what you're getting into. No idea who's behind this." He waved the envelope as if it contained poison, which probably wasn't far from the truth. How had Carrie learned the girl's whereabouts and circumstances? Weren't adoption records sealed?

"But this is my only chance!" Madeleine pleaded. "Ever!" She snatched the envelope out of his hands and removed the letter, pointing out, "It says *without contingency or obligation.* I have nothing to lose."

"Words on a page," Jed replied. "Who will stand behind them down the road?" She was no longer looking him in the eye. "Has your maman written back to this man?"

"I don't know."

"Go home and find out. Maybe she has agreed to cooperate. Or she's made an inquiry."

Madeleine bit down on a fingernail and shook her head doubtfully.

Jed didn't believe it either. He was grasping at straws. A toot from the locomotive whistle at a grade crossing reminded him a station pass was due shortly at Burgess. "Listen," he said. "I have things to tend to." He lowered his wall-mounted stool. "Have a seat here and think about what I said. We'll talk again in a few minutes."

They were about to cross the Oklahoma border. Taking an unrelated, underage girl across a state line was a federal offense under the Mann Act. "White slavery," in common parlance. If Mrs. Robichaux called the police to report her daughter missing, a welcoming party could be waiting at the train's next stop at Ark City.

As Jed tossed envelopes and parcels from the stacks of unsorted mail into the appropriate pouches on the routing grid, the girl retreated into her own thoughts, nibbling absently on her nails. Jed stole a furtive glance her way and felt a pang of tenderness seeing her smooth the padding beneath Cabot's clothes. She'd been audaciously daring and brave. But she was in over her head. Who would protect this girl? Shield her from her vengeful *maman?* Or the conniving Carrie? And who would guard her against the reckless impulses of youth?

"You do know this train doesn't go anywhere near New Orleans," Jed said. "It's going to Enid, and I have work to do all the way there."

"I have a ticket for New Orleans," she said, snippily. "I change trains in Arkansas City."

She'd bought a ticket? How had she worked that out? "Do you plan to keep passing yourself off as a man in that getup?"

She apparently hadn't thought that part through. She shrugged with only mild vexation. "My clothes are packed in Maman's trunk, and I checked it through to New Orleans with the express agent," she said. "But I'm not going back to Beaumont! No matter what."

"Give me your ticket," Jed said. He had to intervene if a colossal mistake was to be avoided.

"No!" the girl said and folded her arms over her chest. "You're not stopping me!"

"Where is it you plan to stay when you get to New Orleans?" Jed asked. "How will you feed yourself? The letter says school doesn't start until August. That's three months from now."

She squared her shoulders and blinked her eyes. "I thought

you were going to tell me the rest of the plan this morning," she said. "I thought you'd arrange something. I thought you …"

… you were my father. Dear, foolish girl. Jed felt as if a child had been abandoned on his doorstep. By default, her welfare was now his responsibility. "When we get to Arkansas City, Madeleine," Jed said, "I want you to wait in the mail car as silent as a mouse. Don't move off the stool. I'll go into the depot and change your ticket and reroute your baggage. You can't go to New Orleans without someplace to stay."

"You are not sending me back to Beaumont! You're not!"

"Just give me the ticket, Madeleine. I won't send you back, I promise. I have another idea altogether."

She looked annoyed and skeptical, but she produced the ticket from Cabot's suit coat.

Her naivety made him wonder, Was this girl really ready for college? Was it even the best course for her future? Wouldn't she be happier finding a husband and having children someday?

"The police might be looking for you when the train stops," Jed said. "It's important you stay out of sight and quiet. This car is federal property. No one is allowed in here without express permission from the post office. And I will refuse to give it." Her eyes darted around the car. "But if they hear you, it will go badly for me when they go over my head up the chain of command."

"Please, Mr. Albright, I'll be quiet. Honestly I will."

Jed uncapped his pen and wrote out an address on his scratch pad. He blew on the ink and tore off the sheet. "This is my wife's address in Joplin, Missouri. You can stay with her until I've had a chance to verify this scholarship offer. All right? And should there be trouble at Ark City, do your best to slip away and take the first available train to Joplin. You'll be safe with my wife. Her name is Amanda. I'll wire her that you're coming from the station."

Madeleine had begun to giggle.

"What's so funny?" Jed asked.

"You have a wife! I'm learning something new about you every minute."

He fingered his wedding ring. "She's a schoolteacher."

Madeleine smiled. "I think I'd like to be a teacher myself

someday.”

“Good,” Jed said, and pointed to a stack of periodicals. “Now, I’m way behind in my work. Grab a magazine out of that stack and browse for a bit until I’ve had a chance to catch up, all right?” He turned and began to sort again, but she pinned his arms to his sides in a bear hug from behind.

“Thank you, Mr. Albright,” she said. She buried her face between his shoulder blades. “You’re my family now, no matter what you say.”

Twenty-Three

Travail

Enid, Oklahoma – May 1930

The hallway stunk of recent cigarette smoke. Jed was surprised to discover it was coming from his own apartment. His mind had been eighty miles away, focused on the girl, wondering if she'd made it to Joplin all right after he'd left her dragging her maman's steamer trunk into the ladies' restroom at the Ark City depot to change clothes.

But now he was on full alert in Enid, alarmed that someone had entered his locked apartment. Arthur's voice rumbled out of the darkness inside as he opened the door. "Close it," his brother said in a grouchy grumble reminiscent of their father.

"Jesus, Arthur. What are you doing here? How did you get in?"

"It wasn't all that hard." A cigarette pack crinkled.

Jed set his valise down and closed the door. "Could we turn on a light?"

A match flared in his brother's cupped hands and a machine-rolled cigarette appeared, dangling from Arthur's tightly compressed lips.

"What's this about?" Jed asked. Something had to be seriously amiss. This was a little over the top, even for his histrionic brother. "Arthur? What is it? What's happened?"

"Tim is dead."

Just like that. Tim is dead, No *sorry I have terrible news.* No *this isn't easy.* Or *you might want to sit down.* Just the blunt, awful truth. Jed stretched out a hand, searching in the dark for the arm of a chair in which he might collapse. His worst fear had come to pass. "What happened?" he asked when he'd sat a moment.

"He was shot," Arthur said. His cigarette glowed brightly as he took another draw. The smoke reemerged as a weary sigh. "They found the body this morning."

"Jesus," Jed whispered. Leaving Tim in the care of the crazy church woman had gotten him murdered by a vigilante mob. Jed's temper had sent Tim to his death. "Do they know who did it? Was it someone in the posse?"

"Afraid not," Arthur said. "Not according to the sheriff, at least. He says Tim was dead when the posse arrived."

"Really? Who shot him then?"

"You tell me. It was your service pistol they found beside the body."

Twenty-Four

Canary Cage

Rolla, Kansas – May 1930

They locked him in a massive cage, seven feet tall and ten feet long, a freestanding monstrosity of woven steel strapping welded together in a back room of the Rolla police station like a ship in a bottle. Just enough wiggle room remained for a tubby constable to waddle around it once an hour, nightstick rattling against the heavy lattice. The constable liked to kick the padlocked door as he left, as if to reaffirm who was in charge.

The extraordinary structure was big enough for two men, but Jed had it to himself. He reclined on the bunk to the right of the door under two high, barred windows. For several hours he distracted himself with the clutter of prolific, lurid inscriptions scratched into the walls. Rectangular shafts of light from the window crept at a sundial's pace across the graffiti. Intermingled with the initials, dates, and places were grievances *(Fella stoll my wife!)* and random drawings, one a cartoon sun radiating beams onto a satellite composed in vague, wavy lines. Had someone drawn a Sun Dog? Could it have been Tim?

A hush settled over the jail and the town at dusk. Horse hooves ceased to clip-clop in the street. A clacking office typewriter went silent. A bird that had chirped a tuneless call all afternoon near the jail window—Tim's ghost come to torture him, Jed thought—took wing and flew on to pester other ears. *Had Tim been trying to perfect bird calls all those years?* Jed wondered.

Around sunset, the constable brought in a bowl of hearty beef stew that made Jed's mouth water. He set it on a table just outside the cage, where Jed could see it but not reach it. Then the lout dragged in a stool to sit and devour the meal himself, smacking his fat lips and laughing raucously when Jed couldn't stop his stomach from growling.

Nightfall came and filled the barred window with stars. The back room grew ghostly in the frigid air. Jed wrapped himself in a ratty, stinking blanket from the second bunk and tried to subdue his tortured conscience. His brother's death wasn't really his fault, was it? He passed the empty hours fighting for sleep.

Just after dawn, Arthur arrived.

"Why haven't you arranged to get me out?" Jed demanded. A stiff neck and back weren't making him any less cranky. "I thought you were going to talk to the judge."

Arthur, startled at the sight of the steel cage, nonetheless ran an admiring hand over it. "Remarkable," he said. Yeah, one of the wonders of the world. "Intimidating as hell."

"Arthur!"

"They didn't tell you?" he said. "The judge is refusing to set bail. He considers you a flight risk."

"Dammit, Arthur! You said it would be just a formality if I turned myself in voluntarily." They'd discussed this in Enid and on the long ride across Kansas. "Remember, I would not be in this awful mess if you'd found my gun like I asked."

"I did what I could," Arthur said. "And I'm doing what I can to get you out. This judge is out for blood."

"Is he going to let me out for Tim's funeral? Let me pay my last respects?" Jed felt desperate to bend a knee in contrition. Beg his dead brother's forgiveness. A terrible weight was pressing down on his battered, remorseful heart.

"Time will tell," Arthur said. "The only funeral a man can really count on going to in this life is his own."

Such a wit, Arthur. "You did tell the judge my gun had been stolen, didn't you?"

"Of course. But it doesn't change anything. It could have been a false report."

"Come on, Arthur. Everyone knows who's behind this, who was out to get Tim."

"It's not so simple," Arthur said. "Hunches and conjecture aren't admissible in court. Hard evidence is."

"How long can they hold me without a proper hearing on this trumped-up evidence?"

"Out here, they do pretty much what they like." Arthur stared out the high windows a moment. "Listen, I did find a lawyer who is willing to take your case."

Making it sound as if it had been no easy trick. Understandable, since taking on the railroad might not be the best career move for a struggling country lawyer. It was hardly much different from stepping in front of one of their locomotives.

The office door opened. The constable had Jed's breakfast—a chunk of hardtack and a tin cup of brackish water. There was a greasy outline where it appeared some eggs had gone missing on the plate. "Your rations," the constable said with a hateful eye on Arthur.

* * *

Lawyer Bob, Arthur called him. Balding. Middle-aged. Slits for eyes. Shirt collar beginning to fray. "I've represented a murderer or two in my time, Mr. Albright," he chuckled, by way of introduction, "and you certainly don't fit the mold."

A patch of wispy hair clung defiantly to the massive outcropping of his shiny pink forehead. When he smiled, the shape of it leaked insincerity. Bob set his briefcase on the floor as Arthur went in search of chairs. Lawyer Bob's eyes rolled like jelly on a plate following Arthur's departing figure.

"So, did you do it?" he grunted when the jelly slid back Jed's direction. "The prosecutor seems to have some dark secret up his sleeve. Care to tell me what that is before it bites me in the ass?"

Jed wasn't sure what the man was talking about, but he hoped it wasn't Martha Wanamaker's terrible accusation. That was the sort of secret you took to the grave if you could, particularly when it might be construed a motive for murder. *You killed your brother because you were furious that he'd had intimate and unlawful knowledge of your sister.* Was Martha Wanamaker blabbing this tale all over town? "Don't know what you're talking about," Jed said.

It was hard to say whether Lawyer Bob's squint was true skepticism or a pose meant to intimidate.

Arthur returned with two milking stools. "All they had," he said. The space between the cage and wall was so tight, he had to shift his knees to one side in order to sit.

A length of rope with a noose fashioned at one end appeared out of Lawyer Bob's briefcase. A soupy burp from Jed's queasy stomach burned his throat. Bob said, "This was on the constable's desk." His eye slits narrowed. Then he chortled. "Course there ain't a tree within a hundred miles to string anybody up from. But it makes an impression, don't it?"

"Put it away," Jed said. "You made your point. What do you charge for trial work?"

"We'll get to that in a bit," Bob said. "I didn't take your case yet, and there ain't exactly a line forming outside to apply for the job, is there?" He let that sink in. "Listen, Albright, I hear tell they have a witness who places you at the scene of the shooting."

The first of many lies, Jed thought. "Is it Martha Wanamaker?"

Bob's face produced a faint rendition of amusement. "No, it's not," he said. "But you're correct in thinking the woman is no friend of yours. Unfortunately, she's also well connected. An hour after I asked her several pointed but perfectly proper questions, I heard from a judge in this circuit that interfering with a witness could land me in here with you."

"What did Martha Wanamaker have to say?"

"She says you lost your temper with your brother the afternoon he was shot. She says there was a mention of some shenanigans in your family's past and that you became belligerent when she told you about it. She also said she didn't see you get on that train to Dodge City."

"Well, she'd taken off with my brother by then," Jed said.

"You *did* get on the train, didn't you Jed?" Arthur asked with unwarranted suspicion.

Jed kept his temper in check, grateful Arthur had ignored the mention of *shenanigans*. "If I hadn't gotten on the train, Arthur," Jed stated firmly, "how could I have gotten back to Enid in time to work my shift the next morning or be in my room in Beaumont that night? My signature is in the hotel register." In no way did the evidence support the charges against him. "Why doesn't that qualify as an alibi? And what about the report I made when the gun was stolen the week before that? Shouldn't that clear me as a suspect?"

"Can you prove it was really stolen?" Lawyer Bob asked. One eye slit closed. "Because they're going to say you had it all along, and the theft was an elaborate ruse. You reported it stolen so you could kill your brother and deflect suspicion elsewhere. Which makes the murder charge first degree."

"But they cooked all that up. Surely it's obvious. The setup. The lies!"

"You need to understand, Albright, it's a jury of emotional townspeople that will decide what is true and what is *not*, and your fate will hang in the balance, if you'll pardon the expression. It'll be a mud fight. The prosecutor will suggest you hitched rides out on the highway. Even find a witness to testify they saw you get in a car. Or a truck. You'd have had plenty of time to go out to Tim's place and shoot him, and still get back to Enid."

Arthur gave Lawyer Bob a cigarette and lit it for him. Bob puffed it up and leveled his slits again on Jed. "Did you have a rather loud confrontation in public with your brother just before he returned home and was murdered?"

Jed's shoulders slumped. Why was Bob harping on facts like a prosecutor instead of working to discover what would prove his innocence? "You don't believe me?" Jed said.

"Did you slap your brother that afternoon, Mr. Albright? In sight of witnesses?"

Jed swallowed hard and nodded.

"Why did you do that?"

"Because of a vile lie that fool woman told me."

"And what was that lie? Tell me."

Jed could feel Arthur's eyes on him.

"What does it matter what lie? It was a *lie*. It provoked me!"

"Well, if it was truly vile and we proved it was false, a slander, it might change some townspeople's opinions, switch their sympathies to you," Lawyer Bob said. "Take away motive."

Not going to happen, Jed thought. He could not prove it was false. And even a hint of such a stain would not earn the family any sympathy. Only more suspicions. Jed said, "Why is no one trying to find Tim's actual killer? I'm going to go crazy if I have to spend one more night in here!"

Bob shifted uncomfortably on his stool.

"You know, Albright, they call this the canary cage because it's been known to make jailbirds sing." He smiled. "So don't go confessing to anything, you understand? I'm going to see about getting you transferred out of here."

"So you're taking my case?" Jed asked, and Lawyer Bob shrugged. Arthur's eyes were as shifty now as Lawyer Bob's. Jed said, "Wait. You haven't told me what your fee would be for representing me. I'm not sure I can afford you."

The blue-backed document Lawyer Bob pulled from his briefcase bore a dreadful resemblance to the one Byron slid across his desk just five days before. This time it was Arthur feeding it through a slot in the cage door. Again there was a legal description of Jed's land packed into the whereases and therefores of legal jargon and a line open at the bottom for Jed's signature.

"You want my land?" Jed asked.

"I'm offering to work for mineral rights to some of your land. It's all spelled out in the agreement."

"So, really, you're no different from the men who killed my brother," Jed said. "You're just another highway robber, demanding my money or my life!"

Bob shrugged nonchalantly and kept smiling. "Mr. Albright, I despise Byron Vanderhorn. And I'm willing to settle for half of what the railroad is going to take from you. Less, really. I'm only asking for the natural gas. That's what the agreement you're holding says. You sell me a half interest in those mineral rights for one dollar." He folded his arms over his chest. "Another big difference between me and the railroad, Mr. Albright: I'll be working to get you acquitted. The railroad will be bribing the prosecutor, the judge, and maybe even the jury to make sure you dangle from this."

He held up the noose. "Did you know men soil themselves when a rope snaps their neck?"

Jed closed his eyes.

"Think about it," Lawyer Bob said.

Jed needed less than a second. He shot the document back through the slot in the steel plate door, where it went fluttering to the floor. Lawyer Bob had talked himself straight out of a fee. Hung himself with his own rope, Jed thought. Because if the trial was to be rigged, there was no way Bob was ever going to save Jed. And he might even deliberately undermine Jed's case to appease the railroad and avoid retaliation from Byron Vanderhorn.

Little wonder he'd been so adamant about Jed not confessing. If Jed confessed, there'd be no trial, and Lawyer Bob would have no chance to take possession of the Albrights' mineral rights.

Twenty-Five

Judge Not

Rolla, Kansas – May 1930

A bargain-basement store's label was sewn into the rayon lining of the suit Arthur laid out on Jed's bunk. The dark fabric was properly somber but badly tailored. Its trendy wide lapels refused to lie flat, and the seams were puckering.

"Put it on," Arthur ordered. "The funeral starts in twenty minutes."

"You really want me to go looking like a hoodlum at a Bible camp?" Jed objected. Arthur's halitosis was particularly revolting this morning, fouling every breath of air in the tiny space. "You said you'd get me a decent suit for the trial."

"This is it," Arthur said. "Just put it on. You can wear it to both. You can't go to Tim's funeral in your jail tunic and those striped balloon britches. And you're not staying here after Bob Johnston called in a favor from the judge to get you a bereavement release."

Lawyer Bob. *Court-sanctioned mourning.* And how was it going to look, a man accused of murder wearing a sad sack suit to his victim's funeral? He'd be wearing it to the gallows next.

Reluctantly, Jed slipped into the trousers and buttoned the fly. "And this Lawyer Bob," Jed said, "is he really the best you could do?"

"Bob is perfectly competent," Arthur replied.

"Right," Jed said. "Putting aside his proposed confiscatory fee for now, you don't think his suggestion that I admit to shooting Tim is the height of reckless ridiculousness? Say Tim pulled his gun first? Put the blame for his death on him? Is it not a serious breach of a lawyer's oath to suggest a client lie on the witness stand? Fabrications his lawyer dreamed up? This man is supposed to be an officer of the court!"

"The idea was just a way to get a discussion started," Arthur said.

"With something totally preposterous? How was that a place to start? What jury is going to believe it when the sheriff is going to tell them Tim died from three bullets fired by *my* gun—two to the chest and one point-blank to the groin that splattered his private parts? How would 'self-defense' or 'fair fight' stand up against those gruesome details?" Not to mention that Martha Wanamaker would be waiting in the wings to give birth to rumors of incest. Was Bob withholding a proper defense until Jed signed away his mineral rights?

"It was just a way to provoke some thought. Drop it."

Jed got into the new white dress shirt Arthur had bought. "And what about my actual alibi? Can't you find a passenger who saw me on the train to Dodge City? Can't you have my gun examined for fingerprints by one of your expert colleagues?"

"My agency has no access to evidence in the custody of local jurisdictions unless specifically invited by local authorities. And I wouldn't count on that."

Arthur was aware that Jed was literally in a fight for his life. Why was he making excuses when he should be out turning over every rock in sight? "Has anyone asked the sheriff to explain how I could arrive in Tim's parlor before Tim did when he was the one who got a ride there in Martha Wanamaker's car?"

"Bob will get into that at the trial."

"That will be too late," Jed said. "I'm so hated in this town that they will probably string me up before then for supposedly shooting his vicious dog." Tim's beloved Arfur had been found dead on his leash in the yard, a bullet in his skull.

Arthur pulled manacles from his coat pockets and tossed them on the bunk when Jed was dressed. "You're required to put these on before they let you out of this cage."

"Leg chains, too? Really?"

"Court order."

The woeful warbling voices of the townsfolk rose in unison in tiny New Mission Church. Hymn 467. "Rock of Ages." Up front, Timothy John Albright lay in waxy repose, mercifully spared the sound of this sour serenade, surrounded by lilies and sunflowers on a catafalque of black velvet. His coffin was absurd. Pretentious. A grease monkey from the world of wrenches and crankcase oil going home to Jesus in a Rolls-Royce.

"Where'd the coffin come from?" Jed whispered to Arthur as they stood just inside the church doorway under the vigilant gaze of the constable.

"No idea," Arthur said. He scowled. "I paid the undertaker for a pine box."

The well-tooled brass coffin made Tim look exceptionally weak and pitiful. So, it was probably Byron who had arranged it to feed the town's appetite for retribution. But other hands had been at work, too. A touch of pink had been applied to Tim's lips and pomade worked into his hair, which was parted on the wrong side. It did nothing to disguise his lifelessness. There would be no whistling past the graveyard for Tim.

Jed's heavy leg irons scraped across the wood floor and heads turned as the constable hastened to unfasten the lock.

The church's wheezing pump organ silenced at the ruckus, Martha Wanamaker at the keyboard, but more than a few of the townsfolk continued to sing the verse a cappella. Jed scowled back at the foolish, sanctimonious woman, who was glaring at Jed as if Satan incarnate had invaded her father's church. The congregation's singing began to peter out, but one determined elderly woman went on—

Naked come to thee for dress
Helpless look to thee for ...

Muffled chuckles could be heard as she was elbowed into silence by the man next to her. Then, waspish heads turned again in Jed's direction.

Just go through the motions, Arthur had advised. Hold your head high. You're there to say your farewell. Do it. Jed tried not to stare back at the weathered faces of old friends and acquaintances, whose stooped shoulders and thickened bellies surprised him.

Old Lady Trutcher, Arthur's mother-in-law, sat just off the center aisle, beneath a crown of pure white hair. Time had shriveled her spine and once-bountiful bosom, but she'd defiantly dodged the scattershot of fatal diseases and accidents that had thinned the pool of Rolla's original settlers over the years. She hadn't been required to work herself to death like the less fortunate inhabitants. Two daughters had succumbed to the influenza pandemic of 1918, leaving only the youngest, Emily, living comfortably in Kansas City as mistress of the Arthur Albright household. Old Lady Trutcher's gaze paused for an instant on her son-in-law and did nothing to acknowledge him. Her hand was resting unabashedly on the knee of the German oompah player, Knoop, seated next to her. Time had savaged him as well. His prominent cheekbones glowed as white as polished ivory. His watery eyes were pools of confusion.

Among the faces in the crowd were two in front who made Jed's knees go weak. *Amanda and Madeleine!* The girl's stricken expression was a match for the horror Jed felt at being seen in handcuffs. What were they doing here? What had Amanda told the girl?

Like a bicyclist on a steep hill, Martha Wanamaker pumped the organ back to life. A fanfare of chords in an ominous key wheezed from it as the Reverend Wanamaker rose from his chair to approach the pulpit in a black satin robe. He moved with theatrical solemnity. His aristocratic nose was undercut by a weak chin, but his dark hair, swept straight back, was thick and vigorous.

"Remember," Arthur whispered hoarsely, pushing Jed into a nearby pew, "poker face." No staring daggers at Martha Wanamaker. "A few of these folks could be your jurors."

Reverend Wanamaker cleared his throat. "Our scripture this morning is taken from the Gospel of Matthew." The gravity of his thundering baritone voice could not conceal a hint of a lisp. Thcripture. Gothpel. And despite its clamorous delivery, his voice failed to penetrate the inner workings of Knoop's ancient, drooping ears. The old oompah player cupped one with his hand as Reverend Wanamaker read, "Blessed are the poor in spirit, for theirs is the Kingdom of Heaven."

A forceful gust of wind rattled the little church's stained glass windows and rocked its steeple bell, which made it ping. Reverend Wanamaker took a deep breath and soldiered on. No Kansas gale was going to outbellow him.

"Blessed are they who mourn ..." he boomed, and stopped again when the back doors of the sanctuary banged open. Two silhouettes occupied the doorway. One was a woman in a voluminous black dress and an even larger black hat, festooned with silk flowers, a long black ostrich plume, and a dark, heavy veil that concealed her face. Just behind her was a huge man whose appearance was black by nature. Jed knew who it was even before he lifted his bowler hat off his straw-colored hair and placed it over his heart. The constable, stationed by the door, shifted uncomfortably, his hand hovering near his revolver. He backed away from the entrance. *There is a new reverend in town,* Jed thought, irreverently. Torch took several steps forward to scan the murmuring mourners, but he glowered at only one. Arthur Albright.

"Crucified Christ," Arthur muttered. "Not today."

When he was satisfied, Torch nodded to the incognito woman, who nodded back. *Jerome.* That was his given name, Jed suddenly recalled. "Don't use that, neither," he'd said. "Folks call me Reverend." Not in this church, they wouldn't. Carrie's aide-de-camp stepped back outside, undoubtedly aware that black men did not accompanying white women to church in Bible Belt Kansas.

The woman who now called herself Rose Starr sashayed down the sanctuary's main aisle in clacking patent leather black pumps, her rump gyrating as she moved toward the open casket. She tugged off a black glove and elicited gasps by gently caressing Tim's cheek. The mourners leaned forward as one, attempting to hear what the woman was muttering to Tim's corpse. A stray note bleeped from the organ as Martha Wanamaker leaned hard that way too.

Carrie Albright had been given up for dead and gone in Rolla years before. Chances were, no one recognized it was her lingering by the casket. Still, she electrified the room. The mystery of her deepened as she lowered her head to whisper in Tim's ear. The congregation gasped collectively when she kissed Tim's corpse! The Reverend Wanamaker's jaw flopped open.

Carrie wheeled around as if to shame the assembled for the commotion behind her, but she froze at the sight of the young woman seated a few feet away next to Amanda Vanderhorn Albright. What passed through her heart at this first glimpse of her long-lost flesh and blood was known only to her, but the shock it delivered was evident in the step she took backward.

Amanda put an arm around Madeleine's shoulder and pulled her tight. The girl bowed her head and closed her eyes. Did she have any idea who the mystery woman was? Jed felt the room sway.

The woman in black turned back to Tim then, bent a bit at the waist, and raised her hands over her heart. "The world never appreciated or deserved your gifted soul," she said, loud enough to be heard. Then she set off for the back of the church.

She stopped, however, at the row where her brothers were seated. Jed could feel the heat of the scowl she directed at Arthur from beneath her veil. And it was clear he didn't care for it even before his snotty voice said, "What the hell is it you think you're doing?"

She gestured at Jed in handcuffs and said, "I'd ask you the same question."

"I'm keeping the peace," Arthur replied.

Carrie's leather glove cracked like a whip across Arthur's face, eliciting a yelp of shock and pain. Several mourners nearby touched their cheeks, as if it had been their faces that were slapped.

The Reverend Wanamaker cleared his throat, his finger hovering over the page of his open Bible. He'd lost his place in the repetitive passage he'd been reading.

Madeleine stood suddenly and looked back at Jed with a confused and troubled expression.

"Look-a-there, Hansie!" Old Lady Trutcher's voice rang out. "That girl! Next to Amanda Vanderhorn! Spitting image of Carrie Albright!" Knoop lifted his hand to his ear and looked blankly at her. She shouted, "The dead boy's missing sister!"

Another blast of wind rattled the church windows, and the daylight outside began to fade. A duster. A cloud of grit scratching and howling its way through town. In the dim confusion, the mysterious woman in black slipped away.

The Reverend Wanamaker, standing in the pulpit with one finger now firmly planted in his Bible, opened and closed his mouth several times. Perhaps not even the man himself knew whether any sounds were coming out.

* * *

The town had been painted a ghostly gray in dust. Merchants were sweeping it away from their doorsteps and off the sidewalks as the funeral procession clomped past. Jed spotted Amanda and Madeleine peering out the train station's clouded windows. They'd fled the church after Carrie's departure. Jed paused, wishing he could explain to the girl how he'd been unjustly accused. Could he count on Amanda to explain that this spectacle of shame was the work of a judge in the pocket of corrupt and powerful men? Probably not. Her brother was deeply involved. "Move along," the constable ordered and gave him a shove. Tripping over his leg irons, Jed went down in the street.

Arthur offered him a hand up. "Don't give 'em the satisfaction," he said. But Jed's humiliation was complete. With the tacky suit streaked in dust, he looked like a derelict.

Bystanders were joining the procession as it moved along Main Street. From the grumbling chatter he was hearing behind him, Jed sensed the procession had turned from solemn to menacing. Bloodthirsty even. Would the constable lift a finger to protect him, if it came to it?

At the cemetery gate, the cortege passed a Buick roadster with four men inside. Earlier, Jed had seen a fancy silver Packard poking out of an alley near the church. Expensive new vehicles were a rarity in Rolla, but he did not know what to make of it.

Tim's coffin rode atop a hearse yoked to two black-plumed mules that plodded along behind Reverend Wanamaker onto the uneven ground of the cemetery. The minister raised his Bible like a drum major to halt the procession at a freshly dug hole where two sweating day laborers stood to one side in a cloud of their own B.O. Pallbearers from the church lifted down the casket for the laborers to lower into the hole using straps.

Jed jumped when a voice seemed to detonate in his ear.

"You!" It was a stern-faced woman in a straw sun hat standing close by. "Yes, you!" she exclaimed. "What are you doing here? You killed him!"

"That's right!" a man at her side concurred. "It's Tim's murderer!"

"Murderer!" someone else shouted, and others repeated it. "Murderer!" they called.

It was Reverend Wanamaker's thunderous voice that rose above the spreading commotion. "Judge not lest ye be judged," he bellowed to Jed's surprise. "Word of the Lord!"

The catcalls diminished to a chorus of confused grumbles. Then a man in a Stetson hat near the back called out, "Time to preach the lesson of Cain and Abel, Reverend!" Murmurs of agreement welcomed this idea.

"Show some respect, sir," the minister answered. "This is a solemn occasion, not some biblical square dance." *Rethpect. Occathion.*

Arthur placed a firm grip on Jed's elbow. "Byron has clearly sent his shills out to stir up the locals. We need to get you back to the jail." But as he said this, the deputy melted quietly into the crowd, taking the keys to the handcuffs with him.

Jed sunk deeper into his despair. How was it that jail was the place he'd be safe now? What hope did that leave for his eventual freedom? And how was he to deal with his guilt over Tim now?

The man in the Stetson hollered, "What happened to an eye for an eye?"

Martha Wanamaker stepped forward to stand at her father's side. "Listen to me," she hissed at this unruly congregation. "All of you! I happened to hear what the woman in the veil said at the casket! Do you want to know what she said?" A hush fell over the assemblage as she looked from face to face. "The woman said, 'Don't you worry, Tim. Jed is not going to hang. I know who did this.'"

From the far reaches of the gathering, the man in the Stetson hat advanced swiftly at Jed, lunging like a football blocker when he arrived. In an instant, Jed was on his back on the tooled brass casket at the bottom of the damp, airless hole.

Above, Arthur could be seen trading punches with the man in the Stetson. Jed's fight was for the next breath. The men from the Buick arrived with badges out. One of them pinned Jed's assailant's arms behind his back.

The shouting sounded muffled and distant down in the shaft. In his solitude, Jed wondered how Carrie could know who killed Tim. Only Tim could have seen who fired the shot that killed him. And he lay lifeless beneath Jed, as cold as the earth, his lips sewn shut by the undertaker.

Twenty-Six

Out of the Frying Pan

Rolla, Kansas – May 1930

His fitful dream had incorporated all of the scuffling noises coming from the next room. But the sharp crack of splintering wood came as a jolt. Chair smashing didn't fit the story that had been playing out in his sleep. Jed bolted upright in the bunk. Alert. Danger had arrived in the night.

He pictured a mob in the street. Lit torches. A rope tied to a buckboard and a skittish horse. A neighboring town had recently hogtied a rapist and dragged him five miles behind a runaway wagon.

Jed held his breath when the scuffle ended. What now? The knob on the office door jiggled. Locked. Angry expletives cursed this discovery. Desk drawers opened and slammed shut. The rattle of keys followed. Jed flinched as one went into the lock, but it did not turn. Nor did the second key. Or the third. When the door finally opened, a very large man filled the doorway blocking most of the light in the office. Like a human eclipse.

"*Shit!* What kinda Rube Goldberg crap we got up in here?"

Jed knew the voice. "Reverend? What's going on? What are you doing?"

"What it look like?" He chuckled.

Like a jailbreak. "Wait, hold on!" Jed said, and sighed as the big man went ahead and yanked hard on the cage door lever. It refused to budge.

"Mother*fucker*," The Reverend groused. He found the troublesome padlock partway down the brace, and another round of trial and error with keys began. Each failure was peppered with a curse.

"Can we discuss this?" Jed asked. Escaping would close the door on returning to a normal life. Escape would mean a fancy price on his head that trigger-happy bounty hunters from here to Dodge and beyond would race to collect by planting a slug in Jed's back. "What did you do to the constable?" Jed asked.

Torch kept trying keys. "Disgusting tub a lard smell like a swamp boot."

"Wait. Stop. You can't do this. It'll just make me look guilty if I run."

"Ha!" Torch said. "You ain't gonna look all that innocent dangling from a rope neither." He tried another key. "They comin' for ya. Po-lice don't put a nincompoop out front if they hopin' to stop a lynch mob."

The padlock popped on the fourth try.

"Let's go," Torch ordered, and heaved the door lever back. "Move your ass. Didn't come busting in here to take *no* for an answer."

Out of the frying pan, Jed thought. *Into the fire.* Trying to outrun the law was a losing gamble, but the bet was out of his hands. He pictured a hanging judge presiding over his trial and Lawyer Bob's shifty eyes pleading his innocence. "I'm coming," Jed said, and reluctantly rose off his foul mattress. "I'm coming."

* * *

Carrie's long silver Packard idled in the starlit alley. She was in the back, still in her flamboyant mourning dress, veil peeled back to reveal her heavily rouged cheeks and the distant stare in her eyes. Torch opened the rear door for Jed. A moment later, the Packard whispered out of the alley and down a side street on its swift exit from town.

The cushiony ride turned jouncy as the wheels dipped off pavement at the city limits.

"Is the Winchester under the seat?" Carrie asked.

Jed saw a revolver in her lap. Rose Starr, the outlaw. In the rear window Rolla looked peaceful and quiet in the night. But how long before the constable revived and raised an alarm? Before Byron's motley army fanned out in pursuit, armed with vintage Spencer repeaters and sawed-off hog pistols? And how would Arthur play it? Would he side with Byron this time?

The Packard raced south across the state line. Thirty-five miles of Oklahoma road lay ahead on the way to Texas. What then? Onto Mexico? New Orleans? "Keep to the back roads," Carrie told Torch. He muttered an oath. "Don't go near anything," Carrie repeated.

"We 'bout as far in the sticks as they is," Torch grumbled. The Packard's headlights carved a narrow tunnel of light out of the darkness. Tumbleweeds pinwheeled into it out of the black void. "Might as well be on the dark side of the moon," Torch carped. Sensing no concession from Carrie's hard line, he tried a fresh argument. "We'd make better time on the highway. Romans didn't invent concrete for nothin'."

Jed thought Torch had a point, but stayed out of it. "Why are you sticking your neck out for me?" he asked Carrie.

"One dead brother is enough, don't you think?" she replied evasively.

She was silent for a time. Then, rather abruptly, she said, "It never happened." She turned to face him. "What that flibbertigibbet church woman said. It's untrue. It never happened."

Torch quietly tilted an ear in their direction.

"I thought you should know," Carrie said. As if closing the subject.

Jed stared into the darkness out his window. Of course she would deny it. Who was there to dispute her?

"Come on, Carrie," Jed said. "Everyone in that church saw you go up and whisper in his ear." And then kiss him.

"I pledged to have his murderer caught, tried, and punished."

"So, you know who it is?" Jed asked.

"Uh, Miss Rose," the Reverend Jerome interrupted, pointing

out the windshield. It was difficult to gauge distances in the dark on the flat prairie, but there was no mistaking the dual halos coming their direction. Vehicle headlights. "Moving fast," the big man said.

"Kill the lamps!" Carrie ordered. Local farmers didn't generally race around at this hour.

Torch turned off the headlights and downshifted a gear, keeping his foot off the brake. Chances were, it was too late, that they'd already been spotted. Outlaws. *Wanted, dead or alive*, Jed thought with a shudder. Would he ever feel safe again?

"Try to look innocent," Arthur had said on the steps into the little church. "I *am* innocent," Jed had replied. "You know what I mean," Arthur grunted.

Without a word of warning, Torch swerved hard to the right, sending the Packard off the road. It felt as if the bottom had dropped out of the car until the drainage ditch rose up to smack its undercarriage with spine-jarring force.

"Quick, the corn!" Carrie shouted as the Packard bumped along on the incline of the ditch, struggling to escape. Carrie's fleshy bulk slid down the tilted rear seat, pinning Jed against his door. The revolver fell to the floor before the car could right itself at the bottom of the channel and begin the challenging ascent out.

At the top, Torch steered into a field of sorghum, snapping off dry stalks as the car became engulfed. Leaves slapped against the bumper, radiator, and fenders. Torch drove blindly, as if guided by an internal clock and compass. He made a sharp left turn and then another as he accelerated through the legion of corn, toppling and shredding row upon row. When the car faced the road six or seven rows in, he stopped, shut off the engine, and pulled the rifle out from under the seat. A vehicle hurtled by out on the road like a shooting star.

"Carrie," Jed said quietly, thinking it might be his last chance, "you need to leave the girl alone. Amanda can take care of it."

"The days of you making everyone's choices for them are over, Jed," Carrie said dismissively.

"Just stay out of it," Jed repeated. "Stay away from the girl."

"Hush now, y'all," Torch growled.

Out the windshield, steam was rising off the radiator around the chrome goddess ornament on the Packard's hood. A trailing plume of dust and debris thrown up by Torch's off-road maneuvers began catching up and washing over the car, clouding its windows. In the distance, the squeal of brakes and skidding tires could be heard. Then the distinctive whine of a transmission working hard in reverse. The speeding vehicle returned and stopped not twenty feet away. A Texas County Oklahoma Sheriff emblem was painted on the door. The car's mounted spotlight switched on.

Jed's heart thudded in his chest.

"Ya'll be cool," Torch urged in a low, rumbling voice.

The spotlight was stirring up swarms of mayflies across the road. Torch repositioned the Winchester in his lap, and Jed ducked lower in the backseat. His prison garb was like a signboard declaring *behold, a fugitive on the loose!*

The uniformed officer who emerged from the car swiveled the spotlight around and inched it along the curtain of dried corn that concealed the Packard. Stalks surrounding the car swayed gently in the breeze and scratched at the Packard's windows and doors.

The patrolman left the spotlight positioned on the corn as he dug a flashlight out of the car's rear boot. He skidded down the slope into the drainage ditch. Torch cocked the rifle. *Why is a cop stopping here?* Jed wondered. If the guy had noticed flattened corn where the Packard bulldozed into the field, why wasn't he searching there? The flashlight went dark and the deputy disappeared at the bottom of the ditch. For several minutes, Jed was aware of Torch's slow, regulated breathing. Then the flashlight switched on again, pointed into a large concrete storm culvert beneath the road. The deputy had drawn his sidearm, but the pipe was empty.

He scratched his head and swung the flashlight in a sweep of the surrounding area. Vehicles didn't just vanish into thin air. After a moment's hesitation, he scrambled back up the incline to the squad car and shined the spotlight forward down the road. His shadow grew long and distorted as he walked a short distance into the pool of light. Nothing but empty road and silent fields were visible for as far as the eye could see. He shook his head.

"Determined son-of-a-bitch," Torch groused.

Carrie pulled a cigarette from a compact case and snapped open a gold-plated lighter.

"Nuh-uh," Torch grunted. "Not yet."

"Yeah," Jed said sarcastically, "one dead brother is enough."

"Yes, I was being overly dramatic," Carrie said truculently. "I know Tim wasn't really our brother. He was a Harpel. You didn't know that, did you?" Jed remembered Clyde Harpel, a widowed miner who'd lived up the street from them in Thurmond. He was a frequent guest at holiday meals. "Dammit, Jed, you had to know Clyde was Tim's father."

He did. And didn't. It had always been obvious something was off, but their ma's insistence that Tim was her boy and her fierce denials of any comments to the contrary had, over time, clouded his thinking.

"Ma admitted the truth on her deathbed, but she asked me to keep it to myself for Tim's sake. Mrs. Harpel died giving him birth, and Clyde had no way to manage alone. Tim was only hours old when our family took him in."

Why mention this now? Of course, Jed thought, it meant that if anything had transpired between Carrie and Tim, it could never be considered incest. It was still depraved.

Jed said, "Why not just tell us? There was no shame in taking in another mining family's child. It was done all the time."

"And you saw how those hand-me-down children were treated. It was wretched. Like outcasts in their new families. Bullied. And likely to become troublemakers themselves. Ma wanted to avoid that. And she was determined to give Tim a regular life."

And they'd all played along. "Look how it turned out anyway," Jed said.

With the spotlight no longer on the corn, they found it easier to follow the officer. See what he was up to. He had returned to his car to smoke a cigarette, and was biding his time.

"Be here all night at this rate," The Reverend muttered.

"What did you tell this Madeleine?" Carrie asked.

This Madeleine. As if the girl was an irritant. "About *you,* you mean."

"Yes."

"Nothing. Which was exactly how much I knew. I told her she reminded me of my sister at her age."

"So, why was she at Tim's funeral?"

"You tell me!" Jed replied indignantly. "Or has your little spy network let you down?" He doubted Carrie would admit to secretly corresponding with Amanda for years. "I know this much," Jed said. "I sent the girl to Amanda when she tried to run away from Beaumont in my mail car. She'd seen a letter offering her a college scholarship and left with no place to stay and no money. You can imagine what might have happened if she hadn't come to me first." Jed studied his sister's face for regret or self-reproach. What he saw instead looked like a smile.

"Sounds like a girl with grit," Carrie said with a touch of admiration. Then her face turned serious. "But you, Jed? You really are getting a little old to be a Boy Scout."

Jed bit his tongue and listened to the cornstalks rattle in the wind.

"Why were *you* at Tim's funeral?" he asked when his composure returned.

"I just told you. To expose Tim's killer. And to come to your rescue, brother. I warned you not to get mixed up in this."

Out on the road, the squad car started up.

"'Bout damn time," Torch said.

The deputy pointed the spotlight back toward the corn before driving slowly along.

"Sheet," Torch grumbled, "fool's gonna see that hole we made up yonder. It leads straight to us."

"So, let's not be here when he arrives," Carrie said.

Torch started the Packard and pulled cautiously forward, lights off, flattening the outer rows of corn. He turned south, staying tucked in tight to the edge of the cornfield, creeping along in low gear, a night creature on the move.

Twenty-Seven

Into the Fire

Joplin, Missouri – May 1930

Out the drugstore's front window, Jed kept watch on Amanda's house down the block. He tried not to pay attention to her neighbor's massive oak tree with the rudimentary rope swing dangling from one branch or at the bare patch worn in the grass beneath. In Jed's tortured mind, they were omens of the hangman and an early grave.

"Don't care for your pie?"

The counter waitress took him by surprise, slipping back to refill his coffee. In his agitated state, he'd become fixated on a horse-drawn tinker's cart rolling past on rusted, noisy wheels. He'd taken his eye off the house for just a minute. But it could have been long enough to miss something. How was he to know if Byron's thugs were already inside, laying in wait?

"Finished, thanks," Jed said. The pie's rubbery cherry filling was stuck to his teeth. And the coffee he'd tried to wash it down with had been strong enough to dissolve tooth enamel. He left a dollar for the eighty-five cent check by his cup, doffed his hat, and left.

Only six dollars remained now out of the twenty Carrie had given him for train fare and expenses. Not even an unscrupulous businessman like Byron Vanderhorn could have started a new life as a fugitive on so little.

Jed patted the pockets of his baggy secondhand suit in search of his watch. Torch had handed it back to him along with his wallet and spectacles on the outskirts of Amarillo, where they'd stopped for Jed to change out of his jail clothes in the dim glow of the Packard's taillight. The seat of the donated pants was shiny and the jacket smelled of pipe smoke. Jed wondered, had it once been worn and abandoned by one of Carrie's johns?

"Good luck," Torch said as he handed Jed the watch and wallet taken from a drawer in the Rolla police station after the big man clubbed the constable senseless.

"No syrupy goodbyes for me, I guess," Jed said when Carrie declined to open her window after he rapped on it. She was angry about his refusal to go with her to New Orleans.

After this rebuffed farewell, Torch had stepped forward to make excuses. "She proud," he said. "But you right to split, ask me." A little grin played at the corners of his mouth. "Don't 'zactly blend in out here, us together."

Jed's finger hovered over the doorbell button on Amanda's porch. He took one last anxious look over his shoulder, which, of course, revealed nothing about what might await inside. But if he was quick, he could escape out the back door in the event of trouble. He wouldn't stay but a minute, just long enough to straighten out any misunderstandings with Amanda and Madeleine. Before his finger touched the doorbell button, however, the front door flew open.

"Jed! Thank God!" Amanda shouted.

Her arms pinned him in a tight, desperate hug, and she squealed a mournful cry. Not wishing to attract attention, Jed arched his back and lifted her back inside and kicked the door shut behind them.

"Good heavens, Amanda! What's wrong?"

"Madeleine!" she bawled. "He's taken her."

"Who has? What's going on? Tell me!"

"Byron!" she wailed. "He's going to hurt her!"

"I don't understand. Byron? Why would he take Madeleine?"

Amanda clung to him, sobbing and gasping, waves of pent-up horror cascading out of the depths. Jed steered her toward the kitchen to pour her a glass of water and calm her down.

Her sputtering account of events managed to convey that her brother had been there when they returned from Rolla. He was cutting up an apple at her kitchen table with an oversized carving knife. "The biggest one I have. And he pointed it at Madeleine. 'I'm Byron,' he says, 'and you're coming with me. We're going to get acquainted.' He frightened her out of her wits."

"Where did he take her?"

"I don't know! I couldn't call for help because he cut the phone line. He told me there was a man watching the house, and if I tried to follow him, the man would kill me. My own brother!"

Byron had come unhinged, Jed thought. "When was this?"

"Two hours ago, maybe." Amanda blinked, grew quiet a second, blinked again, and came to a belated realization. "They've let you out of jail?"

"Not exactly."

"Oh, Jed!" Amanda said.

"Listen, Amanda, I don't know how much time I have. We can talk about all that later. But Byron—I take it he saw you with her in Rolla? Is that what happened?"

"He was in the telegraph office when we got off the train. You'd have thought he'd seen a ghost. Then, suddenly, he was steaming mad. We hurried on then to the church, and I thought that was the end of it. I certainly never expected to see him sitting at this table when we walked in the door."

"Amanda, why on earth did you take her to Rolla?"

"It wasn't my idea. Quite the opposite, I did everything I could to prevent it, short of locking her in her room. But she was determined to go from the moment she saw a notice about your arrest in the newspaper. 'He would never do that,' she said. 'We have to do something.'"

His anger softened. The girl's concern for him touched his heart. "Water over the dam, I suppose," he said. But there was no time to waste. "I'm leaving," Jed said, and started for the front door. "I have a hunch I know where Byron's gone, and he has to be stopped."

"Wait, what are you doing?" Amanda asked.

"Leaving. For New Orleans. On the first train out."

"New Orleans," Amanda said. "Oh? Yes! Of course! I'm coming with you!"

"No, you can't. It wouldn't be safe. Not with armed men after me. You might walk into a crossfire meant for me."

"You let me worry about that, Jed. That girl is going to need me when we catch up with them. And maybe I can talk some sense into Byron. As his sister."

"He didn't listen to you when he was here, did he? No, you're not coming!"

"Don't argue, Jedidiah Albright. I *am* coming. With you or without you. And I have something you don't—an automobile."

* * *

Byron's sleek executive Pullman was in plain sight as they drove past the downtown switchyard. It gleamed like a jewel on its own siding amidst droves of dusty, mothballed boxcars. The Kansas & Western name was emblazoned in cheerful yellow letters on its side. But menace radiated from its dark windows.

"Car 2633," Jed said. "That's his!" Why was it still here? Jed found it peculiar. And just a touch alarming. They pulled over, climbed a low fence into the yard, and crouched behind a flatcar two sidings over. "Stay put," Jed instructed. "I'm going for a closer look."

"Wait, Jed." Amanda put a hand on his arm. "I think we should call the police. Let them deal with this."

"No police," Jed said. "They would arrest me, not him." Before she could detain him any longer, he loped away, bent at the waist to stay beneath the windows of the Pullman as he scurried past on his way to the rear platform. Amanda called after him in a hoarse whisper, "Wait! I would be the one talking to the police."

Jed stopped and squatted next to the Pullman's rear wheels to listen for sounds of a struggle or cries for help. But all he could hear was the huffing of switch engines and the heavy clank of couplers as cars were linked up in the yard.

Swiftly, he mounted the rear steps to the canopied deck and tried the door. It was another unsettling surprise to find it unlocked. He braced for a confrontation as he let himself in, but the office was dim and quiet. The unblinking eyes of the lizard in the glass terrarium fixed on him, the creature as still as a fossil from prehistoric times.

For a makeshift weapon, Jed grabbed a locomotive-shaped paperweight off Byron's desk. It would be better than nothing, he told himself as he stepped into a passage to the right of Byron's desk. There were two doors in the corridor, one on the left and one at the end, both closed. As Jed paused to size up his options, the distinctive multiple clicks of a Colt revolver being cocked filled his ear and sent goosebumps the length of his spine.

"Drop the paperweight, Albright," said a familiar voice that made Jed's stomach lurch. The paperweight thudded to the floor. "There's a good boy," the bully said. The cold barrel of the Colt rested against Jed's neck as the man's free hand made a determined search for weapons in the secondhand suit. "Okay. Turn around. Slowly."

Anticipation did little to soften the shock of facing the ghastly maroon birthmark again. "Well, well," said his gleeful captor. "This is my lucky day. The State of Kansas is offering five hundred dollars to turn you over, alive or *dead*. And you just waltz in here like a moth to the flame. Lucky day, lucky day. To think I wouldn't have collected a dime if that bullet had found its mark back at Winslow! Well, one day's misfortune is another day's windfall. The fickle finger of fate." He nodded. "The gods' hidden plan."

Jed grew weary waiting for the tiresome blowhard to wrap up his little soliloquy.

"Next time, Albright," the Musgrave detective prattled on, "—only there won't be a next time—you might want to check behind a door as you pass. Some fella might just get the drop on you otherwise." He enjoyed a disdainful laugh.

Without regard for his disadvantage, Jed, in a snit, demanded to know, "Where the hell's Byron?"

The Musgrave appeared to blanch at this temerity, but he compensated quickly, driving Jed into a wall with a hand clamped tight to his throat. "Keep that yap shut!"

Jed managed to croak, "A little tin badge isn't going to save you if he murders her …"

A half dozen slugs were poised to go to work from the Colt's fully loaded cylinder, the revolver now pressed up against his nose. "Murder who?" the Musgrave said.

"My niece!" Jed gasped. "Byron kidnapped her. Two hours ago. In front of a witness, who's on her way to the police." At least Jed hoped Amanda had wisely ignored his instructions.

"Man's at a meeting in town," the detective growled, with what sounded like surplus conviction.

"No, he's not," Jed hissed. "And if he's not here in this railcar, he's somewhere on the run with the girl he's taken. And there's going to be trouble if he isn't stopped."

"Don't know shit about any girl."

"Do you think I'd have come here like a moth to the flame, as you put it, if it wasn't true? What's going to happen when your office finds out Byron's abducted a helpless, underage girl? Committed a felony right under your nose. You don't think you might be in the soup, too? Open the door!"

"He *ain't* in there," the Musgrave said, temper flaring. But he pushed the door open. "See for yourself, you little cock-a-roach."

The luxurious wood-paneled room with a massive featherbed and a tufted companion leather armchair was unoccupied.

"Satisfied?" the Musgrave said.

"What about this other room down the hall?"

The second room was more extravagant than the first, as if a Manhattan penthouse had been put on wheels—marble fireplace, dining table for six, built-in buffet, draperies, and chandelier. But again unoccupied.

"So he's disappeared with an innocent girl," Jed said, "and you had no idea?"

The gun swiped hard across Jed's face, sending him to the floor. "Enough of your shit," the Musgrave said. "Man's been delayed at a meeting, that's all."

Jed waited for his ears to stop ringing before he rose to his knees. Then he said, "You want to take the chance that that might turn out not to be true?"

The Musgrave appeared to give this some thought, his resolve developing cracks as he did. One good blow might shatter the man's hard shell, Jed suspected.

"Listen, I have a hunch where he's going," Jed said. "If you take that damn gun off me, I'll tell you where."

The Musgrave hesitated just long enough to demonstrate he was still in charge before tipping the gun toward the ceiling and easing off the hammer. "Shoot," he said, introducing an element of confusion for a moment. "Go on, tell me. But you better not be shittin' me."

The back door of the Pullman beyond Byron's office opened before Jed could explain, and Amanda's voice called in sheepishly, "Jed?"

The Musgrave had Jed on his feet with his arm yanked high behind his back and the Colt against his temple before Jed could shout, "Amanda, no!"

"Who's this, Albright?" the Musgrave said, chuckling as he looked her over. "This the missus? Your witness? Looks like she didn't bring the police."

He locked them in the bedroom and went out into the yard, presumably to make scheduling arrangements for the car. After a time, the Pullman was nudged by a switch engine and pushed backward into a short chain of coal cars loaded with what smelled like locomotive slag and ash.

A long journey lay ahead. And Jed sought comfort in the hope they might still get there in time to save Madeleine.

Twenty-Eight

Night Freight

Joplin, Missouri – May 1930

A switchman popped up in an oil-smeared denim cap to escort Byron's car like a shepherd tending to a stray. The Pullman rocked slowly over switches he opened, directing them to the rear of a waiting southbound freight. When the Musgrave put his Colt to Amanda's head, Jed had managed to appease him with his New Orleans theory. "I don't have the address," he said, "but I'll know it when I see it." Keeping something in reserve was insurance that he and Amanda wouldn't become excess baggage.

Amanda was not on board with his plan. She pounded vigorously on the Pullman's windows at the switchman and shouted for help, but her screaming didn't appear to penetrate the thick glass. Jed could hear the Musgrave chuckle in Byron's office next door, his feet probably propped up on the desk. A lowly yardman wasn't going to stick his nose into what went on in the executive car, not even for a damsel in distress—not if he knew what was good for him.

With the Pullman linked to the idling freight, the switchman departed and Amanda heaved herself down on the gray sateen cover of the stateroom's bed. She nibbled on a fingernail, dumbstruck, it appeared, by how swiftly she'd become a prisoner. Jed wondered what he could say for comfort or consolation as stanchions and switch towers rolled relentlessly by out the windows. He could hear her get up after a time and begin rummaging around. But it surprised him when she said, "Chubby Parker. His favorite."

She had a gramophone record in her hand. A paper sleeve was on the floor at her feet. A wall cabinet door was open behind her with a built-in Victrola on one shelf and a collection of records below it. She gave the record a swift backhand flick of her wrist against the edge of the cabinet's marble countertop, and the molded shellac broke into a dozen bits.

"Smash hit," Amanda said with a scornful laugh. She grabbed another record, shook the disc out of the sleeve to drop it onto the shards of Chubby Parker's music at her feet. Then she stomped it to smithereens as well. Angry tears brightened her eyes. "He won't be enjoying that one again, either," she said.

A lifetime of slavish allegiance to her domineering brother was plainly under duress.

"You always saw him for what he was," she told Jed. "And, honestly, I held that against you. Feel free to tell me I was the fool, believing that he did ugly things only at the bidding of the railroad. That it was the railroad that was heartless and greedy, not Byron. That beneath his hard, demanding surface was a man of principle, standing firm for what he thought was right. But even if it was the railroad that ordered him to kidnap Madeleine Robichaux and threaten me—and it wasn't—that's something you can't do unless you are truly a monster."

Jed put a consoling arm around her shoulders, but she shrugged it off and stormed into the stateroom water closet, where she went through the contents of a mirrored medicine cabinet and pulled out a bottle of cologne. She sniffed it with exaggerated disgust.

"Byron's," she spat. She poured it down the zinc hopper of the commode and it splattered onto the tracks racing by below. "Officially toilet water!" she announced. The sickening fragrance blasted back into the stuffy car in a burst of air. The room smelled like a Sunday school.

Amanda grabbed one of Byron's shirts out of an oak armoire next and began ripping it apart along the seams. She bit off two buttons for good measure and spit them onto the floor. When she couldn't shred a suit the same way (it was made of sturdier stuff), in exasperation she grabbed a shoe from the bottom of the cabinet, declared "Superstition be damned!" and dealt the full-length mirror inside the armoire door a mighty blow. Shards of glass shot everywhere. "Time for my brother to worship a god other than himself!" she muttered.

The Musgrave unbolted the door at the sound of exploding glass and ducked his cruel face in with a thuggish sneer. "Working things out, are we?" He winked at Amanda.

She flung the shoe wildly past his head and charged at him, perhaps to retrieve it and try again. But he pivoted on the ball of one foot as she came and sent her staggering backward with a short, quick uppercut, his arm like a steam piston. Amanda's head snapped back, and she went down like a rag doll on the glass-strewn bedcover. Gene Tunney down for the long count.

The nose of the Musgrave's gun pinned Jed to the chair before he could stand and avenge his wife. "Jesus, Albright. She's a real pistol you got there."

* * *

Discovering a bottle of Seagram's VO hidden in a cavity behind the compartment's paneled wall was a stroke of serendipity. It changed the course of the afternoon—and far more, as it turned out, something Jed would have occasion to think back on again and again with a smile. It turned up on his search for a wall safe, figuring there might be incriminating railroad documents stashed in the car. The bottle and shot glasses appeared almost planted as a consolation prize when the wood panel clicked open.

Jed poured a finger of the whisky into a glass and handed it to Amanda. "Happy hour," he said.

She'd been slow to come around after being punched, and she was fuzzy on the details of what had occurred. Her eye was swollen. She gave the whisky a mordant look but glugged it down in a single gulp. Then she coughed twice. "Is this what my brother drinks?" she queried after clearing her throat. "It's awful."

Jed put an upturned finger to his lips to hush her. "I don't think our friend out there knows you're related to him, and it would be better if he didn't. He might use you as a hostage if he finds out." Safer for her to remain Jed's *missus* than to be the boss's *sister.*

Amanda pondered this a moment, held out her glass, and waggled it expectantly.

Jed poured a very short finger, more like a pinkie, this time. Moderation was in order. "We're after the same thing for now, trying to catch up to Byron and stop him. But once we do, what happens next is anybody's guess."

Amanda's eyes widened. She finished what was in her glass and stared off into space, her tongue absently exploring a tooth loosened by the Musgrave's fist.

The alcohol had begun to catch up with her. "I had to make a choice, Jed," she said dreamily. "Years ago. I wanted to stay friends with Carrie, but I knew you wouldn't have it. Not if you knew what had become of her life. It was wrong, what I did. I understand. Secrets are like termites. You can't see the damage until it's done." She held out her glass again with a don't-you-dare-deny-me look.

"I don't get it. You didn't think I deserved to know?"

"I'm sorry. It's more complicated than that."

"Tell me now," he said. "All of it."

"It's not really mine to tell. It's Carrie's."

"What if I don't get the chance to ask her?"

Amanda's eyes grew misty. She said, "You know what I think, Jed? I think men and women were never meant to be friends. Lovers? Yes. Mates? Sometimes. Never friends."

Enough whisky for her, Jed thought.

"What are we going to do?" she asked softly. "Is he going to kill us?" Alcohol had taken the edge off her fear but not erased it.

"No," Jed offered bravely. "That's not going to happen."

There was not much confidence in the look she returned after this remark. She took the bottle out of his hands, poured two glasses, and handed him one. She clinked his glass with hers and proposed a toast. "Here's to come what may."

Jed scowled. "Come what may," he muttered. Down the hatch.

* * *

The sun melted into a rouge puddle behind distant trees out the Pullman windows in Arkansas. The Seagram's was gone, but it had made them clever. Wise. Powerful.

Amanda laid her head in the crook of Jed's arm. "God, we were young then," she said. "Do you realize if Nathan had lived, he'd be the same age as Madeleine? He'd be a grown man! Probably be a handsome devil like you were back then."

Jed couldn't remember ever hearing her utter Nathan's name.

"You suppose he'd have become a fuddy-duddy like you?" she said with a drunken cackle. She'd earlier wriggled out of her dress under the covers and tossed it onto the floor. She cuddled her soft body now against his boxers and undershirt and appeared to take note of the effect this had on him. She studied his face as she pulled off her corset and bloomers under the blanket and made a show of producing each for his inspection with a bemused smile.

"What if the barbarian at the gate decides to stage a surprise invasion?" Jed asked with an inebriated smile. And he wondered how they would feel about this possible bedroom adventure in the sober light of morning. Would they be able to look each other in the eye?

Amanda giggled. "I expect you to protect the honor of this fair maiden."

When Jed showed no signs of making an advance, she impatiently pulled his hand up between her legs and planted a deep and sensuous kiss on his mouth. Her other hand got busy exploring the vortex between his legs, pleasurably gauging his growing enthusiasm. *Oh my.* A love affair on which the sun had long since set rose again against the darkening sky. Jed closed his eyes, transported to a place in the abandoned past, the thrum and click of train wheels measuring out the diminishing distance to their destination.

Twenty-Nine

Secrets

New Orleans Bound – May 1930

At dawn, Jed awoke to the sour smell of his bedmate's morning breath. He'd developed a sudden apprehension that the train had reversed course as they slept, and that they were now going in the wrong direction, lumbering back toward Joplin. Damn it! There'd be no chance to reach New Orleans in time to stop Byron if it was true! Heart racing, arm pinned under his softly snoring companion, he broke into a hangover sweat, trapped in a post-carnal purgatory and shamed by memories of a sodden night spent carousing.

A tiny, mewling squeak escaped Amanda when Jed coughed. She shifted position, but not enough to free his arm, which was as lifeless as a sausage. He tried turning his face away from her redolent breath, but a strand of her hair had snagged in his teeth, restricting his movement.

The Pullman began to spin like a carnival ride. He closed his eyes and gulped in a frantic effort to keep down the contents of his stomach. Amanda groaned at his squirming and rolled off his arm. He scrambled out of bed.

"God, is there any water?" Amanda croaked.

"There'd better be," Jed said, and staged a quick search. His tongue was thick, his throat parched. He raised a window shade to let in a bit of the gray morning as his arm slowly tingled back to life. Patchy fog clung to the bayou swamp rolling by outside. In the distance was a grove of mist-shrouded cypress trees leaning out over the banks of a river, wide enough to be the Mississippi. Jed's internal compass reversed orientation. They hadn't gone north, thank God.

Amanda asked, "Where are we?"

"Outside Baton Rouge, probably," Jed said, relying on the map of Louisiana's rail hubs he carried around in his head. (He was tested annually on such things to retain his employment.) The names of the towns between Little Rock and New Orleans were a bit fuzzy this morning, his brain as fogged in as the Delta marsh.

Jed kept his gaze discreetly out the window as Amanda untangled herself from the bedcovers and gathered her clothes off the floor. He could hear her grunt struggling into the corset and sigh as she buttoned up her dress. He assumed she was similarly tortured by thoughts of their drunken, scurrilous abandon. He checked her reflection in the glass and tenderly recalled how surprised his hands had been to discover alterations in the contours of her body—the thickening midriff, the breasts as soft as balloons now rather than firm as melons. With an inward smile, he recalled a little growl that had escaped her in the throes of passion.

She brushed behind him to the lavatory, closed the door, and shot the bolt. "I need a bath," she hollered through the door. "And coffee. And a dozen aspirin." And, sadly, there would be none of it, her tone said.

The Pullman roared past a tiny station, scattering crows off the roof. In a station window, a visored postmaster was bent over a stack of mail, canceling stamps. The world went on.

Amanda took her time in the john. Perhaps the cut beneath her eye needed attention. Or perhaps it was her bed-mashed hair she was struggling to fix. He wondered if she felt that her dignity was in question. She could not hide out forever in her brother's Pullman toilet.

After a time, Jed heard the Musgrave detective tramp down the hall and begin rattling pots and pans in the galley in a very grumpy fashion.

Jed was reminded that the shot glasses were still sitting out. Returning them to the wall niche, he saw the bottom shelf wobble.

And when he pressed it down, it popped open to reveal a pearl-handled derringer, a leather ankle holster, and a box of .41-caliber short shells. Good God. It was Byron's last line of defense.

"Is that coffee I smell?" Amanda called from the toilet, as if it might be something she'd consider showing her face for.

"I wouldn't count on getting any," Jed called back as his stomach growled at its frustrated appetite. He turned Byron's little weapon over in his hands, studying it. It was a marvel of miniaturization—compact and sleek. Probably inaccurate beyond a few feet. Nevertheless, it would pack a wallop at close range. It was the sort of weapon Carrie might carry in a clutch purse for dangerous occasions, he thought. He slipped it into his jacket pocket, where it created a noticeable bulge. He tried his trouser pocket, but drawing it from there was slow and clumsy. And if it happened to go off half-cocked, the cost to his manhood would likely be unacceptable. The leather holster felt uncomfortable strapped to his ankle, but it seemed to be his only option.

Jed had never shot a man, and he wasn't sure he'd have the stomach for it. But if he froze and Byron goaded him, the taunts might provide the incentive enough to do it. Shut that mouth once and for all.

* * *

The freight yard at Baton Rouge, Louisiana, was massive, thirty spurs wide and a dozen city blocks long. The overnight freight from Joplin with its unlikely Pullman caboose rattled unimpeded through long strings of idled cars, going left, then right, then left again on the branch switches until it stopped in the shadow of a warehouse with an obsolete railroad's name spelled out in chipping paint across the weathered brick.

"Are we there?" Amanda yelled through the lavatory door, her mood unimproved. "Is this New Orleans?"

"Baton Rouge," Jed called back. He stroked the stubble on his chin, and the trace of a scent from the previous night's escapades wafted out of a crevice of a fingernail.

In the yard, the Musgrave was giving orders in a raised voice to an irritated dispatcher and a slouching brakeman. He hovered while the Pullman was backed onto a siding and hooked to a chain

241

of oil tankers. Soon, they were chugging back onto the main line for New Orleans.

Jed smoothed his trouser leg over the bulky holster and patted the spare rounds of ammunition in his jacket pocket. The derringer held just two bullets. Reloading it in the middle of a gunfight would be impractical. But the extra slugs felt reassuring somehow. You never knew how things might play out.

Amanda unbolted the lavatory door and made an appearance as the train began to slow outside Gonzales, Louisiana. She kept her face turned so the oozing cauliflower of her puffy, prizefighter eye remained in shadow. The Musgrave had a lot to answer for, Jed thought.

"Amanda, listen," Jed said. "I want you to run like hell the moment that bully opens the door. No matter what. No arguments." Jed was planning to knock him down with the whisky bottle the second he laid a hand on Amanda. "You need to keep going—for blocks and blocks—until you're absolutely safe." The derringer would remain in its holster. There was no chance it would scare the Musgrave, and he'd slap it away the moment it came out. Jed didn't want to lose his chance to point it in Byron's face when the time came.

"Why do men think they get to decide *everything*?" Amanda demanded to know.

The woman got up on the wrong side of the bed, Jed thought, and kept it to himself.

"You listen to me, Jedidiah Albright!" she said, using her teacher voice on him now. "You are not going to send me scurrying off like a frightened kitten. Is that clear? I'm seeing this to its conclusion. I'm needed. More than you realize. You really have no idea what's going on here."

Jed snorted, "It seems pretty obvious, actually."

"Well, it isn't. And I'll tell you why. Byron believes that church woman's preposterous story about incest. It's the reason he's taken Madeleine. He's convinced Tim is her actual father."

"What?" Jed scoffed. "Come on, Amanda. That makes no sense. Why wouldn't Byron enjoy a really good laugh and move on if he heard that? It would prove what he'd been saying all along about inbreeding West Virginia hillbillies!" And then, something she'd said stopped him. *Actual father.* "Wait, are you saying Byron had believed he was ..."

"Just listen, would you? Before Carrie ran away, she informed Byron that he'd gotten her in a family way. She demanded that he take responsibility. And he did, I suppose, in his own way. He gave her money to go away. Then all these years later, some woman comes forward with a fictitious *incest* story, and Byron decides Carrie was actually two-timing him with her brother and had played him for a sucker!"

Byron was Madeleine's father?

"Byron is hell-bent for revenge now. He literally has no idea what a hateful, sick thing it is he's planning to do." She had to stop and gulp down a sob. "Oh, Jed. He's going to debase her," Amanda croaked. "Madeleine! He's going to force Carrie to watch the whole thing."

The tears could be held back no longer, it seemed.

Jed wrapped his arms around her and pulled her close. "We'll stop him," he assured her. The little derringer would see to that. "It'll be okay. You'll see."

"No, it won't! It will be horrid! And no one will know just how horrid except Carrie. Forced to relive the worst nightmare of her life! She'll kill him if he doesn't listen."

"What are you talking about?" How could it be worse for Carrie than for Madeleine? "What nightmare?"

"Your father," she blurted, as if directing her hostility at Jed. "He tampered with Carrie."

Stunned, Jed unconsciously took a step back. That filthy bastard had stuck his grime-encrusted fingers into their sister? Defiled her? Without them ever knowing? *The woodshed,* Jed thought, memories jitterbugging back across time. Pa had taken her out there alone when she got the strap. The boys he'd dealt with as a group. Made to drop their pants in front of the others and stifle squeals of pain as welts were raised on their buttocks, legs, and backs.

"It's Carrie's secret!" Amanda said, chin trembling. "No one must ever know. You understand me?"

Jed recalled a look of horror in Carrie's eyes one Christmas when they were children when their pa lifted her onto his lap. The color had drained from her face. "Secret," Jed whispered. "Promise."

"She needs me there for support."

The bolt to the compartment door shot to startling effect then and the muzzle of the Musgrave's gun made an appearance, pointed threateningly at Jed. "Hatching a little plan, are we?" the detective snarled. Before Jed could resist, he'd been knocked down, his face pinned to the floor, and his wrists handcuffed behind him. The Musgrave's knee rested on his neck. *Run, Amanda! Now!* Jed thought. But she'd turned into a statue, staring, terrified. "Okay, lady, get your weepy ass into the W.C.," the detective ordered, "and get down on your knees."

Jed watched helplessly as Amanda was gagged and handcuffed to a drainpipe in the lav. "Your hubby and I have an appointment," the detective told her. "And we don't need you in the way. But when it's finished, I'll be back and we'll get acquainted."

Jed's impotence felt like salt in the wounds to his pride.

"I have to step out here for a minute," the Musgrave said when the train shuddered and jerked to a halt. "I hear yelling, I'll come back and shoot the missus between those pitiful little eyes. No second chances. Is that clear?"

He bolted the door again for good measure as he left.

"You okay?" Jed called to Amanda.

She whimpered valiantly.

"Everything's going to be fine," Jed said. "I promise."

With the toe of his shoe, Jed tugged down the cuff of his pants, which had crept up to expose a bit of holster.

* * *

A Chevy Coupe was parked beneath a switchyard tower in the blazing Gulf sun. The detective shoved Jed onto the scorching seat, his hands still bound behind him. "Give me the address," the detective demanded.

The man's cruelty was unbridled this morning. He was no longer content to play the cat toying with the mouse. His methods were turning sadistic. Jed had the idea that someone up the chain of command had grown impatient. Angry. Someone with the clout to put trains and passenger cars at a detective's disposal. Someone who had a lot to lose.

"I don't know the address," Jed said, and saw stars appear in broad daylight at a blow delivered by the detective's knuckles to his temple.

"A mailman who can't remember an address," the detective mocked. "Sure." He seized a handful of Jed's shirtfront and shook him. "Listen to me, you little shit. Tell me the address or we go back and I get it out of the missus."

"She doesn't know it either!" Jed lied. "But I can find the place. In the Garden District. Tall windows. Green shutters. Street's named for a Roman ruin. Forum? No. Coliseum. Coliseum Street! Once we get close, I can—*ouch!*"

The pain in Jed's ear was intense as the Musgrave twisted it viciously.

"I'm done with your crap, Albright. Tell me that house number now!"

"I don't have it, I tell you," Jed shouted. And he wouldn't say it if he did. He could serve no further purpose afterward, and the Musgrave had made his future intentions clear: He'd be going back to the Pullman alone. With his ear about to rip off, Jed pleaded, "Please! I'll know the place when I see it! But I have to be conscious!"

With an exasperated shove, the Musgrave let go of Jed's shirt. He started the Chevy, ground it into first gear, floored the gas, and shot them forward out a gate, cutting off a streetcar that clanged in complaint. Car horns sounded from all directions as the Chevy barreled along the narrow streets, veering to avoid oncoming trucks and buses, and racing blindly through intersections, the Musgrave muttering like a madman. Jed was tossed sideways as the Chevy tipped, fishtailing through turns. "I'm going to put a hole in her n—'s head, too," the Musgrave said, "and ship him C.O.D. to Sheriff John Law of Morton County, Kansas."

The Chevy nearly sideswiped a parked car on Coliseum, the Musgrave driving like Barney Oldfield. Two men sitting low inside flinched as they roared past, and Jed thought he saw a familiar nose and chin beneath a fedora tugged low over one man's eyes. He swiveled his head for a second look and saw only the sky reflecting off the car's windshield.

"Did we miss it?" the Musgrave snapped.

"No," Jed replied, and faced forward again. "That's it, there!" he said as it shot by out his window. The Chevy's tires squealed to a halt several doors down. So much for not alerting the entire neighborhood to their arrival.

"That one?" The Musgrave pointed back at the green hurricane shutters and white pillars of Rose Starr's notorious establishment, nestled innocuously amidst its flowering shrubs.

"Yes."

The Chevy's gears ground into reverse, and the tires spun again. Jed's pulse raced with the engine. What was about to happen? Was the Musgrave going to lock him in the Chevy's trunk? Shoot him in broad daylight?

Thirty

Nothing to Confess

New Orleans – May 1930

"Any funny business," the Musgrave growled as he unlocked Jed's handcuffs, "you'll have daylight shining through the gap where your guts should be." Jed was kneeling next to the Chevy, tying his shoe, biding his time. When the detective turned his attention momentarily to the house, the derringer slipped silently out of the ankle holster and into Jed's jacket pocket.

The Musgrave turned and kicked him. "Hurry up! Let's go!"

Trouble appeared to already be paying a visit to the house on Coliseum. The front door stood open. The velvet drapes at the tall windows of the parlor were askew. And there was no sign of the ever-present Torch. "A mite late," he might have said if he'd been there to greet them.

A terrified shout came from the house, and butterflies took flight in Jed's belly—butterflies with razors for wings. He raced for the porch.

"Stop!" called a voice from a massive oleander bush next to the steps. A baby-faced man in a dark suit stepped out of the shrubbery covered in pink blossom petals. He blocked their path and held up a preposterously dense gray document with a florid signature at the bottom. "Place is closed. Court order," he said. "Move on!"

The Musgrave snatched the paper out of his hand, eyeballed it, and shoved it back. "Place ain't closed. So, you can stick that thing up your ass."

He drew his gun, backed the man-child off the walk, and yanked Jed up the steps. A blood-curdling shriek echoed through the house, lifting gooseflesh on Jed's neck and arms. Car doors slammed out in the street as the Musgrave hurried inside, closing and bolting the bordello's front door behind them.

"What the hell was that about?" Jed asked. "Who was that?"

The Musgrave replied by twisting Jed's arm up between his shoulder blades and barking at him to shut his yap. Behind a balustrade at the top of the stairs, one of Carrie's saucy girls in hairpins and cold cream ducked down and watched as Jed was frog-marched across the tile floor at the point of the Musgrave's Smith & Wesson. The girl's adolescent breasts bulged sensuously out of her corset as she leaned forward for a better view. Jed winced again at the thought of Pa dragging Carrie back to the woodshed.

The girl squealed dramatically and scampered off when the detective waved his gun in her direction. A door slammed, and excited, urgent chatter broke out behind it. The Musgrave's attention was drawn then to a loud argument in the parlor off the hall.

"You're a liar!" It was Byron's reedy voice. Frantic, unhinged. "A filthy, low-life liar! First, you lied to extort my money. Then you lied again by claiming you'd get rid of it. Because here it is …all grown up!" There was a muffled squeal that Jed took for Madeleine being hit.

The Musgrave pulled Jed back from the doorway to a place of concealment. Jed caught a glimpse of Carrie, hogtied on a wicker chaise, and Madeleine cringing on the carpet, tossed down like pirate's booty, arms lashed behind her back, her wrists bound by twists of insulated copper wire. Carrie sounded undaunted. "Who says that's my daughter?"

"Look at her!" Byron screamed. "It's as if *you* walked in here out of the past!"

Carie said, "Yes, Byron. I see a resemblance. But you didn't come all this way because she might be mine. It's that she might *not* be yours. Isn't that right?"

Jed could hear the girl wheezing hard through the cloth gag wedged in her teeth. Craning his neck to one side, he could see her reflection in a mirror across the room. Her face was ghastly white, her forehead glistening with perspiration, her ears being filled with ugly denials about the facts of her origin. She glanced with distress at the nude painting of Carrie over the fireplace mantel. Hardly the benefactor she had imagined when she left Beaumont.

"Admit it, Byron," Carrie said, "you've been taken in by a silly rumor going around Rolla. It's true, you have. And don't pretend you know the first thing about this girl. You don't. You passed up your chance for that nineteen years ago. And now you're worried this can of worms you kicked down the road is a threat again to your precious reputation. It's no use pretending she's not yours, Byron. She *is*. Look at her. That's your nose. Those are your eyes. Most men would be proud to call this girl their daughter!"

"But she *isn't* mine," Byron hissed. "She's your brother's little bastard! He said as much himself. You just thought you could pass this mistake off as my problem. Play me for a sucker! But you're not getting away with it. You're going to watch me do what you refused to back then—get rid of this mongrel!"

Buttons scattered as Byron yanked open the front of Madeleine's dress. The butcher knife he'd taken from Rolla came out of the waistband of his pants and slit the straps of the girl's rayon undervest. He ripped the rest down, baring her breasts. Madeleine folded over at the waist to lower her bare chest to her knees. The wad of cloth in her mouth did not completely conceal her humiliated cries.

Jed turned away from the mirror. The indignity of it was unbearable to him. Somebody needed to put a stop to it. The cold snout of the Musgrave's Smith & Wesson pressed against his neck said it wouldn't be him. But then the detective unexpectedly shoved him through the parlor door. Jed quickly slipped his hand into his jacket for the derringer. But before he had it in his grip, a second shove sent him stumbling headfirst into a parlor chair.

"Mr. Vanderhorn?" the detective said, his voice dripping with smarmy obsequiousness. "Sir? It's important we get you out of this house at once."

Byron's eyes narrowed and his head swiveled the Musgrave's direction. "Well, if it isn't Judas himself," he sneered. "W. D. Riley! Here to collect thirty pieces of Old Man Chesterton's silver?"

So, Jed thought, the Musgrave devil had a name.

"Sir," Riley said, sounding rushed and short on patience, "agents from the Department of Justice are outside with a search warrant. I spoke with one. You don't want to be in here when the local cops arrive and bust down the door so the Feds can rush the place. They've set a trap—sir."

Byron glanced around and seemed surprised to find Jed in one of the chairs.

Riley said, "There's still time to slip out the back, sir, but we have to be quick."

"No!" Byron shouted. "Nobody's going anywhere until this conniving cunt confesses." He jabbed the knife threateningly in Carrie's direction. "If she doesn't," he said, "her bastard kid is getting sliced to pieces!" He yanked the whimpering Madeleine to her feet by her hair.

Carrie said calmly, "I have nothing to confess, Byron. I really don't know this girl. So, you gain nothing in the way of vengeance if you hurt her. For God's sake, don't be a fool, Byron. You have to know that woman's gossip is sensation-seeking crap."

"Best not to kill the girl in front of witnesses," the Musgrave said for his two cents' worth.

Byron sneered at them, grabbed a bare breast, and swiftly carved a crude letter *T* on it with two swipes of the knife tip. "For Daddy," he announced, sounding amused. "Tim," he told the girl. "That was your daddy's name."

"Sir," Riley said, trying again, "the Feds?"

"Shut up, Riley!" Byron's face contorted. "Run along now. Tell the home office I won't be coming back. Not next week. Not ever. Someone else can take the fall for Consolidated Rail. Samuel Chesterton himself, say. Serve him right."

Samuel Chesterton. The man astride a vast empire of rails, Jed thought, as wealthy and powerful as an emperor.

Riley raised his gun and pointed it at Byron. "Enough!" he declared. "Drop the knife before you don't have a hand to hold it in. I'm done screwing around here."

"Plan to make me another notch in your gun, eh, Riley?" The look that Byron flicked Jed's way insinuated that Riley was Tim's murderer. Byron pulled Madeleine close now to use her as a shield, tucking the knife behind her back. "You planning on trying out for Annie Oakley's roadshow next?" Byron jeered.

"No. But it ain't much of a trick to put a slug in the girl and the next one in you. Put it down. Where I can see it."

Madeleine's eyes were as big as saucers.

Jed worked the derringer out of his pocket and curled his index finger around the trigger. It felt slick in his hand. Two shots. All he'd get. Put the first bullet between Byron's eyes. But the girl might get in the way, and the Musgrave posed a threat that had to be dealt with first.

The derringer felt like an anvil when his arm extended toward the side of Riley's head. His hand bobbed up and down to the thudding of his heart. As a boy, he'd found the secret to bagging a squirrel with his .22 was to slow his breathing and still his mind, to concentrate on squeezing rather than pulling the trigger. But there was no time to gather himself. His voice sounded tight calling out, "Riley! Lay down your gun!"

The Musgrave kept his revolver trained on Madeleine and swiveled his head toward Jed, squinting as though confronted by a child's histrionics. "Got yourself a cap pistol there, Albright?" he hooted. "What about the cojones to pull the trigger?" As if he were a conductor giving a band a downbeat, the Musgrave's arm dipped and lifted again. "Like this?" he said.

The room shrank in an instant of deafening noise. An astringent haze filled the air. Girlish screams spilled down the bordello stairs, and Madeleine toppled over to slump to the floor. Byron blinked dully, his shirtfront splattered with the girl's blood. "What?" he sputtered, looking at his chest in distress. One dot among the crimson array was spurting alarmingly. "But ...," he muttered miserably. What had just happened?

Torch materialized from behind a decorative screen by the parlor piano, valiantly leaping onto the Musgrave's back, seizing his wrist, and pushing the gun aloft. Unnoticed, Byron began to stagger forward, looking lost. He reached out as if to grab something for support, stumbled with the knife still in his hand, and planted the blade deep into Torch's back as he fell. His towering figure howled and went rigid.

Jed saw the Musgrave's fist as a blur out of the corner of his eye an instant before it connected with the derringer. Jed's finger was stuck in the trigger. The Musgrave's head exploded in a spray of flesh, hair, and cartilage that splattered wildly on the surrounding furniture. And then Riley, too, was down, half of his face gone, his jaw and cheekbone poking out of a bed of raw meat, one ear dangling like a mudflap. The pop the derringer made going off arrived late in Jed's buzzing ears, as if a distant memory. And then Carrie's voice emerged, calling, "Untie me, Jed. I have to help Jerome!"

But Jed stayed on his knees beside Madeleine, who was writhing on the carpet in a growing pool of blood. Jed covered her with his jacket and removed the gag. "My shoulder," she rasped. "It's … on fire." When he inspected the wound, Jed could tell that the bullet had passed through the shoulder, away from her lungs and heart, miraculously missing major arteries, before exiting into Byron's chest and drilling straight into his heart.

"You're going to be okay," Jed assured the girl. "Lie still. I'll go for help."

Before he could stand, sounds of a fresh commotion broke out in the front hall. And Jed saw the Musgrave rolling onto his side with a mummy's grimace and lifting his revolver to sight down the barrel at Jed. As Jed tried to wriggle away, a pair of shiny black wingtips strode into view and one of them kicked the gun away.

Arthur stood over Jed cursing a blue streak.

Thirty-One

Criminal Justice

New Orleans – August 1930

The Honorable Hiram Gold, Orleans Parish Criminal District Court, tapped his bulbous, veiny nose as his irritation burned through the midday cocktail mist in his cement gray eyes. The jury was finally out. How could it have taken them so long? What the hell! They were staring at their shoes, too! The judge's hands went ice cold in the muggy heat. Not a mutiny!

Hiram Gold's butt clenched. They abs-o-tively must not convict this man! As they well knew! Perhaps he'd been a bit too strident with his instructions? Or had some prig in this collection of twits gotten wind of the courthouse chatter about his liquid lunches at the speakeasy off Bourbon Street? Or that he played the ponies afternoons at The Fairgrounds? He'd gotten in way over his head with that lately. Markers. Threats. A gun in his ribs to drive home a point. All of it was known to Samuel Chesterton Jr., apparently, as the judge learned in a nasty, confidential phone call. Honest to God. *Samuel Chesterton himself calling! Imagine!* Water cooler gossip was one thing. A tax audit? An ethics probe? End of the line. Public disgrace. Twenty years hard time, possibly. You do not defy the most powerful man in the country. In any event, the cash spigot was about to be shut off. Just when Mrs. Gold was expecting her monthly check.

Trying to mask his rampaging anxiety, Judge Gold closed his

eyes and tried to recite the first line of the Lord's Prayer backward in his head—heaven, in, art, who, Father, our—hoping when he opened his eyes again, the overflow crowd in the gallery would not be staring at him waiting for the fateful question. "Has the jury reached its verdicts on all counts?" But they were.

"We have, your honor." The foreman's tan linen suit made a sticking sound peeling off the chair as he stood. A lowly parish bureaucrat, if memory served. Another snout in the public trough.

"Defendant will rise," bailiff Roscoe called.

The rustling of paper fans in the gallery died away and the judge glared at the bumbling mail clerk down front reaching for his wife's hand and sitting up straighter. All this could have been avoided if the doofus had been a better shot. Out the high arched windows, closed now against the racket on Chartres Street and the mournful tugboat whistles on the river, the sun shone diffidently in the thin overcast. The courtroom held its collective breath.

Judge Gold eased back on his throne chair and cast a glance at the expensive legal talent lined up along the defense table. The razor-cut hair. The crisp shirt collars and cuffs. Silk suit coats that had been slipped back on after testimony was taken in suspenders and rolled-up shirtsleeves. Had these men done all they could? If there was a snafu, could it be blamed on them? The judge might have bestowed a sly wink their way if he hadn't been in such a panic.

"As to Count One," the judge said, "would the foreman read the verdict to the court?"

The verdict form rattled crisply as it was unfolded. From God's lips.

"On the charge of murder in the first degree," the foreman read, "we find the defendant—not guilty."

The uproar from the gallery was swift and pitiless. *Fix! Lies! Crooks!* Marble walls wobbled. In the privacy of his chest, Judge Gold's heart executed a gleeful cartwheel of relief. He kept the surface stern and composed, however. (Sober as a judge.) A small flatulent report from his gimlet lunch surfaced. The outrage of the hoi polloi was no surprise. What the judge hadn't figured on was a demonstration of this magnitude and spite. He toed the satchel under the desk closer to the leg of his chair. Wait it out, he told himself as the shouting and fist shaking refused to abate. He tapped into a reservoir of courage from his imbibed lunch and gave himself a little pep talk. *They don't scare you, these fools. The law is the law. They can just sit down. Shut up. Deal with it.*

"Silence!" the bailiff called. His nostrils were flaring at the scent of danger. Dear Roscoe. Judge Gold's faithful watchdog.

"Order!" the judge grumbled for the record and gave the gavel a light rap. Banging it hard might plant the seeds of a poisonous headache. And he didn't want to draw attention away from Roscoe, rocking like a prizefighter from one foot to the other, meaty hands at the ready, sidearm holstered in plain sight. In a silent show of solidarity, Judge Gold nodded a bit of encouragement at the jury foreman, who was gaping anxiously at the incensed citizenry, creasing and recreasing the verdict sheet along its folded edge, a man entertaining serious second thoughts.

The judge felt a bit sorry for him. The lowly pencil pusher had had no part in the pretrial rulings that crippled the prosecutor's case. Nor did he hold any sway over the Orleans Parish district attorney, who'd been derelict in filing not a single brief objecting to the judge's odious rulings. The D.A. had to be in cahoots, too, the judge had eventually gathered. These backroom maneuvers were just so much legal mumbo jumbo to the public, of course. So the rubberneckers in the seats had only the morons in the jury box on which to vent their outrage. Some of the jurors would be rewarded with Consolidated Rail dividends in perpetuity for their troubles, according to one rumor going around. (If there was tampering, Judge Gold didn't want to know about it. Hear no evil. See no evil.)

Hiram Gold carried enough of a burden as it was, bringing this circus of corruption to its finale. Though it was distasteful—the defendant was guilty as hell—Judge Gold had faithfully undermined the prosecution at every turn and sided with the defense lawyers' arguments at every toss-up point of dispute. He had too much skin in the game not to. At first, his heavy thumb on the scales of justice had been given the benefit of the doubt. He was the hanging judge, after all. The balance would correct itself over time. But then it didn't. And a reporter who could not be bought off dug out suppressed eyewitness accounts and key facts that were being withheld from the jury. And the judge had no choice but to order the panel sequestered.

Judge Gold sighed now, thinking about all that blood splattered on the upholstery, carpet, and wallpaper in Rose Starr's lovely parlor. And no one was more to blame for it than the sociopath at the defense table he was desperately trying to acquit. So, it came as a further offense to the judge to see him turn and point his thumb and index finger at the mail clerk as if he had a pistol. The whole assembly saw it, too, including the damn *Picayune* reporter scribbling grisly details into his spiral notebook with a thick yellow pencil.

"Counselor," Judge Gold barked, and hammered the gavel with abandon this time—consequence be damned—"your client?" The man had quite literally gotten away with murder moments before and now he was willing to risk a mistrial by threatening retaliation against a hapless and ineffective prosecution witness? In plain sight? Was he crazy?

Well, Judge Gold wasn't. And he wasn't going to let down the hush money machine at his back, if he could help it. "Face forward, sir!" he barked at the defendant. *Get that nitwit under control,* his scowl instructed the defense attorneys. The future of a lot of prominent men hinged on safeguarding this verdict. Acquittal on all charges was obligatory. Otherwise this cretin threatened to produce a list of public officials being routinely bribed by the railroad, a record that had recently come into his possession. A federal grand jury was convening to consider indictments, and the judge's name was bound to surface. Hiram Gold's life expectancy at the Louisiana State Pen would be all of thirty seconds in the company of the badasses he'd sent there over the years.

Hiram Gold rocked dejectedly in his chair. Would this circus never end? For comfort, he sought escape in the memory of a raucous and bawdy New Year's Eve charity event at Rose's that closed out 1928. It was a back-slapping, ass-pinching, rip-the-pasties-off affair, not the kind that merited a photo spread in the society pages. It was a night for the judge to speak directly to the governor and a dozen cronies as he stuffed his face with juicy pink prime rib, prawns, finger-fried potatoes, white asparagus, pate, candied figs, hot fresh beignets, and more. A pyramid of champagne on shaved ice stood at the center of Rose's infamous parlor, and her girls strutted in their fishnet stockings for a garter and titty show. Two women in G-strings, gloves, and birthday suits capped off the parade with a show of female-to-female kissing and fondling to boisterous, encouraging male cheers. If you threw five dollars into a fishbowl for the orphanage's benefit, a girl would step forward and give you a boob sandwich around your ears, nose, and cheeks. A jazz trumpeter lay on his back nearby playing "Flight of the Bumblebee" between a third dolly's thighs. The young lady gyrated dreamily to the music, eyebrows and lips parodying puzzlement, shock, and gratification at each shift in the staccato music. She had the men in stitches.

Around midnight in an upstairs room following brandy and cigars, the judge dropped his trousers and bent over a chair for the administration of twelve hard and true, timed to the chimes of the clock as the old year passed. Each blow of the leather on his bare cheeks stung with excruciating precision. Penance, pleasure, and redemption, all in one. A transformative purge! The judge put a hundred bucks in the orphanage fund, and fifty more in the pocket of the darkie who'd delivered the licks.

Yes, the glow lived on. But right now there was the shoveling of more shit to supervise. A boatload of it. Judge Gold hoped the jury had, as instructed, disregarded the prosecutor's sneaky revelation about the murder of the postman's brother. No doubt it was W. D. Riley who'd pulled the trigger on Albright's service revolver to frame him for murder. Yet another can of worms dumped in the judge's lap.

"There will be no mention of this baseless allegation in my court!" he'd thundered in chambers after stopping the proceeding to drag the lawyers in for a lecture. Going down that road would not do the defense a lick of good, of course. "Hearsay, gentlemen. Inadmissible and prejudicial. It is Mr. Albright, in fact, who is charged with that murder in Kansas, not Mr. Riley. It's a matter for the courts of Kansas to sort out, not us! It is not to be mentioned again. If it is, I'll have little choice but to declare a mistrial and lock Albright up on the fugitive warrant issued for him by the State of Kansas."

The mail clerk's wife was staring daggers at Judge Gold now as the courtroom began to finally quiet. She made no effort to break it off when he squinted back at her. Her woeful brown eyes were worming deep into his conscience, and he didn't care for it. Not one bit. She'd worn another of her small-town frocks to court today, quite possibly homemade—something Mrs. Gold wouldn't be caught dead wearing. On Amanda Albright, however, it looked oddly alluring. He had an impulse to invite her to Pierre Paul's for a drink. Just to see what she'd say. She'd been a pain in the ass on the stand. She apparently couldn't see that her despicable brother had gotten exactly what he deserved. Put down like a mad dog. (Thereby saving taxpayers the expense of boarding him for years in a loony bin somewhere—did she really think she'd have enjoyed visiting him in a creepy asylum?) And what possible good would hanging Riley do? It might not even kill him, what with that tree stump he had for a neck.

When the courtroom finally settled, Judge Gold put his gavel back in its mahogany cup. "As to Count Two, reckless endangerment of a minor child," he growled at the cowering foreman, "how do you find?" *Stand up straight, man! Don't be spineless! People are waiting!*

An electric suspense once again emptied the room of oxygen. Would the jury convict the monster this time? The witness list had been thoroughly rigged against it. The potential star witness, Rose Starr (which sounded slightly redundant), had vanished, most likely by arrangements through powerful friends, and the girl, Jane Doe, had been shielded from appearing by the juvenile court. Thought by some to be an illegitimate daughter of Rose Starr, the girl's identity remained a mystery. A subpoena to depose her as Jane Doe had been quashed by her court-appointed *guardian ad litem.* She was convalescing from her gunshot wound at an undisclosed location, and not entirely in her right mind, the judge had been told.

The only available eyewitnesses to the events of that morning were the mail clerk and the defendant, whose accounts could not have been more at odds. Albright went first, setting the grisly scene. But his precise, earnest, and aggrieved testimony was carved up on cross examination with condescending questions by one of Riley's Chicago lawyers. Cunningly, he made the mild-mannered mailman come off as desperate and argumentative.

When W. D. Riley took the stand in his own defense, it felt as if the circus had come to town. He ad-libbed some of his oath to tell the truth on the courtroom Bible. "I swear to God on my mother's sacred memory! Nobody's more truthful than me."

He was the only level head in the room at Rose Starr's that day, to hear him tell it. "If it hadn't been for me, that maniac would have sliced and diced that girl up good!" He had the type of charismatic evil that made listeners want to believe things they knew to be untrue. Once the jury retired to consider the evidence, however, they had asked to see his words set down in black and white in the court transcript, a worrying development for Judge Gold.

"Personally, I was desperate to protect that girl," the transcript quoted him as saying. "And I had matters completely under control. My shot lined up perfectly. Incredibly clean. Beautiful. Would have knocked the knife right out of that nutjob Vanderhorn's hand. Perfect as apple pie with a la mode. Too late to save the colored, unfortunately. No, that N— was done for." The defense attorney interrupted to clarify, "Rose Starr's chauffeur, you mean." "Yeah," Riley agreed, "that monkey on my back."

The Orleans Parish prosecutor had lit up the room on cross-examination. "Let me be sure I understand, Detective Riley. You're saying you shot and seriously wounded a defenseless girl in order to protect her?"

Laughter and applause erupted from the gallery that Judge Gold had to vigorously gavel down. He issued a warning to the D.A., but the prosecutor had become so emboldened that he strolled right up to the jury box as he asked, "Isn't it true, Mr. Riley, that your intention all along was to kill Byron Vanderhorn, and the girl was simply in the way? So, you shot her—even announced that's what you were going to do before you did it? An innocent girl!"

The unexpected shift to aggressive tactics caught Judge Gold with his pants down, adrift in martini-sogged reveries, and slow to react. Where had this come from? There was little more to the man than a dimpled chin and a pile of wavy hair, qualities an adoring female constituency thought sufficient to elect him to office. But he definitely wasn't suited to trial work. And now he'd suddenly decided he could play the rough-and-tumble prosecutor in Judge Gold's courtroom? Well, think again, Judge Gold decided. Perhaps the man was just ass-covering in case the bar association later decided to look at the adequacy of the prosecution.

But the judge ordered the question stricken, and instructed the jury to ignore it. "Counselor, another outburst like that and you'll be joining Mr. Riley in lockup." He fixed the D.A. with one of his stony gazes. "As a consequence of your little ploy, Mr. Riley is going to be permitted to repeat his earlier testimony about the shooting—without interruption. Go ahead, Mr. Riley, tell the court exactly how you saw events play out that morning."

"Happy to, your honor. Because I never once pointed my weapon at that poor girl. Not once. That's something I just don't do, believe me. No, sir. My Colt was lined up perfectly at the knife in the nutjob's hand, but then that fella sitting over there in the front row plugged me in the skull before I could pull the trigger."

The detective had jabbed his finger in Jedidiah Albright's direction. Albright had earlier testified that the little derringer had gone off as a result of Riley's slapping it out of his hand. Which came *after* Riley had shot the girl.

But Riley continued to spin lies out of whole cloth. "A guy can't be expected to shoot straight when he's getting plugged in the skull, can he?" he argued. "Look-a-here what he did."

"Not necessary, Mr. Riley," the judge interjected. But the bandage was already coming off to expose a raw pink gash where his left ear had once been. The nature of the puckered opening brought to mind another bodily orifice not generally put on public display. Gasps rippled through the gallery. "Shot off by that peckerwood over there!" Riley shouted.

"That will do, detective," the judge said. "You are excused. Gentlemen, we will take a brief recess."

The judge had sighed with relief when the jury asked to see a transcript of Jed Albright's testimony during deliberations, as well, in particular his stammering reply to the defense attorney's question: "If he really wanted to kill Byron Vanderhorn, as you claim, Mr. Albright, why didn't Detective Riley simply shoot your brother-in-law in the head? He had that shot open to him, did he not?"

Several jurors sat up a little straighter when the question was asked and even more did so when Albright stammered to a fitful silence. Obviously the answer was yes. The judge's nod of appreciation was barely perceptible. It was the kind of doubt a jury could circle back to again and again in deliberation. A reasonable doubt. The railroad had picked the right lawyers to smother this case. Reasonable doubt became a particular point of emphasis in the judge's instructions to the jury.

He watched for Riley's reaction this time, and wondered what the railroad's plan was for this renegade thug once the verdicts were in. The grotesque, delusional man somehow believed he could bend a vast rail empire to his personal will and get away with it, like a lion tamer who believes he won't be mauled in the end, the judge thought cheerfully.

Once again, the jury foreman unfolded his verdict sheet to read a decision, this one on the second count of the indictment, reckless endangerment leading to the injury of a child.

Thirty-Two

Curse

New Orleans – August 1930

Jed's last desperate hope had fizzled. Arthur was not swooping in at the eleventh hour with a cadre of federal lawyers and boxes of bureau files to put a halt to this travesty. The rigged verdicts were already rolling in. Before long W. D. Riley would be free to pursue his vendetta against Jed and Amanda. What the hell had become of Arthur and the other Justice Department agents? Why hadn't even one of them turned up at the trial? How could nothing have been mentioned in testimony about the government's corruption investigation or that there'd been a host of federal agents at Rose Starr's bordello that day? Apparently, an organization that could bend steel to its purposes across the whole wide country had no trouble doing the same with the truth for a captive jury of twelve gullible fools.

The whole thing stunk to high heaven. On the stand, Jed had been played for a chump by the lawyers, prevented from revealing essential truths. Shouldn't they have wanted to hear the last words Byron ever spoke ("Someone else can take the fall for Consolidated Rail"). Or what W. D. Riley said in reply ("I'm done screwing around here") just before he fired the fatal slug into Byron's heart via Madeleine's shoulder to close Byron's flapping lips—permanently.

Arthur was refusing to answer Jed's letters now. He'd

declared him *persona non grata,* claiming Jed was to blame for the Justice Department's big case falling apart on the doorstep of success. Would his brother's career go in the toilet now as a result?

The squeeze Jed felt on his knee as he held his breath was Amanda's hand offering reassurance. Or perhaps she was bracing herself for the next kick in the teeth from the jury, too. The Musgrave was casting threatening glances over his shoulder at them as they waited. His chair was barely ten feet from Amanda, and the lunatic was flexing his shoulders, as if limbering up to throw a celebratory fist into someone's face upon his return to freedom.

The fault lay partly with Jed. He'd played into the lawyer's hands on the stand, futilely stammering to come up with a counter to a gotcha rhetorical question. Shortly afterward, a newspaper photo had captured his exasperation in the knot of out-of-town reporters who hogged the courthouse steps each day, their words like weapons. "Why'd you shoot the Musgrave, Jed?" "Where's your sister holed up?" "Is Jane Doe your sister's kid?" They'd come from as far away as San Francisco to shout their questions at him and write accounts that spread the Albright family's shame (the known and the merely speculative) clear to Timbuktu. A tawdry private matter had managed to upstage massive corruption that was in fact at the root of the whorehouse slaughter.

A faint smile came to the judge's lips as his gimlet eyes swam languidly across the room from the gallery to the jury box. The old lush, cleaning his spectacles with a handkerchief, was clearly pleased with the way things were going. For a week, he'd steered this charade toward this preordained outcome. Justice might be blind, but in Judge Gold's court it definitely stooped to sniff around for money. If he wasn't bumped off by a bounty hunter first, Jed's murder trial in Kansas would bear a striking similarity. It would have little to do with the truth and everything to do with who owned what and the leverage it gave them to grab whatever else they wanted.

"As to the second count of the indictment," the foreman read, "on the charge of reckless endangerment of a child ..." Another nervous hush fell over the room.

The term *reckless endangerment* grated on Jed every time he heard it. The words were hogwash. Sanitized legalese. The offense could more accurately be described as *heartless savagery*. A paid assassin had shot a defenseless girl through the chest because she was in his way. And the shooter didn't give a fig if it killed her. *Reckless endangerment.* Really. The district attorney practically had to draw a picture for the jury. "Pay no attention to where W. D. Riley said he pointed his gun. The weapon seriously wounded Jane Doe. On the face of it, it's *reckless*. And there is no question Jane Doe was *endangered*. If that bullet had traveled an inch to either side, she'd be dead." Standard met. The Musgrave folded his thick arms over his chest and snorted in derision.

Madeleine had been spared the torment of the trial, stashed away at an undisclosed location, shielded from contentious attorneys, prying reporters, and the stinking masses. Jed was grateful she hadn't been there to see him pummeled on the stand recounting the traumatic morning at Rose Starr's, his words twisted and picked apart by the smoky-voiced defense attorney, strumming the jury like a banjo with his fake bayou colloquialisms and homespun wisdom. You'd never know that the man maintained posh offices in Chicago and New York.

As the jury foreman unfolded the verdict sheet a second time, Jed looked away, and his heart raced at the sight of a stray feather on the floor, a remnant of a crude cork figurine and chicken bones that had been flung at his feet on the opening day of the trial by a Cajun woman.

"It's a voodoo fetish," a reporter for the *Picayune* said. "Used to cast curses. Not unheard of at sensational trials like this. You should say something to someone, though."

What good would that do? Jed wondered. Could you revoke a curse or lock up a vengeful spirit? The damage, if any, was done, the woman scurrying off into thin air. Something awkward about the bend of her back put him in fear for Madeleine's safety, however. He stamped the heel of his shoe on the stray feather now, trying to crush it into the terrazzo floor.

"Not guilty," the jury foreman announced. The jeering shouts from ten rows of spectators packed shoulder to shoulder behind Jed and Amanda exploded, louder and angrier than last time. They'd read the newspaper accounts of the bloody events at Rose

Starr's that described a far different story. All hell seemed about to break loose.

"Sit down!" the bailiff bellowed. "Shut up!" He was on his feet, one hand resting on the butt of his sidearm, staring down nearby agitators. But he'd hardly be able to stop a mob on his own, Jed thought. Above him on his high perch, the judge looked sweaty in his somber robe, idly tapping his gavel, a man determined to hang on to any scrap of dignity he could.

As for his own situation, it occurred to Jed that escaping a melee in a jam-packed courtroom might present problems. A Kansas trooper was stationed at a rear exit with a fugitive warrant undoubtedly in his pocket. Fleeing the demonic Musgrave might drive Jed into the long arm of the law. Being locked away in some hoosegow might protect him for a time, he supposed. But it wouldn't stop the Musgrave forever, jail security being what it was. He recalled with a smile Torch's midnight raid at Rolla, but the cheer faded quickly when he remembered the anguished look on the big man's face as Byron's knife plunged deep into his back. Torch's murder had received short shrift at the trial, mentioned only as corroboration of Byron's deranged and agitated state of mind. The freakish stabbing was an excuse for the Musgrave to pull the trigger on Byron. Or so they implied, the events not really occurring in that order.

Note of Torch's passing was not in the least subdued in the Treme section of New Orleans, however. The gold-trimmed white casket in the clear glass windows of an antique Victorian horse-drawn hearse gleamed in the New Orleans sun. Residents came out of stores and houses, at the sound of ad-libbing riffs by a small brass band on "Just a Closer Walk with Thee." There were loose-limbed dancers, strutting and twirling pastel parasols, and a block-long trail of mourners. It seemed odd to Jed that a death could trigger a celebration unlike anything he'd ever seen. From a distance, he shadowed this spectacle as it weaved from curb to curb for blocks up to the gates of an ancient, crumbling cemetery.

There, six burly pallbearers hoisted the casket onto their shoulders and crunched across the bone white gravel between tombstones deep into the land of the dead. Jed tried to read one of the old inscriptions eroded by weather, a message once held dear by the departed's relatives, friends, and neighbors. Without a scorecard, how were you supposed to tell a scoundrel in one grave from a virtuous, hardworking saint in the next?

Torch's casket was hoisted high into a slot in a masonry grotto crowned by a polished marble capstone with the name *Hardcastle* engraved upon it. Was it the family name? *Jerome Hardcastle?* It seemed too pedestrian and hidebound for a man known for threatening adversaries with wrathful Bible passages.

Once the pallbearers and horn players had departed, Jed moved closer. But at the sound of approaching footsteps on one of the gravel paths, he retreated behind a crypt. Carrie arrived like a dark ghost in her black mourning dress. They'd not spoken since the incident, and it didn't seem to Jed like the time to get reacquainted. He left his sister to the privacy of her grief.

Her bordello did not reopen. The girls scattered, dispersed by federal agents and the local constabulary that had swarmed over the house that morning like ants overrunning a picnic to carry away the crumbs. Fine silk stockings and lacy garters disappeared into the pockets of sleazy detectives, along with packets of ribbed Trojans, scented oils, and dildos. Bizarre sexual paraphernalia ended up as souvenirs on police station desks, according to a reporter who befriended Jed.

Jed thought he'd seen two of Carrie's girls among the bystanders along the route of Torch's funeral procession. A third had turned up at the trial months later. She looked like a stripper stranded at a vaudeville stage door in her false eyelashes, peach rouge, and synthetic blond wig. From the back of the room, she reached up to give the judge a tiny wave, thought better of it, and lowered her hand just before a man in a seersucker suit hooked her arm and escorted her out.

Amanda's elbow nudged Jed out of his reveries. The Musgrave was blowing over the tip of his upturned index finger now, sneering at Jed in a way that sent chills down his spine.

"Counselor," the judge snapped, "your client is reminded to face the bench. There are to be no further public demonstrations or I shall find him in contempt and lock him up for ninety days whatever the final outcome of this trial. Is that clear?"

"Yes, your honor," the lawyer agreed. He placed a calming hand on the Musgrave's shoulder. But Riley impudently shrugged it off. Everybody could just kiss his ass. He was going free. With his bandaged skull, he looked like a guy driving on a blown tire.

"We'll move on," Judge Gold said in a clipped voice. "On the third count of the indictment—wrongful detainment—has the jury reached a verdict?" He leaned forward and reached beneath the desk as if to scratch at his lower leg.

Jed could feel Amanda tensing up again. This was her moment for redress. Riley had denied under oath that he'd punched her or handcuffed her to a lavatory pipe in Byron's private Pullman. She was out to get him, he asserted, made the whole thing up because he'd belittled her prissy manner. The prosecutor produced no corroborating evidence to back up Amanda's story. It was her word against his. The Pullman had vanished in the night, and the cleaning crew that had found Amanda chained up and released her had long since been sent packing. Riley settled back in his chair and smiled at the jurors like a door-to-door vacuum cleaner salesman closing a deal.

Shouldering the defense lawyer's hectoring and feigned incredulity at her claims, Amanda had held her head high on the stand. But when Jed was called on to break the he-said-she-said logjam, the slithering lawyer got under his skin once more.

"Mr. Albright, isn't it true that you broke into Byron Vanderhorn's private rail car? And that your wife physically assaulted Mr. Riley when he confronted the two of you? And that the two of you destroyed some of Mr. Vanderhorn's property aboard that car and used his bedroom as a sort of honeymoon love nest?"

Once again, Jed sputtered at a loss for words.

"How say you?" the judge demanded of the jury foreman. "On the charge of wrongful detainment, how do you find?"

The spectators buzzed like swarming wasps. The jury foreman gaped at them, cleared his throat, his Adam's apple bobbing. A man facing a firing squad. In a strangled voice, he mumbled *not guilty,* just loud enough to set the courtroom chandeliers to swaying.

Riley turned to taunt Jed again at the uproar, but a pair of goons with blackjacks jumped the wood railing near the defense table and began raining blows down on his head and shoulders.

When the Musgrave ducked for cover under the table, his attackers tried to drag him back out. When a third man jumped the rail, the bailiff tried to intervene. The aisles were suddenly filled with spectators, some watching wide-eyed, others picking fights. The donnybrook spread faster than baseball teams clearing their benches for a brawl.

"Let's go!" Jed said. He pulled Amanda to her feet. The Musgrave had his hands full and the trooper was hemmed in by the milling throng. Jed shoved spectators out of his way and steered Amanda up the clogged aisle.

Everyone froze at the sound of the first gunshot. Plaster dust and debris showered down from the ceiling and screams rose up from the startled throng. Behind his desk, Judge Gold had his arm aloft holding an Army officer's pistol. It was still smoking when he lowered it to draw a bead on the Musgrave.

The exit doors burst open from the crush of panicking rioters desperate for escape. Jed and Amanda were swept along in the current of sweaty flesh flooding out the doors, down the stairs, and through the courthouse atrium. A straw fedora bobbed along in the cascade ahead of them, a hat like one Jed had seen on the Cajun woman that first day. Jed was blinded for an instant when a Speed Graphic flashbulb popped with a crackle in his face. By the time his vision returned, the straw hat had vanished.

Swimming against the tide of exiting humanity was the horde of news photographers, fighting to go into the courtroom just before a second gunshot rang out. Cameras were not allowed in court. But neither were guns. As far as the newsboys were concerned, the latter nullified the former.

Thirty-Three

A Blessing

and a Curse

New Orleans – August 1930

Over Jed's objections, they veered off course to the Roosevelt on the dash back to their hotel.

"It's just a couple of blocks out of the way," Amanda assured him after he told her, *no, don't be ridiculous.* They needed to run. But she wouldn't take no for an answer.

Jed paused outside the Roosevelt's glass doors to see if they'd been followed in the sweltering heat. The photo hounds apparently had all turned tail at the courthouse to chase down the new sensation. And there was no sign of the state trooper or Riley.

"This way," Amanda called, mounting the half flight of stairs to the lobby.

"Wait, Amanda? Isn't this Huey Long's hotel?" He practically whispered the governor's name, worried the walls had ears. He was sure this was The Kingfish's unofficial New Orleans residence. Home to his famed "deduct lock box," where "donations" were dropped off by his patronage appointments, favor-seekers, and conniving lobbyists. "Wait!" Jed repeated.

But Amanda didn't break stride as she flew past the box, a bank of house phones, and the elevators. She didn't stop until she reached the door to the Palm Room. It was a sanctuary of potted fronds, crisp table linens, and burnished silver that practically shouted *beyond your means* at Jed. A pianist on a white baby grand near the entrance cranked out standards with titles that reached no further than the tip of Jed's tongue. Three gaudy rings decorated his fingers.

"Order me a sweet tea," Amanda said after they'd been given a table. "I'll be right back." She seemed surprisingly cheerful for a woman who'd endured three days of torment and a disappointing outcome.

"Wait!" Jed pleaded for the third time, still hoping to put a stop to this. But Amanda disappeared into the corridor. Alone at the table, Jed noticed the scuffs on his shoes. He felt a five o'clock shadow when he rubbed his jaw. Damn it. They should be hustling it back to their fleabag hotel, well away from Canal Street, cramming everything into suitcases, and racing for Union Station to catch the first train out. Running for their lives. Who knew how long it might take the Musgrave to track them down?

Jed drummed his fingers on the tablecloth as he glanced at the prices in script on the fancy menu card. Highway robbery! A quarter for sweet tea? Jed's stomach knotted. He was telling a waiter with a pencil-thin mustache that they would not be staying when Amanda came up from behind him, laid a quieting hand on his shoulder, and ordered a glass of sweet tea.

"Good news," she chirped, taking a seat. "Carrie can join us in a minute."

"No!" Jed snapped. Carrie? It was past time he dug in his heels. "We're leaving."

"*After* we've said our goodbyes, Jed. Not before. So, sit down. She's your sister. You don't know when you'll get another chance to see her."

When had he ever known? The woman had a knack for vanishing. Most recently, she'd disappeared the month before the trial, holed up somewhere, perhaps in this hotel under a false name. She'd avoided the process servers and their subpoenas. Was it with the governor's help and protection? So why show her face now in this haven known for swindles?

Amanda gripped his hand in hers. "There's something I have

to tell you, Jed.”

“What?” *Here it comes,* he thought irritably. He cast an anxious eye at the entrance, fearful he would see Riley or the patrolman standing there.

“Look at me, Jed. You need to hear this.” She tightened her grip on his hand. A sheepish smile crept onto her face. Then, surprisingly, tears pooled in her eyes. “We’re going to have a baby,” she said.

“What!” He jerked his hand away with a gasp. He could not have heard that right. “A baby?” His stomach took a terrifying plunge. She couldn’t be serious!

“Yes, Jed. Baby. Us. Shocking, no?” She sucked in an enormous breath and her cheeks puffed out releasing it, as if she’d swallowed a gargantuan meal, not a gulp of air. “So, there you have it—news of a lifetime.”

Words stumbled off Jed’s tongue. “But … but how?”

“I thought you knew how it worked,” Amanda teased. “You do remember our misspent night in the hijacked Pullman? Well, now we shall have a little memento of the occasion.”

Jed’s thumb absently rotated the wedding band on his ring finger. This was nothing to joke about! Not when her life was in peril! “I thought Dr. Atkinson said …” Having another baby might kill her.

“Yes. The old drunk should have stuck to castrating pigs.”

More jokes. Did she really have a reliable medical opinion about her condition?

“It’s going to be fine, Jed,” Amanda assured him with another squeeze of his hand. “Really.” But something in her smile was troubling. She nodded a measure of encouragement his way. “It’s a chance to put everything behind us. Wipe the slate clean. Start over.”

Could they? Could they just forget two decades of misunderstanding, recrimination, and estrangement? Just like that? The bitter circumstances that ensued following Baby Nathan’s death remained open wounds.

He scooted around the table and knelt next to her chair, kissed her cheek, and pulled her close in an embrace as much for his own comfort as hers. There was a tiny speck of life deep in her belly that might possess the miraculous healing power Amanda desired. Or it might turn out to be the author of the last chapter of a long-running tragedy.

Their attention was diverted to the entrance by a noisy fanfare from the Palm Room piano. Jed half expected to see the governor appear. Instead, there stood Carrie, conservatively outfitted in a dark suit and clearly annoyed by the musical salute. She waved the pianist into silence and shooed him from the room with the back of her hand.

Jed rose up off his knees.

"Don't let me interrupt anything," Carrie said with a roguish leer.

"Don't you look wonderful!" Amanda exclaimed, greeting her with open arms.

The women embraced, and then Carrie pushed Amanda out to arm's length. "Oh my goodness, Mandy!" she said with a stealthy glance. "Do we have a special little secret?"

Jed wondered how she could possibly know that. Amanda patted her belly and beamed.

"Fabulous!" Carrie exclaimed. She seized Amanda's arms as if she might dance her around the dining room in celebration. "When?"

"February."

"And … who—?" Carrie asked as her hands sketched a vaguely indecent gesture.

Amanda tossed her head Jed's direction and winked.

"Really!" Carrie's brow shot up in arch surprise. "How about that!"

This playful jab nicked the pride that had swollen quietly in him about becoming a father. A baby could mean the world to him. Did he dare hope this time would be different?

"This calls for champagne," Carrie declared. She snapped her fingers at a waiter standing by the kitchen doors. "A chilled bottle of your best brut," she ordered as he scuttled over. "And a dozen oysters on the half shell."

Jed raised a hand to object to this nonsense, but was roundly ignored.

He eased back in his chair, feeling slighted as they began to chat between themselves. He was envious of their friendship, which had remained steadfast from the day Amanda walked into their lives. Twenty years had passed since that morning at their dugout when she turned up with vinegar pie and lemonade in a basket. Jed had stood back in the shadows, smitten. When she'd departed a half hour later, cradling one of their peeping chicks in her apron, Amanda held his heart in her hands. He never wanted to let her out of his sight again.

"So, you're to be a papa?" Carrie asked, drawing him back from his reveries. "Let's hope the years have taught you a few things."

Had they dragged him here just to insult him? Jed bit his tongue thinking of the abuse Carrie had endured from their father and the recent nightmare she'd been put through by her deranged former lover's violent, psychotic breakdown.

That didn't mean he had to tolerate her lip. "What is it you want, Carrie?" he huffed. "We have a train to catch."

"You know, Jed, you look just like Pa when you're mad."

This was gasoline on the fire. Jed sprang to his feet, nearly dumping the table onto her.

"Come back, Jed," Carrie said. "Please. That was cruel and I'm sorry. I didn't mean it. I apologize." She sounded genuinely abashed. "Would you please sit back down?"

Why? What was it she wanted? It had to be something that deeply mattered to her.

"I have a favor to ask," she said.

Before she could get it out, the waiter was back with glasses and a bottle of champagne in an ice bucket. A platter of oozing oysters followed with an odor faintly reminiscent of Carrie's flophouse. Jed wanted to gag. He diverted his attention to bubbles rising in the champagne that the waiter set at his place with tip-seeking flourish.

"Loosen the laces a little, Jed," Carrie urged. "Drink a toast to the baby."

Jed folded his arms over his chest and looked away. Did

Carrie not know the danger Amanda was in? Why did she have to intrude on such a sensitive, intimate moment in their lives? Inflict her pretentious tastes on them?

She raised her glass. "Here's to a precious new life. May the little bundle of joy shower happiness on two very deserving people." The goodwill alleviated some of his annoyance, but he couldn't very well lift his glass belatedly without admitting pettiness. Carrie gave the first taste of her champagne an approving smile, and tilted an oyster to her lips to slurp it down with a grunt of pleasure. "This favor I want to ask?" she said, and gazed solemnly at Jed. "It's not a small one, I admit."

Jed felt Amanda's eyes on him. She'd been Carrie's staunch defender during her absence from the trial. "Maybe the D.A. thought her testimony would backfire," she told Jed. "Maybe she's unwell, taken to her bed. You don't know. She's been through hell, don't you think?"

The distressing history of Carrie's downfall had filled the moments between court sessions. Amanda filled in details. An abortionist in Kansas City had swindled Carrie, which prevented her from returning to Rolla. She found work as the governess to a widowed church deacon's children, but he'd beaten her half to death when her bulging belly betrayed her condition. She'd survived for a time by begging on the street. And then a saloonkeeper hired her to wash dishes in his kitchen. But he made her a virtual prisoner in the saloon's storeroom, and forced her into carnal accommodations with his customers.

"I don't want to hear this," Jed complained. "She brought it on herself with her terrible judgment."

"You don't feel Byron's to blame at all? He took advantage of her! Charmed her with his flattery and false pledges. Promised to support her in any career she chose to pursue. Said he'd give her chances most women were denied in life. He didn't want to live on the prairie any more than she did. They'd go away and live the high life together in Chicago, at the transportation hub of the world. But the fantasy spell he spun was in tatters after the unwanted pregnancy was discovered. Byron's dark side emerged then. He became hostile. Blamed her. Called her a tramp. Said the baby wasn't his. Claimed she'd set a trap. Marriage was out of the question. He wanted her out of his life. He forced her to take money to leave and make 'the problem' go away."

"And after she went through all that, you're telling me she handed that baby over to a complete stranger who would use her as a child slave?"

"No! It wasn't like that at all. The nuns took the baby away the moment it was born. Carrie never had a chance to hold it. Never found out if she'd had a boy or girl. She spent years trying to locate that child."

"Jed, did you hear what I said?" Carrie's voice was in his ear now, summoning him back to the Palm Room. "The court will be making a decision soon. I'm told it won't be me. Do you understand? It's in the girl's best interest that you be her guardian. She's very fond of you. She trusts you in a way she never would me."

"What makes you say that?" Jed asked.

Her lip curled. "My detective told me how things were in Beaumont," she said. "You can learn a lot about a man when he doesn't know he's being watched."

Jed inhaled sharply. He was unaware she'd spied on him. The faces of the boarders in Beaumont came rushing back. One in particular. Wallace. Forever concealed behind a newspaper in Mrs. Robichaux's parlor while everyone else was jabbering away. And there was that time he'd turned up at the telegraph office in Ark City, mumbling excuses before scurrying away.

"It would only be for three years," Carrie was saying. "Until the girl comes of age. We don't want the court appointing a mercenary attorney whose only interest is collecting a fee, do we?"

Jed said, "No, I suppose not." What else was there to say?

A busboy in a spotless tunic arrived to top up water glasses as Jed puzzled over the question of why Carrie would be willing to give up on guardianship herself. At the time, Jed had not yet learned that his sister had changed her name to Melissa Hardcastle (Torch's family name) and was planning to follow the governor to Washington, D.C., if he was elected the junior senator from Louisiana. She'd been promised a job on the government payroll as an assistant in his office. Although the governor would go on to win the Senate seat, Carrie could not outrun her past.

"All right," Carrie said (on the strength of Jed's ambiguous "suppose not"). "I'll have the attorneys draw up the papers naming you her guardian." As though the matter was settled.

"Just a minute," Jed said. "There's something I don't understand."

"There'll be time to straighten out the details later, Jed," Amanda interrupted to say.

"No, listen. Do you honestly expect a judge would appoint a wanted fugitive to be the girl's guardian? A man who is accused of murder, no less! Or do you just snap your fingers, Carrie, like the world is one big Palm Room at the Roosevelt Hotel and someone will do your bidding?" Perhaps anything was possible with Huey Long's political machine at her back.

Her eyes narrowed. "Apparently you didn't speak to the Kansas state patrolman."

"No. I had no wish to let the press photographers record my arrest."

"The patrolman wasn't there to arrest you. He was there to arrest W. D. Riley. A witness has come forward now who saw your gun in Riley's possession the day Tim was shot. He has given incriminating new evidence. A judge in Dodge has issued a warrant. Wyatt Delaney Riley will be tried for the murder of our beloved brother—not you."

"Very tidy," Jed said, usually a fan of tidy.

But if the witness was recruited and his testimony fabricated, as Jed suspected it was, his reprieve was only as solid as Carrie's willingness to back it. She could snap her fingers and make it disappear. The witness could recant, putting Jed back on the hook. Or in the noose.

"You arranged this," Jed said, grateful and annoyed all at once. Did the ends justify the means?

"Never underestimate the value of money and friends," Carrie replied. She helped herself to another oyster. "A family has a duty to protect family."

As if a moral high ground was to be found in corruption.

And Madeleine was not family. Not yet. Might never be. She

had other ideas.

The first thing she'd murmured to Amanda in the hospital after her lung was reinflated was "I want to go home. Back to Beaumont. To Maman." The cruel, violent world she'd stumbled into since leaving Kansas was not for her. "Better to die of boredom peeling potatoes in Beaumont than be murdered in a Louisiana whorehouse."

Word of her disaffection reached a hospital welfare worker before Amanda could whisk the girl away to Joplin and talk some sense into her. As a runaway, she belonged in the protective custody of juvenile authorities in New Orleans Parish, they were told, and her destiny was to be placed in the hands of a juvenile court. Legally, she remained the daughter of Babet Robichaux until a court ruled otherwise. Mrs. Robichaux had made it known she was rejecting Carrie's scholarship offer. The judge deciding the custody issue wanted briefs from the lawyers of both parties. Carrie's counsel argued that the adoption had been defective from the outset and that the girl's subsequent captivity for housework violated child labor laws. Opposing counsel contended that Carrie was a woman of loose morals and wicked ways and was unsuitable to be the parent of an impressionable young girl. In Jed's mind it was clear that neither placement was appropriate, and the prospect of either outcome horrified him.

"All right," Jed announced, "with Amanda's help, I'll do it."

Jed felt a surge of pleasure at the smile that lit up Amanda's face.

"Great!" Carrie said, and again raised her glass. "To family!"

Jed's hand became clammy and stopped as it traveled toward his glass. The woman in the straw fedora was at their table standing behind Carrie now with a voodoo doll clutched in her hand. She wore seafaring oilcloth overalls and rubber boots that were streaked with seaweed and fish slime. One sleeve of her denim shirt was pinned up at the shoulder like a war veteran's. And her leathery face, despite its deep squint mark lines, bore an unmistakable resemblance to Babet Robichaux, Jed's landlady in Beaumont.

"You like them oysters, do ya?" she jeered. Her thick accent made her difficult to understand. "Dredged 'em up special for ya."

She set the fetish doll on the table and reached into a pocket of the overalls with a gloved hand and produced a misshapen and suspiciously discolored oyster that she set next to the fetish. Evil flickered in the depths of her eyes.

"From the forbidden coast. Same seabed yours. Cut my hand on one like this couple years back. Cost me an arm." She snickered, gesturing at the empty space below the shortened sleeve. "Vibrio," she said.

The word delivered a jolt of panic to Carrie's face. She knew the word. Feared it.

"Can't be too careful with seafood," the monger woman snickered. "Nasty business, eating something thet ain't dead, 'cause it can eat you, too." She bared teeth the color of tobacco with a sneer of satisfaction. "Stealing a girl away from her maman! That ain't safe neither."

Jed was frantic. Had Amanda eaten one of the oysters? So much as touched one?

"So, where is she, eh?" the hag demanded. "What have you done with her? Tell me!"

"Go to hell," Carrie replied, and drew her shoulders back as she stared the woman down. "Your sniveling sister never had any legitimate claim to that child, as the court will soon rule. So, good day to you! Be on your way." She pointed at the fetish. "And take that filthy scrap of trash with you."

The Cajun woman leaned in to Carrie's face, and unsheathed a finely honed fillet knife from her belt. Jed bolted from his chair, and the point of the knife was immediately touching his belly. "Want to see how quick a man can be gutted, do you?" Jed sat back down.

Carrie snapped her fingers and two bruisers rose from a table in a secluded corner of the dining room. They moved with the slow, practiced assurance of private security muscle.

"Can't hide the girl forever," the Cajun woman spat, and waved the knife at Carrie's goons. "And when I find her, she'll disappear in the blink of an eye—off someplace where you and the long arm of the law can't touch her."

A fishing boat in international waters, Jed thought.

The woman fled, racing through the Palm Room's kitchen with the house thugs in hot pursuit. Carrie looked stricken. She was pale and bathed in sweat. Vibrio. Not some idle threat. Five months to the day later, after her body had wasted away, she would take her final gasping breath at nearly the same moment that the premature baby girl born to Amanda and Jed was struggling to take her first.

Thirty-Four

Dust to Dust

Rolla, Kansas – July 1933

The train depot across the street was no longer visible in the
ungodly cloud of soil rampaging through town. Dirt scratched at
the windowpanes of the Rolla Hotel, rattling the sash in Jed's
room. Marauding bits of Oklahoma, Texas, and Colorado dust
were slipping past the tightened latch. Jed's teeth were gritty with
it. His spittle looked like coffee grounds in the enamel basin.

Gas sconces lit the dingy corridor in the middle of the day. Jed
made his way down the hall in their orange glow to the last door,
where Madeleine answered his knock. Terror was visible in her
emerald eyes. Her hair and high-collar dress were dusted a spectral
gray by the storm, and the crevasses around her eyes had
blackened to an other-worldly depth. It was as if she was the ghost
of Carrie standing there.

"Why won't it stop?" she mewled.

"Soon," Jed promised idly, and listened to the thrum of
the wind on the roof. He didn't care to admit to his own
claustrophobia or his worry that drifts could collect on the rails
between Rolla and Dodge and strand them here for days.
"Everything's going to be fine," he assured the girl.

The sky had been azure clear and the winds light just hours
before on their walk to the farm after signing papers at the bank.
The desolate landscape all around had been scraped raw by prior

storms, the topsoil stripped and scattered north and east by the punishing winds. The exposed subsoil of silty clay loam was dotted with husks of dried-out seedlings.

Dust was piled up against the posts of a half-buried fence line they followed past Scruggs's abandoned Victorian. The drifts went as high as the windowsills of the house. His land no longer fit for crops or cattle, Scruggs'd grudgingly joined the great migration west.

The storm pelting Rolla this time had begun as a narrow pitch-black line on the horizon that scoured away blue sky as it came. Another duster hadn't seemed possible so soon after one had blown through two days before. A flock of birds screeched over their heads, and Jed suggested they immediately start for town. They had to pick up their pace when specks of sand began to sting their necks. A tidal wave of dirt rose behind them before they reached the safety of the hotel. It seemed intent on burying them.

Tim's words rattled around in Jed's head. *It's gonna be bad.*

"Not going to be enough grass left around here to feed a rabbit," he'd said in alarm at the rapacious destruction of prairie land by an army of plundering gasoline-powered tractors. "You'll see. Dirt's gonna fly like snow."

"Just a temporary setback," Clarence Ott chortled in greeting at the depot when Jed lamented the shocking amount of devastation they'd seen coming in on the train. "You know, Jed, you could buy Scruggs's place for a song at auction next month. You should, you know. It's dirt cheap." He'd chuckled over his lame pun. "You know this drought won't last forever. And when the rain returns, boom times will return as well."

As part of the morning tour with Madeleine, Jed had made a visit to Tim's workshed. It was tilted from the incessant wind, a relic of times past. The freakish storms had sanded away its blistering paint and polished the rough siding boards to a dull luster. Nearby, the pump jack rocked like a metronome, extracting gas from prehistoric bedrock, almost exactly where Tim had predicted. The well was printing money. The fertile topsoil might be gone, but the land of southwest Kansas was far from done yielding its riches.

Jed had waxed nostalgic about the trials his family had

endured on the frontier as Madeleine watched the methodical motion of the pump. She would be getting mineral royalties thanks to her Uncle Tim, "who sacrificed his life to stop the railroad from stealing the land."

In a futile effort that morning before the storm, they'd hunted for signs of the old footpath. Jed wanted to visit Nathan's grave. But the constant wind had rearranged the soil line along the crest of the short rise, and Tim's homemade marker was buried beneath the mounds of dirt and nowhere to be seen. Jed found this profoundly upsetting, as if his world was unanchored. Ashes to ashes. Dust to dust. Cruel words.

The view out the rear window in Madeleine's room was no different from his in front. All there was to see was flailing dirt. Had they not made it back to town when they did, they might easily have become stranded, disoriented, and at risk of suffocating. "We'll take the first eastbound train out, I promise," Jed said. It was a shame Madeleine would never get to see the place as it once was, the place that he, Amanda, Tim, Carrie, and Arthur had tried so hard to tame. Mired in nostalgia, Jed's voice was wistful. "Somewhere out there," he mused, "is an old schoolhouse where your mother first danced with your father at the harvest ball of 1911."

Madeleine clucked her tongue in annoyance. "Hardly something to treasure," she said.

"Of course," Jed murmured, abashed by his foolish, sentimental jabbering. Couldn't he see he was extolling a calamitous, fatal affair?

Carrie's death had been terribly cruel, done in by her compromised heart and liver, which succumbed to the toxin *vibrio vulnificus*. The bacteria made a distressing hash of her appearance first, raising blisters on her lips and nostrils as it ate away her flesh. "Leave me," she begged them at the end. "I don't want to be seen like this."

The doctor had no answers. "There's not much we can do when it's been ingested," he said. "If it comes into the body through a cut in the skin, we have a chance of saving a patient with an amputation."

Babet Robichaux's Louisiana sister had lost her arm that way.

And now the virus would cost the oyster lady twenty years of her life in prison because she'd deliberately infected Carrie with it. An accomplice in the kitchen got five years.

"What are your classes next semester?" Jed asked, hoping to steer the conversation to a more cheerful place.

For a time, it was as if Madeleine hadn't heard the question or was too caught up in the sound of the noisy wind. She picked up the hat she'd worn on their walk, which had been tossed carelessly on the dresser, and she tried it on again in the mirror.

"The fact is," she said with an edge to her voice, "I've quit school."

"What?" Jed demanded. "You can't! It's already paid for."

"I'm sorry, Uncle Jed. I was going to tell you. It just never seemed the right time. I've met someone, you see. A boy. A lovely boy, and, well …"

Jed's heart was in his throat and his blood boiling. No college Casanova was going to derail this girl's future, not as long as he had any say in the matter. Who did this boy think he was, sweeping an innocent girl off her feet? Had she fallen for another roughneck with a devious heart? Another Lester Barnhart? Had she not mentioned it because she knew the boy was completely unsuitable? Or was that not the worst of it? "You're not in trouble, are you, Madeleine?" Jed demanded.

"No!" she snapped. "And I don't need one of your lectures!" She slumped back on the bed and addressed her next remark to the ceiling. "His name is Spencer, and he's planning to ask for my hand."

"And I will not be giving my consent!" Jed practically shouted. "You're getting your diploma first. Subject closed." Furthermore, he had no intention of accepting this suitor after graduation either. How could the boy possibly be good enough for her?

"Stop acting like I'm a child," Madeleine said. "Really, this isn't any of your business. You're not my father. I'm twenty-one! I'll do as I please. Those papers I signed this morning made me a free woman. You are no longer in charge of my affairs. Not according to the terms of my mother's will."

Could an inexperienced young woman suddenly manage

money *and* independence? Jed didn't think so. Why had Carrie believed she could? Why hadn't she put the money in trust until Madeleine was 25, say? Better yet, 30? Perhaps she had never considered the idea that she might not be around to steer the girl onto a proper path.

"What use is a diploma to me?" Madeleine continued. "What use is it to any woman? You think they're going to allow us to become doctors or lawyers? That they'll appoint a woman to head up one of their corporations?" Now she was just talking silly, Jed thought. "Exactly what am I going to be able to do with a college degree?" she asked. "Nothing I can't do just as well without one—become a wife and mother and tend to some man's comfort and happiness?"

"I thought you wanted to be a teacher," Jed said in a cold, quiet voice.

"After the way they treated Aunt Mandy? Making her quit after fifteen years of teaching just because she was going to have a baby? What's the point of spending four years with your nose in dull textbooks if the sheepskin they hand you at the end can't prevent some man from firing you the minute you're in a family way?"

"Madeleine, you'll never know if you can be a doctor or a lawyer if you don't try."

Madeleine snorted in derision. "Pardon me, Uncle Jed, but you don't know the first thing about it. There's a reason all that the girls talk about at school is boys. They know it's not the grades they get on their exams and papers that will count in life. It's the score they make with boys on weekends that matters. It's the prospects of the boys they catch on weekends that matter."

Jed didn't know what to say.

"And teaching? Really? Who is going to want Rose Starr's daughter teaching their children?"

The girl had been dragged into the cesspool through no fault of her own. The lurid tale of Rose Starr was refusing to go away, kept alive by sensational big-city tabloids and dimestore paperbacks, attaining nearly mythic proportions as one damning new revelation after another spilled out of Carrie's or Byron's pasts. The downfalls of Riley and Judge Gold also breathed new life into the story. At the Joplin Post Office, where Jed had transferred after reuniting with Amanda, they called him "the pistol-packing postman," a phrase first penned by a writer for *Collier's* magazine. Strangers still turned up on his doorstep hoping to find Madeleine. Offers as high as five hundred dollars cash had been received for just a picture of the girl.

"You can't just quit school, Madeleine!" Jed said. "Not for some boy." Had she not listened to their cautionary tales of her father's broken promises to her mother?

"I knew you wouldn't understand," Madeleine said. "I knew you'd try to stop me if I told you. But I'm not going to let you! This is my life. I will decide. Me and nobody else."

She went to the door to her room, opened it, and gestured for Jed to leave.

* * *

She kept her slender back to him on the platform of the Rolla depot, one hip cocked defiantly, arms folded across her chest. They were being watched by an older woman in the shadows with a busybody's scornful squint. She'd seen Jed lug the girl's suitcase out of the hotel, Madeleine keeping her distance. What must the old lady be thinking?

"Don't count on being invited to the wedding," Madeleine announced in a voice loud enough for everyone to hear. Jed could imagine Ott's ear pressed to the window of his depot office. "You'll not be walking me down the aisle, you know."

All he'd asked for on the walk to the depot was for a chance to meet the boy. And this was the way she chose to say no? "Admit it," Madeleine said, milking her tirade, "you were hoping for a chance to scare the boy off with tales of our twisted family tree. Isn't that right? Well, that's not going to happen."

Was the boy as much in the dark about her family and their past as they were about him? Had she managed to conceal her identity at school?

The cloud of Oklahoma dirt had moved on, sweeping northeast toward Hugoton, Copeland, and Dodge City, leaving behind its calling card of tiny particles, like a vapor, floating high in the atmosphere over Rolla.

The sun was pink as it poked through the veil of dust, and it was quickly joined by another, fainter, grayer. And then another, weaker still, as if falling into line. As if the universe had begun splitting apart, forming a new order.

Jed pointed over Madeleine's shoulder at it. *"Sun dogs,"* he said. "Remarkable, yes? A trick of nature. Optical illusion. Your Uncle Tim saw one once. He believed it was a sign from God. A promise of better times." Superstitious foolishness, Jed thought, and wished he hadn't mentioned it.

It surprised him to feel Madeleine's arm circle around his back and her head come to rest on his shoulder. She was trembling. Had the spooky sky generated a change of heart, perhaps?

* * *

They boarded a train from Albuquerque bound for Dodge City when it made an unscheduled stop to repair a temperamental boiler. The conductor told Jed that despite the dust storm, connections were said to be running on time out of Dodge, including a local he wanted to Enid.

At Dodge, they changed for the Enid train, and Madeleine excused herself to use the restroom. But she did not return by the time the train was pulling out. And a search of the cars was fruitless. She'd fled. Jed knew it. There would be no goodbyes.

Thirty-Five

Epilogue

Train 85 – September 1934

A snapshot of a pudgy, rosy-cheeked Annie is thumbtacked to the mail car's bulletin board, where it's been smothered for months by a proliferation of outdated directives and memos. Buried treasure. Jed discovers it as he culls the clutter. How cute she'd looked that day in her embroidered party smock. Her first birthday. An emotional day. An important milestone. The threshold to childhood and the first time Jed had taken a full breath since the day Amanda broke the news in the Roosevelt's Palm Room. With every turn of the calendar, there seemed to be less chance that his heart was about to be broken again. She calls him "Poppy" now, and the pixie ears that stick out in the snapshot are covered by auburn curls now. His beloved Anna Carrie Albright.

It had been Amanda's idea that they name her for Jed's sister.

"Was Benedict Arnold also in the running?" Arthur had quipped at the birthday party, fueled by liberal nips of holiday eggnog. "How about Mata Hari?"

"It was Amanda's idea," Jed said firmly, hoping to shut down the insults.

"You could have said no," Arthur scoffed, and recalled for Jed's benefit how one of their roosters in Rolla was pecked to death by the prodigious hen they called the Duchess.

"Arthur," Jed said to interrupt, "did you know that the first hospital nursery incubators were reconfigured poultry hatchers like the one Carrie had in the dugout? And, you'll recall, it was one of Carrie's hatchlings that I have to thank for winning the favor of my future bride."

It had been a nursery incubator that kept little Annie alive when she arrived in the world six weeks too soon, scrawny and tinged blue. Barely four pounds. "She's a fighter, your little precious," the nurses were fond of saying in their cheerful way. "Not a quitter, this one." Weeks of struggle and setbacks had tested their optimism, guarding a life on the precipice, wrapped in a pink blanket, at the mercy of a glass and metal box distressingly reminiscent of Nathan's coffin. The warmth and extra oxygen it produced aided her for ten weeks until her underdeveloped lungs could manage on their own.

Through sleepless nights and anxious days, Jed began to take comfort from the baby's name. The only other Anna Carrie he'd ever known had bullied her way into feisty adulthood. A path to longevity was possible. And when Arthur's daughter Nancy nicknamed the baby Annie, Jed liked that, too. It seemed to emphasize that little Annie looked nothing like her wayward namesake.

Just before Baxter Springs, the mail car chattered over a short trestle and Jed re-pinned the snapshot to the cork board. He'd found the buff-colored envelope he'd been looking for amidst the clutter of official notices. It had been pinned there, out of sight, since it arrived at the Joplin post office. No postage stamp. No postmark. No return address. Jed's name had been typewritten circumspectly on the envelope. Inside was a name and an Enid address scrawled on a blank scratchpad sheet. It was unmistakably Arthur's dashed-off handwriting, the only clue to the message's origin and meaning. "Can't use taxpayer dollars on personal matters," Arthur had said when Jed asked him to use the bureau's vast resources to find Madeleine. "It's not like the girl was kidnapped," he grumbled.

"You don't know that," Jed replied. "And she is your niece." A month of silence ensued, as if the idea had reached a permanent roadblock. Then, seemingly out of nowhere, this cryptic note turned up with what Jed assumed was the boyfriend's name and address. Was it from the bureau's criminal files? How had Arthur found it with so little to go on?

"Will you go and talk to the boy?" Amanda had asked when Jed told her about it.

"I don't think I should, do you? Madeleine made it clear she wouldn't abide any interference." And there hadn't been a word from her in the eighteen months since.

"She's just taking her time to sort things out," Amanda surmised. "Now that you have an address, we could invite her to Annie's upcoming third birthday. She'd want to see how much our girl has grown."

"She might," Jed agreed. "But she'll also be furious that we tracked her down. I just want to find out if she's okay. Maybe Arthur could tell me. Maybe he knows more than a name and address."

"Not exactly Prince Charming, this punk," Arthur said. The long-distance line scratched with static, and Jed could practically smell the alcohol on his brother's breath. "He's a tomcatting frat boy, this guy. Ladies man. Got several on the string, from what I hear. Would you like me to have him pulled in? Throw a good scare into him? The sheriff in that county is a pal of mine. He'd be only too happy to rough up some arrogant little prick like this."

Jed couldn't tell if the braggadocio was just so much cop talk or if his brother was serious. He thought again of Lester Barnhart's suspicious death. Had it truly been the work of the Musgrave covering his tracks?

"No," Jed said. "Stay out of it. The name and address are all I need."

"Anything you say, brother," Arthur snorted. "Gonna dust off your legendary sucker punch?"

"What?" Jed asked. "No. I'm just going to talk to him."

"Get acquainted, eh?" Arthur said, his breathing husky. "Sure. The Pistol-Packing Postman returns." He chuckled. "Word of advice? Maybe don't aim for the ear this time."

"Cut it out, Arthur," Jed said.

A costly silence stretched out on the long-distance line as Arthur sipped on something and coughed. "Okay, if you should happen to change your mind about my offer ... Personally, I wouldn't let this rake within a mile of my daughter." Then the receiver clattered in Jed's ear as it landed in its cradle in Kansas City. The operator came on to ask if they were finished.

The coffee in Jed's Thermos cup had gone cold. He opened the mail car's loading door and tossed out the dregs. He stood there a moment on the ledge as roadbed gravel raced by below, Jed lost in thought about Madeleine and the boy. Thus did a blind curve in the track take him by surprise and suddenly he was in the train's slipstream, his heart hammering, dangling from a grab bar by one sweaty hand like a kid showboating on a merry-go-round. Centrifugal force from the bending track loosened his grip on the pipe as the buffeting, sooty breeze lifted his legs. He shut his eyes and tasted Annie's slick, salty face on his lips from the kiss goodbye that morning after she'd forced him to chase her, giggling, around the yard. Never thinking it might be the last time.

When the S-curve bent back and the forces reversed, just like that Jedidiah Albright was tossed like a ragdoll onto the hardwood floor of his mail car. A dull pain spread through his chest and upper arm as he lay there gasping. It was a moment of extraordinary clarity. He'd never considered how it might be he breaking his little girl's heart, rather than the other way around.

With his back propped against a pile of mail pouches, Jed fished Arthur's note from his pocket, wadded it up, and threw it out the railcar door into the wind.

A moment later, he was back on his feet, dumping one of the pouches onto the sorting table, where he worked its contents into a neat stack so they could be distributed, one item at a time, into the routing pouches stretched out on the massive grid before him.

The world was a messy place. In the mail car, he could still bring order out of chaos.

Author's Note

Sometime after I'd finished a third draft of this book, I went to work on a daunting box of old photos my mother had kept over the years and left for my attention when she died. In the midst of all the duplicate family vacation pictures, Christmas celebrations, birthday parties, and hundreds of color Polaroids of my dad with his golfing and fishing buddies, I found a tiny black-and-white snapshot of my grandfather. Like a nugget of gold in a box of gravel.

Here was the man I had been writing about for nearly a decade, pictured just as I had him in the opening chapter of the book—standing in the doorway of a railway mail car. How this snapshot had managed to find its way into my hands when it did is the kind of fluke that's hard to pull off in fiction. I stared at it in disbelief, as though I'd conjured it up, just as I had the story of a railway mail clerk named Jed Albright in response to news of my grandfather's hidden past long after he died. I'd had the same feeling standing in a sea of grass at a desolate spot on the Kansas plain where a farmer led me to what could have been the site of my grandfather's primitive dugout. Buried in several feet of sand and soil that had blown in during the great Dust Bowl of the 1930s, we found a broken windmill blade, a rusted milk can, and tractor parts—tangible evidence of his nearly forgotten occupation.

It was only a chance remark my mother made to my father that alerted me to my grandfather's race across Kansas for cheap government grant land. I had never imagined that my family had been part of this history.

I have not tried to chronicle my grandfather's actual life in this book since so much of his history is lost. Instead, I have borrowed a few random specifics of known history as a framework on which to base a work of fiction. My grandfather never spoke to me about homesteading on the Kansas frontier with his siblings or anything about his years as a railway mail clerk. The fact that he didn't greatly excited my curiosity about it all. I pried what I could from my father's failing memory shortly before he died. But he could not say what possessed his own father, two uncles and an aunt to travel west to claim dollar-an-acre land on the frontier in 1911. Or the reason they abandoned that land sometime later. My grandfather was a taciturn man, but his secrecy about this seemed extraordinary to me. I had never heard of these great-uncles or this great-aunt. Why? I asked my father. "I think something happened out there," he replied. It kicked my imagination into high gear.

It has been a long journey since then, and now, after sixteen years, six drafts, and three title changes, it's probably time for my part of this story to be finished.

Acknowledgments

I never got to properly thank the late Randy Edelman for the time he spent taking me exploring on the farm he purchased from my family in the 1980s. We went bounding over the land in his sputtering pickup looking for signs of my grandfather's past. It was an indelibly memorable day in 2007, and I was happy recently to reconnect with his heirs who continue to farm the land.

A lot of family and friends contributed to the eventual completion of this book. I especially want to mention my daughter Christine Dunbar, who propped up my sagging spirits when the project drifted and who played Dr. Kevorkian to some of the darlings I'd left festering in the manuscript after I thought I had snuffed them all out.

Special kudos are due as well to Martha Bergland, Marybeth Jacobson, Terri Sutton, Barbara Miner, Glenda Mehlan, Paul Hayes, Richard Kenyon, and Mary Ritchie for their suggestions, encouragement, and insights as the book slowly developed. Thoughtful readers all.

I am indebted to my artistic son, Patrick, who once again distilled the essence of what I was after in the multiple layers of this novel. For me, his cover captures the spirit of it in a single engaging photograph.

Many thanks to my editor Dulcie Shoener, who knows all about split infinitives, the mysterious workings of the Model T gearbox and clutch, and many things in between. Thank you for keeping it real, accurate, and grammatically correct.

To others who played a vital role in the production of this book—Dave Blank, John and Kathleen Becker, and Don Zoltan—know that you have my gratitude. And I'd be neglectful if I failed to mention my coffee shop buddies—Fred, Scott, Dori, Freddie, and Trish—for lending me their ears when I wandered away from the manuscript to escape the snare of temporary writer's block.

Last but definitely not least, I have to credit my wife for the enduring patience she showed me over these years as the process of creating this book stretched beyond all reasonable bounds. Honey, it's done!

Suggested Reading

The following is a list of the books I found helpful and inspiring in the preparation of this novel. These books may answer questions you have about life on the Kansas plain and elsewhere in frontier times and during the Dust Bowl.

Little Heathens: Hard Time and High Spirits on an Iowa Farm During the Great Depression, by Mildred Armstrong Kalish.

Basin and Range, by John McPhee.

Watching Kansas Wildlife: A Guide to 101 Sites, by Bob Gress and George Potts.

The Great Plains, by Wallace Prescott Webb.

The Worst Hard Time: The Untold Story of Those Who Survived the Great American Dustbowl, by Timothy Egan.

The New Country: A Social History of the American Frontier, 1776-1890, by Richard A. Bartlett.

The Empty Meadow, by Ben Logan.

The Uncertainty of Everyday Life, 1915-1945, by Harvey Green.

The Home Place, by Wright Morris.

Down & Out in the Great Depression: Letters from the Forgotten Man, edited by Robert S. McElvaine.

Time Capsule / 1932: A History of the Year Condensed from the Pages of Time.

The Gentle Farmers: Women of the Old Wild West, by Dee Brown.

Wildflowers and Grasses of Kansas: A Field Guide, by Michael John Haddock.

Pioneer Women: Voices from the Kansas Frontier, by Joanna L. Stratton.

Books by This Author

Even Sunflowers Cast Shadows

Emma Starkey is a spunky little girl trying hard to be charitable and virtuous. But her calculated attempts have a way of backfiring with tumultuous consequences in this poignant story of small-town life in 1920s Kansas.

Life on The Sun

Life on The Sun spans ten days of anger and confusion in a bygone era of love beads, tear gas, and manual typewriters.

Color of The Sun

The murder of a newspaper reporter during a 1967 riot pulls two of his colleagues deep into the contentious issues of race in America and into the secrets of a troubled inner city family.